DEVIL'S DUE

COPYRIGHT

CAST OF CHARACTERS

Colorado Chapter

Officers
Demon – President - Old Lady Violet
Children: Theo
Buzzard – Secretary/Treasurer - Old Lady Sindy
Thunder – Sergeant-At-Arms
Mace – Enforcer
Sparky – Road Captain

Patched Members
Hellfire - Old Lady – Moira
Children – Demon, Kennedy, Samuel
Bomber - Old Lady – Jeannie
Cad
Ink
Lizard
Pyro
Paladin - Old Lady Jayden
Rusty
Skull

Prospects
Dan
Wills
Smithy – Failed Prospect

Sweet Butts
Bella
Breezy
Sheila
Titsy
Tulia

Deceased Members
Blackie – Previous President
Furnace – Previous VP
Ingot – Previous Enforcer
Taser

Arizona Chapter

<u>*Officers*</u>
Drummer – President- Old Lady – Sam
Children – Eli
Wraith – Vice President - Old Lady – Sophie
Children – Olivia
Heart – Secretary - Old Lady – Marcia
Children – Amy, Jacob, Isabel
Dollar – Treasurer
Peg – Sergeant-At-Arms - Old Lady – Darcy
Children – Noah
Blade – Enforcer - Old Lady – Tash
Joker – Road Captain
Children: Maya (niece)
Mouse – Computer Expert - Old Lady – Marianna

<u>*Patched Members*</u>
Bullet - Old Lady – Carmen
Beef
Hyde
Jekyll
Lady
Marvel
Roadrunner
Rock - Old Lady – Becca
Slick - Old Lady – Ella
Shooter
Viper Old Lady – Sandy
Drifter
Truck

<u>*Prospects*</u>
Matt
Hound

Roadkill

Deceased Members

Adam

Buster

Tongue

Hank

Bertram

SATAN'S DEVILS MC

CHAPTER ONE

"Fuck! Break it up. Get them a-fuckin'-part."

Four arms come around me, two bodies pulling me back. I continue to swing blindly for a moment, hearing swearing and an oomph before I'm better restrained.

"For fuck's sake, Beef. What's got into you?" Lady, far stronger than he looks, snarls into my ear.

"You want to take me next?" Peg, the sergeant-at-arms of the Satan's Devils Tucson chapter, growls. "'Cos I'll fuckin' break you in two."

The voices at last seep through the red fog in my mind. As the mist clears, Rock comes into view, standing in front of me, ruefully rubbing his jaw while moving it side to side as if to test it. One of his eyes is already swelling and is surely going to be black tomorrow. *What the fuck have I done?*

"Becca's going to be fuckin' furious with you, Beef," Rock warns, as he shrugs off Drummer's assistance and question as to whether he should call Doc. "What the fuck just happened?"

I don't know. That's the plain truth of it. Rock's my best friend. Has been since we prospected together. Tonight, at our monthly sparring match, I just lost my fucking mind and took out all my frustration on him. My eyes catch his, wincing at his left eye that's closing more by the second.

"Brother, I…" I stop. How can I apologise when I don't know what the fuck happened?

"Suggest you go cool off," barks our president, Drummer. "Whatever's between you two, sort it the fuck out, and not with your fists, Beef."

Rock's looking at me, more curious than pissed off. He knows better than anyone, losing control is so unlike me. Shit, Becca. That little girl doesn't deserve me sending her man back to her in pieces. Tomorrow she'll no doubt give me a piece of her mind, and I won't stop her. I love that girl like a sister. *Or more than that,* I admit to myself. *Maybe that's part of the problem.*

It hits me then, why my anger came out and why the target was Rock, the man who's now confidently turning his back on me, his action showing he knows whatever drove me to act out of character has left me. Peg and Lady feel my body relaxing and release me at the same time. I follow Rock down from the ring, squeezing my large body through the ropes and dropping down to the floor.

Instead of going off to examine his injuries, he's waiting for me. "Want to talk about it?"

My shoulders rise and fall. "Probably need to, Rock. But not now, okay?"

"You gonna sort," the prez's hand waves between Rock and me, "whatever this is, out?"

"Sure, Drummer. Look, I'm sorry, okay?" It's not okay. But the lame apology is all I can offer. Hitting out at Rock, taking out my frustration on him as I can't hit or shout at the person to whom my anger is really directed. Or, more realistically, at myself, and the situation I've found myself in.

"Go home, Beef," Rock tells me, his eye now completely shut. "We'll talk tomorrow."

But I don't want to talk, tomorrow, the next day, or the one after. The mess I'm in is completely of my own making.

"My office, ten o'clock. You hear me, Beef?"

I hear Drummer loud and clear. Seems my president has had enough of my recent behaviour, my sour moods, my sulks, which culminated tonight in turning what should have been a friendly bout into something that could have become a murder scene had I not been pulled off by my brothers.

A chin raise to him, then I purse my lips as I view Rock again, his hand stroking his jaw as he tries to ease the ache there. I got off uninjured as he, at least, was pulling his punches. If he hadn't, one of us may well have ended up dead.

Prez has a right to be concerned.

Eyes follow me as I leave. Wraith, the VP, shaking his head. Blade looking confused. Joker looking from me to his partner Lady, even Heart's face is set and angry. All I can do is raise my hands in general apology and stride out through the clubroom into the fresh night air.

Home. That was where Rock suggested I go. Home. *But where the fuck is that now?* The home I want to go to is my suite adjacent to Rock's that I had occupied since the Satan's Devils had moved to this compound. I've given that up though, allowing him and Becca to have more space. They needed it, having added baby Rose to their family.

Around me, my brothers have fallen like flies, all capturing their *one.* Their old lady, the love of their lives. While I would never have made a move on Becca—she was Rock's from the start even though he'd had his head up his ass for a while—she's the image of the woman I want.

Rock had taken time making up his mind, allowing me to become close to his woman. No one knows it was only my loyalty to him that had stopped me from stepping up and claiming her. She'd got under my skin. Those long hours when she'd stayed with me in my hospital room while I lay close to death. She'd been there, when I came back to life, but she was never for me, only for Rock. I knew it and hadn't interfered. The perfect woman for Rock had entered his life when he least likely expected it.

Just like it had happened with the others. Wraith's girl, Sophie, turned up out of the blue when she needed somewhere to hide and be safe. Drummer found Sam when she came searching for her father. Peg found his by the side of the road. One by one, Slick, Mouse, Blade and even Dart, who subsequently transferred to San Diego, stumbled across their old lady. Even young Pal eventually got the girl he'd been waiting for. It seemed so easy. No one can doubt my brothers have all found the woman they know they can be faithful to for the rest of their lives.

That's what I had in mind, what I wanted for myself. A wife and a family. It wouldn't have mattered if those kids had come readymade, if she'd been the right woman for me. I thought I'd found her, but, as it turned out, I'd been too hasty. Thought because she'd fallen into my path, that I should make her my old lady.

Starting my engine, I head out through the gates the prospect slides open for me, pointing my bike as Rock had instructed, toward what everyone else calls my home.

As I ride, I think how I couldn't describe it as that. It's a house the club owns, the property where Heart had lived with his first wife. The single storey building which now houses the woman I claimed, and her two children.

I should be happy, I muse, as I kick down the stand, before reluctantly taking the few steps toward the front door. This is what I wanted after all, a woman I could call mine waiting for me to come home. It hurts to say it's not working out and will be painful when I have to admit that to my brothers.

They already know.

Yeah. They probably do, though no one has said as much. All waiting for me to give them the words. The signs have been there, almost from the beginning. I'd jumped in with both feet far too fast, and now I've no idea how to extricate myself. I'm a coward, knowing what I should do, but not being brave enough to cause the hurt I know will result.

I open the front door as quietly as I can. The clock once belonging to Heart, well, we moved into this place fully furnished, shows it's eleven o'clock, and I might be lucky. She might have gone to bed. As I'm wondering whether I can get away with sleeping on the couch, tomorrow's excuse running through my head, *I didn't want to disturb you,* footsteps sound.

"Beef. You're back."

A tinge of guilt at the joy in her voice. A suggestion that maybe she'd thought I wouldn't come home. I may have considered sinking my cock into a sweet butt, Allie's perhaps, she's sweet as pie, or taking Paige and Diva together as I have many times in the past, but I'm not so much of a bastard to do that to the woman who's trying so hard to make things right between us. An impossible task, though she doesn't realise it.

"The kids are down, Beef. They've left some pictures for you. They were trying to draw your bike."

Yeah, guilt me why don't you? I don't need the reminder it's not just her I'd disappoint if I came out with the truth. Since her ex-husband went to prison and she got her divorce, she's pushed the kids at me at every opportunity. They're good kids, no complaints there, she's brought them up right. I like them well enough, if they had a different mother, maybe it would work out. But the woman who'd come into my life, the person I thought was meant for me, isn't the one I've been waiting for. *She isn't Becca, or anything like her.*

"Sally," I begin, my voice tired.

"Beef," she interrupts. A look of concern on her face. "What's happened?" Taking a step forward, she raises her hand and touches my eye. I flinch. *Rock must have got a lucky shot in.* I hadn't even felt it. "Have you been fighting?"

That right there. The look of disgust that she can't hide. I'm a biker. Yeah, tonight I went too far, but I regularly spar with my brothers. It keeps us fit, sharp. She didn't mind violence when it rescued her from the situation she'd been in. But now? Her background shows. A gentle woman from a moneyed family.

"Just sparred with Rock," I explain. "You know what we do, Sally."

"I'll clean it for you."

Another woman's attentions might be welcomed, not hers. Becca will probably be doctoring Rock and, after she's fussed him enough, with the birth of Rose a few months back, her touch will probably end up with him having his cock deep inside her. "Nah, Sal, I'm fine. I'll do it myself."

Sally might not be the right woman for me, but it's not because she's stupid. A wistfulness crosses her face, a clear sign she wants me to let her help. "I'll get you a beer."

I don't need serving. But how do you turn down a well-meant gesture? "Sure. I'll be right back."

While she disappears into the kitchen, I take myself off to the half bath, take a much-needed piss, then examine my reflection in the mirror. There's a small cut above my eye, no wonder it didn't register. Nothing to worry about at all. Still, to ease Sally's mind I splash my face with water, getting rid of the dried blood. So tiny a wound, it doesn't bleed after.

I stare at my reflected image as though it might have more answers than me. How can I tell a woman like her that things are not working out? I hadn't lifted a finger nor been an active participant when we got together, no effort required on my part at all. When she stayed at the clubhouse waiting for the media to lose interest in her husband's high-profile court case, she'd latched onto me. To my shame and regret, I hadn't put up much objection, it had been easier to go along with it. When it was suggested she move into Heart's place, along with her kids, the thought of being alone had caused her stress. When she'd hinted she'd like company, I said I'd go with her, just to help ease her into her new life.

Playing house had been a novelty at first. A woman I could call mine to come home to. When she invited me into her bed, what can I say? I'm a man, I went. It was okay, I got off, made sure she did too. When my brothers asked if I was claiming her, I said yes.

It soon became clear, my preferred style of loving wasn't hers. My adventurous nature a complete turn off. Missionary position was the only way she permitted me to take her. After years of variety, I soon got bored. Wouldn't step out on her though. Not while I was with her.

Her husband had beaten her, badly. Had agreed to stay away from her and had for two years. until a wife and family was helpful in his desire to have a political career. She'd been afraid of him, with good reason. In front of her, he admitted he'd get the sympathetic vote if she was killed.

She's already been told she's worthless. How could I do that to her too? I never realised Sebastian Lawson had been her first and only boyfriend, her family had kept her sheltered until they'd found her a suitable man. Now that I know, it influences what I can do. She's no knowledge of break-ups, of relationships which don't work. Her husband wanted her dead, and I'm thinking of discarding her like, what, a worn-out shoe?

Nah. Can't do that to her. I'll have to stay and make this work.

"Beef? You okay?"

"Coming." I flush the toilet. Then I take a deep breath to fortify myself.

In the living room she pats the seat beside her. "Got your beer, Beef. I wanted to talk to you."

Please tell me you know this isn't working out. As I place my ass on the cushion, it dips, moving her body closer to mine. I lean forward to pick up the glass she's just placed there. Normally I drink beer straight from the bottle but am not given the choice when Sally's around. I risk a glance at her, there's an excited gleam in her eyes.

"You know how you want me to ride your bike?"

I'm not one to place any particular emphasis of who the

woman is riding up behind me. But as far as anyone's concerned Sally's my old lady, and as such her place should be pillion on my bike. But she'd quickly disavowed me of any notion she'd be doing that. *Too dangerous,* she told me.

"You changed your mind?" Now, that would be a good start. Along with perhaps letting me stick my cock in her when she's on her hands and knees. One thing about Sally, she's got a great ass, with hips a man could hang onto.

"Well, I might." The words are said triumphantly.

"Yeah?" Maybe things have started looking up. Now if I could get her…

"Look Beef. I'd feel safe on that."

She turns her tablet toward me. My eyes roll back in my head. She's showing me a Goldwing, with a rear passenger seat like a fucking armchair. Safe? Yeah. "Sal, that's a fuckin' Honda. I'd be thrown out of the club." Probably wouldn't. If push came to shove, we'd change our by-laws rather than expel a member due to his choice of bike. But all the members ride Harleys, well, a couple in other chapters have Indians, and some have vintage bikes they ride time to time, but what she's showing me? I can just imagine doing a high-speed chase or getaway on it. It would be a complete joke. Her idea is not going to work.

Seeing the disdainful expression on my face, she pouts. "If you don't like the make, doesn't Harley do a similar model?"

"Yeah, they do, Sal…"

"Well why not get one of them?"

Because I like the speed and manoeuvrability of my Fat Bob. "Haven't got the money to buy a new bike. Those cost close to thirty big ones."

"I've got the money."

Abruptly I stand, the cushion bouncing back displaces her, causing her to reach out her hand to regain her balance. "I said no, Sally. You wanted to be with a biker? Well, you have to love the man, the club, and his choice of bike. I'm going to bed."

CHAPTER TWO

I pretended to sleep but spent most of the night awake worrying about three things. How badly I may have damaged my long-time relationship with Rock, what was going to happen with Sally, and on top of the list, what would happen at the promised morning's meeting with Drummer?

Not only is Drummer the president of the Tucson Chapter of the Satan's Devils MC, he's also the national prez as Tucson is the mother chapter, the club having been started way back in Bastard's day. When Drummer, Bastard's son, took the helm, he got us out of a lot of the shit we'd previously been into. Easy money, but an easy way to die. It takes a strong man to lead not just one, but all the chapters of an MC, and Drummer hasn't maintained the top spot for as many years as he has by being weak. A fair man, he'll give it to you straight when you've fucked up. Words out of his mouth, that withering stare from those steel-grey eyes, and even a muscle man like me wants to slide under the table.

After last night's fiasco, I reckon I'll be flayed alive.

"Mornin'."

"Ah, fuck, man. You okay?" I step toward Rock, my eyes squinting to take in the damage.

"Becca's not happy with you," he replies, shrugging off my concern.

"Shit."

"Aw, come on. Messin' with you, man. She's fine. Worried about you more than me, I think."

Flashing him a grin I laugh, "And so she should be. Me and her? We're close." I press my forefinger and thumb tightly together and hold them up in front of his face. For which, not unsurprisingly, I get a clout around the head. Then, flicking worried eyes toward the clubhouse, add, "Well, I better get inside."

"Yeah, you're seeing the head teacher, aren't you? You might have detention. Oooh. Or homework. You might have to write out 'I must not hit Rock' fifty times."

"Shut it," I growl, shaking my head.

"Or you could get expelled."

I shoot my middle finger toward him as I walk inside. One thing you're not when you're summoned to see Drummer, is late. Pleased to see I'm right on time, I knock on his door.

"Yeah."

Entering, I pause until he waves me to the chair in front of his desk. I suppose this is going to take time. Prez asking me what the fuck happened last night, and me being unable to explain, or admit I know the reason why. I decide to take the initiative and sit forward. "Look, Prez, I'm..."

"Sorry you beat the shit out of your brother?" Drummer leans back in his chair, linking his hands behind his head. "Gonna give me a fuck load of excuses about why?" Suddenly he lurches forward. "Why don't we cut to the chase and I'll tell you?"

I suspect he's going to give me a few home truths I don't want to hear. But what can I do? He's my prez.

"You've let that woman get her hooks into you. Every fuckin' brother here could see she wasn't right for you, but you let her lead you along by your dick."

My dick makes bad choices. Even he ain't happy now.

As I shrug, Drummer reaches behind him. I could count the number of times on one hand that I've been in Drummer's office and have been offered a glass of his pure malt whisky. It's a sign this will be a serious conversation. I would have thought it was a bit too early to be hitting the hard stuff, but if he doesn't care it's not even the middle of the day, then who am I to object? If he's offering, I may need it.

He waits until I've taken a sip and have sighed in appreciation. "I don't get between men and their old ladies. Only a fool would do that, and I like to think I'm not such a fool." As I give the grin he expects, he resumes, "You've been the muscle at my back more times than I care to remember, Beef. Ready to back it up too. Not shy to get into a fight beside your brothers. But when it comes to women? Soft as fuckin' cotton wool."

Another raise and dip of my shoulders. Can't really argue with that. Wouldn't let a man get one up on me, but a woman? Yeah, perhaps spineless does describe it.

"Way I see it, Sally saw you, thought you were a good thing, and you simply went along with it. You probably saw it as a chance to have something that I, and your other brothers, have. Easy choice, Beef. Doesn't mean it was the right one."

"Wasn't hard for you, Prez. Sam dropped into your lap, so to speak."

The corners of his mouth curve. "I saw her, knew I wasn't going to let her go. Sure, I fought it, but she was mine from then on. Sally? Nah, don't think you can say the same Beef. I've watched you together, can't see she's your one."

"She wants me to get a fuckin' Goldwing," I input grumpily.

"What?" His laugh sounds incredulous. "An armchair on wheels?"

"I said no."

"Didn't need to add that, Brother." He chuckles, then frowns. "As I said, you're a fuckin' good man to have at my back, Beef. But you haven't got the guts to do what you need to do. I'm stepping in as I don't want a brother killed." He shakes his head as if remembering last night. "I'm telling you, not giving advice. Move back to the club. Viper's done up some new suites, take one of those."

"Sally's not going to like that."

"Don't give a fuck. I'm worried about you."

He lets that sink in. I know he's right, but it's not so easy for me to put his suggestion into action.

"It's an order, Beef. Dress it up to her as you will. I'm not risking last night happening again."

I'm not averse to his suggestion, it's just the acting on it that's going to be hard.

Sally needed a man, I needed a woman to take my mind off the one I wanted but couldn't have. Thought we could make it work, but it's turned out to be the worst mistake of my life. Problem is, there's no way I can get myself out of what I've got into without causing more harm.

It's easy for Drummer to suggest I cut her loose, but he's forgetting her background. She was married to a man who'd hurt and abused her, and in the end, had told her to her face she was worth more to him dead than alive. Any self-confidence she'd had had been slashed apart. If I outright tell her I don't want her, she'll blame herself. It's not her fault I can't be the man she wants. It's not on either of us our relationship doesn't work, it's that we're two different people who should never have teamed up together.

Yeah, I'm a marshmallow when it comes to dealing with her, but it's not just hurting her, it's trying not to deal a blow that could add to her existing insecurities and destroy her.

For my sanity, I have to get out. For her sake, I have to ease away, and not simply cut her from my life. Moving back to the club while letting her believe it's not final could be the first step. Loosen the ropes that bind us. Trouble is, I know my woman better than that, and she won't take me putting distance between us well.

Delaying the proposal won't help, and I won't be able to come up with a better solution however much time I give to my thoughts. Best do it now, while Drummer's voice is still echoing in my head, giving me some of the fortitude that, where women are concerned, I usually lack.

Leaving the relative sanctuary of the compound, I ride back into Tucson, for once not enjoying the wind therapy, too wound up about the conversation to come, a discussion long overdue. As my wheels spin beneath me, I berate myself yet again for getting into this mess, and not having the guts to get out of the situation as soon as I knew it was wrong.

Sally's at home alone, the kids are at school. If we're going to have tears and remonstrations, now's a good time as any. I lean against the washer as she separates the laundry into different piles, a small frown playing on my face as I see her sort my socks and underwear. I'm perfectly capable of washing my own shit, but it's the one area where she insists she's in charge.

"I'm moving back to the club."

Swinging around, her eyes are wide. "What did you say?"

"I'm going to stay at the club for a while."

"Beef!" She comes flying at me, her arms holding me tight, her cheek already wet with tears dampen my tee. "Don't leave me. I need you. What will I do without you? Don't go, please?" She starts to sob.

Oh fuck. I'm so fucking weak. "Hey, don't' cry, Sal. I'm not leaving you. It's just I need my own space for a bit. I'm not in a good headspace right now, and I'll only take my shit out on you and the kids if I'm around, and I don't want to do that."

"Is it me? Have I done or said something? Or are things upsetting you at the club?"

As good an excuse as any. "The club," I lie.

I can see her biting back words and am half expecting her to tell me I could leave the Satan's Devils, jumping at the perfect excuse I've given her. But when she ends up asking simply,

"You'll come back?" I wonder whether she's got some inkling it is *her*, and wants to skirt away from the truth as much as I.

"Uh huh," I lie again.

She pulls back and stares into my face. "How long, Beef?"

"I don't know, Sal. Until my head's screwed on right."

"I'll still see you. When I come to the club?"

"Of course."

"Okay. As long as I know I can call on you."

Her tears dry, but she hovers, checking how much I'm packing. In the end, it's not much, just the bare necessities to keep me going. It leaves her satisfied, but I'll have to come back.

All Drummer knows is that I bring a duffle of clothes and move into the suite he's made available. I don't fess up and tell him I haven't broken things off with Sally. Unfortunately, it isn't long before he gets the first hint, as all my brothers do.

"Beef. The bathroom tap is dripping, can you come fix it?"

"Beef, the timer on the cooker is wrong, can you reset it for me?"

Beef this, Beef that.

Sally's friendship with Tash and the other women is used as an excuse, so, acting out of character, she's at the club almost every day. Just as often it seems, I'm back at the house with odd jobs to do.

My concentration is fucked. Culminating in me forgetting to tighten the nuts properly when I put a wheel on a bike. Luckily Slick noticed the wobble before he hit speed.

I deserved his fist in my face.

As well as the dressing down that's now to come from Drummer.

I approach the prez's office, pausing for a moment outside, wiping my hands down my face. Two weeks ago, he told me to end it with Sally. Sure, I'm staying most nights at the clubhouse, but as for her getting the message? No fucking chance.

Inside, I open my mouth to apologise.

He raises his hand. "Called you here for a reason, Beef." *To give me shit about Slick's bike. Of course you did.* I wait for it.

"Need you to do something for me."

"Yeah, I… what?" His opening gambit has floored me. "Er, yeah. Whatever you need, Prez."

He chuckles. "Like that, Brother. But I think you best hear me out before agreeing off the top of your head. Might be something you don't want to do."

I *like* that it sounds like I'm going to be useful to him. Rather do Drummer a favour any day of the week than have him tear me off a strip for making a rookie mistake. "What's up?"

"Colorado."

Whatever I expected him to say, it wasn't that. "Prez?"

"You were there with us a few weeks back, Beef. You must have noticed Demon's new to wearing the prez's patch. I expected Hellfire would back him up more, stand up by his side, but it hasn't worked out like I thought. Hell's all but into his retirement now, just wants a comfortable life. Demon's VP, Thunder, only took the job on temporarily, as he reminds him and anyone else who'll listen, all the time."

I nod. "Heard him say that myself." Hellfire was the ex-prez who'd stepped down to allow his VP, and son, Demon, to move into the top spot. Problem is, that's left a hole in the officer ranks which, as Drummer has pointed out, is for the meantime, being filled reluctantly by the sergeant-at-arms.

"I want someone to go and check things out. Report back to me how the club's running, and whether I need to step in."

"And you want that to be me?" I'm stunned. Not that I don't think I could do what he's asking, I didn't expect to be his first choice.

"Yeah. Trust you Beef. You and I have ridden together a long time. Most of the men here are now family men, haven't got much choice in who to send. Road? Hyde? Jekyll? Not been patched in that long. Drifter? He's even newer than the others. Marvel? He can be too much of a joker, and Dollar I need here. Don't have much choice out of the men unencumbered by ol' ladies."

"There's Sally," I remind him. I'm not exactly a free man myself.

There's the stare. The one that sees deep inside you. "Yeah." If possible his eyes sharpen. "We gonna talk about that?"

I raise and lower my shoulders. "She's weak, Drum. I tell her I'm walking out for good? I just don't know how she'd cope. She relies on me. She needs me."

"And you need to be needed. But there comes a limit, Brother."

He's right about that. I'd reached mine long ago.

"Which brings me back to my suggestion. Thought getting you to the club would provide the break you needed but underestimated the depth of Sally's claws. So, Colorado. That enough space?"

My mind loops back to his proposal. "Effectively she'd be kicking me out of my home, out of Tucson." I live for this club. Ire starts to burn inside me at the thought *I'm* the one who has to go. *Yeah, but I'm the one who's running from hurting a woman.*

"You tell me you don't want to do this? My choice might not be my first one, but I'll find someone else. I got a need, Beef, and decided you can fill it. The fact that my need provides you with a solution is just happy coincidence."

Morosely I stare down at my hands. "Sally won't do well on her own."

"Vulnerable and helpless, yeah? That's why you're giving into her every demand. She's got you all twisted up. You say how you really feel, and she'll pull out every sympathy card going. Am I right?"

That and then some. I don't bother using words. Just raise my chin.

"So you heading up to Pueblo for a few weeks, this gives her a chance to learn how to cope. If she prefers, she can go back to her family. There's no longer a problem now that her ex, Lawson, has been jailed."

"She likes being independent, Prez. Doesn't want to go back."

Drummer exasperatedly shakes his head. "But she's not being independent. Not when you're at her beck and call."

I think over what he's just said. Then I come to a decision. "I'll go." My initial impulse to refuse had, as Drummer rightly surmised, been guilt about Sally. If he thinks this is the right way to force a break, then I'll do it. It's the thought of leaving my brothers behind that's fucking hard to take. I patched into Tucson many years ago, never thought about transferring to a different chapter. Living with the Satan's Devils has been the only home I've known since I left the army. Now my main concern isn't about leaving Sally, but my friends here. "How long, Prez?"

"As long as it takes. I need to know I've a man there who I've complete faith in. Want you to be my eyes and ears, maybe see if you can push Demon into appointing a second."

"Is he going to like that, Prez?" My brows knit together at the thought of the kind of welcome I'd get. A nobody like me turning up and telling a president how to run his own club.

I underestimated Drummer. "Don't see anyone would question you wanting to visit with Pal and Jayden?" His eyebrow rises.

I catch up with him fast. "Under the circumstances, yeah. I can play it that way if you want, Prez." I narrow my eyes. "You've spoken to Demon? How much have you told him? Has he any idea why I'm really going?"

"Nah. Just told him I had a member who needed some time to get his head on straight. What you tell him when you get there, well, I'll leave that to you. You'll be on the ground, you make the calls. I did tell him you put in a request to go nomad."

I sit up straight, that puts a different perspective on matters. "Lose my fuckin' Tucson rocker?" I rapidly shake my head. Don't like that. Don't like that at all.

"It makes sense, and it's the role I'm asking you to play. The mother chapter's representative checking out the other chapters."

"Chapters?" I thought a few weeks away and then I'd be back. This is a more serious decision than I expected.

"We can revisit when you've sorted out Colorado." He shrugs.

Nomad. A biker, on his own. Essentially Drummer's traveling enforcer. It's not that I can't do it. It's the thought of the loss of the rocker denoting me without a permanent chapter that concerns me. Tucson's my home, I'm not ready to say goodbye to it.

"Makes it easier for your brothers to accept, Beef." Drummer's tone is persuasive. "A request from you to go nomad, without having to explain your personal circumstances. Someone has to do it. No pressure. Your choice."

"I *can* come back, Prez. Can't I?" If my voice has a hint of desperation in it, I can't help it.

Drummer suddenly snarls, "Be fuckin' hard to see you go, Brother. Believe that. But I need someone in Colorado, you need some distance from your life here. Of course, you can fuckin' return when you're ready, and when Demon's got his top team sorted."

Simple, really. A chance to get out of Sally's life, or rather, her out of mine. A break away from the love and perfect relationships I see all around me. Time to catch my breath and decide what I really want, without hankering after a woman called Becca. A task that Drummer thinks I'm up to. "Prez." The determination in my voice has him grinning. "I'd like to put in a request to become nomad."

"Bring it to the table," Drummer replies, standing, his hand outstretched. I stand too and take it.

CHAPTER THREE

Normally I'd include my best friend in any plans I'm making. This time, I keep my thoughts to myself. When I eventually tell my brothers my intentions, my decision doesn't go unchallenged.

"You are fuckin' jokin'." Rock stares at me across the table. I'd waited until all other business had been sorted at Friday night's church, then tabled my request. "You knew about this, Prez?"

Drummer eyes my best friend. "Of course I fuckin' did. Beef has my blessin'."

"You're really walking out on us?" Peg's shaking his head.

"Sergeant-at-arms," Drummer snaps. "Beef's request fits in with my plans. I need eyes and ears in Pueblo."

"Yeah, but Beef?" Blade's looking utterly shocked. "We need him here, Prez."

"This have anything to do with the woman you're shacking up with? She been putting pressure on you to move?"

Drummer was right. I really don't want to air what a failure I've been at having an old lady at the table. My response to Rock is simply to tell him, "Nothing at all. She won't be coming with me."

"Christ, she's going to love that. You told her?" Lady seems to have got her measure.

I just glare at him. The fact that I haven't, *yet*, is none of his business. Got that pleasure to come.

"If you don't want to agree to Beef removing his Tucson rocker, who else do you suggest? Who's volunteering?" Drummer asks in a reasonable tone.

We've got the best clubhouse in the charter. Swimming pool, houses being built at the top of the compound for any couple who wants one, enough women snapping whips so the prospects keep the clubroom clean and tidy. Anyone would be a fool to want to leave. A wave of homesickness crashes over me, even though I haven't yet packed my bags, and I remind myself, one word to Drummer and I'll be back. I tell them that, too. "It's not forever. Just until I've sorted business."

"And after Colorado. Where will you send him then?" Dollar asks.

My eyes snap to Drum's. Hoping he won't say that I'll be wandering clubhouse to clubhouse.

Prez gazes at me intently. "Wherever there's a need."

He means until Sally's given up on me coming back, doesn't he?

Rock's stare is almost worse than that of the prez. "You un-claiming your ol' lady?"

"I can't take her with me, not that she'd want to go. Seems wrong to keep her tied down when my future's uncertain. So, yeah, Brother." It's not like I've patched her yet. Since she's not shown any inclination to be on my bike, nor party at the clubhouse, I haven't given her a vest.

"Your mind's set?" a voice sounds resigned.

I've an affinity with Road. After Rock met Becca, and before I had Sally, I'd taken to sharing women with him. You get a certain closeness when you feel another man's cock as he's sliding into their ass, and you're in their cunt. Or vice versa.

I take a moment to look around this table, realising this is the last time for fuck knows how long. The table I first sat at when, like Drifter who's keeping silent, I'd first got my patch. *I'm gonna miss this. Miss every-fuckin'-one.* I then focus on Road and raise my chin. "Yeah, it is."

He stares back, then nods in resignation. "Then let me wish you good luck, Brother."

There's silence. A few eyes look toward Rock as though for guidance. It's no secret that while we'd all give our lives for each other, Rock and I have a bond that's stronger than most. I took a bullet while sheltering his injured body under my own, and had no problem doing it, knowing he would have done the same were the positions reversed.

I watch him dropping his head into his hands as he realises things will change. His friend who he's relied on for so many years, who's always had his back, will no longer be sitting opposite him. No longer will we high five each other across the table when we share a joke.

Everyone gives him the time he needs until finally he looks up and meets my eyes. "Will miss the fuck out of you, Beef, but you have to do what you need to."

That's all everyone needs. They go from suspicious to full one-hundred percent support. My eyes water. This is my family, and I'm leaving them. *Not forever.* But being nomad is dangerous, riding without a brother at your back. There's always the chance, however much I want to, I won't be sat around this table ever again.

A thought Peg seems to echo. "Prez, we're leeching members instead of trying to build up the club. Aren't you worried about that? Dart went to San Diego, and now Beef's going off to Colorado. And Truck…"

"Truck will be back," Drummer says firmly.

"You think?" Blade challenges. "Man refuses to see us, or his fellow firefighters. All we know is that he's fucked up. Might not be able to take his place around this table even if he wanted to."

There's a moment of silence as we all think about the new member. Patched him in on the eve of his transfer to a hotshot wildfire fighting team in California. He's didn't die, but that's as far as anyone knows.

"If you do get to see him," I offer into the quiet, "give him my best."

"A message from Satan?"

I snort. A reference to us both having come far too close to Hell's door.

CHAPTER FOUR

Telling my brothers I was going nomad ended up being easy, compared with trying to explain my absence to Sally.

"What will I do while you're gone, Beef?" She pauses, dabbing her eyes with a tissue, then loudly blowing her nose. "What will the *kids* do?"

I *hate* seeing a woman cry. My reaction is always to stop their tears, and if that means saying what they want to hear, that's what I normally do. Where a woman's concerned, I'm the ultimate peacemaker. If it had been just me, I'd back down, tell her I'll stay, that I won't walk out the door. But Drummer's relying on me.

It wasn't garbage he'd spouted, wasn't an excuse he'd made up. I'd been in Pueblo with him. While I respect the hell out of Demon, he's been thrust into the role of president and needs a good strong number two. Thunder, his sergeant-at-arms, is wearing the VP hat reluctantly. No one else in the chapter wants to step up, and remembering what I'd seen of them, while I respect them all as members, there's no one I could point to and say they'd be right in that spot.

I'm far from VP material myself—I only have to look at Wraith to know that. But maybe I can advise someone else, build them up, so they are capable of being at Demon's side. Or, even, suggest a transfer in from another chapter. Dart, who used to be a member in Tucson, is now Lost's VP in San Diego, and by all accounts, is doing very well too.

Drummer's right to identify the weakness in Colorado. So I'm not going off on a fool's errand, I've got a job to do. The fact Sally can't understand how the club comes first is another sign she'd never make it as an old lady.

"Why Beef, why? Can't one of the single men go?"

I don't explain that deep down I still view myself as single, though I don't the freedom which comes with that. I haven't told her much about why I'm leaving, that's club business. But I've said what I can. Now I repeat it again. "Sally, my president has asked me to do a job. I can't refuse. I'm a member of the club. He says I've got the right tools, and I go where he needs me."

"If he doesn't need you here, why don't you leave the club? You must be able to do something else. You're a vet…"

She breaks off as my eyes roll. Has she any idea how many vets are homeless with no work to do? What skills do we return with? Oh yeah, how to kill a man with our bare hands. Skills only something like an MC find useful. Leave the club? Never. I'll die a member.

"Can I talk to him? Tell him how much I, and the kids, need you?"

My eyes roll again and widen. I clamp my mouth shut. It's not like I'm a kid at school needing her to go to bat on my behalf with the teacher.

"Sally, we've only been together a few months. For years it was just you and the kids. They like me, I like them, but I haven't been around long enough for them to see me as a substitute father."

"Can we come with you?"

"We've been through this, Sal. I'm expected to live on the compound. It's not like Tucson at all. It's a converted steel factory. Not suitable for kids."

"We could rent a house."

"No, Sally. Just, no. I'm leaving, and that's final." My words in a tone I've not used with her before echo around the room. The irrevocability of my statement leaving her no room for a comeback. She's tried all the weapons she has, persuasion, coercion; nothing has worked.

She sobs, then tries to angrily wipe the tears away. "You don't want me, do you?"

"It's not you, Sal, it's my job." She's given me an out, I'm a weak man, I can't take it. I don't want her to think there's anything wrong with her.

"You'll come back to visit?"

I can't even promise her that. "I don't know if I'll have the time."

"And how long will you be away for?"

"I don't know."

A little gasp, then she forces the issue. "You're not coming back, are you?"

"I'm coming back." My tone is positive at that.

"But not to me."

"Let's see how things go, shall we?" I give a half smile. "You might not miss me at all." When her mouth drops open, I step closer, gentling my voice. "Sal, I don't want to lead you on, but it's not working out how I thought. Maybe I'm not old man material."

But when she scoffs and says, "The old 'it's not you it's me' talk." I realise I have to give her some of the truth.

"It's not you, it's not me, it's us, Sal. I know you think it's working out, but it isn't. The man I am around you, isn't the man I want to be."

"Look, my last marriage wasn't perfect. Maybe I'm trying too hard to be the good wife I thought you'd want. I can change Beef. Give me a chance."

But she couldn't change into the woman I need her to be. Someone more adventurous, someone who wants to be part of my life rather than just fitting me in as part of hers. "If nothing else, Sal, this time apart will give us a chance to examine our feelings for each other."

"I know mine. I love you."

But she doesn't, not really. She loves the idea of a man who comes home to her each night. And the most I've got going for me is that I don't use my fists on her. Not the ideal for a perfect relationship. I don't reply. I can't say I love her back. I never have, and while I tried hard, now I know, I never will.

Had I led her on? Maybe. But as Drummer said, she was the one chasing me. I'd agreed to move in until she settled and got comfortable, not realising that time would never come. I've got my escape route now. I'm going to use it.

"Let's sleep on it. Things will look different in the morning. I'm going to bed. You coming with me?"

She doesn't get it or won't accept it. A few hours aren't going to change my mind. I don't reply as she walks down the hall leaving me feeling like the biggest heel in the world. My brothers had made relationships look easy, but this experiment proves they're not, at least for me. I'm taking this experience as a serious warning not to let another woman get close. I'll do okay on my own. I'm off to a clubhouse of mainly single men. Sweet butts on tap. That will do for me. I never want to be in this position again. Nah. I gave a relationship a chance once, and it's shown it isn't for me. I wonder how my brothers do it, being at their old lady's beck and call? Nope. Definitely not for me.

The sounds of her using the bathroom fade, water running into the sink, a flush, then the bedroom door opens and shuts. I start walking around, looking at the shit of mine I moved in. A few Harley magazines, they go in the trash. A parts manual, that I'll take. I open drawers and cabinets slowly realising how little of me is here. The remainder of my clothes I hadn't already taken to the clubhouse, I'll pack in the morning. Shooter volunteered to bring the truck to take what I can't fit in my saddle bags and put it into storage at the club, but to be honest, there won't be much.

After puttering around for a while, I sit down on the couch, lean back my head and try to sleep.

"You didn't come to bed," her accusing voice wakes me the next morning.

"I thought you'd prefer to be on your own," I lie. Then stand and stretch. "Shooter will be here soon, I'll go grab my shit." I don't want to rehash last night's conversation. I want to get out of here as fast as I can. It doesn't take me long to get my toiletries from the bathroom, then separate my clothes into those I'm taking and those I'm leaving behind. There's just one more thing I need to do.

I take out my knife and slice the Tucson Chapter patch off my cut, then, raiding Sally's sewing kit get a needle and thread and sew the Nomad one on instead. Christ, by the time I've finished I've pricked my finger more than once, as it's hard to see through the tears that had fallen when I took off the Tucson insignia. The residual wetness on my face reminding me, I'm shedding none at the thought of leaving her.

She tries one more time. "Am I still your old lady, Beef?"

"Beef, you ready?" Shooter shouts from outside the door.

"Give me a minute," I respond, then turn back. "Sal. It's been..." *Good? Interesting? A lesson learned?* "Say goodbye to the kids for me."

"Beef. Don't go."

"I have to Sal. It's what I've been asked to do. And to be honest, it's best for us to have a break too."

"Will you be faithful?"

What? Oh fuck, why did she have to go there? I'm itching for my cock to get the sort of workout it loves. I'm already salivating at the thoughts of the sweet butts in the Colorado club. "Sal, babe. I'll be gone a while."

"No, Beef. You said we're on a break, not that we've broken up. My feelings for you won't change. I don't want you sleeping with anyone else."

Not sleeping I can promise her. But that's not fair.

"Beef?" Shooter yells.

"I've got to go, babe." One more look at her face, and I know I have to leave her with something. With a silent apology to my dick, I offer the words she wants to hear. "I promise."

She goes on her tiptoes to kiss me. I turn my cheek so her lips press only against my skin, then, I open the door and leave. Shooter takes a bag of clothes and throws it in the back of the truck.

I stand wiping my brow with my hand, then pass it down my face. I'm a fucking idiot with no one to blame but myself. I could simply have said the words, *it's over*, yet couldn't force them out of my mouth. I'm postponing the inevitable, not cancelling it. Well, I only got what I deserve.

"Man, you look like shit," Shooter tells me when he catches sight of my face. *Thanks for that, friend.* "You going to be okay for the ride?"

I just toss him a glare. *I could ride in my sleep, I'll be fine.* Right now I'm trying to get my head around the fact that I, an over-sexed biker, have just promised to be celibate. For a woman I've no feelings for. *She'll never know.* But I will.

What a fucking mess.

Rock and the others had wanted to give me an escort out of our territory, but I'd turned them down, wanting to start as I am meant to go on. I'm now nomad, a biker riding alone, best get used to it. It was tempting to ride one last time alongside my brothers, but I'd preferred to say my goodbyes at the clubhouse. There would never be a good time to part company.

I follow Shooter as he drives back to the compound, but when he turns off, I carry straight on. I swear I have to fight my bike for a moment as it seems to want to steer in the direction of what I consider my true home.

Instead, I resolutely face my bike north and keep my hand to the throttle.

It's an eleven-hour ride to Pueblo. I know, it was only a few weeks ago that I last rode there. At first, the sun on my face, the wind cooling my body, the pavement rolling by beneath my wheels gives me the sense of freedom I need. Slowly though, I'm twisting the nut to hold the throttle in position, as my hand starts to cramp. My ass begins to feel bruised, and the loneliness of riding without companions gets to me. I can't remember when I last made a journey this long without riding with a pack, or at least one brother for company. *But that's what being a nomad means.* I knew this when I accepted.

Has it all been for nothing? Damn. My hand slaps my leg as I realise Sally's still got me in her hold even though I'll be eight hundred miles away.

Nope. No old lady for me. Never again. Never letting someone close to me. My one example is still controlling me. Stupid, stupid Beef. I should have made the clean break then and there. Now I've committed to only my hand being on my cock.

I pull over when a rainstorm gets too heavy, taking the opportunity to top both me and my tank off with fuel. Then it's back on the road again as steam from the fast evaporating standing water starts to rise when the clouds clear.

Weary, almost in a trance I arrive in Pueblo just when the sun's beginning to set. A clock above a store front tells me it's six-forty pm. I get lost and have to backtrack, see a distant sign and take a shortcut up a backstreet, wondering if I'll be here long enough to feel familiar with the layout of the roads. I'm stopped at a junction, waiting for a safe gap in the traffic that's steadily going past, knowing I'm too tired to take chances right now, when to my horror I take in the sight on the opposite side of the road. A car, moving fast, and mounting the sidewalk.

"Get out of the way!" but my roared instruction is drowned out by the traffic. It's as though I see it happen in slow motion. A girl, a woman, who the fuck knows, with her hand on a dog's harness… Christ, the car's heading straight for her. The vehicles continuing to roar past on the main road cause almost a strobe effect. My eyes can't look away as I see the dog react, it pushes the woman, she falls…

A woman's startled cry. A piercing, ear-splitting heart-rending scream from the dog. The squeal of brakes, the shouting. I'm off my bike and tearing across the road dodging traffic that hasn't bothered to stop. The woman is half sitting, half lying against a brick wall.

I reach her before anyone else and appear to be the only one getting involved. The car which struck her is disappearing in the distance, hopefully someone took note of the licence plate.

"You okay?" I snap.

"My dog! Max. My dog." She's crying hysterically, repeatedly calling out the name. It's when her hands start touching the pavement, feeling around her that I realise she's blind, and that the dog who's gone silent isn't just a pet, it's her lifeline.

"Someone call a fuckin' vet!" I yell out. "It's an assistance dog." I stand, the woman doesn't seem to be badly hurt, more concerned and upset than anything else. Touching her briefly on the shoulder, I then go to the canine, expecting to find it dead. *It saved her.* If it hadn't seen what was going on, she'd have taken a direct hit. She couldn't have evaded it, literally wouldn't have seen the car coming.

The dog's breathing. I don't want to move or touch it. A man's injuries I could assess, but the closest I've got to a dog is Grunt back in the Tucson clubhouse. I walk to a man who's got his phone in his hand.

"You called a fuckin' vet?" I grab his jacket.

"You'll need to find one and take the dog to him," a woman with her hand over her mouth tells me. She looks like she's trying not to be sick. "Vet's don't come out."

"I called an ambulance, man." The guy I'm holding looks scared out of his wits but manages to convey disgust that I seem to care more about the dog than the woman. But I'm pretty sure the car didn't hit her, and that the dog has the more serious injuries. I'd had a prime seat from across the other side of the junction after all.

With a wailing of sirens, an ambulance appears. The medics examine the woman and get her up.

"Max. Max. Max? Where are you, boy?"

"Ma'am, we've got to take you in. You seemed to have banged your head."

"I'm not leaving my dog. Where is he? I need to go to him."

"Ma'am." I don't know why I offer, it's none of my business at all. But of the few people who've stopped, they all seem to lose interest now the woman's got help. "I'll stay with the dog, I'll make sure I get a vet for him. Find out how he's doing, then I'll let you know. Where are you taking her?" I direct my question to the paramedic, and then mentally note his answer of the name of the hospital I'll need help to find.

"You promise?" Her head is tilted in my direction, locating me only by the sound of my voice, hers is full of desperation as she repeats. "You really promise? You'll see he gets help?"

"I promise." My teeth are gritted. I've no reason to help. I'm tired as hell and want nothing more than a beer and a bed. But something about this situation gets to me, and I know I can't walk away.

"Is he, is he...?"

"He's breathing—" I start answering the question I know she's asking in the only way I can. Then I pause. She seems to realise I'm asking a question.

"Stevie."

"Yeah, well, he's breathing Stevie. But unconscious."

"He's my, he's my..."

"I know," I say firmly, knowing she was going to tell me he wasn't just a pet. "Believe me, I know."

"I want to stay with him."

I see the medic shaking his head, and again I find myself repeating a promise while half of me wonders why the fuck I'm getting involved. "I'll stay with him. I'll update you as soon as I know anything, but I won't leave him alone."

What am I getting myself into? Instead of drinking with

brothers in the clubhouse, I'll probably be sitting in a waiting room. That's if the dog survives a visit to the vet. A journey which at the moment, I've no idea how to take.

She sniffs, loudly, making an effort to hold back the sobs which I can tell aren't too far away. She holds out her hand in my general direction. When I grasp it, her fingers wrap around mine and squeeze. "I don't know who you are, but I trust you. He, he's my everything. Please do what you can to help."

As the medic takes her arm to lead her to the ambulance, I feel a loss when her hand leaves mine.

CHAPTER FIVE

I t wasn't how I envisioned my arrival in Pueblo. I wouldn't have been surprised, as no biker turns down the opportunity for a party, that my visit to Pal may have been sufficient for a celebration to have been arranged. Satan's Devils don't need much of an excuse to break out the drink.

Even if it was just to be a quiet night that would have been fine. What I hadn't anticipated was to have taken responsibility for a Labrador retriever who's currently lying injured or quite possibly dying at my feet. Quickly I compute my options and know I can't do this alone. Taking my phone out of my cut, I place a call.

"Pal… Yeah, look. I'm here… Yes. But I fuckin' need help." I go on to explain the situation. Pal might be young, but as soon as he knows what the emergency is, thank fuck he stops asking questions and simply wants my location. Looking around, *how the fuck do I know what street I'm on?* I give him enough clues to guess, and he agrees to come meet me.

He pulls up with another brother on his bike, and a prospect and someone else in a truck. It's my luck the clubhouse isn't far away, and they arrive fast. I'm relieved help has now arrived, as my bike's still where I left it, abandoned on the opposite side of the junction. I couldn't move it as I didn't want to leave the dog. I recognise Pyro as the man who's come with Pal and nod my thanks as he immediately goes over to wheel it across the road.

"I brought Rusty," Pal points to the man beside him. I nod, recognising him as someone I'd fought beside just a few weeks back. "He's our medic. Thought he might be able to help."

Wasting no time, Rusty kneels beside the stricken dog. After a moment he looks up. "He's still breathing, but I'm no vet. Wouldn't know where to fuckin' start."

"Know where we should take him?"

Rusty scratches his head. "Not had any reason to go see an animal doctor."

Pal's tapping at his phone. "According to Google, there's one quite close. Whether he's any good or not…"

"Let's go." Having stated my intent, I eye the dog. If it had been a man, I'd have been able to assess better how to pick him up without doing more damage. A fucking dog? I've no idea. All I know is my promise to Stevie, a blind woman who I've only just met.

Rusty's looking at me and shaking his head as I hesitate. "Thought we were going."

"I don't want to hurt him worse," I reply lamely.

"Fuck, man." He throws me a scathing look, and immediately bends down, huffing as he picks up the eighty or so pound dog.

The dog makes no sound or movement as he's lifted into the air, then placed on the rear seat of the truck. That, to me, doesn't seem to be a good sign.

"Just called the vet." Pal's in the process of sliding his phone back into his cut. "It's good timing. He's finishing up his consultations and will be ready for us."

"He sound like he knows what he's doing?"

Pal's eyes widen. "How the fuck should I know?"

I have no idea what to do with an injured animal, or whether a service dog should go to a specialist hospital or not. I go to my ride that Pyro had rescued from the other side of the road and am right behind the prospect and the truck as he pulls away, glad to see he's got the sense to move off gently. I'm surprised when two bikes fall in behind me. While Rusty's making his way back to the club, it looks like Pal and Pyro are coming to keep me company. Can't say I object to that. Whatever chapter we're from, Devils are Devils, it's good to have my brothers at my back.

"Leave him," I instruct the prospect sharply, when he opens the back door of the truck after we arrive at the veterinary hospital. Not wanting to move Max and hurt him further, I walk inside to see if I can find someone to help. It's only a small place. There's a woman in scrubs at reception, it looks like she doubles as a nurse.

Her eyes widen when she sees me, and I'm not surprised. I'm a big man and I'm wearing a leather cut, clearly denoting I'm a member of an MC. It's such a common reaction I barely register her taking a step closer to the phone as if ready to summon help.

"Er, can I help?"

"Got a dog outside. Hit by a car. Needs attention. We rang…"

"That the service dog?" At my nod she becomes all business. "Hang on, I'll get James." Now she knows we're not here to rob the place, her attitude completely changes. A man rushes out of the back and passes with barely a glance at me. Within moments they've got Max on some sort of gurney and are wheeling him inside.

"He's a service dog," I say with emphasis, as the vet passes by for the second time.

"I've got eyes and can read," the man who's clearly the vet replies sharply.

Of course he'd seen that. I hadn't wanted to remove the harness in case it was holding something vital together.

"You might have eyes, his owner hasn't," I snap back copying his tone. "She needs that dog to be alright. You heal him, you hear me?"

James, or whatever his name is, pauses briefly. "You think I wouldn't do everything I can? Doesn't matter if he's a service dog or the family pet. If it's possible to help him through this, I will, but I'm not God."

"Sorry man." Yeah, maybe I'd been a bit rough on him, but watching that accident happen? Well, it had been a shock for me. The way the dog knew danger was coming and bore the brunt of it himself. Well that takes bravery, and this biker, for one, is fucking impressed.

"I'm taking him in the back. I'm not happy with his breathing. He'll need X-rays. It might be helpful if I know how the injury happened. Give a summary to Vera, will you?" he nods at the nurse. "Then, Vera, I'll need your help."

She jerks her head in agreement, then narrows her eyes at me. "What happened? You knock him over with your bike?"

"Christ, no," I snap, disliking her attitude. Then, for the second time this evening, I explain how things went down.

Immediately her bearing relaxes, and a sympathetic expression crosses her face. "Who's the owner?"

"Girl called Stevie. I didn't get the rest of her name." I tell her the hospital, where she was taken, but that's as much as I know. As she frowns, I realise what could be an issue. "Look, I'll pay. Whatever."

"It could get expensive," she warns.

Fuck knows why, I wasn't responsible for Max's injuries, but I've got some money saved and if need be, this seems as good a use as any for it. I wouldn't want him to go untreated because of the cost. There was just something about how Max saved his mistress that got to me. Loyalty like that? Can't be ignored. "I'll pay," I tell her again.

"Could be the association that supplied him might pay the bills. Won't know the arrangements until we can talk to this Stevie. Now, excuse me, I've got to go back and assist James. Have you a number I can call with an update?"

I'd promised I wouldn't leave him, or at least not until there was news. "I'll wait." Before she can attempt to throw me out, I walk to a hard-plastic seat that's far too small for my ass but ignoring that, sit. Then I fold my arms and stare back at her with determination.

She doesn't argue. Well, it's not like she could move me. Her eyes flick to the door, then, with a shrug that suggests her canine patient is more important than any protest, she disappears after the vet.

I hadn't noticed Pyro and Pal come in. They squeeze themselves into seats one away and to either side of myself. I look from one to the other as if I'm watching a tennis ball bounce between two rackets. "You don't have to stay."

"No worries." Pyro stretches out his long legs, putting his arms over the backs of the seats to either side of him.

"Not got anything better to do." Pal folds one leg over the other.

It's Saturday night. Okay, so Pal's got an old lady, but Pyro looks like a party type of man, in a beer and pussy type of way, of course. I suspect that they're both lying. It warms my heart they intend to keep me company.

"So how was the journey, Beef?" Pal asks when the silence becomes too heavy.

"Fuckin' long. Good to start with, but after a few hours I could feel my age." My back twinges as I'm speaking, and I lean forward and reaching back, try to rub a few kinks out.

"You're not old," Pyro scoffs. "Look about my age."

"Thirty-seven," I tell him, feeling every minute of it. It's the first time I've relaxed in hours, and the ride has caught up with me. "How old are you?"

"Told you. Your age or thereabouts. Thirty-six."

"Christ, you two are ancient."

Leaning over I scuff Pal's hair. "You're just a baby."

He swipes my hand away. "I'm twenty-one."

"You even start shaving yet?" Pyro leans forward, peering

around me and looking at our companion as if trying to see for himself.

"Fuck off."

I smirk, glad they're waiting with me. Hanging around here isn't much different than being in the waiting room of a hospital. The smell of disinfectant seems to permeate every breath that you take until you feel your lungs are coated in it. Worrying about a diagnosis, having nothing to do, and feeling useless you're unable to help. It's damn ridiculous, but I'm willing that dog behind the closed door to come through. I hope the girl's okay too. I feel for her, but I don't want to call the number she gave me, not without any news.

Pyro leans forward and takes a magazine off the rack, something about dogs from the cover, I think. Pal gets up and goes to read the notice board.

"Christ! Have we wormed Bitch recently?"

"What the fuck?"

Pal's turned, looking green. "If not, she could have those growing inside." He points to a rather disgusting picture of internal parasites. "Or fleas. Hell. Never knew they looked like that." A blown-up photo is displayed in full view. "Fuck, might ask that nurse when she comes back if we can buy some shit for her."

"That's why they do it," Pyro says sagely. "Show you all that shit so you spend good money."

"Bitch?" I can't remember seeing a dog in the clubhouse.

"Club cat." Pal's answer is more puzzling than illuminating.

"Club pain in the ass you mean." Pyro doesn't look impressed. He raises his hand which has scratch marks on it. "She got me last night. Anything up there about declawing, Pal?"

Now I recall seeing a massive feline last time I was in the clubhouse. It had been sitting on a couch. Alone. Perhaps the state of Pyro's hand shows why no one had gone near it.

"Demon's worried about her now that he's got a kid to consider?"

"Yeah, Prez might be impressed if we go back with some shit to sort her out." Pal still seems intent on studying the various leaflets.

"There is that," Pyro says as he idly flicks through the pages of the magazine he'd picked up.

We fall into silence. As it would be with my brothers I'd left behind, it's companionable rather than awkward. A clock on the wall ticks away the minutes, but no one appears from the back to give us an update. When the door finally opens, it takes me by surprise.

I stand. "What we talking about, Doc?" I'm holding my breath in case he announces the dog is dead.

"Sorry, I didn't introduce myself earlier. I'm James Ransom. We don't stand on ceremony here, so call me James." Now he's lost that sense of urgency, he seems to be an affable sort. Slightly younger than me, with sand coloured hair, cut short. "Max is doing well all things considered, but he's got a long way to go until he's out of the woods."

"What are his chances?"

"Let me explain his condition, then you'll see why I can't offer guarantees." James brushes his hand over his head. "He's got a little trouble breathing, so we're giving him flow-by oxygen administered using a mask. We've fitted him with a catheter, and he's got a line in. I've given him buprenorphine for the pain." He pauses, sees the look on my face and wryly translates. "In other words, the first thing we've done is to make him as comfortable as possible."

"He wake up?"

"Awake, but drowsy. He's a good dog. Used to being handled, but that's what I'd expect from a service dog."

"You know what damage was done yet?"

James looks serious. "I've taken thoracic radiographs. It's possible he has a slow bleed in the chest that those don't show which could start to affect him hours after the initial trauma. The x-ray helps to evaluate the chest for pulmonary contusions but is only a picture of what's happening now. He has a broken rib, but like humans, that should heal by itself. His left rear leg has a mid-diaphyseal transverse complete fracture of the left femur, but I won't do anything about that until he's stabilised."

"You mean he's got a broken leg?"

As if not realising he's just spoken in a foreign language, James gives a sharp nod.

"How long will stabilising him take?" I want to get to Stevie and tell her Max is going to be okay.

"At least a day, possibly two, before I'd risk the necessary anaesthetic to fix his leg." James shakes his head. "I wish I could be more positive, but the next twenty-four hours are critical. There's a possibility of lung injuries that aren't immediately apparent. As you will have noticed yourself, he's got multiple abrasions on his skin affecting the dorsum and ventrum, sorry, back and belly." He grins slightly seeing my confusion. "I've given him convenia, an antibiotic. You're paying?"

Having listened to the long list of things wrong with him, I begin to regret saying that. But the memory of long hair, wide unseeing eyes that brimmed with tears and panic together with the utter helplessness of Stevie, for some reason not immediately apparent, it seems worth anything to put the smile back on her face. "Yes," I say firmly.

A respectful chin raise, then James continues, "He's on intravenous fluids, and we'll monitor what pain control he needs and give it as necessary to keep him comfortable. He may need a light sedation if he gets agitated, but at the moment he's quiet enough. We're going to have to auscultate the chest every two hours."

"You're going to stay with him?"

James takes a deep breath and straightens his back. "Yeah." He looks at me intently. "I'd do it for a normal pet, but dog like that? From what you told Vera, he saved his owner today, probably all in his day's work, though normally he wouldn't get hurt. I've got every respect for a service dog. Let's hope this one hasn't paid the ultimate price."

"What's his prognosis?"

James sighs. "If I can operate, I reckon I can keep him with four legs. But it's too early to say—the next twenty-four, even forty-eight hours are crucial. All I can tell you is that I'll do my best. I'll also keep the costs as low as I can. I understand you were just a passer-by." His eyes harden. "Do you know anything about the car or the driver? He should be sued for the fucking cost."

Good point. "It happened so fast. I wasn't at a good vantage point." But it might have been caught on camera, someone's dash cam perhaps. "I'll see what I can find out."

James holds out his hand. First I, then Pal and Pyro, who've been carefully listening shake it as well. His grip is firm. "I'll do my best."

Somehow I have no doubt of that. James Ransom seems to be one of the good guys.

CHAPTER SIX

"You going to call the owner?" Pyro asks as we get outside. "Fuck me, but I couldn't work out if that was good news or bad."

My shoulders rise then lower. "Not much different from when Heart came off his bike. A jumble of medical terms that meant fuck all to us. It seems vets and doctors are the same in that they won't commit themselves."

My phone is in my cut, I make no move to take it. "Look, I think I'll deliver what news I can in person. She cares for that dog." Four-legged creatures can worm their way into your hearts. Something like that happened to Heart and Marcia's dog Grunt back in Tucson? Whole fucking club would be down at the vet's. It's the thought of how I'd feel if it had happened to Grunt that makes me wary of delivering uncertain news via the phone.

"You know where she is?"

"I'll try the hospital. If she's already discharged, it will have to be a call."

"If she's in the hospital, she's probably already got family or friends with her," Pyro warns.

I think about it. "I hope she has. I can't exactly say Max will be fine. I can give her a bit of hope, but someone will need to prepare her." If she's got a husband, family member or friend with her, perhaps I'll have a word with them first. Then they can pass the news on. Then, finally, I'll be able to get to the club-house, unpack my shit and have a beer at fucking last.

"What you waiting for? Let's get rollin'." Pyro slings his leg over his bike as Pal gets on his.

I look at them with my eyebrow raised.

Pyro interprets it correctly. "You know where this fucking hospital is?"

Of course I don't. I've only just arrived.

Without batting an eye or complaining he's got better things to do, Pyro just indicates he'll take the lead. "Best show you the way then."

Pal, yeah, I've known him, what, coming up four years now? He'd started prospecting when he was eighteen, patched in a year later. Sat around the table with him for nearly three years. I might give him shit, but he's a man I call friend. Pyro? I've barely spoken to before. Hell, I might have removed the bottom rocker off my patch, but the significance of the top patch hits me. Satan's Devils are brothers whatever city or state they are in.

I don't put my thanks into words, but a jerk of my chin conveys my gratefulness for a second time tonight.

Pyro takes the lead, I fall in with Pal behind him. On the way I'm running through the vet's complicated explanation in my head, while hoping to fuck that Max is going to pull through and make sufficient recovery so he'll be able to perform his role for Stevie again.

I hate hospitals with a vengeance, and with very good reason. Ten months ago, I took a bullet and needed surgery. That wasn't the problem, I was healing okay from that when I developed septicaemia and ended up as close to death as anyone could be. There have been jokes that Satan didn't want me and sent me back, but whether the Devil or God had a hand in it, in the end I hadn't died. Much to the astonishment of the medical profession who prodded and poked me far too much, trying to analyse what I'd done to fight such a serious infection. I came through and made a complete recovery. But I'd spent far too much time in that hospital bed, and the smell of the hospital, like at the vet's, tends to bring it all back. I'd be happier if I never had to step foot in such a place ever again.

Although the parking lot seems to be busy, fitting in three motorcycles is easier than parking the same number of cars, and we're soon walking toward the emergency entrance. Although the place is busy as places like this usually are on a late Saturday evening, I'm hoping there's not been too many blind women called Stevie who have been brought in after being hit by a car.

I take a deep breath of fresh air before stepping up to the entrance, pausing to hold open the door for a man walking out with his arm in a sling, then I step inside, unsurprised to find the waiting room crowded. There's a bunch of youths congregating around a friend who's holding a cloth to a bloody wound on his face, a couple of the others looking like they too have been in a fight. Not uncommon at the weekend. There's an elderly gentleman who's coughing a lot, and a young child wailing, and that's just part of the selection. I spare a thought for the doctors and nurses who are going to have to deal with this lot.

As the three of us enter, the room quiets. Ignoring the looks and the whispered comments, I start walking toward the queue at reception, the question I'm going to be asking already framed on my lips, when a nurse emerges, her hand on the elbow of a woman, leading her to an empty chair. If I wasn't so tall and able to see over most other people, I'd have missed her.

I recognise her immediately, she's the woman I'm seeking.

Changing direction, I push my way through the milling throng, making my way over to her. Suddenly quickening my pace when a drunk lurches into her. I get there in time to pull him off.

"Get the fuck out of the way," I snarl at him.

Her head snaps up in my direction, but her eyes don't find my face. If I was shorter, she'd have made a good approximation. "How… how's Max?" she asks immediately, her voice shakes and her lip is trembling.

Every medical explanation goes out of my head. "Alive, broken leg."

"Short, and to the fuckin' point," Pyro mumbles beside me.

Ignoring him, I continue, "How the fuck did you know it was me? Can you see?" Had I been wrong? Is she not completely blind after all?

"Your voice and you smell of engine oil and leather." Her explanation is as succinct as my assessment of Max's diagnosis. "Is Max going to be okay?" Her voice falters. "His leg, is he going to lose it?"

Crouching down to her level, I take both her hands in mine, squeezing them gently. "I stayed until we had news, now the vet and nurse are with him, he'll be monitored all through the night. We won't know much more until tomorrow or the next day. At the moment, the vet doesn't know if there are problems that haven't materialised yet." And don't I know all about those. It wasn't the bullet that had almost killed me. "He didn't say he'd need to amputate."

Her head bows, I think I hear a sob, then she does that strange looking straight at me thing again. I take the time to notice her eyes are beautiful. "Thank you. Have you got the vet's number? Can you put it into my phone for me? Name it Max Vet?" She fumbles in her purse then passes her phone over.

As I tap the number in, copying it off the card the vet gave me, I ask my next concern. "How are you, sweetheart?"

"I'm fine. Bruised but not broken. Oh, and a cop came to speak to me."

"Any leads on who ran into you?"

"Who are you?" Her brow creases and her head tilts toward my left.

"Pyro."

Now her hand reaches out toward me. For a second I'm puzzled, until she says, "Can I touch you?" As her hand traces my face as if trying to memorise the shape of it, I realise this is her way of discovering what I look like. "I don't even know your name." She says it as though surprised that it's only just occurred to her.

"I'm Beef,"

"Beef?" While her principal emotions are worry and concern, there's an undercurrent of mirth in her tone as she repeats my name.

"Yeah," I grin. "Because I'm a big ugly fucker."

Her fingers touch my face again. "No, you're not ugly." A fleeting smile curves her mouth, and I realise I'm enjoying her touch.

"You can't see him," Pal interjects bluntly, contradicting. As her head tilts, he adds, "I'm Paladin."

Now her smile is larger. "Like the knight?"

"You got it."

"Are you from an MC?"

I'm still crouching, and my muscles are complaining, but her comment makes me look at her sharply. "What do you know about MCs?"

"Nothing." Her skin has got a pink tinge. "Only what I picked up from watching Sons of Anarchy and the books that I read."

I note the strange use of the words *watching* and *reading*, but now's not the time to question her. I just want to put her mind at rest. "Yeah, we're from the Satan's Devils MC, sweetheart, but mean no harm to you."

"I know that. I know there are people here frightened of you, but I'm not. You looked after Max, Beef. You've taken the time to come to tell me about him when you could have called. You've got friends with you. That's what I know of you. I heard people move aside as you were coming over, the whispered comments they made. But actions speak louder than anything else."

The more I talk to her, the more she impresses me. Maybe it's because she knows who I ride with and accepts it, not from any pre-conceived notions, but only judging from experience. Extrapolating from a man spending a Saturday evening at a vet's, that he must be a good person. I might not be able to say I haven't got a stain on my character, but I don't think of myself as bad. It's refreshing to find someone who doesn't start with poor judgement as soon as they know who I ride with.

A shift by my side. Glancing up I see Pyro glaring. The room's filled up more since we've been talking. The man Pyro's directing his expression at holds up his hands, but his eyes indicate the room around him. Yeah, probably wasn't his fault that he bumped him. I don't need to hear what Pyro's murmuring to Pal to know they want to get out of here.

"You got anyone coming for you?" My attention turns back to Stevie.

"No, I'll call an Uber to take me home."

No family or friends? I frown. What will she do when her ride arrives? Ask someone to take her to the entrance? Ask the Uber driver to come in and collect her? How will she know she can trust whoever comes along? She could end up getting in a car with anyone.

"You up to riding a bike?" I surprise myself with the question.

"A bike?"

"Yeah, I'll take you home. Don't like the idea of you going off with a stranger."

She frowns, then snaps out, "I'm blind, not helpless."

I nearly smile at the vehemence in her tone. "Not suggesting you are. But this place is crammed, Stevie. Don't know how long you'll need to wait for a ride. It is late on a Saturday. Fastest way to get you back is for you to come with me."

A snort makes me look up. Pyro's eyes have widened. But he doesn't know my philosophy of thinking the pillion seat comes in useful for anyone needing to hitch a ride. Doesn't mean anything more to me. Waste of time having one if you're not going to have a passenger, and no point me reserving it for an old lady seeing as I'm not going to go down that route again.

"Ever been on a bike?" Pal asks, dubiously, his eyes studying hers. I'm just about to reply and say her sight or lack of has nothing to do with her ability to hang on when she replies.

"Not for a while, but back in my late teens I used to ride on the back of a bike."

"So, not a virgin?" I grin, though she won't be able to see it.

Her cheeks flash red. "No."

"Well, come on then. Let's get you home." At last I get to my feet and hold out my hand.

She hesitates.

It hits me I'm exactly what I warned her of. "Hey, I know I'm a stranger…"

"It's not that. I don't think of you that way, not after everything you've done for me. But, could you give me your hand?"

Well, fuck. Stupid fucking idiot. This time, my hand reaches out further and grasps hold of hers.

She takes it but doesn't keep hold of it. Instead, once she's standing, she moves it until she rests her fingers in the crook of my arm. "Lead on."

Pyro's watching her, then giving a jerk of his head, steps in front of me. He clears a path ahead, and I lead her through. All's well until we get to the door and instead of taking the ramp, I step down…

Luckily my reactions are fast and I manage to catch hold of her before she topples right over. I hear a muttered *'fuck'* under her breath.

"Jeez, babe, I'm sorry."

"Beef, if I had a dollar for the number of times people have forgotten to warn me about a step, or a curb, I'd be a very rich woman. That's where Max is good."

"Your dog warns you?"

"Yes. He stops."

"Dog's got more fuckin' brains than you, Beef."

"Can it," I growl. But Pyro's observation has made Stevie giggle, even though she'd stiffened at the reminder she was without her dog.

Steps, curbs. Stop at them. If a dog can be trained then so can I. But why the fuck am I trying to commit that to memory? I'll take her home, drop her off, make sure she's okay, then go get that fucking beer that has my name written on it.

CHAPTER SEVEN

The lamps around the parking lot cast good light in places, poor in others. For the first time in my life I'm studying where to place my feet. While Pyro and Pal squeeze through narrow gaps between the cars making a direct beeline to our bikes, I lead Stevie up and down the rows taking care there's no obstacle in her path.

By the time I've reached my bike, I've a new admiration for Max. While I've only led Stevie a short distance, it's clear that no distractions are allowed, and the job requires complete concentration. Somewhere in the depths of my memory I recall being told you shouldn't interact with a service dog while it's working, and now I understand the reason why.

When we reach my bike, I remember that my saddle bags are still full of my clothing, and the pillion seat is heaped high with the rest of the shit I brought with me. But I needn't have worried. Pal's already unhooking the bungee cords and Pyro's piling my bags on his bike. True brothers jumping in and sorting out a problem you didn't even know you had. Pal even extracts a helmet from his pannier.

"Jay's," he explains, "but I think it will fit."

I approach Stevie. When the helmet touches her head, she

jumps. "Fuck, sorry. Just putting a helmet on you, okay?" *She can't see, dumbass.*

"Yeah, sure. Thanks." But my unexpected action has shocked her, I can see how her breathing sped up.

"Stevie, I'm going to make a lot of mistakes, okay? I'm going to fuck up."

She must use the sound of my voice to guide her, but her hand finds my arm, then slides down until she's gripping my hand, squeezing it gently. "You're doing fine."

"I'm gonna get you on the bike now, sweetheart. Take a step to the side and put your hand out. There, lower. Got it. That's the seat. I'm going to get on, then when I do, put your leg over it, okay?"

"I'll help her if she needs it," Pal offers.

But she's got the idea of it, swinging her leg over like a pro. She hadn't lied, she has done this before. As she doesn't weigh much, the bike hardly notices her extra weight on it as I kick up the stand and balance it. Before turning on the engine, I give her a few instructions about hanging onto my waist and moving with me around the corners just in case she's forgotten. I take a second to admire her bravery and trust, she's on a bike with a stranger, but offers no plea for me to take it carefully.

"Okay. Let's get moving. You going to tell me where we're going?"

"We'll see you back at the clubhouse," Pyro says. Then he and Pal take off.

She gives me the general idea, then fine-tunes the directions as we draw closer. It takes a lot of communication, me describing where we are, then her telling me which way to turn. When we arrive, there's a drive I can park on. It's a pleasant house from what I can see of it in the darkness, set back a little from the road, flowers lining the driveway. As I help her off and hang the helmet on the handlebar, I notice a perfume in the air as I walk her down to the front door.

She takes out her key and uses it, then steps inside, placing her purse and key on a table near the door.

Then she turns. "Thank you, Beef. Thank you for everything. I don't know what would have happened had you not been there..."

"Fuck, babe. Someone would have helped. Just glad I was there. I hope Max does okay." I don't tell her, but I'll be checking up on him myself.

It's awkward. I don't know her, she doesn't know me. Just strangers really that met in the night. I've got this strange impulse to know more about her, how she lives her life, what she does for a living. There's no one at home, so presumably there's no husband or kids, but she may have a boyfriend. Woman looking like her must attract interest. I'd love a peep into her home, wondering if it's drab and dreary, or whether she has a colour scheme. Fuck knows why she would, she can't see it. Is it fancy or plain and utilitarian? And why am I so fucking interested?

She's not inviting me in, and there's no reason for her to. "Well, I'll be off. Stevie, I took the liberty of putting my number into your phone. If you need anything—"

"Thank you, but I'll be fine, Beef."

I start leaning in with the intention of placing a kiss to her cheek, then pull myself back. *Not got that kind of relationship.* Not got any kind of relationship at all. As I realise this is the last I'll see of her, I feel a pang of regret.

"Okay. Right. Goodnight." Nothing else to say.

"Goodnight, Beef. And, thank you again."

She steps forward, reaches for the handle. I step back, and the door closes.

Some bizarre instinct has me glued to the spot. My protective nature would have liked to check out the house before she stepped into it. *What if there was an intruder inside?* How would she know? It's not like me to just walk off and leave someone, but I've not had an encounter like this before. If I've ever taken a woman back to her house, it was with the intention of fucking her. That's not the situation here. Not that I wouldn't have turned down the offer, but it wouldn't have come. She's not the type to want to casually take a ride on a biker's cock.

Why is my mind going there? Last night, like a dumbass, I'd made a commitment to Sally that I wouldn't touch another woman. Even had she offered, I wouldn't have been able to take her up on it.

I stand there, staring at nothing, thinking about the difference between the woman I'd left and the woman who's behind the other side of the door. I might not know much about Stevie, but am impressed as hell about how well she's able to cope. Her independence shines through, and she's brave. Didn't balk at riding my bike, didn't fear falling off. *Trusted me to keep her safe.*

Sally might think she needs me, but it dawns on me that's what is missing. *Trust.*

I'm brought out of my reverie by a disturbing sound. A distraught wail followed by weeping.

I'm frozen to the spot, uncertain of my next actions. Do I quietly go? Leave her to her privacy? Or, do I try to offer comfort and help? Would me witnessing her breakdown cause embarrassment, or would she welcome the support?

Before I have second thoughts, my hand lifts and my knuckles knock against the wood. Getting no answer, I rap louder, then call out, "Stevie, you alright?"

The cries fade, then I get a response. "I'm… fine. I'm…" Each word is punctuated with heart wrenching sobs.

"Babe, let me in. You've had one hell of a shock. You shouldn't be alone." She must have a friend I can call for her.

"Beef, I…"

"Let me in." Bracing my arm against the wood, I lean forward and gentle my voice. "Open the door, babe."

For a moment nothing happens. I'm just accepting I've done

all I can when there's the sound of the deadbolt being slid back and the latch turning. The sight I see on the other side breaks my heart. Already her eyes are red, tracks of tears running down her cheeks and those not yet fallen are glistening in her eyes. She looks the picture of desperation. It's natural for me to take the step that closes the distance between us, kicking the door shut behind me with my boot, and pulling her into my arms.

Her hands clutch at my cut as she avails herself of human kindness. Her sobs that she was trying to hold back come forth. I rub my hands up and down her back.

"Let it out, babe. Let it all out. I'm here, Stevie. I'm here. You cry babe, you need it."

Loosening her fingers, she's now gently beating at my chest. I don't think she's got a clue what she's doing. "Why, Beef, why? Why did Max get hurt? Why did that car run us down? What was it doing on the sidewalk? Why Beef? Why?"

Well fuck me. I'd been so tied up in dealing with the aftermath, I hadn't given the *why* much thought. An accident or lack of concentration was what I'd put it down to, but I'm a biker used to a criminal world. Now she's got me wondering whether there could be more to it.

"I don't know, Stevie. But I do know Max is a fuckin' brave dog who saved your life."

"I don't know what I'll do without him." Her tears might have started to dry, but her voice still breaks at the thought.

"You'll have him back. He'll be fine, Stevie."

"You don't know that. You told me yourself."

"Look, why don't we sit down? I'll call James—he's the vet. Get a progress update, how about that?" Anything to give her some hope. And if the dog's taken a turn for the worse, at least I'll be here to help her deal with it.

"At this time of night?"

Somehow I think James will have been true to his word, and will be keeping a close watch on his canine patient. "I'll give it a try, okay?"

Another sob, this one less violent, and she takes out a tissue blowing her nose noisily. Her hands touch my chest again. "I've made your cut wet."

"Not a thing for you to worry about. Where are we going to sit?" I fumble for a light switch and when I find it by the side of the door, flick it on. She might be able to find her way around in the darkness, but I'll break my neck.

She lets me go, then points to a sofa. She makes her way unwaveringly to it, avoiding the low coffee table in her path. Before she sits, she turns back. "One rule in this house, Beef. Don't move anything. No furniture, not even the waste basket. Leave everything in its place, okay?"

She's clearly used to issuing that instruction. The reason why is obvious. I nod my head. Then realising the futility of the gesture, give her words instead, "Got it."

She sits at one end of the three-seater sofa, leaving the other two seats for my bulk. It dips as I place my ass on it. True to my word and mentally crossing my fingers, I waste no time in calling the vet.

"You got James."

"How's Max?" I ask without even an introduction. I doubt he's caring for more than one animal of that name.

"Resting comfortably. Have you seen the owner?" James is equally brief.

"Yeah, I'm with her now."

"She alright?"

Stevie's making gimme gestures, and I guess she wants to hear the update herself. I pass the phone over, carefully wrapping her fingers around it.

"James, sorry, I don't know… Ransom. Got it. Yes, I'm fine. Not much more than a headache. How's Max?"

I'm only able to hear her side of the conversation which consists mainly of, *uh huhs* and *okay* and *yeah, I got that*. I take the opportunity to watch her face. She bites her lip, grimaces, frowns, then there's a small smile. Then her brow creases again.

"What time are you open?" she says at last. Followed by, "I'll be there. Thank you. And yes, I'll be prepared."

When she holds the phone out to me I take it, watching as she leans her head into her hands.

"Well?"

"He used a lot of medical jargon, but at the end of it you were right. Good news is that so far he hasn't deteriorated. I'm going to go in at eight tomorrow and see him."

The words, "I'll take you," immediately come out of my mouth.

Her head comes up, and she stares at a point just over my shoulder. "You don't need to do that."

I don't know what drove me to make the offer. "You got family or friends that can take you?"

That streak of independence appears again. "No, but there are things called taxis."

I may not know her, but she's cute and pretty. It's hard to imagine she's got no one to call on. "No friends who support you?"

"I've got family, yes. But they're not close by. I only moved here fairly recently, so I haven't got any contacts yet."

"Workmates?"

"No, what I do, I do from home.

I'm interested. "What do you do?"

"I'm a computer programmer."

Don't you need to be able to see to do that? My respect for her grows. But so does a feeling of responsibility for her. I settle back on the couch. "Well, you do now."

Her brow furrows again. "I do now what?"

"Have a friend who'll be there for you."

She laughs incredulously. "We've only just met."

I shrug. Then use words. "Doesn't matter. Maybe it's because I know how I'd feel if something of mine was hurt, maybe I took a liking to Max. No doubt he's a hero and that I can respect.

Maybe it's because I think we've connected. Look, you don't know me, but I'm no threat. I don't want anything from you. You want the truth? This is strange to me too. I've only moved to Pueblo today myself. Perhaps I could do with a friend too." It's true. Especially as I'll be in a new clubhouse. Sure, I'll have brothers, but there may also be times when I need privacy and a break. The Pueblo clubhouse isn't like Tucson with acres of room on the compound and the suites with only one neighbour. Here my room will be in the midst of all the others.

"You moved here today?"

"Yes. I rode up from Tucson, was on my way to the clubhouse when I saw that car hit Max."

She swings her body around to fully face me, one leg drawn up beneath her. "Let me get this straight. You rode up from Tucson. How long did that take?"

"Eleven hours, perhaps a bit extra for stops to stretch my legs."

"Your luggage? That was what your friends took off your bike?" At my look of confusion, she explains, "I heard sounds, elastic pinging. Heard them struggling to get, what, bungee cord done up?"

"That's right." Her ears, her interpretation of what she's hearing, are fucking amazing. I'm stunned she was able to tell.

She looks thoughtful, and her head moves to one side and back. "You spent all evening at the vet's because I asked you to, then brought me home. Then came in to make sure I was okay."

For the umpteenth time I shrug.

"Am I right?"

I feel like slapping myself around the head. *Must remember to speak.* "Sums it up, babe."

"Are you hungry? Thirsty? Stupid question. Of course you are. How about I make you a sandwich? And I've got beer."

"I'm alright," I reply automatically. My stomach, seeming to have heard the mention of food, growls loudly.

She giggles, then gets up. "I'll be right back."

"I'll help—"

"You stay here." After issuing an instruction in a tone I can't argue with, she strides confidently across the room and into a kitchen. There are sounds of something opening and closing, then two opened bottles are brought back and placed in the exact middle of the coffee table. Then she's off again.

Beer. At fucking last. And it's a brand I like. I raise the bottle to my lips and take a long thirst-quenching swallow. Stretching out my legs I hear my knees creak. *Getting old.* The couch is comfy, the back just the right height for me to rest back my head. Closing my eyes, I breathe out, feeling tension seep away.

"Your sandwich."

It's said quietly but is enough to make my eyes open. Pushing down on my hands I pull myself upright. "Nearly drifted off there for a moment."

"That's why I spoke quietly. Didn't want to wake you if you were asleep." Again, she interprets my unspoken question. "Your breathing, it was different."

"You notice a fuck of a lot, don't you?"

She resumes her place at the other end of the couch as I tuck into a ham, cheese and lettuce sandwich. Good shit it is. "You're not eating?"

"I just had a piece of cheese while I was making that for you. I'm not hungry."

I eye her critically. What she hadn't added out loud was that she was too concerned about Max. She doesn't look tired, just worried. Maybe it will take her mind off things she can't control if I get her talking. I could talk about bikes, my favourite topic, or I could ask about her.

Choosing the latter, I begin. "So, you recently moved to Pueblo? For work?" *For a lover?*

"Something like that." Her legs, which she had curled up under her, straighten out. She's tense, I can see it. Okay, I don't know her well enough to pursue a topic she's uncomfortable with. It's none of my business.

"Are you alright, I didn't ask. Hurting?"

"I was just bruised and shocked, Beef. I'm fine. I've got a bit of a headache, but nothing too bad. Probably more tension than injury. And God knows bruises don't bother me. I get enough of them. You should have seen my legs when I first moved in."

"This your furniture?"

A shake of her head, making her hair fly around her shoulders. "No, I… rented it furnished. Didn't know where anything was." She chuckles. "Spent enough time on my hands and knees mapping it all out."

"You've got amazing hearing."

"Yes. I'm lucky that way." When I think that's all I'm going to get, she tilts her head on one side. "I don't mind you asking, if you're interested."

I am. "Have you always been blind?"

Her head moves side to side. "I've got a condition called retinitis pigmentosa. It's an inherited condition, but for generations it hasn't appeared in the family. I was born fully sighted, but my vision started to deteriorate early on. I was about five when my parents acknowledged something was wrong with me. If they approached from the side, I didn't notice them until they were right in front of me. They took me for tests and got the diagnosis. Nothing to be done, and eventually I'd lose more of my vision. Some people retain some, I've lost most. In good daylight I can sometimes make out shapes, but not always. I was lucky though. My condition is often related to another that also causes deafness." She shudders. "Thank God I don't suffer from that."

"When did you lose your sight to the extent you have now?"

"When I was in my early twenties. You mentioned my hearing. Going back to when I couldn't see people in my peripheral vision, I started listening more. Because I had some vision it helped to distinguish what made what sound, if that makes sense? It helped when I lost my sight entirely."

"You have Max to help you. What will you do while he's recovering?"

Her lips purse. "Be a hermit?" Her comment is followed by a self-deprecating laugh. "I have a white stick, but it's not as good as a dog."

Putting down my empty plate I ask, "Why not? Not all blind people have dogs, surely?"

"They don't. Looking after a dog is too much of a chore for them, and they manage with just a stick. But have you seen someone waving one? Weaving it back and forth to see what's in front of them?"

I nod automatically, then give myself a mental slap. "Uh uh."

"Imagine a table. Imagine trying to walk through a restaurant, an unexpected chair pushed out in front of you." She laughs again, a sound I find endearing. "The stick hits empty air if I'm waving it between the legs. Told you, I'm no stranger to bruises, tripping up or falling down."

I can't help it. I'm interested, but tired. I yawn.

"You're half asleep. Anyone would be after that long ride. Rather than heading on to your clubhouse, why don't you stay here tonight? I've got a spare room."

I look at her sharply. "You wouldn't mind?"

"Why should I?"

"You don't know me at all. I could be an axe murderer or jump your bones in the night and molest you."

That laugh again. The one I prefer over her tears earlier. It's followed by chuckles, and then she can't seem to stop. "I'm not afraid of you, Beef. I don't really know why. Not offering to share my bed, but something tells me it wouldn't be the worst thing in the world to have your hands on me. Not an offer, but no, I don't think you're a threat. As for being an axe murderer? I'll take my chances." She chuckles again.

It wouldn't be bad for me either. Except, I couldn't take her up on the offer if she actually made it. Not when I'd promised Sally.

But a bed for the night, that would be welcome. Better than trying to drive through unfamiliar streets and locate the clubhouse in the dark.

I shoot off a quick text to Pal explaining the situation, then follow Stevie into her spare room.

CHAPTER EIGHT

Despite nearly falling asleep on her couch, the moment my head hits the pillow in Stevie's spare room, I'm wide awake. The bed's comfortable, the pillow is soft just how I like it. I've got the ability to sleep anywhere, but for some reason, I can't drop off.

I can't stop thinking how terrible it must have been for Stevie and her family to receive the information so early in her life that she was going to go blind. Does knowing help you prepare? Did she have counselling? She seems to be such a well-balanced person, proud of how she's adapted, not ranting or raving about what she's lost. I can't help but admire her. In the darkness I grin. That comment about me jumping her bones not being unwelcome? That took me by surprise and shows she's no shrinking violet.

But in the same way I hadn't made a move on her, she hadn't on me. It wasn't a suggestion to be acted upon, just put out there. *Was she serious?* Hell, I don't even know if she's available. We didn't talk about partners.

Problem is, even if she's free, I'm not.

At first, when my brothers had started finding their soul-mates, I couldn't understand how they believed one pussy could satisfy them for the rest of their lives, until a certain woman came to the compound. But she could never be mine, she was Rock's. Becca never had a notion that while she viewed me as a big brother, what I managed to successfully hide from both her and everyone else, was that my feelings for her were far from fraternal. Rock never knew thank fuck, if he had, being his friend wouldn't stop him putting me six feet under.

I was happy for Rock that he'd found his other half but viewed their relationship with some jealousy. The answer, in my eyes, was to find a good woman for myself. But despite the luck my brothers have had, it seems finding one is like searching for an elusive unicorn.

Before Becca, I was perfectly happy with a variety of pussy in my bed every night. That I was happy to share with my brothers shows I'm not a possessive man. That's who I am, not a partner or husband. Perhaps Sally and I would never have worked as I'm not the settling down type.

Maybe there's not a woman out there for me, and maybe I don't really want one. The thought of being serviced by sweet butts is enough to get my dick to perk up. I can get female companionship from the old ladies in the club. What more do I want?

If God had blessed me with features women admire, maybe my choice would be wider. But he hadn't, and it's not.

I have nothing to offer a woman like Stevie except one night in my bed.

But even that's forbidden, I'm still shackled to Sally by the foolish promise I'd made. I'm a man of my word, but by God it's going to be hard to keep it.

Stevie's attractive, no denying that. Probably the type I'd lust after but couldn't have. She'd step out with someone far better looking—if she could see them. But she's no sweet butt, and I couldn't live up to any other type of expectation. I've experienced living with a demanding woman once, and I won't be leaving myself open to that again. Selfishly I suspect there would be even greater challenges with Stevie. Remembering to speak all the time rather than gesturing is one change I already need to make, and I've enough difficulty remembering that. I might be tidy—learned that in the army—but hey, I'm a man. Sometimes I leave my boots where I drop them.

Maybe that's why she's alone? Perhaps she doesn't like dealing with anyone else's shit lying around? I wouldn't blame her, if untidiness results in her repeatedly falling over and hurting herself.

I like Stevie, but I'll need to be ruthless. If she's serious about me spending time in her bed, I'll have to refuse. Don't want to raise expectation. But I can be her friend. Seems there's no one else, so I'll be there when she needs someone to take her to visit with her dog. Sure, she could take a taxi, but if she's going to receive bad news, she needs support. I can do that. As long as she respects my boundaries. Friends. Nothing more.

I don't remember when, or what was my last thought, but eventually, I must have dropped off. When I wake it's because the door of the guest room opening disturbs me. I sit up fast, my hand reaching for the gun that I keep in my cut as I come around totally disorientated and not knowing where I am.

"Stay there," she instructs. "Let me put this down. I don't know how you like it, so I did it like mine, with cream, but no sugar."

As she comes closer, the welcome aroma of coffee wafts up. I keep still as steadily and surely she makes her way over and places the cup on the bedside table. "It's half-past-six. I hope that's not too early for you. I'd like to be there eight on the dot, if you're still okay with that offer you made last night."

"No problem, babe. You sleep okay?"

She sits on the side of the bed. Having watched her carefully I read her intentions and shift my ass to accommodate her. "Not really. I tossed and turned worried about Max." She bites her lip. "I don't know what I'll do, Beef, if I lose him."

She'd come in all composed. My innocent question had brought her worries to the forefront. Immediately I feel guilty. "Babe, let me hold you." When she doesn't protest, I put my arms around her and pull her against my naked chest. Her hand touches my pecs.

I don't even think she's conscious of it when her hand starts to explore, just like she'd done when she'd been mapping my face.

Then she lifts her hand away. "I'm sorry…"

I place her hand back. "Knock yourself out." It's nothing more than a sighted woman checking me out.

Her fingers explore, moving across my chest one side to the other, and down over my muscles. "A six pack?"

I nudge her hand downwards. "Eight."

"Hmm." Her mind, for a moment seems to have been taken off her dog. While I'm realising she's going to stop soon, my cock is getting very interested and swelling in hope of some attention.

But she seems focused on my chest, and now, on my arms. "You're very big and muscular, Beef. I can see how you got your name." The same touch from another woman would give me completely the wrong idea. Hers, well, it's just like someone else staring. As I look down at the tight tee she's wearing over figure hugging jeans, I'm wishing I could take the same liberty. But feasting my eyes will have to do.

"Are you looking at my tits?" she asks, her voice amused.

"What? No?" I lie. "Why do you ask?"

"Because that's what men do, isn't it?"

It feels natural to lean forward and place my lips against her cheek. "You caught me. I may have told a small fib."

"Have you got tattoos?"

"One or two." The laughter comes through my voice. There's not much of my skin that isn't inked.

"A stereotypical biker?" She smiles. "Describe them?"

"Well, on my back I've got a full back patch. It's the Satan's

Devils insignia, the Devil with a scythe looming over three demons."

Her smile widens. "I'm picturing it. What else?"

I run through some of my other tats, her hand tracing them as I describe them. "Let's leave the rest for later." My cock is currently going mad with her tactile exploration and I've got to stop this before I do something stupid like tell her my dick is tattooed.

"Yes." To my combined relief and disappointment, she stands. "Drink your coffee. Bathroom's down the hall. Clean towels are in there if you want a shower. I'll get some breakfast going. Bacon and eggs?"

"Thank you."

By the time I'm showered and dressed—a quick trip to my bike to grab a clean tee in the saddle bag—she's got breakfast on the table.

"I did scrambled eggs. Fried can be a bit hit and miss."

"It's perfect." Indeed it is. It might be because I'm extra hungry, but it's one of the most delicious breakfasts I've had. I'm still amazed how she managed to cook it. Intrigued, I ask her.

"By smell," she replies. Her face completely straight.

"Really?" My eyes widen. "You can tell when something's cooked by the smell?"

Her head bobs up and down fast. "Yup."

"Wow, that's amazing."

"When I smell smoke, I know it's overcooked."

It takes me a second then I roar with laughter. "You're pulling my leg," I complain.

"A bit," she agrees with a smile.

Her smile is even broader when half an hour later we're allowed to go in and see Max. James takes her to an indoor kennel where Max is lying, tubes and wires attached to him. I'm glad she can't see them, but James takes her hand and gently traces them with her, explaining the gadgets that monitor his heart rate, and the IV running into his leg providing him with sustenance. He explains he's quiet because of the pain relievers and mild sedative he's been given to help him keep still.

Stevie's not the only one over the moon to learn he's progressing well, and, that if there are no problems today, James will operate on his leg the next morning.

The best bit? Well that was when Max opened his eyes and his tongue came out to lick the hand of his mistress. I had a tear in my eye at that point, which I turned and rubbed discretely away.

We visit for an hour. When she leaves with assurances James will call if anything changes, and a promise that yes, she can visit this evening, all too soon we're standing in front of her house, and I suddenly don't want to leave her. She's easy company, while, apart from Paladin, I have virtual strangers waiting for me at the clubhouse.

"Want me to take you back later?"

"I can't ask you to do that."

"You didn't. I offered." Watching the sunlight play on her gorgeous hair, highlighting streaks of natural red in it, I know more time in her company would be no hardship at all. "Honestly, babe. I feel invested in Max's recovery. I'd like to check up on how he's doing too."

"Well, if you're sure. Thanks Beef." She turns and starts to walk to her door, then takes the same number of steps back. "Beef, look. I've had enough pity, strangers thinking I need help. If that's all you're doing it for, thank you, but I don't need it. I'd rather you said it now, then string me along."

"Stevie," I trap her hand, partly because I want to feel her skin against mine and partly to stop her from moving away. "Apart from my brothers you're the only person I know in Pueblo. You said you were new here too. Seems like two newcomers could do worse than spend a bit of time finding out about the place together. I'm not pitying you. Fuck, you know what? It's the total opposite. I have immense respect and admiration for you. And fuck strangers, you know what? They don't look beneath the surface. They see me, big fella with tattoos and wearing a cut? They walk the other way. You *see* me, babe. They think as you're blind you need help? That's because their eyes might work, but they don't *see* you."

She's quiet for a moment. Then she rises on tiptoe. Whether she was going to place a kiss against my cheek or whether her intention was for us to touch lip to lip I don't know, but our mouths meet. Briefly. My cock jerks. One fucking kiss, no tongues, and I swear it felt like an electric shock.

I'm doubting the wisdom of seeing her again when she touches her hand to her lip, smiles and says, "See you tonight, Beef. About six?"

With no hesitation, I agree, "Six it is, babe."

Finally, after something like a sixteen-hour delay, I arrive at the clubhouse. Demon's leaning on the bar, a cup by his side, deep in discussion with Cad. I go straight across to pay my respects. After the back slapping and handshaking is done, he steps back and I await the expected interrogation as Cad nods and wanders off.

"How's the blind bitch and her dog?"

"Girl's fine, Prez, dog seems to be coming along okay. Took her to see him this morning."

"There's our Beef. Brief and concise."

I swing around. "Morning, Pyro. Thanks for your help yesterday."

"Bet that vet went into all sorts of details you can't even remember." He grins.

"Fuckin' can. He's on dexmedetomidine for the pain and the antibiotic Convenia given subcutaneously." I raise my eyebrow, expecting a further comment. He doesn't disappoint.

"Well, look at you. Spouting that shit. Bet you made all that up." The laughter in his eyes belies his mocking tone.

Demon clips him around the head. "Just because you don't know shit, don't mock those who do."

I could be back in the Tucson clubhouse. I grin.

"Bit of a strange welcome to the town. You know who drove into her?" Demon takes a sip of his coffee while staring at me.

"Not a clue. According to the cops, no one thought to get the license plate." I shake my head.

"Someone fall asleep at the wheel?" Pyro's stopped laughing and looks serious now.

"Hard to tell. But you'd expect that on a freeway, not in the middle of town." I'm kicking myself as I didn't check the plate out myself. But Max's scream of pain had been distracting, and I hadn't known at the time whether Stevie had been hit or not.

Demon whistles and shouts, "Cad."

A head pops up from the other side of the bar. "Can you see what you can pick up on any security cameras out where the hit and run happened?"

"Where was it?"

I glance at Pyro, who nods and goes over to where Cad is sitting to explain exactly where it was. I have no fucking idea.

"Thing I don't like about it, is that the fucker drove off. If it was an accident, why didn't he stop?"

Shrugging, I respond, "Could be any number of reasons. He could have been shocked. Worried about getting a ticket. Embarrassed as fuck."

"Or, it could have been a hit."

I round on the man who's spoken. "Thunder. Good to see you." Another exchange of back slaps.

"Good to see you too, Brother."

"I can't see how it could be a hit," I respond to his first statement. "She hasn't been in Pueblo long, not long enough to make friends let alone enemies. That was the reason I stayed last night. She had no one to call or to help her. She works from home, so couldn't rely on any co-workers. Don't see why anyone would want to hurt her." Or, if Max hadn't pushed her out of the way, worse, killed her.

Cad's head reappears again. "Want me to check up on her? Got her name?"

I do, but do I want to invade her privacy like that? "Nah, Cad, thanks, but not now."

"Is that it?" Demon asks. "Or are you seeing her again?"

Feeling sheepish, but not understanding why, I look him in the eye. "I'm taking her back to visit her dog this evening."

"Can't say I blame you." Pyro wanders back. "Bitch was hot."

CHAPTER NINE

My temper flares. Man's got no right to talk about her like that. Doesn't he know she's... *Huh? Where did that come from?* Instead of ranting, I sling my arm over his shoulder. "You're not wrong. Hey, meant what I said. I appreciated what you did last night."

"Not a problem. Can see what caught your interest Brother. You tapped that, yet?"

"Nah, and I'm not going there."

His brow creases as if he's considering for a moment. Then he shrugs. "Just wondering what it would be like to fuck a woman who's blind."

Not much different to anyone else I wouldn't think. "A hole's a hole, Brother."

"Hmm." He doesn't sound convinced. "You ever had a girl let you blindfold her?"

"Nah, never," I truthfully reply.

He nods sagely. "Takes a lot of trust, that. Did it once, but she wasn't into it. Had to untie her as she was too worried what I'd do to her. S'pose the bitch girl's a bit like that."

I eye him thoughtfully, never considered that. I wonder what it would be like? Then push those thoughts away. "Well, neither of us are going to find out. She's a nice woman, way out of our league."

"Nah, she wouldn't be worth the bother. Her problems would be hard to cope with."

Demon's obviously bored waiting for us to finish our conversation. He suddenly asks, "You want to dump your shit in your room, Beef? I'd like a word with you when you're done."

"Sure, Prez." God. I had to force that word out. I've only called two men that before, the first was Bastard, then after he was killed, Drummer. It seems strange and wrong, making me suddenly homesick.

"Prospect?" Demon yells.

When the prospect who I remember is called Wills appears at a run, Demon has a few words, then the prospect's raising the saddlebags I'd dropped at my feet and is leading the way up the stairs. I follow, wondering what kind of room I'll be in. I know there're two types here, a few basic rooms with a shared bathroom, and others with an en-suite of their own. I'm praying mine will be one of the latter as I've been spoiled in Tucson for years.

When Wills unlocks the door then hands me the key, I poke my head around, quickly spying the doorway through to the adjacent bathroom, and relief comes over me that I'm not going to have to share. I'm too old for that shit.

"Keep your door locked at all times," he warns.

"Who don't we trust?" I narrow my eyes.

"Not who, what. Bitch can open these door handles and she doesn't like men so be careful." Turning around I eye the door handle, thinking with some quick work with a screwdriver it could easily be turned upside down. I wonder why no one else has thought of it.

Crossing the room to the bed, Wills places my bags there, then turns back. "You've got a mini-fridge." He points it out. "If you want anything else just call me."

"How long you been prospecting, Wills?" I ask conversationally, as I catalogue the contents of the room. There's a desk, a comfortable looking armchair, a wardrobe, a chest of drawers and a bedside table. It's quite a large room too.

"Getting on twelve months. Oh, and I put beer in the fridge and condoms in the top drawer."

I grin. Everything a man needs. Yeah, prospect's probably near done his time and knows what a brother needs. "Thanks."

As he leaves without fanfare, reluctantly I start emptying my bags. The other shit Pal brought back for me is sitting in the corner waiting to be put away. It feels wrong and permanent. I make myself remember this is just temporary, that Drummer sent me here to do a job. Soon as I help Demon choose his new VP, and know Colorado is running smoothly, then I'll be able to return home. Unless Drummer has other plans for me. *I hope not.*

My phone rings. I pause halfway through putting away my tee-shirts, fumbling with the armful I'm holding, shoving them in a drawer, then trying to get to the device before it goes to voicemail. I make it just in time without checking who's calling.

"You got Beef."

"Beef, I need help."

I breathe in deeply. "Sally…"

"The air conditioning isn't working," she hurriedly explains the reason for her call. "I didn't want to bother you, but I don't know who to call."

"You know what to do, Sal. In the top desk drawer in the office, there's a bunch of paperwork. The rental agent's details are on the top, and there's the emergency contact on it." It's Sunday, she'll need that. "You really didn't need to call."

"I thought you might have an idea what I could do."

The Tucson club owns the property, but through a shell company. We like to keep some things under the radar. We use managing agents to deal with all the shit so if we need to house anyone there without people knowing our connection, there's no trail to be followed for anyone to find out. For the amount we pay the agents, they can get a call out on a Sunday and fix whatever's necessary.

"Sally, you've got to get yourself together, you know? This time will be good for you to start learning some independence."

"I didn't think, Beef. Just panicked. The kids are so fractious in the heat."

"Yeah, I can imagine. Get in touch with the agent, then why not take them out? That play place will be nice and cool." I'm sympathetic enough to offer a solution.

"Okay. Good suggestion. I'll do that. I'm glad you got there okay, Beef. I was worried."

"Yeah. Got here fine. Gotta go now, Sally. Prez wants to meet with me."

"Sure. Beef?" She poses her question hesitantly.

"What, Sal?"

"Did you party last night?"

My teeth grind together. "No, I did not. And I don't appreciate you checking up on me, Sally. I made you a promise." *Which I'm already fucking regretting.* "If I'm having a problem keeping to that, we'll have that conversation first."

I hear the sob down the line. "You're not coming back, are you?"

I'm sure she can hear my sigh. "I've every fuckin' intention of returning, Sal. Got a job to do for Drummer. I told you that, but you know how we left things. We've both got thinking to do."

She's quiet for a moment, then, "I've got to put the trash out. Can you go through the recycling again, Beef? What goes into what?" It's an excuse to keep me talking.

"Top drawer of the desk there's a leaflet, Sal. Easier for you to read it and keep it to refer to." *So you don't ring me every Sunday to check.*

She promises to do that. We exchange goodbyes, hers taking a little longer than mine, then I end the call. My thinking is done, she's just got to come around to the same conclusion. For a second I sit, ignoring the rest of the unpacking. The contrast between a blind woman who's so intent on keeping her independence, and Sally who wants none at all, is striking.

Not for the first time I regret snapping up something offered to me on a platter. Not going to make the same mistake again. The last thing I want to do is become another woman's support.

Sally would be capable of a lot if she'd just put her mind to it, and hopefully she'll start to do that now I'm gone. She can see what she's doing for a start. Those everyday things that shouldn't be a challenge to Sally would be impossible for the woman I met last night.

Veering between finishing my unpacking, and giving up and going downstairs, in the end my sense of needing everything in its place wins out, and I continue putting my shit away, including dumping the bag of toiletries in the bathroom. Finally, I place a photo of me, Rock and Becca next to the bed, take one look around my new domain, and go down to formally meet my new prez.

While I've been upstairs, a mountain of pizzas have been brought in. As Pal waves me across he pushes one of the boxes toward me.

"Saved this one for you. It doesn't have anchovies."

Thank fuck. I hate those salty little fishes, can't see why people like them ruining their pizza, then settle down to feed my stomach. Demon can wait a little while longer. The room is mainly silent as everyone devours the takeaway, and I take a chance to go over names and faces in my head.

Thunder, the sergeant-at-arms and acting VP is eating his standing by the bar. Now if I could persuade him to take on the role permanently, my job here would be done and I could go home. Nah, that wouldn't work, not unless someone would step up to the SAA role he'd be leaving vacant, and that seems unlikely. Fuck, what a mess.

Beside him is the enforcer, Mace. He's a decent enough guy, though still a bit green. Hasn't got that hard look around him like Blade wears. I wonder whether he's been sufficiently tested.

Probably won't know how to scalp a man. Yeah, I might have watched Blade do that, under Mouse, our part-Navajo's, careful instruction. Jeez, I can't keep comparing these men to my Tucson brothers. *Gotta give them a chance man.* But Sally's call has unsettled me, made me realise all over again it's down to her why I've got the nomad patch on my back.

"Who are they?" I point out two men I hadn't seen before.

"Karl and Beaver. Hangarounds," Pal replies. "Got a vote coming up in church as to whether to take them on as prospects. Seem to be willing enough."

"Beaver?"

"Yeah, it's his fucking surname, would you believe?"

Poor man.

"Settled in, Beef?" Jay plops herself at her man's side and snags a piece of his pizza.

As I've just taken a mouthful of my own, I simply raise my chin in reply. A burst of laughter catches my attention. Hellfire, the president who's just abdicated, is holding court by the bar with Buzzard, the treasurer, and Rusty and Bomber, two other old-timers. At the other end, clanking beer bottles together, are Sparky, the road captain, Ink and Lizard, and the newest patched in member Skull. Skull's an interesting one, the gossip around the circumstances of how he got patched even reached Tucson. Hell thought he had evidence against him when Jayden went missing, tortured the shit out of him, but the kid couldn't tell what he didn't know. Left the club for a month to get his body healed and his head together. Surprised the fuck out of everyone when he returned, seemingly bearing no grudges. If he's straight up, I've got a hell of a lot of respect for the man, but there has to be some doubt he'd want no retaliation. I'll best keep out a careful eye. Some folks can wait for revenge.

Raising my head I can just see Cad, he's taken over the right-hand end of the bar, and has computers and monitors set up there. Man's so pale like the cadaver he was named for, looks like he never goes outside. Pyro's talking to him. That's all the brothers. I've met them before, spoken to all of them, fought beside them. I know them, but don't really *know* them. A few are sending curious glances toward me. It goes both ways, takes time to learn all there is about someone. The head start I've got is that we're all Satan's Devils. We wear the same patch and have all been tried in the same way to earn it. Any man found wanting gets his ass kicked out the door. These men would already die for me, as I would for them. Takes a certain brand of man to put his life on the line for another.

Apart from Jay there are no old ladies around at the moment. With the exception of her and Pal, the few old ladies who belong to various Colorado members don't live on the compound. Such a different vibe to Tucson. A welcome change, a return to the true biker life. Partying, drinking and fucking, without having to worry about falling over kids all the time. Yeah, this will suit me fine. Just got to get Sally off my back so I can fully immerse myself in the lifestyle, the one that I've chosen and want.

With a kiss to her man, Jay gets up and leaves. Looks like she only came to steal his food.

"You comfortable with the nomad patch, Beef?" Pal asks, then leans forward, and adds quietly, "Can see why Drummer sent you here. Good club, don't get me wrong, but Demon's not settled as the head of the table as he's got no second to rely on. Unsettles all of us that no one is stepping up."

Glancing around to confirm no one's in ear shot, I murmur back, "No one suitable, or everyone just goddamn lazy?"

"Bit of both." Pal grins suddenly. "I heard my name was thrown into the hat, but fuckin' glad it wasn't pulled out. Don't want that kind of responsibility, or not just yet. I'm not stupid, looking as young as I do isn't a good look on a VP."

"You're right there. But otherwise, I think you'd be a good choice."

"Nah, just started life with my ol' lady. Prefer to concentrate on doing that right for now. After you sort us here, Beef, do you know where you'll go next?"

Straight back to Tucson. But Pal's reminded me, I'm essentially a roving enforcer. Drummer can send me where he wants.

"Not aware other chapters have issues," I tell him.

"There's Utah."

Hmm. Utah. Snatcher runs a tight ship. Only problem I can see is that none of us quite knows what goes on there. *Shit. Drummer wouldn't send me to find out, would he?* Was that why he insisted I change the rocker? Nah. It was just so I could have as much time as I need and in case I outstay my welcome in Colorado. *That's why, isn't it?*

CHAPTER TEN

"**P**rez." I raise my chin respectfully at the man sitting behind the desk.

Sliding his laptop to one side, Demon regards me with tired eyes. "We got the welcome out of the way, Beef, so let's cut through this shit. You've got the nomad patch on your back. Why the fuck does Drummer believe he needs to send an enforcer to Colorado?"

He's asked me out straight, no dancing around the subject. I scratch my head, debating whether to tell him the story Drummer and I concocted that conveniently skirts around the truth. I eye him for a moment, trying to get his measure. As he stares back confidently, I decide to be just as up front in return. "Don't want to blow smoke up your ass, Demon. The answer's as fuckin' plain as the nose on your face. You've got a hole in your ranks."

"Drummer thinks I'm leaving myself exposed." Sitting back in his chair, he folds his arms across his chest.

"That's about the way of it." I lean forward. "You take a slide on your bike? Get caught up in something with the cops? Who's going to step up and lead?"

"Thunder knows what has to be done."

"Then you're short of someone looking out for the safety of the club. Whichever way you look at it, Prez, you're fucked. What's Hellfire's position?"

Demon presses his lips together. "Hellfire has stepped down. He carried this shit too long to want to take the gavel back. Yeah, in an emergency he'd be there to lean on, but his time's come and gone." As I go to speak he holds his hands up. "Not my choice, not the way I wanted it, but it's water under the bridge now."

"Hell must have been around your age when he got top spot."

"He was." Dark eyes flare. "Ain't gonna fuck this up, Beef. You can report that back."

"Let's have no misunderstanding. I *know* you're not going to fuck up. Drummer's point is you need a second to help you out and have your back. Without one, you're exposed and that's a weakness we can't have. I know he's not happy wearing the patch, but is Thunder pulling his weight?"

"No misunderstanding, you say? Okay, let's show all our cards. No, he's not. Oh, he sits in the right seat, but he's constantly reminding me how much he doesn't like it. He's scared shitless of me taking that slide as you put it."

"So, what are the options?"

Demon seems to have calmed. He presses his fingers against his temples, then pinches the bridge of his nose. "No brother here wants it. Thunder's shown it doesn't work if a man is forced into the role."

"Got anyone in mind if it's a bit of persuasion they need?"

"To be honest, no. No one's ready."

"Then that means looking at other chapters. Want me to ask around?"

Demon scoffs, "If someone has a good man, you think they'd want to lose them?"

I breathe in, then let out a sigh. "You're acting defeated before we start. Could be a man wanting a change of scenery. Someone with a personal reason for wanting to get away. Until you ask, can't know what's possible."

I've caught his interest.

"I'll put out some feelers. I'm not some kid fresh off the block, Demon. Got connections I can use. Get information quietly."

"I don't want you to make any formal approach…"

"Not going to. Just think who could be suitable, then we'll discuss what to do next." After speaking, I sit back, and let him digest my proposal.

After a minute's passed, he raises his chin. "You talk sense, Brother."

"Nah, not so much. Just been doing some thinkin'. Sometimes an outsider is better placed to sort out a problem."

"Drummer did right."

My brow creases and I shake my head.

"Sending you here. I wasn't certain, felt he thought I was a failure."

"Nah, he doesn't think that. You're not a big chapter, Demon. Ain't got many to choose from."

"I don't want this discussed at church. Not the reason why Drummer sent you." He frowns, and I understand his position. He doesn't want to appear weak.

It's my turn to come clean. "Then we'll go with the other truth. My personal reason for wanting to get away from Tucson. That should sound credible enough." Having caught his interest, I carry on, "There's a woman—"

"There always is," he interrupts, huffing a laugh.

I grin quickly, then grow serious. "You know what Tucson's like. Christ, hear the jokes about something in the water often enough. But yeah, the club has changed. Majority of brothers are no longer single, and most have kids. Wanted me some of that."

"Can understand it." His eyes stray to a photo on the side of the desk. His wife and child. "Nothing better than the right woman in your life."

"Yeah, well, the woman I chose, or, who chose me to be honest, turns out she wasn't the right one. But she had expectations when we got together and won't believe I can't meet them. Needed a break to get away. She thinks she can't function on her own. My absence will show her she can. Or, if she really can't, she's got family she can go back to."

He stares at me. His eyes grow wide, then narrow again. "You could have just told her to fuck off."

Most men probably would have, but that's not how I'm made. "Would say it like it is to any brother. Even you, Prez. But a bitch? Nah, they need gentler handling. Would it have been better to rip off the band-aid? I think this wound needs to be nurtured better than that."

"Drummer know?"

"Is there anything he doesn't?" I smile, again shaking my head. "Drum knows me, could see for himself this shit with Sal wasn't right. Well, kinda gave it away when I lost my temper with Rock. Me coming here filled both our needs. Yeah, if I'd have stayed in Tucson, I'd have cut ties with Sal sooner rather than later, but she's a woman who needs someone. While we're keeping up this pretence, she doesn't have to feel she's completely alone."

"You supporting her?"

"Don't need to. She's got money of her own. Her family's still paying her an allowance, and she's got money coming in from her ex."

He looks surprised, but it's clearly not something on the top of his agenda to be bothered about one way or another. He chuckles, then enlightens me, "And now you've bumped into someone else who, according to Pyro, is hot."

"Not getting involved with another bitch before I've extricated myself from the one I'm still, unfortunately, with. Maybe never again. Kind of reminded me why I stayed single for so long."

He laughs, but it sounds dutiful. "I was like you. But it turns out I was waiting for my one. Now I've found her? Well, have to say, the grass is fuckin' green and tender this side of the fence."

"Glad to hear it, Prez." But I doubt it's for me.

A considering look comes my way, then a grin slowly slides onto his face. "Well, you won't go wanting. Got five sweet butts here who'd be interested in a new cock."

That's all I'll be to them. For a moment I do miss having a woman to call my own. Problem is, the girl who I have in mind doesn't yet have a face, and certainly isn't called Sally. Which reminds me. I offer an explanation in advance. "Can't do that just yet, Prez."

His eyes sharpen. "You got the clap or something?"

"Nothing like that," I say fast. "Fact is, I promised Sally…"

"Oh man," he gives a deep belly laugh, "you're so fucked."

He's right. I am.

His observation marks the end of our conversation. I leave his office feeling slightly adrift. I don't know what the members think of me turning up here, nor yet understand the dynamics of the club. In Tucson I wouldn't have hesitated, knowing what to say to whom, and where each brother's interests lay. Here, I'm a stranger among strangers.

It would be easy to gravitate to Pal and spend time updating him on shit going down in Tucson. But mindful I need to get to know the brothers not only to make my life easier, but also as I'm here to make my own assessment of whether one just needs a nudge and encouragement to step up to the VP spot. The job Drummer assigned requires me to mingle and get to know the men as well as I do those back home.

Glancing around I notice Pyro, Buzz, Skull and Bomber have a card game going on. Seems as good a way as any to while away a few hours on a Sunday afternoon.

I saunter over to their table. "Got space for one more?"

Bomber gives me an assessing look. "Don't know you, do we? Might be a fuckin' card shark for all we know."

"Don't know you either. Could be dealin' from the back of the pack, old man."

"Now that settles it." He glares. "You ain't joining in. No way I'm fuckin' old."

Grinning, I note he didn't refute he could be cheating.

"You looked in the mirror recently, Bomb?" Skull, the youngest, asks with wide eyes, his head shaking side to side.

Buzz kicks out a seat, he's chuckling like everyone else. "Tucson's money is the same as ours. Don't mind taking a load off you, Brother."

I keep my face impassive as I eye the pile of bills in front of the treasurer. *He'll be the one to watch.* I've played with Rock for years, lost more than I can count to him, but also have learned a trick or two. It will be interesting to see if any of those can be applied here. Strictly above board, of course. When it comes to my brothers I don't hold with dishonesty, in any form.

A couple of hours later I glance at my phone as the current game comes to a close. Bomb starts to deal the cards again, but I hold up my hand, indicating he should leave me out.

His brows meet. "You're taking the money and running? Not giving us a chance to win it back? Just starting to get a feel for you, man."

Which means it's a good time to go. Before they recognise my tells.

It's Pyro that comes to my rescue. "Yeah, you're going to take that bitch to see her dog. Or," he frowns, "feel him I suppose."

"Yeah. Picking her up soon." *Just need a piss then I'm ready to go.*

"Say hi from me. Hope the dog's no worse."

Standing I place my hand on his shoulder. "So do I." My response is heartfelt. The afternoon's entertainment has cleared Stevie from my mind, but now she, and her problems, return. I hope that dog's okay. If it's not? I don't know what the fuck she'll do.

Beside hers, Sally's problems pale into insignificance. Sure, Sal was upset when she'd been forced to return to her abusive husband, but she'd not had long at his side until he had been exposed for the fraud he was. She'd stayed on the compound, sheltered from all the media attention, then had me by her side when she started to build a life for herself in Tucson. Marcia had helped her get the schools arranged for her kids, I'd got her a car. She was fine driving to the shops by herself, taking the kids to school and all the household chores. While I was out working for the club, she'd get on just fine.

Except.

What we should eat, what brand of fucking toilet paper we should use? Which store we should go to? Even what clothes she should wear became a topic. At the start I thought she was just learning my preferences, but it went on and on. Not one decision would she make for herself. I know there are some men with a dominant personality that like a personal slave, but I'm not one of those. I don't even insist on the dominant role in bed, in fact, I find it sexy when a woman turns the tables on me.

I became tired. Worn. My head, buzzing with club problems, I wanted to relax when I came home. Not go through a shopping list for a week.

I hadn't realised at first, hadn't diagnosed the problem. Until one night she'd been sitting beside me on the couch, her eyes slowly closing, then she'd jerk back awake, and force a smile onto her face, and ask if there was anything I needed. I'd told her to go to bed. When I'd stated it clearly, she'd got up and done what I said. Yeah. She was actually waiting to be instructed. My head shakes as I remember. Even after I'd explained she didn't need me to tell her what to do, she'd ask for permission instead.

If I ever dip my toe in the water again I'd want the woman by my side to be my partner, just like Rock, Mouse, Peg, hell, all the brothers with old ladies have. It had been too exhausting, when all I wanted to do was be me, not the man she wanted.

That's why I'm so leery of getting involved again. There's no way I want to be caught in the same trap.

I'm not late, but when I pull up outside, the front door's

already opening, and Stevie's standing at the door. As I approach, my eyes look her up and down. She's got on tight narrow-leg jeans which hug the curvature of her perfect thighs, boots more suited to winter weather but perfect for going on the bike, and another of her tight tees that shows she's got more than enough breast for me. Her hair is tied back in a ponytail. She might not have been prepared for yesterday's ride but has made up for it today. Surprisingly, she looks a biker chick in every way. I'm not complaining, I love the look on her.

But I have to admonish her. "Shouldn't open the door, babe. Not before checking who's come knocking."

Shit, how can she do that? She can't look out.

"Beef," she sighs, and points. "Intercom right there. Not one hundred percent if someone really wants to fool me, but I can probably tell more from a voice than most people. And I knew it was going to be you, Beef."

"Babe, just because you knew I was coming—"

"Your bike. The engine is unique. When you shift down into first, there's a tiny rattle."

My mouth drops open. I'll be fucked. I hadn't even noticed that myself. Doubt it's anything to worry about, I'd have heard it if it was serious.

"Not much gets past you, does it?"

She grins at the compliment. "I think my brain uses the processing power it used to apply to vision to understand what my other senses are telling me. I see the world, just in a different way than most people."

"Do you visualise shit?" I don't know why I ask her. But when she says *see*, what does she mean by it?

"I've a memory of what a motorcycle looks like, but no, I don't bother translating what I hear or touch anymore. To me something is what it sounds like, feels like, smells like." She leans in and sniffs. "Leather and diesel. Beer and cigarettes. Do you smoke?"

"Nah, well, the odd joint. But the men in the clubhouse here do."

"Here? Not where you came from?"

I laugh. "Too many kids around."

"Lots of changes to get used to." Her head dips as though she understands. I suppose she does, she's in a new environment too.

She's right, but I don't comment on it. "You need anything? Or are you ready to go see how Max is?"

"I can't wait to see him. Let me just get my purse." She turns, confidently walks back into her house and within moments comes out with a strap slung over her shoulder. "But I know how he's doing. I rang James just now. I didn't want any nasty surprises."

I can understand. "How is he?"

"Holding his own and fighting."

Good boy.

CHAPTER ELEVEN

Max is indeed holding his own, I'm certain I can see an improvement. His eyes look better and more focused, and he licked Stevie's hand more than once. James wasn't on duty, but another vet who seemed to be just as competent was there. While Stevie was with her canine friend, I took the vet to one side.

"Will James be able to operate tomorrow?"

"In my professional opinion, yes." He glances at me, then at Stevie. His eyes soften as she gently runs her hands over her dog's fur. "He's a service dog. He's got an important job to do. You can be sure that we will do our best to get him back on his feet. Normally I'd warn this is expensive, but in the circumstances, I'd be surprised if he doesn't have a very good insurance plan. Maybe from the organisation that supplied him."

I might have won a few dollars earlier, but the vet's assumption makes me feel better.

"I'll get the details from Ms Nichols before you go. We've gone this far on your assurance to pay."

"What happens after the op?"

"Normally he'd be ready to go home that evening, but he will need care." He lowers his voice. "James and I have been discussing his situation. I take it you're not Ms Nichols' partner?" At the shake of my head, he continues, "We're not convinced that alone she'd be able to care for him as needed. He'll need to be brought back in for bandage changes, given an assortment of tablets. If it's easier for her, we'll keep him here for a few days. How long depends on him really."

I agree. While Stevie would be delighted to have her dog home with her, his needs will be challenging. I can't commit to being there to help out, hell, she might not even want me to offer. We're little more than acquaintances. The vets' solution is generous, and under the circumstances, makes sense.

I'm staring at Stevie, my thoughts whirring. "And after that? As you say, he's a working dog. How long until he makes a full recovery?"

"I've seen dogs bouncing around as if nothing's happened after a couple of weeks. But technically, bones will heal in six to twelve weeks. It depends on him, it could be a lot longer before he's back to his old self. I haven't got a crystal ball, though I often wish I had. What you want to know is when he'll be able to wear a harness again and take on his responsibilities, well, I don't know. But I'd say you're looking at three months or more. He will be able to go for gentle walks earlier than that. I'm sorry I can't be more definite, but dogs, like people, are different."

"Rod?"

"Ah, excuse me, will you? Oh, and tell Ms Nichols we need all her details for payment."

I nod automatically, then stare again at Stevie. She's going to be lost without that dog. For the first week or so, she isn't even going to have him at home.

She turns, unaware I'm watching her. "He feels so much better, Beef. Yesterday I could barely feel his heart beating, today it feels stronger. They're going to operate aren't they?"

"They are. I trust James, and this guy seems to know what he's talking about too." I walk closer and crouch down beside her. "They wouldn't put him under so soon if there was any risk."

"I know. It's still going to be hard though."

"He wants to know the insurance details, Stevie."

A flicker of something comes over her face. "Oh, I've got them at home. Can I just leave my credit card details for now? I'll have to dig all that info out."

When we go out to the reception area, there's a woman sitting behind the desk. Apparently today a vet nurse isn't doing double duties. "Ah, Ms Nichols." She looks up as we pass. "I'm glad your boy's doing well." As Stevie nods in her direction, she continues, "We didn't get all the information from you the other night. Can you provide it now?"

Feeling Stevie stiffen by my side, I interrupt, "I left my details for payment."

"Yes, but I take it Max is insured?"

Stevie seems flustered. "He is. But I don't have the information at hand. I'll give you my credit card and start the claim later."

"This will run into thousands of dollars. And I mean *thousands*," she emphasises. "You must get that claim initiated."

"I know," Stevie insists. "But I have difficulty completing forms as you can see." Her mouth trembles.

The way she's said it has the receptionist sitting back, her features rearranged in an expression of regret. "I'm sorry. Take your time. Yes, your credit card will be fine for now."

I'm about to offer help filling in any fucking form, but it's the first time Stevie's offered the *I'm blind* card. I frown as I look down at her, wondering why.

The vet, Rod, reappears from the back. "Ah, Ms Nichols. Before you go. Any idea where Max's microchip might be? James couldn't find it in his neck, and we didn't want to move him around too much to search for it. Has a vet told you where it is before?"

At my obvious confusion, Rod goes on to explain, "They're

implanted in the neck, but it's not uncommon for them to migrate around the body. Sometimes even ending up in a leg. I'm sure he'll have one, all service dogs do."

"He has one," Stevie confirms, "but I don't know where it is." There's a tic at the side of her eye that another person might not notice, but I'm used to looking for things that give people away. *She's lying.* She's also biting her lip, her brow furrowing, her mouth opens and shuts.

"Well, no worries. James will find it tomorrow when he's got him sedated for the op."

Her expression lightens, and she decides to speak up. "I'm afraid I didn't change the details. It's still in the name of the woman who bred him. I," again her lip tremors. "I didn't bother as it was too hard for me to do."

Surely there's something on the computer that would help her? A conversation comes into my head. *What do you do for a living? I'm a computer programmer.* Something doesn't add up. All I know is when the vet finds the microchip, Max won't be registered in her name. *Could he be stolen?* I, of all people, don't give a fuck about that. But I'd like to know what I'm dealing with. She might need help.

"That's fine, Ms Nichols. A lot of people don't bother changing the registration, and it's perfectly understandable in your case. As long as your insurance company is happy with that, I don't see a problem."

If I hadn't spent most of my adult life, or at least, since I left the Army, living with an outlaw MC, I'd have taken every-thing Stevie had said at face value. But I have. Although we try to exist on the right side of the law, losing men to prison isn't easy, we do stumble back and forth across that line. Back in Bastard's day we were firmly on the wrong side. Then, I'd been involved in debt collection, learning from one of the old-timers. When a man said he couldn't pay up, there were ways to tell whether it was because he simply had no desire to, or truly lacked the ability. If I'd gone to her to collect a debt, I'd say she just didn't want to part with the cash while pleading poverty.

I'd actually been out flexing my muscles when the club had been decimated. That had saved me, along with Rock who'd been doing prison time when all the shit went down. We were two of the few survivors.

But my reminiscing is beside the point.

Why is she lying? I dismiss the notion her having Max was the result of a theft. He's too well trained. *Perhaps she's not kept up with the insurance?* Well, at times anyone can struggle to make ends meet.

I think more on it as I lead her out to my bike and decide that's probably the most likely explanation. She wants, *needs*, her dog back and is saying all the right things to get him fixed. She'll worry about paying for it when he's fit. Yeah, I'm sure I'll find money at the root of it. I'd meant it when I said I'd step in and help. I've got money doing little more than sitting in a bank account and earning more of it, thanks to Dollar's advice. Using it for a charitable purpose, don't people do that all the time?

For now the vet's got two assurances of payment, one on her card, one on mine. We'll worry about everything else later.

Almost an expert now, she climbs on the bike behind me without hesitation. As her arms go around my waist, I can feel slight vibrations as if she's shaking. It's clear she's upset. Worrying about Max? Or about the money.

"Babe. Got some winnings burning a hole in my pocket. Feel like stopping off and getting something to eat?"

She doesn't answer immediately. "It's a nice idea Beef, but not tonight, okay? I'm worried about Max, and not in the mood for company."

"Those forms. You want help with them?"

This time her answer comes fast. "No, I can do it myself."

Can she though? Or, will she even bother?

I've no choice but to take her home, walk her to the front door just to be gentlemanly, then it's awkward on the doorstep.

For some reason her demeanour has completely changed, it's as if I'm a stranger, no longer a friend. *That hurts.*

I try once again. "I'd like to help you, Stevie."

She stiffens. "I don't need help."

Not knowing her well enough to press it, I'm going to have to leave it for now. "Okay. Call if you need me. I'll check in with you about Max tomorrow, see how he does after the op."

"There's no need, Beef."

"It's no trouble. You want to visit him? You call me, not a taxi, okay?"

A nod, which doesn't tell me anything. Then her key is placed directly into the lock, the door opens then closes behind her. I'm left staring at the wood, wondering why I have this feeling that anything between us had just turned into dust. *I've known her for twenty-four hours.* Why should her dismissal matter?

I have no idea. But it does. Maybe it's because I'm a natural carer. I see a problem, I want to help solve it. *Yeah, and that's how I got chained to Sally.*

Riding back to the compound, my uneasy feeling doesn't get any better. In fact, it gets worse. Something about the woman I just left is worrying me. As I back into a free parking space against the wall of the clubhouse, I come to the conclusion that if she won't tell me, I'll find out about her myself. Then, if she needs assistance, I can be prepared to provide it. As long as I maintain the boundaries, can't be any harm in that. She's apparently got no one else.

If I was walking into the Tucson clubhouse it would take more than a minute to get to the bar, brothers would be stopping me, engaging me in conversation. Might be questions about my bike, might, under these circumstances, be right up in my business about the blind woman and her dog. Here I'm still a visitor rather than a trusted friend, so apart from Pyro calling out, "How's the dog?" and my raised thumb to show he's still okay, that's the end of any impedance.

Soon I have a beer in my hand and am making my way to Cad's corner.

Back in Tucson, Mouse had his own office, preferring to work in quiet and secrecy. I wonder why Cad is so different.

"Can't they find you an office space, Cad?" I wave at the chair opposite him, then at his chin jerk sit down.

He offers a quick grin. "There's no room. I have thought about emptying out a storeroom, but to be honest, I prefer it out here. I can keep my finger on what's going on. And, of course, it's closer to get my drink refreshed." As his eyes fall on his empty bottle, then rise to meet mine, I bark a laugh.

Taking the hint I stand, rap the bar, and get Wills' attention.

"Okay," Cad's eyes narrow when I bring his beer back. "Don't think you've come to pass the time of day. What's on your mind?"

Hoping I'm doing the right thing as I'm about to stomp all over her independence, I take a deep breath. "You made an offer to find out about that woman I met. Got a feeling she might have money troubles or some such shit. I'll admit I'm curious. She shut down when the clues started coming. If she's in trouble, I'd like to offer help."

"She need it, you reckon?"

Do I? Had all I saw just been worry and concern about her dog? Nah, my gut is telling me something different, and I've done well before to listen to it.

Cad sees my reluctance. He leans forward. "You're not sure if you're doing the right thing prying into her business. It can't hurt. We don't find anything? No one needs to know we looked."

But it is a risky step. If I want to pursue a friendship with her, I'll need to be fucking careful never to reveal I know something about her which she hasn't told me herself.

But the feeling inside me tells me this could be important. "I want to know, Cad. I don't know what, but something's not right, and she doesn't seem to have many in her corner."

"Well, let me take a look." He raises his bottle to his lips, puts it down, and pulls his laptop closer, flexing his fingers as he rests them on the keys. "What do you know about her? Full name would be a good start."

"Stevie Nichols."

His eyes narrow. "You're kidding me, right?"

CHAPTER TWELVE

"**Y**ou know her?" If he does, that would cut the investigation time in half. *How does he know her?* Suspicions flick through my head. *Is she a criminal that he's read about?* But how can a blind woman commit a crime? *Computer fraud?* Yeah, that would be something Cad would know about.

His head moves to left then right. "Nah, I don't know her. How old is she?"

"Late twenties, early thirties?" I frown. It's not something you ask a lady, not when you've only just met. Well, not without risking getting your face smacked.

He raises his eyes. "Reckon her parents liked music."

He's lost me. My confusion shows.

"Stevie? Stevie Nicks? Sang with Fleetwood Mac? Was inducted into the Hall of Fame with the band in nineteen-ninety-eight, and in her own right as a solo artist in two-thousand-nine-teen. She's a fuckin' legend. Love her voice."

He must be a fan to have an encyclopaedic knowledge of the bitch.

"Oh, well, never mind. It could just be coincidence. So, Stevie. You reckon she's a Stephanie?"

"Assume so."

He leans his head back and closes his eyes. After a moment he looks down. "We know she's blind, let's start there. You know what kind of blindness? Was she born that way?"

"Nah. Degenerative disease started back when she was a kid." It's my turn for my eyelids to shutter my pupils as I try to recall the conversation in my mind. I've got quite good recall for technical details and at last can hear her saying it again. "Something to do with retinal pigment." Not quite that, but close enough.

A chin jerk, then he starts tapping. "This is going to take me some time, Beef. You want to go do something else while I check?"

"Yeah, okay. I'll be around. Give me a shout when you know something."

"Beef! Wanna game?" Pal yells from the other side of the room and holds up a pool cue.

Indicating yes, I detour via the bar and get a fresh beer.

As the hours pass and Pal and I are joined by Lizard and Thunder, I lose some, win some, par for the course. All of us are about evenly matched, which makes the games interesting. It's getting late when I realise Cad hasn't appeared with information. Putting away my cue, I wander over in his direction. I see him sitting, deep in concentration, a phone under one ear as he taps at the keys.

"Hold on a sec," he says into the phone, then looks at me. "Not proving as easy as I expected. Got some searches running that may take all night. Catch up in the morning?" As soon as I nod, he returns to his call.

I suppose I hadn't given him much to go on. I don't know where she moved from, and if she hasn't been in Pueblo long, maybe she's not registered anywhere here.

Another couple of beers. A nice chat with Pyro about some of the bikes that he's worked on, then I go to bed having turned down an offer from Titsy and Breezy, who if I'm not mistaken are offering their services together. I regret once again that rash promise to Sally. As I undress, I wonder if there's anything strange in not being able to get immediate information about Stevie, but if there's something I need to know, I'm certain Cad will find it. If he's not up to it, there's always Mouse, our computer guy back in Tucson.

Jeannie, Bomber's old lady, is in the kitchen when I go down the next morning. Violet, Demon's wife is with her. They seem to be directing the sweet butts whose duties apparently include cooking and serving the men. I take a plate full of a breakfast that looks as good as it smells.

"What are you doing today, Beef?" Thunder asks conversationally. "Prez put you to work?"

"Sorted that out with Pyro yesterday." I point my fork at the man I've named. "Gonna be working in the shop alongside him."

"Know what you're doing?"

"Reckon I know the ins and outs of an engine," I respond, not taking his question as anything other than a polite enquiry.

All of us work. I'm happy to turn my hand to anything and will never turn down a chance to work on a bike. Cages too, though I'm not so keen on them. Especially the modern shit which are more like mobile computers than anything mechanical. Mind you, some of the recent models of bikes are becoming that way too.

"Beef? Prez wants to see you."

"Just come when you're ready." Pyro waves off my apology about being delayed. "Sure Prez's business takes priority."

It would in any of our chapters.

When the prez wants to see you, he wants to see you. Swallowing my last piece of bacon and carrying my half-drunk cup of coffee, I head straight for his office. When I enter, I'm surprised to find Cad standing there.

"Beef, sit." Demon waits until I've done so. He notices me looking at Cad, trying to calculate why he's there. "Don't know how it works in Tucson, but here? If we think there's something that might affect the club, or a member, then I want to know about it immediately."

I've only asked Cad to do one thing. "Stevie."

"Beef, I'm sorry, but…"

"But Cad quite rightly brought it to me." Demon raises his eyebrow as if daring me to object. I don't.

But going around my head is a question. *How the fuck can a blind woman have anything to do with an MC?* I finish my coffee then sit back and fold my arms and raise my eyebrows expectantly.

Cad clears his throat. "Stevie Nichols doesn't exist."

I bark a laugh. "She's not a figment of my fuckin' imagination, and if you don't believe me, Pyro and Pal saw her as well. Dan too."

"I'm not saying the woman isn't real." Cad ignores my reaction. "What I'm saying is, whoever she is, that's not her name."

Absentmindedly I reach for my cup, see it's empty—*damn, forgot I'd drunk it*—and replace it on the desk.

Cad continues, "I looked in every database I could. Called on Mouse, he worked some magic and got that sheikh's wife, Cara looking into the government databases."

That makes me grin. Sheikh Nijad is a Dom who doesn't like his wife using her amazing hacking skills. When she helps Mouse out, he doles out punishment—of the type that apparently does nothing to stop Cara doing what she shouldn't. Yeah, Mouse has described some of his threats in great detail. But if she's got involved, she's the best. Whatever Cad has to tell me I can take to the bank.

"And?" I prompt.

"There's been no registered blind person with that name, with or without a guide dog for the past thirty years. No one on Medicare, in no fuckin' database. Retinal pigment you told me. Retinitis pigmentosa is the correct term, but we've checked databases of registered sufferers to no avail."

I shake my head. "You can't have run through everyone with that name…"

"Well, with Cara's help we investigated everything."

"Jeez, Cad. You're saying she's a ghost?"

"Nah. Think about what I said. *For the past thirty years.* Found a spanking brand-new identity though. Six months old. Cara could even pin point the person who added the records. And unlike her, they were legit, or someone with legitimate access."

"Unless your girl was only born six months back, she's using a fake identity," Prez puts it simply, slightly annoyed eyes flicking at Cad. "Which is what he should have said in the first place."

"She's hiding." My teeth are gritted.

"Seems to be the case. But it's the why that concerns me, seeing as you've become involved with her. Which brings me back to how you met her and my question then. Was it an accident or deliberate?"

Cad nods. "That question is exactly why I brought it to Prez. She's hiding. Just might be that she's been found and the car heading straight for her wasn't a coincidence."

Fuck! If Cad's suspicions are right, she's in danger. My stomach churns. If that's true, she's at a great disadvantage. She can't even see who's at her door. Her hearing may not be enough to protect her. She wouldn't hear the gun a visitor was pointing at her, not until it was too late, and a shot was fired.

Demon's fingers rap on the desk. "I don't like this, Beef. Don't like any woman being hounded, but a woman with a service dog by her side? Can't see how she could have done anything bad enough to have someone gunning for her."

Resting my elbows on my knees, I steeple my hands and place my chin on them. "I might only have just met her, but I can read people well, Prez. Have enough experience not letting someone get one over on me." He meets my eye and nods. There are skills you learn to stay alive when you ride with an MC. I continue to think aloud. "The thought of her doing something criminal is crazy, so my gut feel is she's not running from the authorities."

"On the scant facts we know, I agree," inputs Demon.

I raise the fingers of one hand then lower them to their original position. "Unless she's robbing someone from behind her computer."

"How can she do that shit?" Cad asks. "Hard enough for me, and I've got good eyesight."

I shrug, don't know, hadn't asked.

"It's possible," Demon says. "Even blackmail can be done remotely."

"Or she's totally innocent and has been caught up in shit not of her own making."

"So she goes into hiding. Hard to do on her own."

"She's an expert with computers. Maybe she set up her new identity?"

Cad's shaking his head. "Cara said the way the entries were done was good enough to throw most people off the scent. She suggested there'd need to be official sanction to alter the database like that."

"She's had help." I think for a moment. "Witness protection?"

"That would make sense." Prez raps his knuckles this time. "And if that hit and run wasn't a fuckin' accident, all her carefully laid plans have come undone."

"If that's the case and if she's sensible, she'll be talking to her handler. Moving on."

"Did she suspect it wasn't an accident?"

I go back over our conversations in my head. "No, she didn't seem at all suspicious. Was more fuckin' concerned about the dog. Don't think she saw herself as a target." Which is a worry in itself. If she's in danger, she doesn't know it. Damn, I need to warn her. Then she can contact whoever made arrangements for her and do it all over again. I frown, thinking how she explained she was so used to bruises. Now, with just a white stick to help her around, she'll be picking up a load more of them if she has to start all over again.

But she had dismissed me fast yesterday. Maybe she might not have seen the car as deliberate, but something else has spooked her. Max. *Jeez*. "For fuck's sake." I slam my fist onto my leg. "The vet is tracing the microchip. Of course that won't be fucking registered to her current name. If, and it's a big if, that accident was simply carelessness, that he's checking the dog's identity will be raising a red flag somewhere. She's fucked whichever way you look at it."

"I hadn't even thought about something like that." Cad's shaking his head now, his eyes sharp. "Of course all service dogs are chipped."

There's more too. "She was reticent about filling out forms for the dog's insurance."

"It's possible that's one detail that was missed. Her new identity was set up to be watertight, from what you say, it didn't occur to them to set one up for her fuckin' pet."

Not a pet. But I don't correct him.

"She's a fuckin' wise girl if that's the case. Careful, as she should be. I bet she'd never thought about it until she was asked for the details."

I nod. It was at that point her demeanour had changed.

"She'll know better than to start filling in forms. You know what those companies are like, they'll want to know every detail. Including where she is." Cad sighs. "Companies like to think they're secure, but you'll no doubt have heard about all the high-profile data leaks. Most times, when there's a breach people just patch over the hole and get on with it. Young kids try to get into databases for fun. Someone like me? If I'm just looking for info, no one knows I've even been there."

"You saying if she puts in a claim then they'll find her?"

"Her dog's hurt, everyone will expect her to claim." Cad pauses, then looks from me to the prez. "People go into Wit Sec for one of two reasons. Either because they need a permanent change, they've been a witness in a high-profile case and they never can return to their old life. Or, they are moved temporarily until a trial is over. If the latter, whoever sorted out her new identity may not have thought of all the details."

"If she's a programmer, maybe you're wrong, Cad. Maybe she does have the skills to do it herself?" Maybe that's why she wanted to get rid of me. A flicker of hope that she might be helping herself.

But Cad knocks that on the head. "Not necessarily. She might know code, but unless she's committed a computer crime which is why she's in the system—" he breaks off as I give a violent shake of my head.

"In that case," he resumes, "she's probably never used her knowledge nefariously. People like Mouse, Cara and I spend a large part of our time on underground forums learning tricks and how to look for weaknesses. Doesn't mean she can."

"We've got one fuck of too many 'don't knows' here, and a brother who's been seen with her wearing our cut." Demon uses a prez's stare on me. "That's what I'm concerned about. I want to know what's at the bottom of this to know whether there could be any blowback on us."

Drummer would have done the same thing in Tucson. Make sure a member didn't step in shit and then brought it back to the club.

"Of course, all this conjecture about Wit Sec might be completely the wrong tree we're barking at. Could be she's trying to escape an abusive ex, in which case, her preparation could be flimsy."

My turn to eye Demon. He's correct. But there's the worry that my cut might have signalled to someone that the Satan's Devils are involved. I understand why he's worrying. And fuck, here am I, not even a Pueblo member. Anything I've inadvertently put wrong, it's down to me to right. "What do you want from me, Prez?"

"Can you get her here? So we can talk to her?"

I remember the way she dismissed me last night. "Pretty damn certain I can't. I wouldn't even count myself as being in the friend zone right now." She'd wanted me gone. But then, if she's got all this worry on her shoulders, I'm not surprised. Being reminded Max's microchip would reveal details that she wanted hidden would have been a shock. If she's in Wit Sec, she would have wanted to talk to her handler. Of course, if she is here under a new identity, her safety means her keeping everything to herself. She's not likely to spill everything to a virtual stranger.

Demon sees my dismissive shake. "Okay, if you can't get her here, can you at least approach her? Find out what's going on for yourself? You taking her to see the dog after his op?"

"She told me she'd sort herself out. I did tell her I'd call and find out how he's doing."

Demon stares down at his hands for a moment, then he looks up. "Force the issue. Go see her, Beef. Do your best to get her to open up."

Cad scoffs. "If she's scared for her life, she's not going to say anything."

He's right. At the first sniff of trouble, she'll run. But then, she might want to, but it's not so easy for her. She could change her looks but the one thing she can't pass for is a sighted person. Far easier for the world to have disappeared from her, than for her to disappear from the world. She can't merge in with the background, however hard she tries.

"Got an idea, Prez."

Demon nods at Cad.

"We found her. If her new identity hasn't been found already, then it's only a matter of time before it is. In the end, Cara said, it was easy."

"Hold up. You only found her as you were looking backward. You still haven't found who she was before she became Stevie Nichols." I note Prez is sharp remembering everything Cad had said. He goes up in my estimation.

It seems Cad has taken that as criticism. His mouth tightens. "We'll know soon. Cara's still trying to track back. Would have started with that if I'd thought."

I point out what they have forgotten. "Hang on, there was the accident. Her location could be already known if that car was targeting her."

"What if it was just that? Someone falling asleep at the wheel as we first thought?"

I breathe out. It could well have been, that's what I'd accepted at first. "So she could still be safe. If that fucking accident wasn't deliberate." Then I sigh. "But there's the problem with the dog and his fuckin' microchip. If…"

"Lots of 'if's' there, Beef. Just hear me out?" When I nod, he continues, "Pal's setting up a security business. He's looking at security gigs at venues. Not too much of a leap to extend that to personal security. He even joked that you would be a good addition if we got into that."

"Hang on." I try and catch up. "You suggesting I become her bodyguard?"

Demon's head tilts to one side. "Way to broach the subject, Brother. Rather than scaring her saying *I know you're a fake,* offer something up. Tell her you know she needs help, and you can provide it. In an official capacity."

There's no doubt in my head. "I'd do it anyway."

"We know that. But she doesn't. It at least gives you a place to start."

CHAPTER THIRTEEN

"You recognised the sound of my bike." I'd spent an hour yesterday listening for a rattle, but I'll be fucked if I could hear it. I'd also parked a little way down the road, but clearly I hadn't fooled her.

She's holding the door open, enough so I can see lines on her face which weren't there yesterday. Immediately I'm concerned.

"How's Max?"

"He's doing as well as can be expected. Came through the op, James put in a plate to support the bones, just got to wait now. He's still under heavy sedation, no point me going to see him tonight. I thought you were going to call, not come around."

"I wanted to talk to you."

"I'm tired, Beef. I think it's all caught up with me."

She's probably telling the truth, but I'm going to insist. "Babe, let me in. There are things we need to discuss."

Her sightless eyes stare at me. "Is it money? Have the vets taken it out of your account? I'll pay you back, Beef."

"Babe, this isn't about fuckin' money. It's about you and your life." I've had enough. I step forward, crowding her. As she gasps my hands go to her biceps and carefully, watching what's behind her, I push her back. Enough so I can kick the door shut behind me, then release her.

It strikes me she's not the only blind person here. I'm used to being able to stare someone down, to see their pupils change with different emotions, to use their small giveaways to see into their souls. As her eyes give nothing away, I'm relying on other clues just as she leans on her senses.

"We need to talk," I tell her again.

"I don't think so." Her hands raise, she moves closer until they touch my chest. She pushes but has no chance of moving me even an inch. "Please leave."

"No. Not without you listening to what I have to say."

"I don't have to talk to you. I don't want you in my home. I'm very grateful for your help with Max, but now, please *leave.*"

I'm conscious she's starting to look unnerved, and I can't blame her for that. She's got six foot five of well-muscled biker standing uninvited in her house. I slide a card out of my cut, and hand it over to her, pressing her fingers against it.

"Read that."

"What?" she almost screams at me. Then her mouth opens in an O, and her other hand comes up to hold it. Her forefinger traces the front.

"SD Security Colorado. Dwayne Carson *Security Consultant?* Who's that?"

"Me." As of this morning. Well, obviously it's my true government name, but the job is new.

"You had this made special," she throws at me accusingly. "No one walks around carrying business cards in braille. Not unless there's one hell of a lot of blind people you do business with."

"Nope. Just one. You're right. Made that special. But I wanted you to know who I was and doubted you'd listen otherwise."

"So what else is fake? Just how long has this company been in existence?"

"A few months. It's a new business venture we've been getting into."

She shakes her head, disbelieving. "Are you going to tell me that's why you came to Pueblo? To join a security company?" Then she frowns and says contemptuously, "What are you then, the muscle?"

My hand snakes out and slides around the back of her neck. She jumps at my sudden touch, but I don't feel apologetic. "I might be muscular, babe, but I've got a fuckin' brain as well. I won't be dismissed as nothing more than brawn by anyone, not even you." She's touched on a sensitive point. All the times Drummer had me going to meets just as a dumb-ass threat. All I needed to do was stand looking like I could kill someone with my bare hands. I didn't object but had had to bite my tongue more than once, feeling frustrated I couldn't add to the discussion, particularly when I saw a point someone had let slide.

"I'm sorry."

Releasing her as the apology comes, I step away, giving her space. "Stevie, come sit down. Let me talk to you."

She knows she can't physically remove me from her house, and her requests have failed. Her shoulders slump, but before she moves to the couch, she has one more thing to say, "You can talk to me, *Dwayne*, doesn't mean I want to talk to you."

How long was it since someone called me by my real name? Even Sally hadn't used it. Coming from Stevie's mouth in that softly spoken voice shouldn't have caused my cock to twitch, but it did.

Forcing my brain to kick back into gear, and my dick back under control, I nod, agreeing to her terms. Hoping she'll change her mind when she hears me out.

"Beef, I can't see if you're nodding or shaking your head."

"I'm agreeing, babe, sorry."

It's her turn to raise and dip her head, then she walks straight to the couch, sitting down on one end. As before, I sit on the other side, and the sagging cushions dip. Her head tilts expectantly.

"Your name isn't Stevie Nichols," I begin, ignoring her sharp intake of breath. "It's hard, isn't it, when you choose a new identity? Hard to respond to a name that isn't your own? You risk ignoring people however good your hearing is and stumbling over giving a handle when you can't remember it. So you choose something you wouldn't forget. You a fan of Stevie Nicks? Your parents' favourite singer?"

She makes no move, not admitting or agreeing to anything. But if we were wrong, she'd have denied it by now.

"You could be a criminal, or you're in witness protection, or you're just running as you don't want to be found." I pass a hand over my face. "I might not know you, but from the little interaction we've had, I don't reckon it's you that's done wrong."

If I had a statue sitting beside me, it wouldn't have been more still. Only the slight rise and fall of her chest gives away she's a living woman.

"You've got family, yet you're in a strange town without them. You can work anywhere, as you said, so why here? Why not stay where it's familiar? Because you had to get away. Because someone is after you."

I can almost see the wheels whirring in her head. Eventually she responds, "Perhaps I'm escaping an abusive relationship."

"Nah. Dismissed that. Whoever set up your identity knew what they were doing."

"I'm a programmer," she objects. "You don't know what I'm capable of."

"Is there an ex somewhere? And did you do it yourself?" I ask direct.

Her mouth opens, but she can't force a lie from her lips. Yeah, just as I called it.

I change tact. "What are your thoughts about the car that almost killed you?"

"An accident. I spoke to the cops earlier. They've still had no luck finding out what car it was. They think, because they hit the dog and not me, that they felt they needn't stop. Should have, but maybe acted in panic."

"That might be what the cops think. But how about you? What conclusion have you arrived at?"

"I haven't had the time, or the want to think about it, Beef." She throws herself off the couch and starts pacing, expertly avoiding everything in her way. "I've been too tied up with worrying about Max. Since I've had him he's made my life worth living. I couldn't have come here without him. Now he's not here, I don't know what I'm going to do."

I stand. I move into her space, my hands stopping her forward motion. Again she tries to push me away, her fists hitting my cut. I pull them away before she damages herself, knowing she'd bruise before I do. "You're fuckin' worried, aren't you? Whatever you're running from may have caught up with you, and while you're trying to ignore it, you can't."

"They can't have found me, Beef," she admits at last. "I was assured it was impossible. Yeah, what do you think? Of course I'm wondering if I was deliberately targeted, but the driver probably just made a mistake. That's more likely than someone finding where I am when I'm halfway across country."

"Where do you come from, babe?"

Her mouth slams shut.

"I'm not here to hassle you. You really want me to go? Then that's what I'll do." It wouldn't sit well with me, and she'd probably hear my bike more times than she'd like as I kept a careful eye on her from a distance. I'm more protective over her as she can't see what's coming for her. A sighted person would have been able to jump out of the path of that car, but she'd had no warning. "Before you show me the door, can we talk a little more? You don't need to tell me where you're from or who's after you. But I'll tell you what I can do, and you can tell me what you need."

Her brow furrows as she considers my words. Her frown disappearing shows me the moment of capitulation. "Okay." I'd expected it might take more to persuade her. Then I remember, she doesn't appear to have anyone else.

"Okay." I take her hand and lead her back to the couch. Once there, I let her go again, then flex my fingers, missing her touch. "Can you tell me this, has your move, and the reason for it, been legit?"

"Yes. I've done nothing illegal."

That's what I expected. "Is it permanent, or temporary?"

"Hopefully just for a few months."

"Way I see it, sweetheart, is that it would be hard for you to relocate unless you have Max fit and well with you. That may not be for another three months. Any chance you can be assigned a new dog?"

Her lips purse as though she's not really taken that in. She's quiet. I give her space. "A new dog is out of the question. Even if I could come out into the open, there's a waiting list, then you have a month's training to pair you up with the right dog and learn how to interact with each other." She sighs. "Yeah, you're right. I've got dependent on having him with me. Some people manage with a white stick or have friends who can help. But I can't go anywhere that I know someone. Can't go to a place that's familiar. It's important I don't stick out. Max allowed me to explore and stopped me from making a fool of myself, by falling over curbs or crashing into obstacles."

"If whoever wants to silence you has found you and was behind the car almost running you down, then they're going to make another move. My feeling is it will be soon. First thing they'll expect is that you'll run, and this time they may lose you for good. I reckon if anyone wants to make another attempt on your life, that it will happen before you, or whoever's helping you, has time to make new arrangements."

"You're not exactly helping me feel better."

"That's not what I'm trying to do. I want you to face up to what I think's happening. Get ready to fight it head on."

"I can't fight…"

"You can with me beside you." Stupidly I indicate the business card which had dropped from her hand onto the floor. "Won't lie and tell you this isn't my first assignment, but I was telling you the truth. Satan's Devils have a security company, and I'm now on their payroll."

"You're suggesting I employ you and pay you? As what? A bodyguard?"

"That could work."

Her lips press together. "And just how much will this cost?"

If I say nothing, she won't believe me. Which will mean I lose the opportunity to learn who's after her, and who may now have the club in their sights. "We can work out the details later, but it won't be at full cost. I'm doing this on a trial basis myself."

"I'm a test? You keep me alive and they'll take you on permanently?" she scoffs.

I chuckle. "Something like that."

Another woman might have turned toward me, her expression trying to read mine to see whether I was serious. I only notice that's missing when she doesn't. If she could see, her gaze would be fixed at a point on the floor.

Another woman might be in hysterics. Her dog is fighting to be able to walk again if not for its life, and I've just forced her to face up to the fact, whatever she's running from may have caught up with her. But then she's faced more adversity and challenges than most other people I've met in my life. I suppose she's had years to get used to it, but that she doesn't berate how much she's lost makes me admire her.

"You got a good family?"

Now she smiles. "The best, yes."

"Well let me help you get back to them in one piece, yeah?"

"How can I trust you? And what help can you provide?"

"Well," reminiscent of the position I'd take in Demon's office, my elbows go back on my knees and my chin rests on my clasped hands, "have I done you wrong, so far?"

"What if you were working with them? What if you're trying to trick me? Getting on my right side, sucking me in. Then… hurting me? You were there right at the time the car ran me down." Her mouth twists as if she's tasting something unpleasant. "You've quickly reached the assumption I'm not who I say I am. How did you do that, Beef? Or did you already know?"

As the thought hits her, she shudders. Her visionless eyes search for my face.

Quickly I rush to reassure her. "Once I pieced everything together it was obvious. I picked up on the clues you let slip. Maybe someone else wouldn't have put it all together. I assure you, Stevie, I have no idea of this 'them' you think I might be working with. I have no idea of your real name or what you're involved with." She doesn't seem convinced, so I try to explain. "Think about it, babe. Think about how we met. Sure, I was there when you had your accident. I always hang around to watch women being run over with my bike loaded up with all my clothes. Oh, and don't forget, immediately coming up with a plan to worm my way into your good books by looking after your dog. Kinda proves I'm not just muscle, doesn't it babe?"

Fuck me, she giggles. *Down, fella, I instruct my cock.*

CHAPTER FOURTEEN

After the brief moment of mirth, she stands as though she's uncomfortable. It's hard to accept she can't see a fucking thing as she confidently walks from one side of the room to the other, and then back. Then she does it again. I can well appreciate her warning about not moving furniture. If that stool, for example, was put in her path she'd end up flat on her face. She needs a moment, I give it to her, watching the fleeting expressions come and go as they rearrange her features. Her brow furrows, then smooths, her lips press together. Her mouth twists as though she's remembering something that's painful.

Several minutes pass before she turns her face in my direction. "I was warned not to tell anybody anything. They impressed on me just one careless word could lead them to me."

I'm hanging onto every clue here. She's referred to *them* a few times. That rules out an ex. I know she'd told me that herself, but it's good to have confirmation.

It's not easy for just anyone to set up a new identity, so I'm pretty certain we're on the right track thinking she's in witness protection. If there wasn't a mystery surrounding her, I could have written off that car as just an accident as we first thought. Now I know more, it seems unlikely to be a coincidence. I'd bet good money, someone has got the information about where she is, and that that someone shouldn't have. I can do nothing to help her unless I know who that is.

"Who knows where you are, babe? Your family? Have you had any contact with them? Could someone have let anything slip?"

"Don't you think I'd love to talk to my mom? To my dad? My sisters? Have you any idea how hard it is to be so far away and unable to even pick up the phone?"

I don't. Sure, I've left my family to come to Pueblo, but I can call, go back to visit, hell, go home for good if that's what I wanted. Drummer would probably give my Tucson patch back in a flash if I explained staying away was too hard. To be so alone, unable to hear a friendly voice when she wants to. I can't imagine that. My respect for her increases yet again.

My brow furrows in sympathy. "Did you know how hard it would be?"

"I knew." Her head dips and rises. "I just had to harden myself. I have to do what is right. It's just for a few months, then I'll be able to pick up my old life again."

"You sure about that, babe?"

"Beef," she suddenly cries, "I'm not sure of anything. *I'm* not the one who did anything wrong, yet I'm the one being punished for it." She paces again, then stops. "I was in danger, I couldn't have stayed. Not when it wasn't just me, they threatened my family too."

I try to join the dots and come up with a likely explanation. "You're going to testify against someone." It seems obvious now. She's being kept off the radar until the court case. Then she'll resurface, give her testimony, and hopefully put whoever it is away, and it will be safe for her to return. *Will it be that easy?* To be given a new identity, to be moved, from what I've picked up, halfway across the country means it isn't a small case of shoplifting. *Corporate crime?* That seems likely, it can't have been something she could have seen, so something she knows, perhaps. Through her work? Maybe.

She hasn't replied. *How can I get her to trust me?* "You got a beer, babe?"

"Sure, yes."

"It's okay, I'll go." Getting to my feet I go into her kitchen and get two beers. Returning, I put one into her hand. "Come sit by me."

I'm pleased when she does. She takes a drink and then places her bottle on the coffee table.

"I'm running too, babe," I start to tell her.

"From the law?"

I laugh, then grow serious. "Babe, sometimes I think that would be easier. You want to hear a story?"

"Stops me from worrying about mine."

I nod at her reply. "One of my brothers met a woman. She'd got involved with a crooked politician. She had shit on him that could have put him away, well, let's just say her life was in danger."

Her head is tilted toward me. Her mouth is open. "What happened? And one of your brothers? How many do you have?"

Dozens. I grin. "Not a blood brother, one in the MC. In many ways, we're closer than blood."

"The woman?" she prompts.

"Blade, my brother, well, he was an ass. But once he got his head screwed on, he, *us*, well, we took down that piece of scum."

"You killed him?" Her voice squeaks.

"Nah. He's going away for a very long time. We got the evidence he'd committed murder to clear his way through for the nomination." I hear the sigh of relief.

"Are you telling me you're the good guys?"

"Like to think we are, but that's not why I'm telling you this." I'm going to bare my soul to her, so I take a few sips of beer to prepare. "Man had a wife. They were separated as he'd used his fists on her once too often. But, politician that he was, he'd do anything to make himself appear to be the right candidate, and that included bringing his wife back to his side."

"He hurt her again?"

I won't go into everything. But yeah. "He kinda did."

"I hope she's divorced his ass."

"It's just been made final, babe. He didn't contest it," we might have had a hand in that, "so it was a formality. Went through quickly. Sally, that's her name. She stayed at the club when she was hiding out from the press. There was quite a lot of coverage."

"I can imagine there would be. What does this have to do with you being in Pueblo?"

"My brothers in Tucson, well, a lot of them have found their ol' ladies. Wives," I quickly explain, seeing the look on her face. "I sort of wanted me some of that. A biker's not short of a woman when he needs one, but someone to come home to every night? Having a partner, someone to be on your side, well, that was starting to look very attractive. My brothers, they seemed so happy."

"So you got together with this Sally? She's what, your old lady now?" A flicker of something crosses her face that I can't comprehend. I wonder if it's disappointment. Wishful thinking perhaps.

Not going there even if it is. I realise I should reply. "Yes and no. It's complicated."

"Relationships often are."

"Sally, well… Sally, she's not a strong person. She's been told what to do all her life, by her parents who'd pushed her into the marriage, then by her husband who picked up where they left off. Thought I was getting her out of that situation, giving her space to start thinking for herself. Fact is," I check to see she still looks interested and I'm not boring her, seems I'm not so I continue, "Sally needs that, needs someone to give her instructions on every part of her life. I'm not that man, couldn't be what she wanted."

"So you left her?"

"Not proud of what I've done, babe. But, yeah. My prez saw I'd got myself into something that was hard to extricate myself from. So he made me a nomad—that's a biker with no affiliation to any particular chapter, and goes where there's a problem. That's why I'm in Pueblo, to sort some shit out. Sally equates that with working away."

"But you're not going back to her?"

"Makes me sound an asshole, but what I'm doing is giving her space to realise she can exist on her own. That she doesn't need a man to complete her. But no, I'm not going back. To Tucson, yeah, but not to her. I'm hoping she'll come to that realisation herself."

She's quiet for a moment. "I can't work out if you're a big softy or an utter asshole, Beef."

I chuckle. "I think I'm a bit of both."

"This came about because you thought you needed a woman to complete you, Beef. Not much difference between Sally and you from what you've said."

"World of difference, babe," I refute. "I wanted the dream, which was what I didn't get. What you've got to understand is that my brothers seemed to come across that one special woman much the same way as Sally came into my life. Thought that was a sign, read it wrong. Nah, I don't *need* a woman, especially now. It's a trap I won't fall into again." I don't explain the club whores are there to take care of my sexual needs, or that there's no problem being a single man in an MC. "The Pueblo chapter is completely different from Tucson. There, men are dropping like flies into the ol' lady trap. Here? Most are like me, single."

"But you're not. Not while this woman thinks there's a chance you can get back together."

She's not wrong. I swear my cock's starting to shrivel through lack of action. Even before I'd left town it had been weeks since I'd last made polite love to Sally. If I don't get back in the game soon, I might forget how to use it. "I'm going to cut her loose. Soon as I can do it without hurting her."

Her hand hovers in the air. It seems like an invitation to take it. As soon as I do, her fingers tighten around mine, well, circling my big paw with her tiny one as much as she can. "She'll hurt, Beef. May be kinder to pull off that band-aid rather than letting futile hope fester."

I'd come clean with her to try and get her to trust me. By laying my own soul bare, thought I could get her to reciprocate, or start that in motion at least. I didn't expect to find talking to another woman so helpful, giving me a clarity which hadn't been there before. "I've done this all wrong, haven't I? Should have been honest as soon as things started going wrong."

"How long have you been with her?"

"I've known her four months, lived with her two. Not very long."

She squeezes again. "Beef, I might not be able to see you, but I'm a fair judge of character for all that. You've told me you and your brothers were on the right side of the law when you took down that politician. You're here because you hate letting someone down. If I had someone like you in my life, I probably wouldn't want to lose them either."

"I'm not a good man," I warn her.

"I think you are." She bites her lip. "I'm in witness protection."

Jesus H Christ. It worked. "You gonna tell me enough so I can help you?"

Her expression isn't what I expected. Her head swivels on her neck, but not in my direction, she's focused on something behind me.

"What...?"

"Shush," she says fast and quietly. Her brow creases. "I heard something. At the back door."

Her hearing must be acute. There's nothing wrong with

mine, but her ears are definitely sharper, I'd heard no sound at all.

Not doubting her for one minute, I stand. She does too. "Stay here. I'll go check."

Seeing she clearly has no intention of obeying me, I half wish she'd be more like Sally and just do what she was told. But too eager to find it's a cat foraging so I can put her mind at ease, I slide my gun out of my cut—just in case—and waste no time heading into the kitchen. The view afforded by the window, looking out onto a backyard shows nothing of any concern. The door has frosted glass in the top panel, I'd be able to see a shape if anyone was there.

"*Stay* here," I use a sharper tone. "I'm going outside to check. Lock the door behind me, okay?"

She nods. "Yes."

I place my hand on the handle and pull. The door doesn't budge. I glance up and down, there are bolts, but she hasn't slid them. There's a key in the lock. *Fucking idiot, Beef.* I turn it. The door though, gives a fraction, but won't open.

"You got problems with this, babe?"

"What? No."

Someone's already tried to kill her. My brain computes facts fast as my body is already surrounding her, pushing her back as a blast comes from the front of the house.

My ears are ringing, my nostrils suddenly fill with acrid smoke coming through from the living room. *Someone's thrown a bomb into her house and locked the back door, so she couldn't get out.*

"Beef!" she screams.

"Stand still." I turn back and kick the door. It won't budge, not even with all my strength directed at it. "We've got to get out of here," I spit at her. One glance into the living room where the fire has already taken hold shows me there's no way we're getting passed that and to the front door. I grab hold of her hand. The window might have a good view, but it's too small for us to use to get out. I've got to find one that's bigger. Yanking her along behind me, I'm pulled up by her oomph of pain. *Fucking idiot that I am, I forgot she couldn't see.*

I sweep her up into my arms, kicking doors open. The bathroom's no good. Ah, her bedroom. Yeah, we can get out of that. I open the window.

Is someone waiting outside? But that's the least of my worries, I already feel heat at my back, we'll have to chance it. Thank fuck the window opens easily. In other circumstances I'd make sure she's out before me, but if anyone's waiting to stop her escaping, I'd rather him deal with me first.

"I'm going out. You come after."

She's shaking with fear and the smoke's making her choke. But like everything, she takes the destruction of her house and her need to escape in stride. Within seconds I'm in the fresh air, taking a moment to survey my surroundings. *No one in sight.*

"Come on," I urgently instruct, watching her hands and feet, giving her precise instructions. As soon as she's out I have my body around her. A bullet will have to go through me first, and with my size, I should stop it. I eye her worriedly, she's coughing. Having been in there a few seconds longer, she'd inhaled more shit than myself. *Doctor? Ambulance?* Nah, I'll take the risk she'll be alright. Need to get her to a place of safety.

"My bike's out front." Thank fuck I had the foresight to park it away from her house, though originally that had been for a different reason. "We've got to get out of here."

"Don't I need to stay to talk to the authorities? Beef, can the house be saved?"

I'm carrying her again, simply because it's easier than trying to navigate her around to where I want her to go. People are coming out of their houses.

"She alright? I called 911," asks and states a concerned neighbour.

"I'm taking her to get checked out," I shout back, hoping no one stops us as I go to my bike. People look stunned, but luckily no one steps up to prevent me whisking her away. My quick glance around shows various expressions from shock, to sympathy, to onlookers' enjoyment and curiosity seeing someone else's house burn.

Then, I'm at my bike. "Get on babe."

"Where are we going?"

"Somewhere a lot fuckin' safer than this."

CHAPTER FIFTEEN

She's hanging onto my waist so fucking tightly. Taking my left hand off the handlebars once I've shifted into top, I reach down and squeeze her hand tightly, giving her what little comfort I can as I get to my destination as fast as possible. My senses are on high alert, I can almost feel danger breathing down my neck.

My head whirls with the implications. Someone locked a blind woman's escape route and then set fire to her house. There had been no one waiting out back, they were that confident she wouldn't get out. I'm filled with rage, wondering what the fuck would have happened if I hadn't been there today, and if Stevie hadn't had such good hearing that got us out of the living room at the right time?

I could have been killed too.

There's no doubt now. Someone wants Stevie dead. They are not going to succeed. Not if I've got anything to say about it. That I myself had been in danger now makes this personal for me too.

I've been checking my rearview as I've been riding, no one seems to be following me, even when I'd made the diversion I had. I'm pleased as fuck when at last the gates of the clubhouse, reinforced after the attack a few weeks back, appear before me. The prospect has those gates opening as soon as he recognises my bike.

"Prospect!" I yell, as I dismount. After quite closing the gates he comes running over. I explain fast, "Don't think I've got a tail—"

I don't need to explain what I want when he interrupts, "I'll keep my eyes open."

I may not know him, but something tells me Dan's good. He knew immediately what I wanted.

"Where am I?" Instead of looking around, Stevie's clearly listening hard. Someone is working on their bike, revving the engine. Loud voices reach us from the clubroom.

"I've brought you to the clubhouse…"

"Take me to a motel," she immediately insists, for the first time seeming frightened and wary.

I can see how coming to a biker compound could be scary, even for a sighted woman. For her? I'd had no time to prepare her. It must be terrifying. To be honest, all I had on my mind was getting her away from whoever wanted her dead, and what place could be safer than being among my brothers? I hadn't spared a thought for how she would feel about it. I take hold of her hand, she grasps it like an anchor.

"Babe," I'm thinking aloud. "You've been found. That's a definite. I don't know who's after you or how many. You haven't told me anything, so you probably know better than I. If they found you once, they could find you again. If I took you to a motel, you wouldn't have the same protection we can give you here."

"You say *we*." She's keeping her voice down. "Why should your friends help me?"

"Don't forget, it was my brother's suggestion to extend our security services to you. And even if that wasn't the case, they'll do it for me."

Her eyes squeeze tightly. "But you said your brothers were in Tucson…"

"Any man in any chapter is my brother." Dan's watching the gate, but I'm only too aware the strong steel slats will keep out most things, but not a bullet. "Babe, let's get you inside. Don't like that you're out in the open."

"Describe it to me, Beef. What type of building is this?"

Information. That's what she needs. "It's an old steel mill that's been converted."

She raises her chin slightly. "Going to need you to help me, Beef." She doesn't ask helplessly, just matter of fact.

"I'll be by your side, Stevie. And if I'm not, I'll make sure one of the women is with you. You won't be alone." I'll need to fill in Demon and the rest of his men, can't personally guarantee to stick with her.

I watch as she draws her shoulders back and takes a deep breath. "Okay, lead on."

I'm a quick learner. I put my arm firmly around her. "There's a curb here, Stevie. Only a couple of inches. Yeah, that's it, you got it. Now three steps to the door. You okay?" We get to the door, I open it, noticing the strip at the bottom in time to warn her so she doesn't trip. That darn mat that's always slipping and bunching up is the next obstacle, I ease her over it.

I'm concentrating so hard on watching her feet that I don't see what's in front of me until…

Christ. "What the fuck?"

At the sound of the slap Stevie stiffens and moves closer to my side seeking protection for dangers unseen while I stare at the woman who's just walloped me around the face.

"Beef! You fucking cheat! I knew I couldn't trust you. You wouldn't go with a whore, that's what you said, and now you're walking in with one."

"Mommy," a voice wails.

Without taking her accusing eyes off me, Sally holds out her hand for her middle child, Eliza.

Well fuck. I'm shocked enough that she's here, but not only that, she's brought all three fucking kids.

I've just been almost burned to death in a fire, I do not need this. Having cheated death for a second time, I'm not at my best, and at a complete loss as to what to say.

The silence extends until someone else speaks.

"Sally isn't it?" I start to open my mouth, but Stevie continues, "I know what this looks like, but there is nothing between Beef and myself."

"He's holding you freaking close," Sally complains.

"Because I've not been here before and I'm blind."

Sally's mouth drops. "You're blind?" Her voice rises incredulously. "But you don't *look* like you are."

"I wouldn't know." Stevie's mouth quirks. "Now, Beef. Can you plant me somewhere I can sit down? It would seem you need to have a discussion with Sally."

"Can't you see anything at all?" Aden, at seven has always impressed me. He's staring with wonder at the woman by my side. "I've never met a blind person before."

Kaylee takes her three-year-old thumb out of her mouth. "What's blind?"

"She can't see anything," Aden patiently explains.

"The lady can't see?" Kaylee repeats, then puts her palms over her eyes as though trying it out for herself.

Stevie may have no sight, but she's not *blind*. "Why don't you kids come sit with me and I'll tell you what it's like not to have your sight. Then your mommy and Beef can have a chat."

I lead her to a couch. An amused Pyro and Ink stand, making room for Stevie. Pyro leans in, then his expression changes rapidly to one of concern. "You smell like you've been in a fire, Beef. What happened?"

I'm not surprised Pyro sussed it out so fast. Fires and he have a certain relationship. Mimicking him, I incline my body toward his. "Fucker locked her back door and threw a fuckin' bomb in the house she was living in."

"Jesus." Ink, overhearing, looks from me to Stevie and then to Sally who's standing at the bar with her arms folded over her chest watching me talk with a suspicious expression on her face. "And you came back to this? All you fuckin' need."

"Er," Stevie speaks, her head tilted toward us. "I don't know what their mom would say, but can we hold off on the swearing in front of the kids?"

Sally wouldn't have the nerve to say shit. To me, perhaps, but not to men she doesn't know, or can't even see.

"You okay, babe?" Ink's looking down at her in concern. His worried eyes flick to me.

"Shocked, but okay," she replies. "Don't think I've got my head around it yet." She coughs, making me frown.

Pyro catches my unease and tilts his head toward the bar. "Go sort her out." Her being the woman glaring at me. "I'll fill Demon in and Ink can look after the girl. We'll get Rusty to look at her too."

"Good to see you again," Stevie speaks up. "Pyro wasn't it? And pleased to meet you." As she holds out her hand, I'm pleased one after the other Ink and Pyro take it then Ink starts introducing himself.

After exchanging chin lifts with Pyro, I feel confident I'm leaving Stevie in safe hands. I turn away and stride toward the last woman I expected to see in the Pueblo clubhouse.

For a moment I just stand in front of her, noticing she's staring at my cheek which must be red by now. I almost don't trust myself to speak. Half-turning, I see Stevie's entertaining the kids, if that's the right word. She's got all three of them with their hands covering their eyes and has already got them passing a glass between them. I suspect she's encouraging them to explore it by touch.

"Come." If Sally and I are going to have words, I don't want everyone overhearing. Having entered my home and in such an explosive manner, there's only one way this is going to end, and that's not how she wants it. I lead her out the back of the clubhouse and over to one of the picnic benches, noting as I do, Stevie can never come out here, or not by herself. Even Max would find it hard to navigate. The ground is covered in crap, bricks, pieces of concrete, half-demolished walls. That great fucking fire pit, the furnace where they used to melt down half a train at a time, would be a death trap.

"Sit." I point. She does. I plant my ass on the opposite side of the picnic bench.

She stares at me, then looks down. "I'm sorry, I got it wrong." Her bottom lip is trembling. "I thought…"

"Know what it looked like Sal. That girl's not been here before."

"Don't you hold people like them by the arm, not cuddle them?" Her question shows me she's not convinced. And Stevie's people, not *people like her*. Christ, Sally can't cope as well as her and she's got full use of her eyes.

"Told you what happened. That's all the explanation you're going to get. Now, why the fuck are you here?"

Sally finds her hands interesting. "The kids missed you."

I shake my head. "First thing Sal, we've been through this. Never played dad to those kids." For this very reason. So they wouldn't get attached if things didn't work out. Somehow, deep inside, I'd had my doubts from the start. Like the kids well enough, played with them too, but always remained on the sideline. "Second, I've only been gone two days."

"It's been longer than that. You've been living at the club, I missed you," she admits at last. "You weren't around much, but you were there to do stuff. When the air conditioning stopped working, and I called you, you sounded so cold. I thought something was wrong. I couldn't sleep for worry. It was different when you were in Tucson. Tash had told me you weren't—"

"You didn't trust me," I reply, stopping her from saying my brother's woman had reported back I wasn't sleeping with whores. Looks like me and Blade will have words.

I gaze at her, not sure whether I'm angry or upset. She's got no spy here. She's clearly been sitting on her own putting herself through hell thinking as soon as I arrived I was dipping my cock in every available pussy, despite the promise I'd made. So much so, she did what I didn't think she was capable of and came to seek me out. In some ways I'm impressed. "How the fuck did you get here, Sal?"

"We flew. I booked the tickets when I couldn't sleep."

Makes sense. Well, they can just fly back. "Impressed you did that, Sally. I'm glad you did." I feel guilt at the smile which appears on her face, but my next words wipe it off fast. "We need to talk."

"Beef—"

"No. It's my turn, Sally. The fact you don't trust me fuckin' hurts. No, don't deny it. Your reaction without asking questions first; when you saw me walk in with Stevie you thought I'd confirmed your suspicions. I've barely been here two days, and yet already you had to come find me. You don't trust me, I've got a job to do here. Seems you'd be happier without worrying what I'm getting up to, and I'll be able to concentrate better, if we part ways now."

"Beef," she starts, pleadingly. "I thought you'd let us stay. I wanted you to be pleased that you had your family with you. Hoped you'd be missing us as much as we miss you."

Hoped, yeah. But I notice she hadn't said it had been her expectation. It was fear that had driven her here, she was afraid she'd already lost me. She has, she's just moved me telling her up on the agenda.

"No, Sally. You've got more strength than you realise. Coming here? Well that's shown me that. Should show it to you, too. Takes guts to walk into a strange clubhouse."

She doesn't look like I'm paying her a compliment, but I am. Her lip trembles again. "I'm sorry, I shouldn't have come here."

"Nah, Sal. You only advanced the timetable a bit. We were never going to work out, long term."

"Have you been faithful, Beef?"

I hate that she has to ask. But I give her the words she needs. "Yeah, Sal. I have."

She goes quiet. Then asks, "Are we really over?"

I settle for nodding my head. She wipes a tear from her eye as I try and think of ways to help her out. "You've got options, Sally. You should plan for your future. You could go home, back to where your parents are. They might be helpful with the kids."

Surprisingly, she shakes her head. "No, I don't want to do that. Eliza's settled in school. Aden too. Even Kaylee likes her playgroup. I still see Tash and Marcia from the club." She nibbles her lip. "In fact, Sam came to see me yesterday. It's why I'm here."

Sam? Drummer's old lady? What's she doing talking to Sally and making her come all this way to see me? Inwardly I bristle. I'll be calling my old prez very soon and demanding to know why Sam's been interfering in what should be something between a woman and a man. Then I'll speak to Blade too and get them all sorted at once.

"Sam suggested I should let you go. Well, not in so many words, but that was her meaning."

My assessment of Sam has done a dramatic one-eighty.

"She worried me. Suggested how I could be independent, and that I really don't need you."

"No?" My lips quirk. Not to be needed? That doesn't bother me at all.

"I, also, I, er…"

"Spit it out, Sal."

"In the, er, bedroom. You want more, don't you?"

I don't immediately reply. What do I say without making her think she's a failure? After some deliberation, I decide to be honest. "Yeah. Sometimes, Sal, I need someone to know my needs before I do myself. It's not me to always be in control. There's nothing wrong with you, just you're—"

"Wrong for you?" she replies. Then nods. "I knew, Beef, I

knew. But I've been relying on people so long, I panicked. That's why I'm here, to reach you before you started to look elsewhere. I wanted to, I don't know. Yes, I do. I wanted you to take one look at me and see what you were missing."

Trouble is. I haven't missed her at all. I keep quiet about that.

She goes quiet. I keep my face impassive. I fucking hate situations and conversations like this, it's why I avoid them. Hate disappointing people, not being able to live up to what they want. Exactly why I was a coward and wanted things to just fizzle out between us. My heart breaks for her, almost as much as it would if our situations were reversed.

She watches me, then seems to focus on a handful of birds pecking at the ground, trying to find crumbs left over from a barbeque or perhaps just insects and worms. A glance back at me, then defeat comes into her eyes.

"Can you arrange a motel for us? We'll fly home in the morning."

She's on her own in a strange town. I'll have to get Stevie settled first, but making this offer seems the least I can do. "Want me to stay with you?"

Her eyes close. She seems to have an internal battle with herself, then she opens them and says with fresh determination, "No, Beef. We'll say goodbye here. If you can make the arrangements, then point me to somewhere the kids can have some fun. I'll turn this trip into something about them."

I regard her before nodding. Her acceptance I'm not coming back to her is welcome, and so too, is the way she's straightening her back, taking responsibility. It's what I wanted for her all along. *Was I holding her back?* Quite possibly.

As to a suggestion for the kid's entertainment, I'm too new here to know, but I'm sure one of my brothers will have an idea.

It turns out to be easy. Pal knows a hotel close to a pizza parlour and an ice rink. Apparently, that will do. He even offers to give Sally a lift there as Demon, not surprisingly, wants a word with me. It's not after all, every day that a member almost gets killed in a house fire.

I say goodbye to the kids, who Stevie's been keeping entertained, then watch the four walk out the door.

I'd love to say I feel some regret as Sally leaves, but I can't. Instead, I'm filled with relief.

CHAPTER SIXTEEN

The door closing behind Sally and the kids makes me feel like I'm on the brink of a new life. One where I don't see the need for a woman. I give myself a moment to draw in a deep breath, then a hacking cough draws my attention to Stevie, still seated on the couch.

She's my responsibility now. She's my job. I suppose, as she's alive, you could say I've been successful doing it, but hell, it was sheer luck we escaped with our lives today. But, in her case at least, not totally unscathed.

"Beef."

"How the fuck do you do that?" Ink asks, amazed.

She gives that typical shrug I've come to expect from her. "He walks a little unevenly. I heard his boots on the floor."

Well, of course, we all look down and examine my feet. Must admit I'm feeling a bit self-conscious as I complete my journey to her. "You okay?" I didn't like the sound of that cough.

Ink gets in fast, "I got Rusty to take a look at her. He's not particularly worried. Just said if her cough gets worse, she may need to get checked out."

"I said all that without speaking," she says, drily. "I don't want to go to a hospital. When they find out I'm not dead, that's the first place they'll check."

Pyro's eyes meet mine. *Who?* he mouths.

I shake my head. *Fuck knows.*

"You okay here, babe? I've got to update the prez on what's gone on."

She presses her lips together, a sign which I've noticed means she's thinking. "Can I speak?"

I give a quick look around. It's just members, no old ladies, sweet butts or prospects within hearing. "Yeah."

"I'd be dead if you hadn't been there, Beef. Those kids? Well, they took that off my mind for a while, but now I've got to face up to the facts. I need someone on my side. And someone who saves me rather than tries to kill me is someone I know I can trust. Your prez is your boss, isn't he?"

I remember a nod isn't sufficient. "Yes."

"Then if he wants me to, I'll speak to you both."

"I want that," a voice bellows from the direction of Demon's office.

She stands. "Lead on, MacDuff."

Chuckling slightly, I go to put my arm around her. "Take hold of my elbow, Beef. Just steer me in the right direction."

"While you're in with Demon, I'm gonna head out to her place. See what's going on."

"Can you see if you can find my white stick? It was in my bedroom…"

"Cops will be there, Ink," I warn.

Stevie's expressive face shows she hadn't thought of that.

He nods. "I'll do what I can, Stevie."

She thanks him. I'm more interested in what he can find out rather than anything that can be saved.

I'm not surprised to see Pyro going with him. He's got fire-fighter friends who may well be in attendance and who might be able to give him a clue as to what accelerant was used or anything useful.

I just remember to stop her in time to move a low stool out of her way, then we're walking in to Demon's office. I place her hand on the back of a chair. She takes a second before she sits down. Anyone else I would think she's taking in her surroundings, but clearly she can't be. After a moment she nods and holds out her hand in Demon's general direction.

He reaches over the desk to take it. "I'm Demon, President of the club."

"Stevie Nichols," she responds. "Though I expect you already know who I am."

"I might," Demon replies, the smirk showing through in his voice. "If you were who you say you are. Sit." When she does, I take the seat next to her. "First off, Stevie, are you alright?"

She closes her eyes briefly. "I'm fine, apart from a bit of a cough. That's nothing. I shouldn't be, wouldn't be fine if Beef hadn't been there. I don't think what's happened has really caught up with me yet. I'm just so pleased I wasn't alone."

Demon's eyes catch mine. We don't need words for the sentiment to be exchanged between us that we're both fucking glad I was too. We all know if I hadn't been she most likely wouldn't have made it out alive.

"I told you I was the prez. My role is leading this motley crew, running our businesses and keeping everyone in the club safe. If we're providing you protection, you are our business. But if that's going to cause any harm to come to my club, I need to know about it. Beef got you out of the house, as he should. But from the soot on his cut he was wearing it. Anyone watching would have seen him take you away."

"Not necessarily here," I tell him. "Fuck, they'd already know I was involved with her, Prez, from the amount of times I've been to her home and have been checking up on the dog. But I wasn't followed here, I made sure of that. I could have stashed her anywhere." But I can't deny someone might know the Satan's Devils are involved.

Stevie's nodding. "I don't want to bring more people into it.

That's why I left home in the first place, couldn't risk putting my family in danger."

Again, Demon and I exchange glances. Her leaving wouldn't necessarily guarantee they'd leave her folks alone, but now's not the time to tell her that.

"She's in Witness Protection," I tell him.

"Have you a handler? Someone you can call? Get you moved on?"

"That's the point. That's what he'd do."

It doesn't take a genius to realise why she doesn't want to do this officially. "She can't go anywhere without Max, her dog," I tell him.

Prez digests that for a moment. If she refuses to go to her handler, it means we can't get her off our hands. I wait, wondering what he's going to do. His next words show me he's not going to run her off, or not immediately.

"Who's after you, Stevie? What do you know?"

Her lips press together. "I don't want to say. Suffice to tell you, I saw something I shouldn't."

Demon shakes his head. "Is this from before you went blind?"

Stevie gives a short laugh. "No, sorry. The use of my word was confusing. I have ways of identifying people without using my eyes."

Demon's staring at me. "Have you got any suggestions how we handle this, Beef?"

Instead of answering, I stare at Stevie. Now the adrenaline rush of getting away from the fire has died down, and my anger, then sorrow at seeing the end between me and Sally, welcome, but the admittance of failure all the same, I've started to think more rationally. There are some questions I want answered.

"Leaving aside the hows and whys of your situation. Who knows you've come to Pueblo?"

"My handler. Who he's told, I don't know."

"Who's he with? FBI or cops?"

"Er, FBI."

My eyes meet Demon's again. A federal case is more serious. "They usually play it close to their chests. Only people who know are those that need to."

"I know," she says, adamantly. "That's why I thought I was safe. I haven't done anything to draw attention to myself. I'm not stupid. It's my life after all. I looked into everything before I accepted leaving my old life behind. The US Marshals providing witness protection haven't lost anyone, *ever*. Unless the person slipped up themselves."

"Have you?" Demon asks.

A vigorous shake of her head. "Absolutely not."

I lean back, my hands clasped behind my head. For a moment I stare at the ceiling above. It doesn't provide inspiration. I start speaking my thoughts aloud. "Most people in Wit Sec are criminals. Only a very small proportion are innocents. You sure you're not involved in something you shouldn't be?" Changing my viewpoint, I bring my eyes down to stare at her. "Babe, whatever you've done we don't give a damn. Wouldn't call us criminals, but we live outside the citizen world as much as we can."

"Beef!" she cries out in frustration. "*I've* done nothing wrong. I've been caught up in something that I'd give anything to have avoided. I should have been safe here. No one should have been able to find me. I've got a new life, and I've done everything I can to protect it. I assure you, the very last thing I want to do is die."

That's where I do believe her.

Demon is staring at me. I've brought a woman onto the compound, involved my brothers, when I don't a clue what's going on. I've been seen around her wearing my cut, it's almost a certainty that someone, somewhere, suspects where she is. If I was in Demon's shoes, hell, even wearing mine, I'd want to know what we're up against.

"Come clean, Stevie," I instruct her, using the tone which would have had Sally shaking.

Maybe it's because she can't see my fierce expression, but Stevie, unlike Sally, doesn't comply. Instead she suggests again, "Take me to a motel. I'll wait it out there until I can collect Max, then I'll contact my handler—"

"No," I interrupt. The thought of abandoning any woman in her situation wouldn't sit well on my shoulders. But her? I've got a vision in my mind of her innocently opening the door to someone who says they're a motel employee, then of her lying dead or bleeding out on the floor. "If you're going anywhere, you won't be alone."

Demon has remained quiet for a while. He now steps back into the conversation. "Beef wears a cut. Clearly shows which club he belongs to. Chances are whoever is after you knows exactly where you are. Might be too dangerous you staying here. Nah, hear me out. You've got challenges, shall we say? Don't want to play on them or make you out to be less of a woman than you obviously are, but things which we take for granted, you struggle with. Only a fool would ignore that. So, I think you're in danger staying here, and as you won't tell us who's coming for you, I can't rule out collateral damage to the club." His eyes meet mine briefly. Only a couple of months back and they had to rebuild. If she could see she'd be able to tell that for herself. Be a few years yet before the new brickwork starts merging in with the old. "But a motel isn't a good option, and I'd have concerns about you going alone."

There are two things I'm reading loud and clear. One, is Demon's got an idea, and two is I'll be the one going with her. I haven't got a problem with that, though I'll have to run it past Drummer. He sent me here for a reason after all, and I haven't had much of a chance to sit down with Demon and discuss it except for our one brief chat.

Demon doesn't disappoint me. "You need somewhere to hole

up until your dog is back on his feet. Club's got a cabin up in the woods. Less than an hour's drive from here. Hellfire used it when we were kids and had had enough of the city. Club members use it from time to time. Might need a bit of cleaning, but hey, that's what prospects are for. You can stay up there with Beef."

"Max…"

"We'll keep an eye on him for you. Soon as he's fixed, bring him to you. You'll be off the radar and safe there until you can talk to your handler and get yourself moved on."

"No records linking the cabin to us?" I sit forward, interested in his proposal.

"Nah. Club's owned it almost from the start, but never been our name or any one of the members on the deeds. Be hard as fuck to trace. From forty years ago more likely to be paper records covered in dust."

I can imagine the various purposes it was probably used for. Back forty years this particular club wasn't part of the Satan's Devils, and Blackie, the first prez, was into things we no longer touch. Probably more than one member needing to keep his head low from time to time.

"It's a nice place once it's clean and tidy. Got water and electric. Remember it well from when I was a kid. Jeannie and Bomber have used it from time to time as well."

Stevie looks like she's thinking. "You sure no one other than your club knows about it?"

"Wouldn't have suggested it if I thought there was a chance. If you agree, I'll get the prospects to clean it up, and you can go there with Beef tomorrow."

"You sure you don't mind?" Her teeth worry her lip. "I know you offered your protection as part of the security service you run, but I can't afford to pay you much."

"We're branching out." It's Demon who answers her. "If you've been straight with the information you've given, when you can, you contact your handler. Put in a word for us. We might get more work out of it."

My eyes open wide as I wonder whether she'll swallow that. Us work with the US Marshals? I very much doubt it. But I'm happy that Demon is foregoing payment. No Devil likes a woman being hunted, killed or tortured. If Demon hadn't agreed to extend his protection, I'd have contacted Drummer. I'd briefly considered taking her to the Tucson chapter, but without knowing who's after her, I can't risk it. If they were determined enough, they'd search for her at any of our chapters. They probably still will, but this way, they won't find her. I'll need to talk to Demon about it and get him to warn the other clubs.

"I want to stay alive," Stevie says. "And I need my seeing eye dog back. If you're sure I'm not putting Beef or your club in any danger, then yes, I'll go to the cabin. But..." She must have heard our intake of breath as both Demon and I open our mouths, and she holds up her hand to stop us. "*But*. Once I know my way around the cabin, Beef doesn't need to stay. I'm sure he's got better things to do with his time. I'll be fine once I've learned the layout. Perhaps give me a burner phone in case I need help, but I don't need a babysitter."

I suppose I've got so used to Sally, she's taken me by surprise, and damn it if I don't feel disappointed. What she's suggested would probably work, if the cabin is as far off the radar as Demon has stated.

One thing I'm fast learning, is Stevie's not helpless. To do the right thing she's already uprooted and left everything she's ever known. Why wouldn't she be fine staying alone?

Demon raises his eyebrow toward me, then raises his chin. "Get settled in, Stevie, see how the ground lies, then Beef can make the calls."

The meeting is over, or at least the one with Stevie in it. Demon has used gestures to make it obvious he wants me to return. Helping her stand, I take her elbow. Once in the clubroom I see Wills and Dan, and point them in the direction of Demon's office. Then thankfully I spy Violet and take Stevie over.

"Violet. This is Stevie. Can you take her under your wing for a moment while I have a chat with your old man?"

CHAPTER SEVENTEEN

Returning to Demon's office I patiently wait until he finishes giving instructions to the prospects. From the brief chats I've had during the short time I've been here, I've discovered both are more than ready to patch in. Might not know enough about them to give them my vote, but everyone here thinks they've served their time and earned enough trust to be brought to the table. When that happens, Beaver and Karl, the hangarounds, will take their places as new prospects. But even when they are, the club will wait a time before trusting them with information that could bring harm to the club. Hence, it's Wills and Dan who'll take the lead on preparing the cabin. They've shown they can be trusted to keep their mouths shut about where they are going, what they are doing, and why.

Watching Demon, I admire his style, appreciating how he's addressing the prospects. His manner of showing the job will be done to his satisfaction or else neither will be getting their patch makes me hide my smile. This close they won't want to fuck up. I doubt I'll find a speck of dust when we go to the cabin tomorrow.

Wills' face is serious as he takes an old-fashioned looking set of keys from Demon. His eyes meet mine and he jerks his chin as he goes out the door. It's a silent promise they'll do what's needed.

I retake the seat I'd vacated moments before. "I'd take her back to Tucson, but—"

He's there before me. "No Satan's Devils chapter would be safe, Beef. I commend that she doesn't want to give herself and who she's hiding from away, but it's making our lives fuckin' difficult. I don't know how to prepare us. Are we facing one man? Two? A gang or an organisation?"

"Someone with reach, that's for sure."

"I agree. That's your number one priority. Get her to tell you exactly what we're dealing with."

I'll try. That's all I can promise. Stevie's protecting herself, and quite rightly. But in doing so, she's not protecting us. Club first above everything. Something occurs to me. "D'you reckon she might believe our sympathies would lie with who's trying to silence her?"

Demon taps his fingers against his desk. "Must admit it had occurred to me. But nothing immediately springs to mind."

"Not all MCs are as clean as ours."

"True. Would be easier if we knew where she came from: north, south, east or west. It could be anywhere."

We both go quiet. Each dredging the depths of our minds thinking of shit that we've heard on the grapevine in which she could be involved, but nothing immediately comes to mind. Feds are always chasing MCs trying to get something on the gangs as they call us. But likewise, it could be the Mafia or, my personal favourite, something she's learned about a corporate organisation from working behind her PC. Demon's right, I've got to get her to tell me. There's just a chance it might affect where our loyalties lie. Of course I wouldn't let any harm come to her, but persuade her against testifying? Yeah, that I could do. Though my leanings are against it. I'll want nothing to do with people who're trying to take out an innocent woman.

Thinking time is over with no productive result, so I ask

something else. "What do you think about leaving her alone, Prez?"

"You'll find the cabin is out of the way. Biggest danger is someone seeing you coming or going and following you. My view is that it's best if you stay with her and out of sight. Anyone who's seen you will have noticed your nomad patch. If we're questioned, we can say you took off and we don't know where, they'll probably believe us."

Demon sounds certain there will be a 'they' turning up. I'm right there with him. It makes sense that not only Stevie, but I will stay off the grid. "Biggest risk is when the dog gets out of the vet's. We'll have to get him up there without being followed."

"You let me worry about that. You're right, that's where they'll focus, so we'll have to do some kind of diversion."

"Decoys," I suggest. "Get a load of trucks. Send them off in all directions. They won't know which one is carrying Max."

"Max may need check-ups when he's released," Demon muses aloud. "I'll contact this vet. See what he's made of. It's possible he can be persuaded to make a house call, if necessary, instead." I've got a feeling James might. I'm happy to leave that with Demon. "Pick up a couple of burners from Cad."

"Sure."

"Want you at church next week."

So I'll be making the trip back anyway. I don't tell him he's just contradicted himself, but maybe he means for me not to be seen around town or working at the shop on a daily basis. Should be able to get there and back without being followed, but how much can I get out of her between now and then? He's given me a week to earn her trust. "May not have much to share," I warn him. "Reckon it's going to take more than a minute to get Stevie to open up."

"It probably will. But the brothers will want to hear anything you do find out from your own mouth."

There's a knock at the door. Demon calls out they can enter, and Ink comes in. His face is grim, and he brings with him a faint acrid smell of smoke. "Pyro's pal from the fire service was there and got his team to turn their backs while I had a look around. The back door was fastened shut with heavy duty wire. No way she could have opened it."

I know that myself. If a big fucker like me couldn't budge it, she wouldn't have had a chance.

"You go inside?"

"Nah. The fire was intense, man. Continued to burn after you got out. There's virtually nothing left. Anything she had is gone. If anything survived, it would be badly smoke or water damaged."

I doubt if she'd have brought many personal possessions with her. Anything she had would have pointed to her past. Having escaped with her life, I doubt there was anything gone she'll be too worried about. This won't be the first time Stevie has had to start all over again.

Except for some stuff. "She needs clothes."

"She's about the same size as Jayden. Ask Pal if she's got anything spare that will keep her going for a few days."

"Can you send Vi out to stock up? I'll pick it up when I come back for church."

"That's a plan." Prez nods.

My mind circles back to the fire. "You see anyone other than firefighters?"

"Like who?" Uninvited, Ink takes the second chair.

"Cops? Marshal?"

Ink's eyes shutter as though he's trying to remember. "Cops, yeah. Hanging around waiting for the firefighters to get what they need." He pauses. "What does a US Marshal look like?"

Demon and I look at each other. I see his mouth turning up at the corners. Ink's got a good point. A marshal checking on a woman who doesn't exist would hardly be wearing his badge. "All the cops in uniform?"

"Nah, looked like a detective there."

It was obviously arson. A detective is likely to be assigned to investigate a crime.

"If the marshal knows he's lost his witness, they'll be searching everywhere," Ink notes. "Firefighters have already determined there's no body in the ruins of her house." I look at him assessing, wondering if Demon's considered tapping him for VP.

He's come up with another good point. Wiping my hand down my face, resting my fingers on my chin, I shake my head. "Got more than one group of people searching for her, Prez. Starting to wonder whether we've bitten off more than we can chew."

Demon studies me for a moment. "She's right, though. Marshals will move her fast if they know she's exposed. It's not something that's gone into lightly. The info she's got must be hellishly important for them to give her a new identity in a new town."

"And the people coming after her scary enough that she's given up everything." Ink looks impressed. "She either hates these people she's up against, or puts society's needs above her own. Pretty damned impressed with that myself. Now it's likely she'll have to do that all over again."

A little earlier I'd been considering telling the authorities where she is so she could be looked after by people who, to date, have never lost a man. Or woman, come to that. Now I'm realising, if the US Marshals knew, they'd take her away and I'd never know where she was, would never see her again. It's just my need to protect her that makes me want to keep her close, isn't it? Along with my desire to want to reunite her with her dog. Sure, she's an attractive bitch, wouldn't turn down someone with her looks, but I've got a stable of sweet butts here I haven't tried yet. Nah, that's not influencing me at all.

I glance at Ink, then at Demon. "Someone who isn't meant to know where she is, found out. Unless we discover the how and the who, we could be putting her back into danger again. Sure, the US Marshals have an impeccable record. Doesn't mean they can't fuck up a time or two."

Ink nods. "There's a leak somewhere. Could be within the US Marshals' outfit, or with the cops."

"Or someone just got lucky, or she herself slipped up."

Demon looks sharply from me to Ink, then back again. "You're right, Beef. Anyone can fuck up. We didn't know Taser would go off the rails, but Ingot certainly found out. He'd prospected, earned his patch, spent more than a few years sitting around this table, then killed Ingot off in the hope he'd get an officer patch. Maybe a marshal wants something more. It will be a big case, possibly big money involved. Maybe enough to prove tempting. We need to know more. Right now, I'm as much in the dark as she is, and that's what I don't like. We get her to contact her handler, might be the very man she shouldn't trust."

Ink's shaking his head. "Bad business with Taser. Man must have had a screw loose. Who'd want an officer patch when that comes with responsibility."

Okay, then. Ink doesn't want a seat at the head of the table. I'm beginning to understand Demon's problems.

I start pulling at my fingers as I sum up. "First, Stevie doesn't want to be parted from her guide dog. Not only is Max her salvation, but also her friend. The likelihood is if she's whisked somewhere else, the dog will be left behind. Second, we don't know who she's running from, who might have turned, or who to trust; the leak could have come from the very people who have guaranteed to keep her safe. Third, we do have somewhere we can hide her, at least until Max is recovered enough to go with her, wherever she might go."

"And four," Demon takes over with a glint in his eye, "you would never see her again."

I shrug as if that's no matter while ignoring the thought deep down that it is.

"Alright. Beef, we go with the plan we discussed earlier. But you stay with her, talk to her, get her fuckin' drunk, don't care how you do it, but I want to know what we're fighting here, who we should be looking out for."

"You got it, Prez."

By the time we've finished all the discussions, it's late in the evening. Violet informed me that the events of the day had caught up with Stevie, and she showed her the bed in my room. I resign myself to an uncomfortable night on the sofa, can't intrude or ask if she wants to share. We're barely friends, and far from lovers.

The lack of accommodation here makes me long for Tucson. The clubhouse is quieting down but still a few brothers are talking and drinking. Knowing there's no point in trying to get my head down right now, I grab a beer and take myself outside into the pleasant warmth of a Colorado summer evening and place a call to my prez. My *real* prez.

"You got Drummer."

Knowing him of old, I don't introduce myself. He'd only tell me my name's displayed on his phone. "Sorry to call so late, Prez."

"Nah, I was still awake. Zane's got a cold and don't we all know about it." I don't hear complaint in his voice, just sympathy tinged with pride. In the background I can hear a baby wailing, and Sam's voice soothing him. "What you got for me, Beef?"

Pleasantries over, I get right down to business. "First off, Prez, my situation has been resolved. Sally was here." When he stays silent, I go on, "Did what I should have done in the first place. Told her how it is."

"She accept it?" When I reply in the affirmative, he continues, "So, you telling me you already want to come home? You haven't been there five minutes."

"Got a job to do here, Prez. Not plannin' on lettin' you down."

I believe I hear a sigh of relief.

"How's it going? You have a sit-down with Demon yet?"

I shift to get comfortable on the hard wooden bench. "I can see his problem. At least one man here could do the job from what I've seen, but no one possible has any desire to step up. I've made a few suggestions, but nothing positive has been decided about a new VP yet. I've, er, I've been distracted."

"Tell me it doesn't involve a woman. You only just got rid of one bitch."

I laugh, as I'm meant to. "Nothing like that, Prez. But yeah, there is a woman involved. And a dog." I raise the beer bottle and take a long swig. Then, my throat wetted, I explain what's been going on, and what Demon has proposed.

"You go off the grid, that means you're not doing the job I wanted you to do." Drummer's not so much complaining, as stating the facts. "Demon should have run this past me, not you."

"I expect he'll make contact, Drummer. But I'm sort of doing this on my own. I was there, he wasn't. Can't walk away from this, Prez."

"Knowing you, I'd expect nothing less." He goes quiet for a few seconds. I've no worries he'll object, he's just thinking it through. When he speaks again, as I thought, he gives me his blessing. "Yeah, you do what you have to, Beef. You need any help from this end? Need somewhere else to go? You come back home. Bring this woman with you if you need to."

I explain the Satan's Devils connection. He agrees to warn the other chapters too. They all might get visitors trying to find where Stevie could have gone. As the national president Drummer takes the protection of all his chapters seriously.

I promise to let him have the number of my burner, then end the call.

In the end my night turns out not to be as bad as I feared. Due to the explosion that destroyed a lot of the clubhouse, the sofas are new and not lumpy, just short for my tall frame. The ability to catch a nap anytime, anyplace, was honed when I was a soldier, and this is far from the worst I've ever experienced. But as I try to get comfortable, I hope there will be more than one bed in the cabin. I'm getting old and prefer my creature comforts.

The next morning we get an early start, leaving immediately after we've grabbed some breakfast. Driving the club's SUV with darkened windows out of the compound, I decide to take the opportunity to discover the back streets of Pueblo, to ensure I haven't picked up a tail. Leaving the clubhouse, I thought I saw a truck pull out behind us, but I lost him a while back, then a white Chevy seemed to be getting a bit close, but after a few twists and turns and a short stay in a parking lot out of sight of the road, he disappeared as well. Eventually when it's all clear, I start following the instructions that Demon had imprinted onto my mind.

Stevie's quiet in the back seat. A precaution we'd taken so she wouldn't be visible as a passenger. Beside her is a bag crammed full of essentials that she and I might need over the following days. Luckily it's summer, so lightweight tees, shorts and jeans, don't take up much space. We've also both got a couple of sweaters, having been warned the nights can get chilly. Both Violet and Jay contributed to Stevie's haul. She's also got shampoo, conditioner and other, what the girls called, essential stuff. I'm no stranger to living with a woman, so suspect that includes tampons, the item they didn't want to discuss. Like I hadn't told them about the condoms. Hey, I've been a boy scout.

We've both got burner phones—hers fancier than mine. She'd been holed up in a corner with Cad for a while, why she got a brand-new model we haven't discussed.

I know she hates leaving Max, hates that she can't keep checking up on him. Demon's promised a brother will find out how he is every day and let her know if there are any problems. The other worry she must have is that she's literally putting her life in my hands. She's only known me a few days, knows nothing about me at all except I'm a biker.

What would I have done in her place? Part of me is pleased it's me she's decided to trust. Not that she's got much choice, the authorities haven't done a good job to date, and if they found her, they'd whisk her out of my life. She would lose her dog, and I'd never see her again. That thought bothers me causes me to wonder whether that would be for the best. Still, I've agreed on this plan, now I've got to go along with it.

It's less than an hour's drive to get to the cabin, though with the backtracking I've done it takes a good sixty minutes more. While Stevie's content to be alone with her thoughts, I use the time to think. No one should have discovered where she was. If she moved on, what guarantee is there that the same rat won't resurface? She's escaped two attempts on her life. Would she survive a third? I doubt it. Unlike a cat she probably doesn't have nine lives. Three is a stretch for any human.

She's blind, and while I know that doesn't make her completely helpless, the thought that there's someone after her must be terrifying, but at least she hadn't seen the car heading toward her. She might have smelled smoke, felt the heat of the flames, but hadn't seen how close her escape from the fire had been. On the other hand, I had. Maybe watching her face death twice explains the strange urge I have to protect her. I'm glad Demon hadn't suggested anyone else. Or maybe he just thought I would have a better chance of getting her to open up.

If I'd been back in Tucson I could have reassured her any of my brothers would look after her. Here? I'm sure the brothers are good men, but I can't personally vouch for them. Not yet.

Did Demon take the opportunity to get me out of the way? So I wouldn't be able to do the job I was sent here for. Hmm. Something to ponder.

Then it hits me. Sally and I are over. There's no longer a reason for me to stay away from Tucson. *I could go back.*

But I can't. For starters, I haven't done what I came here to do. Have been so tied up with the woman in the back seat, I haven't had a chance. Need to get that sorted for Drummer.

Then there's Stevie herself. What would happen if she

contacted her handler? Something tells me they wouldn't give a damn about her dog. While we haven't discussed it, there's a chance he might not make a full recovery, that he won't be a working dog any more. Would the marshals just put her in line to get a new service animal? Would they understand the bond that's grown between woman and canine? To them she's not a person, she's a commodity, her only use the information she carries with her, the evidence that will maybe break their big case. What would they care of her mental wellbeing? Their job simply to keep her alive, until she has her day in court.

CHAPTER EIGHTEEN

The road has been fairly flat for a while after we left Pueblo, but then it starts to climb. I follow the directions, a couple of times checking what's written on a piece of paper I have resting on my lap. As I turn off the freeway, it's like I'm driving into a different world.

I'm no stranger to mountains, Tucson is surrounded by three ranges, but here the vegetation seems different. Evergreen trees start to close in rather than open desert. I begin to anticipate some time to simply chill out. Since moving in with Sally I've had a tension inside me, it would be nice to enjoy some down time and relax. I crack the window an inch, breathing in the smell of spruce and pine.

"That's nice," Stevie murmurs from the back seat. "Are we in a forest?"

"Getting there," I reply.

"Is it much further?"

"Don't think so. Looking out for the track now."

Demon warned me it wasn't particularly easy to find. He was right. When the milometer shows me I've clearly overshot the turning, I find a place to manoeuvre the car around and go back. I'm not surprised I missed it. There are tire tracks from the vehicle the prospects had brought, but the gate is almost invisible with a fallen tree in front of it, and only possible to spot if you're watching for it. I stop the SUV.

"Just got to open the gate," I explain, remembering to voice everything.

The barbed wire fence and gate are hidden by the dead branches of a tree. It looks impossible to move but is actually easy. Taking a leaf from the prospects' book, I drive through, stop, relock the gate, and swing that tree in front again. Anyone passing without knowing it was there would never notice it. I'm pleased with this first level of security.

The road climbs steeply for another mile or so, and around us the forest becomes dense. The road divides, but I'm prepared, taking the right-hand fork. Another few hundred yards and there's another gate. I'm surprised to find it opens automatically on my approach, then closes behind me.

Cad's standing on the other side, nodding with satisfaction.

I hang my head out of the window. "Didn't expect to see you here?"

"I came up with Sparky to check everything out."

"That gate electric?"

He both nods and shakes his head. "Yeah, solar powered. This time of year should work okay, as long as the panel's kept clear. That SUV you're driving has the trigger to open it. It's easy enough to pull aside manually if needed though."

I'm surprised at the sophistication, it's not what I expected.

"Mind if I hitch a ride?"

"Be my guest."

"Hi Stevie."

"Cad."

That she recognises his voice doesn't surprise me.

It's about a quarter of a mile from here to the cabin. As Cad points out the potholes to avoid, I mention my surprise, "Thought this was going to be a primitive escape."

"Yeah, it would have been in the past, but this is Sparky's

and my baby. We both like to hunt, so use it as a base. Fixed it up with some surprises. You know the history?"

I nod, conscious of Stevie in the back.

Cad raises his chin back. "Let's just say, your woman there is not the first to need somewhere to hole up."

The Colorado MC, before Hellfire patched the club over to the Satan's Devils, had had a bad rep. I have my suspicions this cabin was used more than once to provide refuge for someone to lie low.

"It's also a good retreat for the club. Bigger than you expect, I think."

"Electricity?"

"Via solar panels again. Sparky put that in. Provides enough for the basics. Cooking and heating is via the wood-burning stove."

"Water?"

"We've diverted some from a stream that keeps a tank filled. Toilet is a porta potty though. Prospects have brought plenty of bottled water for you to drink."

"I'm looking forward to this." Stevie's voice actually sounds excited. "How old is the cabin?"

"The original frame must have been built a couple hundred years ago. It's been added onto since."

I smile to myself. It could be a lot worse. She could be complaining about the lack of facilities. Glancing in the rearview mirror I notice her brief spell of delight has gone.

"What is it?"

"I was just thinking how much Max would have loved it here."

Cad replies for me, "Won't be long before he's here with you. May not be running around quite how he used to yet, but he'll enjoy sniffing out the squirrels and deer."

A cabin, indeed larger than I was expecting, appears ahead. We're here. Cad directs me to a lean-to where I can park.

I help Stevie out as Cad grabs her bag.

"Ground's flat, but a little uneven." She nods and grips my elbow. I lead her slowly up to the front door. "There's a step."

Once the door is opened, various smells greet us. Disinfectant, polish, and an underlying mustiness as though the place has been shut up for some time. I nod at the men finishing cleaning up.

"Who's here?"

Damn. Forgot again. "Wills and Dan, the prospects. They've cleaned it for us, Stevie. Done a fine job too."

"Clean sheets on the beds."

"Thanks Dan." Beds. Plural. Good. I won't be sleeping on that very uncomfortable-for-my-size looking couch.

"I'm Sparky." He comes up and introduces himself. "You've got lights, hot water, fridge but that's about all. No AC I'm afraid. Fixed up a charging point for your phones and shit." He points over to a corner. "Got a TV but you won't get a signal. There's a DVD player and a stack of DVDs."

"Board games in the cupboard," Cad adds. I ignore that. No use for Stevie.

"Wi-Fi?"

"Nah. Not out here. And to be honest, haven't tried to put it in. Too tempting and too fuckin' easy to slip up."

Guess I don't have to worry about her posting to Facebook.

"Any chance I could get something I could listen to books on?" Stevie asks. "I love to read."

"I've got something back at the club. I'll ask the girls what they recommend."

"In the circumstances, a good MC romance series would be good." Stevie nudges me. "I could get an idea of what I can expect from you and your brothers."

"Fiction, woman, those authors have no fuckin' idea, 'cept for the handsome part. We're all handsome as fuck. Except for Beef that is."

I growl deep down in my throat as I glare at Sparky. And

what's he got to talk about? Yeah, he's okay, a bit rough around the edges, but handsome? Not my type.

"We're finished." Dan and Wills reappear. "We'll be back on Saturday to empty the porta potty, and we'll bring more water. Any particular food you want? We've stocked up with the basics."

While Stevie gives them a short list including the brand of cereal she likes, I muse it's a shame the hunting season hasn't started just yet. I could see myself being the man and shooting a bow and arrow to bag some fresh meat.

With the excuse they're just showing me where it is, Sparky and Cad grab themselves beers, and drink them fast. Then, they're gone.

As the sound of the engines fades into the distance, quiet, apart from the sounds of nature outside, descends. We're alone. Two virtual strangers who are going to be living together for the foreseeable future. The strangeness of it hits me with a force I didn't expect. I can't remember a time when I've had no brothers around. Despite the woman standing close, loneliness floods through me.

Stevie clears her throat. "Um, could you show me around, Beef?"

Her request gives me something to do, something to focus on. It's no problem, I want to explore too. Get to know where everything is. Make sure I can reach the hidden weapons when I need to and where the spare ammunition is kept.

The cabin has a main living area, its focal point a huge fireplace with a log-burning stove. Off to the side is a kitchen area, sink, fridge, cupboards and a pantry. Off that is a small bathroom with a rudimentary shower and sink. There's a double bed curtained off to the opposite side of the living area, and steep rickety stairs leading up to the loft which has been divided into two rooms, each with a queen-sized bed. All beds have been made up, so we have a choice.

Even though it was warm, verging on hot in Pueblo, though nothing like the temperatures I've been used to back home, up here in the mountains it's pleasantly cool. The prospects have opened the windows presumably to air the place, and I'm pleased to see screens have been installed to keep out the worst of the bugs. A nice breeze is blowing through. I make a note to close them later, when the sun goes down. I expect it will grow chilly.

Stevie's counted the stairs and is feeling her way around the room. She'd asked me to place her hand on the furniture, and there's a little frown on her face that suggests she's mapping it out in her head.

I'm trying to work out sleeping arrangements. It must be easier for her to sleep downstairs, but then that's my place, where I can be the first obstacle anyone would face if they came to the cabin.

"I like this room."

"You gonna be okay with the stairs?" I'm thinking about her needing to use the outhouse in the night.

"I'll be fine. Might take me a short while to get my bearings, but I've got this, Beef."

Her confidence continues to surprise me. I wonder whether it helps that she lost her sight gradually, rather than suddenly, or whether she'd have been the same if she was born that way. I close my eyes, trying to experience the world as she knows it. Immediately I feel unsafe, and don't want to move in case I forget where the stairs are and fall down them.

She, though, admittedly with her hand to the wall, starts walking purposefully to the staircase, and quickly is back on the ground floor. But then, she stops, and more hesitantly moves across the open space making her way back to the couch. She's moving slowly, and she finds it when her foot touches it.

Having been watching her carefully, I have an idea. "I'll just be a moment."

Leaving her to think I'm taking a piss or whatever, I step out the front door. I'd seen something on the way in as I'd been examining our surroundings, getting to know the lay of the land. There, along with the pile of chopped wood, are some sticks. Not sure why they're here, ready to be made into kindling, perhaps? They're the type used to prop up plants. I think it might do the job. I pick up a likely one and with my knife, strip anything sharp from it. Soon I have a workable cane.

Taking it back inside, I raise her hand and pass it to her. "A stick. It's not white, but will it help?"

"Jeez, the colour doesn't matter. But yeah, this is great, Beef." She stands, and with her makeshift cane waving back and forth in front of her, now has a more purposeful stride as she walks in the direction of the kitchen. "You hungry, Beef?"

Always.

I follow her, making an assessment of our options. A wood-burning stove is not something you can switch on and off, and it will take a while to warm. But opening the fridge I see a couple of steaks and had noticed a grill outside.

"Steaks? I'll cook them. There are the makings of a salad here."

"That will do. I'll make the salad, you go do your man thing." She starts opening drawers and feeling around for what's there.

When I first see her with a sharp knife attacking the lettuce I'm worried, but then realise she's been fending for herself a long time and knows exactly what to do. There's actually something sexy in the ways she's so competent, so self-sufficient. When I offer to help, she shoos me away.

We work well together, with me outside cooking and her doing the rest of the stuff. It's not long before the meat's done, and the trimmings prepared. We sit on the couch to eat, with plates propped on our knees.

It's easy, conversation flows naturally. She seems to be relaxed so I take my chance.

"You going to tell me why you're in hiding?" I ask, swallowing a mouthful of steak, which I swear always tastes better when it's been cooked outdoors.

"No." Her hair flies around her face with her negative action. "I don't want to embroil you any deeper than you already are." She puts down her fork. "Beef, I can tell you're a man who thinks they can sort out the world for everyone else, but this is one situation you have no control over. The short story is what you already know, I have to keep out of sight until the court case, then I give my testimony. The bad guys get sent down, and hopefully I'll be able to return to my life."

"Really?" I frown. "Usually people give up their old life for good. You really think you're going to be able to return home?"

For the first time since I've met her, her face falls. Apart from her sorrow and worry about Max, she always manages to stay positive. Within seconds, her mask is back in place. "The marshals did suggest this could be for good, but I can't believe that. Once the men are put away, I'll be free again."

She's naïve if she thinks that. Whoever she's up against will have friends on the outside or will make ones on the inside who are coming up for release. If her life's at risk now, even when it's all over, going home will likely mean she ends up dead. Even if the damage has already been done, if people end up convicted, they may want revenge. Can't tell until I know who she's going up against.

"Tell me, Stevie. I might be able to help. Tell me who they are." If I know, maybe I can assess whether there could be a lingering threat. The Mafia, for example, would never forget or forgive.

Again, her head moves side to side. "What if you think I'm wrong, Beef? What if you don't agree with what I'm doing?"

"Fuck, woman," I snarl. "There're people wanting to kill you. You think I'd side with them? Running Max down, setting fire to your house… You think I'll take their side rather than yours? Don't give a damn who they are. They're already dead for what they've tried to do to you."

<hr>

CHAPTER NINETEEN

<hr>

Over the next couple of days I try at odd times to catch her out at a weak moment, but she continues to refuse to enlighten me. I grow more concerned about why she's not sharing who's after her. *Why would she think there's a chance I'd side with them?* The thought concerns me, and I begin to grow suspicious.

When I push, she clams up and while it's normally easy to get along, my reference to what info she's holding makes things awkward between us, an awkwardness that's uncomfortable. Knowing the door is firmly closed, I decide to avoid the issue until I find a key to unlock it. Surely, she'll weaken and let something slip?

So after my futile and clumsy attempts to get her to open up, we skirt around the reason why she's here, and instead start learning about our new home. Cooking on the wood-burning stove is a bit of a test, for us both, but our endeavours do provide fodder for a lot of laughs.

It's like being on a vacation, I don't think I've felt so relaxed for years. Sure, living on the compound in Tucson was easy: the women did most of the cooking, the prospects kept the place clean, I had little to do but work, drink, sleep with whores and enjoy the company of the men. There's something about being here with Stevie that's taken me by surprise. I forget I'm missing the company of my brothers and simply appreciate being with *her*.

With Sally I'd always felt on tenterhooks, waiting to do or say the wrong thing. Me clomping in too heavily would get her startling as though expecting me to raise my hand to her. Stevie just laughs and tells me there's no way she'd ever mistake me for anyone else. I'm a big man, I stomp. I can't help it.

She constantly amazes me. One afternoon I walk in to find her cooking, opening a can of tomatoes and adding them to a pan. It takes me a moment to decide what's wrong about the situation.

"How the fuck did you know?"

"Know what?"

"That cupboard is full of tins. How did you know there're tomatoes in that can?"

"Tomatoes? Damn. I wanted beans." She pouts and frowns.

Realising she's pulling my leg. I walk closer. "Woman," I growl.

She sighs and takes sympathy on me. "In the old days I'd do it a number of ways. Have someone help me unpack my shopping and put on different tags so I could tell the difference. Elastic bands around certain things for example, raised stickers for another. Sometimes you can get a feel for the contents by shaking it. Obviously no one's helped me here, so I'm afraid there are a lot of opened cans in the trash."

Fuck. *I should have helped her. She hadn't asked.* Guiltily, I take a step toward the bin to see just how much food she's wasted simply to find the right can.

Her giggling stops me. "I'm joking. Now, I have better tools." She reaches into her pocket and takes out the high-end phone I notice she'd got from Cad. "Come here, watch."

Waving me nearer, she asks the phone to call up an app. She

then places it in front of the tin. Her phone reads the writing on the front, clearly telling her it contains the contents she wanted.

"Christ, that's neat."

"Yeah, makes life much easier. Another app recognises bank notes and tells me the denomination. Technology has really helped me become more independent."

"You have to check your bills every time?"

"No. Once I know what it is, I fold the corner or fold it in half. I've got my system."

Again, I nod admiringly.

Seeing I'm interested, she takes the pan off the heat, and leans back against the counter. "Then there are clothes. All the ones I lost in the fire were marked. I use different shaped buttons to separate the different colours."

"How do you know what to start with?"

A look of pain briefly crosses her face. "That's where my sisters helped. They'd separate them into colours, and I'd sew the buttons on. After that I didn't need help."

Damn, I hadn't realised the significance of losing her own clothes, had just asked for her to be lent some.

She's on the same wavelength as me. "Of course, I don't know what I'm wearing now. But denim's usually black or blue, so this top should go with my shorts whatever colour it is."

I've been with her a couple of days, and I'd never thought about things that have no everyday significance in my life.

My brow creases. "Seems like you have to spend a lot of time and effort doing things everyone else takes for granted," I observe.

"Time? What's time? We all have to do chores, Beef."

I suppose she's right, we do. But the insight into her world has been intriguing, and I admire her more than ever.

It's the fourth day when I fuck up. Those boots which make my feet so loud? Well, yeah, I may have taken them off and not kicked them under the couch.

I'm reading a book I grabbed off the shelf, a history of Harley

Davidson, when suddenly there's a loud exclamation of 'shit', and a stunned and irate little woman lands in my lap. I'm not too sure whose oomph is louder.

"Beef! Did you leave something lying around?" she cries out indignantly.

Keeping my arms around her, I lean forward to check for myself if I had. "Fuck, sorry, babe. My boots."

"Did I hurt you?"

"Fuck no. But keep still and stop wriggling." I'm half expecting her to leap up as soon as she realises that her movements have caused her to straddle me, and she's now sitting over a cock which I couldn't bring under control if my life depended on it. It really doesn't help that I'd already been admiring her walking around in tiny shorts and a tee shirt with the Satan's Devils logo on it.

"Um, is this me, or would you get hard if any woman landed in your lap?" Her tone is gently mocking.

She's correct on both counts, but on balance, the fact it's her has most to do with it. What's the right answer? As her head tilts to one side waiting for a response, I realise I could press for more, or back out of this situation gracefully. Trouble is, I don't know what I want. My hands move of their own volition, gently resting on the side of her hips. She's rounded with curves, soft, not hard and angular.

She's still waiting. Oh fuck it. "Babe, doesn't take much to get me hard, I'm a fuckin' man. Don't let it worry you. Doesn't mean I need sex, or that I intend to act on it. If I need to, I'll take care of it myself later."

She gives a soft laugh as her fingers come up to trace my face, her touch so soft and soothing. "You don't scare me. You could have been walking around with a hard-on for days, I'd never have noticed."

I wait for her to get up, but she doesn't move. As her hands start to explore, I do nothing to stop her. All she's doing is mapping me, like she had that first morning which seems a lifetime ago now. But as we've learned more about each other, this afternoon her touch feels more intimate. A long session in the shower relieving my cock with my hands becomes more and more likely.

She smells like a summer's day, maybe a flowery comparison for a biker, and it must be down to her shampoo, but that's the only way I can describe it. Her fingers are gentle as they roam across my body, her little sighs of appreciation as she discovers something she likes does nothing to deflate my hard dick.

After diving into the deep end with Sally, I'd promised myself I'd stop searching for my one, had realised the dangers of getting in with the wrong woman again. I'd learned about my own shortcomings as a man, and that while I'll give everything I can to the woman I love, I can't take being constantly depended upon.

I'd be up for a quick fuck, what man wouldn't? But what would be her expectations after that? A ring on her finger?

"Beef, am I making you uncomfortable?"

My hands haven't strayed from where they lightly rest on her hips. She's noticed I'm not reciprocating, but she can't see I'm using my eyes where she has to use her hands. Feasting on her gorgeous tits covered only by a thin tee. I haven't told her her nipples show, not when there's just the two of us here. One of my brothers comes calling? I'd tell her to put on a bra.

How best to answer her question? Am I uncomfortable? Yes, no. Affirmative because my cock's so fucking hard, no because I don't want her to move. I'm enjoying the sensation of having a beautiful woman sitting on my dick even though I'd prefer there to be no clothes between us.

"Babe. You must know what you're doing. Meant what I said, ain't going to act on it, but..." I tell her at last, "you're an attractive woman. And I'm a red-blooded man. Think you need to move."

"You think I'm attractive?"

"Of course, I do."

"Hmm. I like the feel of you." Her hands trace my chest. "I think you're attractive too."

"You can't see me." I chuckle.

"Are you butt ass ugly?"

I laugh as she asks me outright and taken aback as to how to reply. I settle for, "I wouldn't win a beauty pageant if that's what you're asking, but I do alright. No one's ever complained."

"Can I kiss you?"

I still.

"Just a kiss. Beef?"

A kiss. But if our mouths meet, the signals from my cock tell me that's not all I'd like to do. Would I be able to stop there? Would she?

What if she wants to take things further? I promised myself I wouldn't leap into another relationship. Go with a sweet butt with no expectations? Sure. But Stevie? We're living together, for fuck's sake. Neither of us able to walk away.

It would be a very bad idea. *Wouldn't it?*

I hadn't realised I'd murmured the last thought aloud, but I must have.

"Why bad, Beef? As you've said, you're a man, I'm a woman. I've got needs too. We're friends, aren't we? How about friends with benefits?" She bites her lip, and inhales deeply, the action causing her breasts to thrust pushing up against that tee, stretching the Satan's Devils logo. "I'm not asking for a future, I don't have one. Not here, not with you. But to be in your arms, just once?"

I'm silent. *Christ, she's offering herself to me on a platter. No strings.*

I'm quiet for so long, she starts to move. "I can understand you're worried after what you went through with Sally. You've only just got yourself out of that mess. Beef, I'm sorry. I shouldn't have suggested it, I'll respect your boundaries and won't ask again. This wouldn't be a good idea."

Now she's said it, perversely I want to change her mind back again. As she goes to get up, my arms move around her and tighten. "Stevie…"

There's the sound of engines approaching the cabin. I push her off my lap urgently and stand. My hand goes to my gun.

"It's alright, it's your bike," she tells me in her sweet soft voice, "and the truck your friends were driving."

With my hand on the butt of my gun, I walk to the window, standing at the side and peering out. She's not wrong.

Saved? Well, maybe. Pushing thoughts about what they interrupted out of my head, I focus on the scene in front of me.

I'm not too happy to see the prospect swinging his leg over my ride, hoping he rode carefully up the rutted drive else he won't be getting his patch. Seeing there are no immediately apparent new dents in the fairing, I check to see who else has come visiting. It's only Wills. Christ, how could I have forgotten it's already Saturday? Days seem to have flown past, Stevie's company is that good.

My cock, realising it won't see any action, has deflated at the sound and sight of the prospects. Half of me thinks I had a lucky escape, being pulled back from the brink of making a mistake I'll only regret, while the other half is cursing them for their timing. Mind you, it could have been worse. I could have been balls deep in her when they'd turned up.

"Hope you rode fuckin' carefully," I snarl, as Dan is first through the door.

"Course I did." He chucks me my keys, I catch them one handed. "She's a beaut, man."

"Still got that rattle," Stevie sings out behind me.

Dan's eyes narrow. "Ain't got no rattle."

I sigh. I can't hear it either, but I might get Pyro to take a look at some point. Right now, I'm curious as to why he's brought it. Turns out I don't even have to ask.

"Prez wants you back at the compound. He's called church for six."

The reference to the hour makes me glance at the old-fashioned clock over the mantelpiece, it might have ticked its way through a fair number of years but seems to keep good time. The big hand's already close to five. I'll have to get moving if I want to get there on time.

"We're going to stay here while you're gone. If that's alright with you, Stevie?" Dan continues.

Stevie dips and raises her head. I walk over to her, shoving down the strange impulse to lean over and kiss her. "I won't be long. I'll be back as soon as I can."

"Take your time. I'll be fine. I really don't need a babysitter."

She probably doesn't, but I'm not leaving her on her own. Dan raises his chin and taps the gun in his belt. A signal he's prepared for anything. Wills, just entering, carrying some bags, jerks his head in a similar confirmation.

I close the door behind me on the way out, pausing before getting on my bike, shaking my head as I think about what they had interrupted. *All for the best.*

I get on my bike, start the engine, and once away from the hard-to-navigate road, enjoy the ride and the fresh air rushing past, realising I've missed having it available. Last time I hadn't ridden for a few days was when I'd been holed up in the hospital, that time I nearly died.

I'm fully recovered now, though it took some time to get back to full fitness. The memory, however, lingers.

I'm no stranger to bullets flying, and half expect one day one will take me out. Living this life, no one would think it extraordinary. What I hadn't realised was that it would be something invisible to the naked eye that could take me down. I could neither evade nor fight it. Having done the impossible and unexpected and come around, it's left me with various considerations. One, how fragile life is, another how I should relish every moment now given to me, but there's a part of me which wonders, why? Why was I saved? Why was I brought back? Was there a purpose or reason, or was it just how my cards fell?

Not wanting to waste any precious minute was part of the

reason I got involved with Sally so fast. My mortality had been brought home to me, and I live every day thinking I'm on borrowed time.

The memory of how close I'd come to leaving this life makes me appreciate today's ride even more. I notice the little things, like how it gets noticeably warmer as I descend in altitude. By the time I reach the city I'm wiping sweat from my brow. The sweater I'm wearing over my t-shirt too heavy now. First thing I do when I reach the compound is tear it off.

"Beef!" Pyro calls out, also just pulling in on his bike. "How are the mountains?"

"All good," I reply. I wait for him to draw closer. "Getting to feel like home already."

"It strange living with a blind bitch?"

Strange? Nah. "Half the time you wouldn't know there was anything different about her," I tell him, seriously. "I don't want to kill her yet if that's what you're asking."

Dutifully, he laughs. "Oh, by the way, been checking in with the vet. Max is progressing nicely, as he put it."

I thank him, then, following his lead, I grab a beer from Beaver who's bartending, then walk into church. As I take out my phone to drop it into the basket, I notice I've made it just in time.

Pyro and I are the last in. Planting my ass on the spare seat at the bottom of the table, it hits me this is my first time in the Colorado church. Things have happened so fast in the week that I've been here. I wait to see how different or similar it is to the ones we hold in Tucson.

"Ok, settle down." Demon's mild knocking of the gavel on the table has the desired effect. "Some of you," he looks pointedly at Thunder and Mace, "already know why I've interrupted your Saturday. The rest of you need to be brought up to speed."

I sit up straighter. *What's coming for us now?* I get a twitchy feeling in my gut, especially when the prez's eyes land on me.

"You got any more information out of the woman?"

I respond to his direct question, "Nah, sorry Prez. I've tried pushing her, but she's staying dumb."

"There's a good reason for that." Demon pinches the bridge of his nose, then shakes his head. "Had a visit yesterday. The local prez of the Wretched Soulz. Filled me in on a few details."

My eyes sharpen. What the fuck has Stevie got to do with the dominant MC whose area covers a large part of the states and beyond? Any MC setting up in the dominant's territory does so only with its blessing. Satan's Devils coexist by permission, and for the most part, have a friendly arrangement with them.

Having let the importance of his visitor sink in, Demon resumes, "You've all heard of the Warped Jokers?"

"Club out of LA, aren't they?" Cad asks. "Into some bad shit from what I've heard."

Most, including myself, nod. Unlike the Satan's Devils who've got a rep we don't nowadays deserve, the Warped Jokers live up to every citizen's nefarious expectations of what an MC gets up to. Drugs, guns, extortion. If it can be named they're probably up to their necks in it. We might not approve, but we turn a blind eye. Live and let live—our motto as far as clubs like that are concerned. As we don't have an LA chapter, we don't often cross paths with the Warped Jokers.

"Feds have busted them. Half of them are in prison awaiting trial, the rest out on bail."

That's news I haven't heard. I sit up straighter, the dots joining fast in my head.

"It's a RICO indictment."

Christ! That will take out the whole club if proven. Every fucking member will go down and for a very long time. *RICO.* The word no MC wants to hear. It's the way feds take down organised crime. Doesn't matter if he never had his hand anywhere near a gun, if they think a killing or robbery was planned from the top, everyone in the club is guilty by association in the eyes of that law. Twenty-year sentences will be handed out, the club's assets seized.

I've got a horrible feeling I'm right, enough signs are there. Hoping I'm going to be contradicted, I state, "Stevie's a witness in the case."

Demon nods. "The star witness."

I don't like this. Don't like it at all. "Why come to you, Demon? Why tell you?" The bad feeling in my gut worsens.

"We knew there was a leak somewhere, and that someone knew where she was and had eyes on her. Beef, you were clocked when you rode her around town as we thought you might be."

I swear my heart stops beating. "You confirmed where she is?"

"Nah. Not until I had this meeting. I wanted to get us together to decide what to do."

With a thump my vital organ starts working again, and my lungs take in oxygen once more. But maybe it's just a temporary reprieve.

I hardly dare ask the question that's on the tip of my tongue, but I need to know the answer. "Why are the Wretched Soulz involved, and why are *they* trying to find her?"

CHAPTER TWENTY

It's not just me who wants to hear the answer. Everyone's sitting forward, their heads craned to face the prez sitting at the top of the table. The answer most likely is that they want her taken out of the equation so she can't testify, the least possible response is that the dominant is fed up with the Warped Jokers and want her kept alive, and use her to get rid of a thorn in their side.

Demon's eyes flare, and his mouth twists. "They want to make sure she doesn't turn up in court."

My hand smashes down on the table. "Why, Prez? Why are they protecting those motherfuckers? We all know what they're like. Wouldn't we be better off without them?"

Demon lurches ending up hunched over the table, both his fists come crashing down on the wood. "We're all bikers, aren't we? We're all living on the wrong side of the line. Some of us just with a foot or two over it, but the spectrum is wide. The Warped Jokers just happen to be at the far end of it. Feds get one success, they'll be looking for more. No one wants eyes on our business, no one wants dirt being dug up. Whether we like it or not, the Warped Jokers are a legitimate club set up with the dominant's permission. They're our biker brothers."

They're not my fucking brothers. And there's one thing we haven't discussed.

"What did they do, Prez? You're suggesting we off a woman to let them walk free. What fuckin' crime are you proposing we help cover up?" I realise there's something else too. "And how can a fuckin' blind woman be a credible witness? Surely their lawyer could shred her in court. Surely you aren't suggesting we hand her over?"

Demon stands so fast his chair falls over backward. His palms flat on the table he looms over making me pleased there's distance between us. Beside me, Hellfire, Demon's dad and previous president sucks in an audible breath.

"I'm not suggesting fuckin' anything. If you think for one second I'd condone killing an innocent woman, or anyone, who's done nothing wrong but tell the truth, then you're not a fit for this chapter. I don't care if Drummer sent you here, I'll be sending you back."

The rest of the brothers look like they're watching a tennis match, their heads turning one way and the other, checking me then Demon. I suspect they're wondering if we're going to settle this with our fists.

Thunder's hand shoots out and grasps Demon's arm. "We're not on the side of the fuckin' Jokers, Demon. Think you ought to explain that. And you, Beef," he turns and meets my stare head on, "you don't know the workings of this chapter, don't know Demon's approach. I suggest you hold back on your accusations until after you've heard everything Prez has got to say."

Hellfire speaks from beside me, "If this club raised a finger against an innocent, I'd be the first to walk out." He doesn't face me as he says it.

I realise I've jumped in too fast. They're right, I don't know this chapter or how Demon leads it. I took the silence around me as agreement for anything he proposed, including harming Stevie. I drop my head into my hands, then look up. "Coming to a different chapter isn't easy. You're all brothers, but you roll a different way. Likewise, you don't know me either. I apologise, Demon. I meant no offence."

Slowly, very slowly, the tension leaves Demon's arms. As he straightens, Mace slips out of his seat and discreetly picks Demon's chair up. When the prez is re-seated, he dips his head. "Apology accepted. Now, if you let me, I'll answer your questions with what I was able to find out." His hand pushes his long hair back from his face, and he sighs. "Got some discussions necessary to decide, *as a club,* where we take this. But for that, you need facts."

Lizard gets out his cigarettes. Mace wiggles his fingers and the packet is slid across the table. Before it returns to the tattoo artist, Sparky and Ink each take one out. Demon waits until the air's become tinged with blue, and Mace has taken two ashtrays from a shelf behind him.

"Fuck knows why they thought it was a good idea, but the Warped Jokers decided to go down the old-fashioned route. A bank holdup. Things didn't go as planned, one of the customers decided to be a hero, received a bullet for his pains. They'd taken their eyes off the cashier who got shot when she went for the panic button. Another customer tried to disarm one of the Jokers and managed to pull his mask off." Demon breaks off and looks grim. "There were five customers and two cashiers in the bank at the time. Seven potential witnesses. The Joker whose face was revealed decided he didn't want any left alive, except for the blind girl who couldn't see anything."

"They were right, weren't they? She couldn't see. Couldn't tell who they were. Whether they were black, white or fuckin' purple," Rusty says, his brow creasing. "How the fuck could she be a witness?"

"It's not what she saw, but what she heard," I tell them, not even having to think about it. Living with her, seeing how her other senses compensate for the loss of her sight, I can well understand it.

"Heard, felt and smelled," Demon agrees. "It's not like RIP to be chatty, but I get the feeling he was impressed. I asked the question, he answered. Smell, leather, oil and sweat. They weren't wearing cuts but had been. She suggested they could be bikers, which got the cops looking in that direction. There was more than that, her memory is spot on. They hadn't realised, but they'd used a name, One-Eye. Cops homed in on the Jokers. Got them in a line-up, she identified them by their voices."

"Would that stand up in court?" It seems flimsy at best.

Demon catches my eye. "They left her alive but impressed on her she had to stay silent. One hit her around her face, his ring left bruising. Another grabbed her in her struggle to get free, she felt his hand, it had one finger missing."

"They weren't wearing gloves?" Buzzard asks incredulously, shaking his head, as though he's an expert bank robber.

"Yes, but only thin latex ones. That too, she said."

"Her info? That's enough to get a conviction?" I ask.

Demon nods. "She's convincing as hell. Feds think yes."

I could easily see how she could convince them. Sure she couldn't see the bank robbers in the same way as I could, but those details she remembered using her other senses were presumably just as reliable.

"No other witness?" I'm grasping at straws. "Anyone outside see the getaway vehicle? The driver?"

A shadow falls over the prez's face. "No one. Anyone inside was dead. They'd used silencers and picked a quiet time. If anyone did see anything, they haven't come forward as a witness."

Probably wouldn't. The Warped Jokers are not a crew you'd want to get on the wrong side of. And if anyone had, they'd be suffering the same fate as Stevie—moved away from everything they'd ever known.

"What are we going to do, Prez?" Rusty asks the direct question I wanted to. My eyes shoot to Demon to see how he's going to handle it.

Demon's head is moving side to side. "Fuck knows," he

responds after a moment. "Here's the situation. The dominant, *our* dominant, wants the feds' attention off MC clubs in LA and beyond."

"Fat fuckin' chance," I scoff. "They're always looking to bring us down."

"I agree. But the heat has intensified with the Jokers' recent caper."

"They're fuckin' criminals," Hellfire says scornfully. "They might call themselves an MC and ride bikes, but they're way out the other end of the spectrum to us. Satan's Devils, even the Wretched Soulz, would never be so crass as to rob banks and certainly wouldn't gun down innocent citizens if there was any way to avoid it."

"But," Demon plays devil's advocate, "they are an MC. Do we want a reputation of turning rat on our biker brothers?"

I want to vomit at the thought of calling any man who wants Stevie dead my brother, but technically, that's what they are. My fingers tap on the table, my head spinning. "As long as clubs have existed," I start, "we've been fighting each other."

"Sure have," Rusty agrees. He nudges Ink who gets out his cigarettes and passes him one. "Big clubs fought it out in Denver back in the day."

Demon's eyes have narrowed. "You're suggesting we go head-to-head with the Warped Jokers?"

"With half of them inside that wouldn't be hard." Bomber's got a gleam in his eyes as Pyro nudges him appreciatively.

"You're forgetting something," Thunder observes. "They're in LA."

I hold up my hand. "Not suggesting we get physical, just that we help bring them down by keeping Stevie out of their way. Let her turn up in court and see where the cards fall."

In a move reminiscent of Drummer, for a second making me homesick, knowing there'd be a different vibe if we were talking around the table in Tucson, Demon runs his hand over his short beard. "So let's start there. We refuse the request of the Wretched Soulz, pitting us against the dominant club."

"We're not here to do their bidding, Prez," Sparky interjects.

"You're right," Demon says calmly, "but we've always co-existed with the dominant. Couldn't be here without their approval to set up the club."

That's spot on. Any club wanting to establish themselves in the dominant's territory has got to jump through a number of hoops. Technically we don't need approval, but if we hadn't allowed them to review our charter and regs, then, well, ride with a patch not recognised by the Wretched Soulz? Any biker who does that is facing a severe beatdown, or even death. Satan's Devils have done it right. Have given our support to the Wretched Soulz a time or two as well, and sometimes, they've helped us out. What none of us want is an out-and-out war. We'd have no chance of winning.

"Beef's a nomad. Yet he's brought this bitch to our door and landed us in this shit. Why don't we just leave it to him to sort out? We can wash our hands of him."

There's quiet as Mace lays out the cold facts. He's completely right. Trouble is, if Stevie's and my presence is bringing trouble to this club, it would follow to any other chapter who took us in. I'm not going to leave her unprotected, whatever they decide. I'd be out on my own with a blind woman to protect. Hate thinking of her as disabled, but I have to face facts. There are things a fully sighted woman can do which she can't. The main one being, she can't see trouble coming.

I hold my breath, waiting for the answer. "I vote to dismiss that," Skull, unusually pipes up. "That's signing both her death warrant and our brother's. I know he's not of this chapter, but he's a Satan's Devil all the same."

"Drummer would never agree to it," Ink observes.

It's Demon's reaction I'm interested in, inwardly squirming during the moment he takes to voice his opinion. "While Beef's here, he's one of ours." His tone is final.

Grateful for that, I'm still aware my actions are bringing down heat on a chapter I don't even belong to. Now Demon's given me support, I can't suggest I take the problem back to Tucson and Drummer, as that would be disrespecting my new prez, however temporary that situation is. But there is another solution.

"I go it alone," I find myself suggesting. "Sure, I'm staying at the cabin owned by the club, but you needn't know who I've got with me. Could be I just needed time to decompress. I'll get more out of Stevie now that I can tell her I know most of it anyway. Cad?"

Cad glances up from his tablet.

"If I find out who she's dealing with, her handler and stuff, can you dig up the info? Now we know the facts, there's no need for her to keep things quiet." When he nods, I continue, "We try to find out where the leak came from, then locate someone who isn't going to rat on her. When Max is back on his feet, we pass her back to the marshals and they can take over her protection. At that point, the club's clean."

"In the meantime, I lie to the Wretched Soulz." Demon's brow furrows.

"Plan's a good one, Prez," Thunder observes. "And it's not lying, just concealing the truth. You just need to be inventive. They don't know we've got the girl. Sure, they know we had contact, but we could let them assume we washed our hands of her."

Slowly Demon grins. "I can make that work. I just omit some of what's pertinent." He picks up the gavel, turning it over in his hands. "We continue to help Beef in his sojourn at the cabin. That's the motion on the table. If he's got a bitch there, well, it's none of our business."

The ayes around the table are resounding, More than one brother glances at his neighbour and nods. It saves us from an outright war with either the Jokers or the Wretched Soulz. Of course, it also means we're helping the feds with their business.

But in this instance, if it means Stevie stays breathing, they're the lesser evil.

"Motion carried. But I think we all know we'll be revisiting this again."

Demon's right. At least we're not as much in the dark as we were, we know who's after her and why. Just not who betrayed and outed her.

"Prez?" Hellfire raises his hand. "All this talk about possible outcomes, is it time to consider strengthening our ranks? It was going to come up soon anyway; how about bringing Wills and Dan to the table and giving Beaver and Karl their prospect patches?"

With his lips curved sarcastically, Demon responds, "Is this the right time to bring new blood around the table?"

What he means is the more people in the know, the more risk of something slipping. I have a contrary view, one which supports Hell's desire to have a larger pool of men. "Wills and Dan done their time?"

"And then some." Demon's eyes stare at me, and he raises his chin.

He knows I'm going somewhere, just not where yet. "Then you trust them to know where the bodies are buried." A round of low laughter and smirks. Of course they do, wouldn't be near getting a patch if they didn't. "Beaver and Karl. Investigated enough to bring them on board as prospects?"

Cad perks up. "I have. Nothing in their backgrounds looked off."

"Where you going with this, Beef?"

"Wills and Dan. If there's nothing else in their way, bring them to the table. Can't trust them with the life of a brother, then we shouldn't even be discussing giving them their patch. And they already know Stevie's staying with me." Nods of agreement from everyone. "Beaver and Karl, though, they stay in the dark. Get them to bring shit up to the cabin, but warn me, for fuck's sake. I'll get it looking like a bachelor pad, find somewhere to stash Stevie while they're visiting. If they're on the up and up they won't spout shit in any event, if not, they won't see anything to talk about."

"Like that idea, Prez." Hellfire's regarding me carefully.

Prez raises and dips his chin. A silent communication goes between him and his father. Then he picks up the gavel again. "Next church we patch them in. Think we're all talked out tonight, Brothers. I, for one, want a drink and to fuck my ol' lady."

The gavel starts to descend. "Prez, before you finish up, can I say something?"

Skull's spoken for only the second time this meeting. There are sighs that their gratification in whatever way they prefer is going to be delayed for a moment, but Skull gets the nod to continue.

He shifts awkwardly in his seat. "I, er, I, well. There's a woman."

"You want some advice?" I ask, my lips curving. "You know your dick, well…"

"I know what to do with my dick, thank you, *Brother.*" But his lips quirk as he continues, "I'm pretty serious about her. Would like to bring her to the club."

"You talkin' claimin' an ol' lady?" Demon's eyes are wide. So are everyone else's. "She a civilian?"

"Yeah, that's why I'd like her to come around. See if she'll be a good fit."

"Give me her name, Skull. I'll look into her."

"If she passes Cad's investigation, sure, Skull. Be interested to see what's got your motor revving."

There's laughter, but also shock. Unlike in Tucson where brothers are dropping like flies falling into the old lady trap, here in Pueblo, most are single. Looks like another one's going down soon though. I eye Skull thoughtfully. Whoever this woman is, he seems pretty smitten.

"She comes here? She's mine." Showing more determination than I've noticed before, Skull goes on the offensive.

"We'll behave," Ink reassures him.

"Gotta test her out though." As Skull starts to stand, Pyro continues fast, "Not gonna fuck her, man. Whether her pussy is tight is your business. Nah, just gotta make sure she understands club business ain't hers. Ain't gonna put up with a bitch whining she's not being told shit."

This time the gavel does hit the table. "Church fuckin' over."

CHAPTER TWENTY-ONE

I could have hung around to have a beer, but I've got enough back at the cabin. I could have fucked a sweet butt, but I've got... *Damn it.* I've no idea what I've got waiting for me on my return. As I pass the brothers stopping only to exchange a few necessary pleasantries, I try to make as direct a line as possible to my bike. Once outside in the fresh air, I'm suddenly not so impatient, and my mind starts whirring.

Will Stevie be waiting to continue what was interrupted this afternoon?

Part of me is hoping she'll be waiting for me in my bed, wearing some sort of negligee, half of me is hoping she's not. It's the latter that my head is hoping for, my cock, needless to say, the former. But my brain has to win out.

I've had my share of casual hook-ups, but only those where I, or they, don't hang around until morning. If I thought Stevie would fuck then be happy being kicked out of my bed, I'd be over that like a rash. Problem is, we're living together for the foreseeable future. I enjoy being around her, life's easy and comfortable. I fuck her, it could upset what we have. Relief for my cock in exchange for what? Awkwardness, and one of us getting more involved than we should.

I could do her once and walk away without a look back. Not sure I could say the same for Stevie.

She's got needs too. Perhaps it wouldn't hurt to take care of them? I laugh to myself, confident that I wouldn't leave her wanting. Except, perhaps, for more.

What if it was me who wanted a repeat performance? Nah, once has satisfied me before, can't think of a woman who I'd become addicted to. Except for the one I never had.

"Hey, Beef. You got a minute?" a voice hollers. I turn to see Prez standing just outside the door, and mentally berate myself for not escaping when I had the chance.

A prez is a prez. When one queries your availability the only thing to do is make time and look cheerful doing it. "Yeah. Your office?"

His nod is all the invitation I need. Suppressing a sigh, I make my way back across the parking lot, retrace my steps through the clubroom, and enter his domain.

Demon is standing with his back toward me, seemingly studying the Satan's Devils' flag hanging behind his desk. If I squint and look at nothing but the image of Lucifer and the three little demons, I could be back in Tucson. The same flag hangs in all our chapters.

He half turns as though to check it is me, and that I've closed the door, then studies our insignia again. "You okay with what we agreed?"

Kicking out a chair, I sit. "Fine, Prez."

"You want anyone up there with you, just in case, now that we know the Wretched Soulz are sniffing around? Boys won't mind drawing up a rotation."

I give his suggestion a moment of thought. "Don't think it's worth it at present. If something goes wrong and word gets out about where she is, then, yeah, I'd welcome support at that stage."

"Your call, Beef. If and when you want to make it."

"Thank you," I say to his back. It's becoming habit with Stevie not to rely on chin lifts the whole time.

At last, he turns, propping his hip onto the desk. "What do you make of Skull, Beef?"

I haven't really had time to get to know him. Again, I take a moment to gather my thoughts. "He's quiet. Doesn't contribute, but he takes in everything."

Demon nods as though I've echoed what's on his mind. "That he does."

"Still finding his place at the table?" I suggest. "Sometimes it takes time. Particularly after what happened to him."

"You know about that?" At my nod, he resumes, "We made him hurt. I accepted it when he understood why and said he would have done the same thing were the positions reversed. That nothing is more important than our family. Clues pointed his way, he could see that."

"He returned," I state the obvious.

"He did."

My brow creases. "You think there's another reason behind it? That he wants vengeance?"

"Wraith warned me to watch him."

"Bringing this woman on board might steady him." I hope for Skull's sake she's a good fit and they vote to allow him to claim her.

"Took me by surprise, didn't see it coming. Skull keeps himself to himself."

"You think he's got an ulterior motive?" Can't see it myself. What nefarious purpose could bringing a woman onto the compound serve? "Just get Cad to investigate her thoroughly if you're concerned."

"Yeah, that was already my plan. I'm just worried Wraith sees something I'm missing."

Ah. So that's what's behind it. Demon's still wet behind the ears in his president's role. They've already had one traitor in the club. Is he doubting his own ability to read people? "How long were you VP, Demon?"

My question takes him by surprise. "Um, er, ten years?"

I nod. "Then you know your club. You know your men. Sure, you didn't know Taser had a screw loose, but one bad apple doesn't mean there's more. What do *you* think, Demon?"

My reminder about the length of time he sat at his father's left hand seems to have made him straighten. "Christ, Beef. You're right. As VP or Prez I'd put money on Skull being exactly what he appears, a fresh patch around a strange table, worried about saying something out of line. Listening to learn how to behave. Have seen it before, will see it again. Wills and Dan will probably be much the same for the first couple of months." His gaze is now assessing. "Wearing the prez's hat is harder than I expected. Before I had Hell there to knock me around the head if I started taking a ride on the crazy train."

"You need a VP," I tell him abruptly. "Someone to bounce your ideas off. Thunder would help if you let him."

"Thunder's too busy telling me I'm not what he needs, to try to become that for me," he says, drily.

Which brings me to the point of my visit to Pueblo. Maybe I can get this sorted, get Stevie back with the marshals again, and return to my home. Nothing stopping me now. Sally knows where she stands. Home. Fuck, I can almost smell Tucson in the air.

"I'm sure you're aware of my difficulty," Demon responds with a sharp look at me. "After all, that's why you're here. You've got a job to do, and Drummer won't let you leave until it's done."

"You want me gone?"

His head bobs back and forth fast. "Not what I'm saying. But a president like Drummer doesn't send out one of his most trusted men as an enforcer to another chapter unless there's something to enforce."

I lean forward, clasping my hands between my knees. "It's not anything to do with you, Demon. Drummer's just concerned you're not running at full strength."

His finger and thumb pinch the bridge of his nose. "I've been thinking on your suggestion about bringing someone in from the other chapters. Should have brought it up at church, but I'm concerned about the brothers' reaction."

I can't see an alternative. "Then tell them to suck it up or stand up themselves."

He huffs a laugh. "Just like that?"

"Just like that."

His head now moves up, then down, then slowly rises again. "Have you got anyone in mind?"

"Other prezes won't like it if you start poaching one of their VPs. So I think you need to start looking down, maybe an enforcer or sergeant-at-arms ready to move on."

"Like?"

"I won't suggest anyone from San Diego. They're still finding their feet after what went down a couple of years back." A bad business. The old president, Snake, and seven of his members had hatched a plan to get rid of Drummer, become the mother chapter, and point the Devils in the direction of the drug running game. Snake and the ringleaders are dead, the rest of the traitors out bad. I shudder just thinking about such a fate, preferring death myself. No reputable MC would take in a member who'd been put out in bad standing by his club. Not being a brother would kill me for sure.

"Understandable. Lost and Dart are making a go of it."

Yes, Lost moved up to the top spot, Dart, his new VP, was a member from Tucson who'd gone to help the club out, found his place and stayed. He's doing well, settled in now. "Vegas is more stable. How did you take to Indian and Twister while they were here?" Indian's the sergeant-at-arms, Twister the enforcer.

Demon snorts. "Look, our clubhouse was burning down

around us. Men acted okay, had our backs, but it wasn't particularly conducive to conducting interviews."

I run through the other men that I know in my head. I don't know much about any of them. Rope and Cuff I know best, and certainly not for any ability that shows they would shine as a new VP. "Maybe ask Red?"

"Could. But then I've got the problem of men here not trusting them to have our backs."

"It's simple. Find a possible. Get them here under some pretext. Let them sit around the table, drink with the men, share the whores. Let everyone see what they're made of. Gives them a chance to see if Pueblo suits them, and your members the chance to know their mettle."

Demon's eyes flare, for a second giving me the reason for his name. "Good fuckin' idea, Beef." His hand thumps the table. "That's what I'll do. If they don't like it here, or don't match up, no harm no foul. I'll get onto Red in the morning."

My mind can work on two things at once. Now we've at least got an approach to him getting a new VP, it circles back to the problem he called me in here for. "Getting back to Skull. You can't go on gut feelings or crediting him with shit in his head that isn't there. Take Rock, for example." My reference brings a wistful smile to my lips. I miss my best friend. We're still close, though not so much as when we used to share women before his girl Becca came along. She's one he won't share, and I can't blame him for that, however much I'd like to persuade him.

"Rock?" His brow creases.

"When Drummer set him up and we thought he'd turned traitor? I was the last person to believe it, but Drummer had set all the evidence in place. Before he painted Rock in such a bad light, he had it in black and white so no one could question it." With a grimace I continue, "Even I believed my best friend had turned bad."

"Your point?"

"You're looking for a problem which might not exist because

Wraith said something. Best way to piss a brother off is to keep watching for him to take a step out of line. You let him prospect, patched him in. Give him the same trust you do everyone else until the point where you think he's fucked up. Then look at it all twice and make sure your case against him is watertight. That brother's already been on the right side when you thought he was wrong once, don't make the same mistake again."

Demon takes in a deep breath, holds it, then lets it out. "You talk a lot of fuckin' sense, Brother."

Do I? I frown. Not sure I've ever been accused of that. Then I grin. "Has to be a first time for everything, I suppose. While I'm apparently being wise, give this woman of Skull's a good welcome. Get Violet to take her under her wing. If Skull's fallen for her, having her getting along with the ol' ladies will cement his loyalty to the club."

Demon digests that for a moment. Then he stands, walks around to me, and his meaty hand lands on the back of my cut. "You gonna stay for a drink?"

He's offering, but my original intention to get back to Stevie hasn't changed. "Nah, I think I'll head back. Stevie's all alone." Well, she's got the prospects with her, but I'd rather I was there.

Demon shakes his head. "I can't imagine it, you know? Being isolated at that cabin and not being able to see? She must jump at every fuckin' sound."

"She's pretty damn smart. We hear a twig snapping. She could probably fuckin' tell you the weight of whatever walked on it."

"Yeah?" At my nod, he resumes, "Christ. We could use her as a lookout sometime." He grins, obviously seeing a use for her talents. "Girl seems smart."

She is. I find myself preening at the compliment he's given her, but fuck knows why. She's my job, that's all.

I'm still grinning when I make my way, finally, to my bike. Before I mount up, I slap the palm of my hand against my forehead. I really must stop thinking about her as anything other than someone I need to keep safe. If she makes any offer to me tonight, I'll have to turn it down and for more than one reason.

She's a target for a killer, we already know that. Letting my guard drop might lead to her death, and there's no way in hell I want to be responsible for that. My job is just to keep her safe until Max can take up his guide dog duties again and we hand her over to the marshals. They'll give her a new identity for a second time, she'll drop out of sight and be in another state where I'll never be able to find her.

The dog's doing as well as can be expected, at least I can tell Stevie that. I pause with my finger over the engine start button, wondering how long it will be before the dog's fit. My days guarding the woman could soon be over, and if our plan works out, Demon will get his VP. Not too long and I'll be breathing the air of Tucson. Sounds fucking good to me.

The brothers know I'm at the cabin, but until we get the message out I'm there by myself, or for all intents and purposes I am, I still need to be careful not to be followed. I go this way and that, turning an hour's ride into two as I carefully make sure I've got no tail.

Once out on the open road and able to relax, my fucking head goes there, throwing up memories of Stevie sitting on my cock earlier today. I'd seen brothers fucking unconcerned in the clubroom after my impromptu meeting with Demon, it must have been that which reminded me and brings into my mind ideas of what I could do to Stevie.

It would be different, for sure. She wouldn't be able to see what I was doing. What difference would that make? I wouldn't be able to make love with my eyes, it would be my hands and tongue that would paint the picture of my desire for her.

Does she like being tied up? Sally certainly hadn't. Not that we'd tried it. The look of horror in her eyes when I jokingly suggested it had made me backtrack fast. Nah, straight missionary was how Sally wanted it.

But Stevie? Yeah, I reckon she'd be quite adventurous. The

thought of being in control with my hand twisted in her hair as I guide her lips to my cock, then start fucking her mouth…

For fuck's sake! The vibration of the engine isn't calming my cock at all. The only plus is that I'll be able to hide it. Just got to keep my distance is all.

CHAPTER TWENTY-TWO

After my conversation with Demon and my circuitous route back to the cabin, it's late by the time I draw up outside. Dan and Wills are hanging out by the railing and look impatient to be off. I just raise my chin at them, and then watch as they walk smartly to the truck and drive away, the noise of the engine gradually fading into the distance.

The need to concentrate on the road in the dark had, at least, calmed my unruly dick. As I wheel my bike the last few feet into the lean-to, I hope it will stay that way. I also hope that Stevie will be in her own bed and sleeping, but, on entering the cabin, I have no such luck.

When I unlock the door and quietly enter the main room, she's rousing herself on the couch, wiping sleep from bleary eyes. I take a moment to soak in the sight. Her hair is awry, strands coming down over her face, one cheek is red from having been pressed into the cushion. *She's fucking adorable.*

Red embers are glowing in the wood burner. She laid a fire or had the prospects? Kept it going all night? *Isn't that dangerous?* What if a log fell out and she burned the place, and herself, down? What were Dan and Wills thinking?

"What time is it?"

"Past midnight. You should be asleep in bed." I wish you were. Then I'd be better able to control myself. My dick, which I had got behaving, has perked up in interest again.

"I was too comfortable in front of the fire," she pouts. "I didn't want to move." When she shivers, I pull the blanket down from the back of the couch and pull it over her. "Well, I was, before I fell asleep and the fire burned down."

"Didn't you ask Dan or Wills to build it up again?"

She gives me a look as though saying she's perfectly capable herself. I change the subject, knowing the thought of her throwing logs into the fire is the making of nightmares.

"Want me to make you a hot chocolate before you go to bed?"

"No, I'm fine. Did you have a good meeting?"

I should tell her yes, or no. Make some shit up. Tomorrow's soon enough to have the conversation that's well past time, but somehow the words come out of my mouth. "Why the fuck weren't you scared of me, Stevie? Why weren't you worried when you came to the clubhouse?"

Her head tilts as though she can't understand my question.

"We're *bikers*, Stevie. Like them."

Her mouth opens in an O, and her breathing seems to stop.

"We know it all, Stevie. What you're running from and why."

Her unseeing eyes shutter and close. "I didn't have any choice but to accept your help. I knew you were different, I know not all MCs were alike. I knew you were good people, Beef, you saved Max and you saved me. I just couldn't tell you, just in case..."

The reasons for her reticence drop into place. "I'm from an MC, and you thought we might be involved."

"Not you, Beef," she says fast. "You could never condone what they did. But your club? I don't know what affiliations you have." Swinging her legs off the couch, she sits up. "Will this change anything?" As her head tilts accurately in my direction, I see her brow is creased and her teeth are worrying her lip.

"No." I go over and sit beside her. It seems natural to take her hand in mine. "You've heard of the Wretched Soulz?"

"Of course," she scoffs. "I wasn't born under a rock. They're that huge club, everyone knows of them." She shudders, the gesture gives away what she thinks of them.

She turns her hand in mine, and her fingers press mine gently. "You know it all?"

"The Warped Jokers robbing a bank, yeah. That you're the star witness? That too."

Her head rises, she stares in the direction of the dying fire. "I try not to think about it, else I'll hear it all the time, Beef. Those muffled shots, those screams. The begging, pleading for mercy. The cries of fear and pain. They were firing again and again, gradually the sound getting louder. I smell the cordite, I breathe the odour of the man who held me and threatened me. I could feel their evil."

She pauses, then adds, "I was powerless to do anything then, all I can do is help put those men away." She pauses, her lips press together. "I feel guilty that they left me alive. How crazy is that? They thought I was a nothing, not even a person good enough to kill. I should have been one of those bodies, instead I wasn't worth a bullet."

"Fuckin' glad they underestimated you." It seems natural to pull her toward me, to wrap my arms around her and hold her close. This near, I can feel her shaking. It's me who's feeling at fault right now. I hadn't considered how terrifying her ordeal had been, nor its lasting effect on her.

"Do I scare you?" I ask suddenly.

"You? No, why?"

"Because I smell like them. Oil and leather."

Her head shakes against me. "You're different. They smelled bad, your leather smells of some sort of polish."

It smells of the conditioner I use to keep it supple. Care of my cut comes second only to the care of my bike.

"Why did you mention the Wretched Soulz?"

"You know they are a big club." I explain as best I can. "They cover a lot of the states, other countries too. They're what's known as the dominant club, at least in this area. Any club that sets up in their territory has to get their permission. We live alongside them, know the boundaries, and don't step out of line."

"They've got a bad reputation."

"All MCs have, darlin'. It's par for the course. People don't understand us. But one club is not like the next. We keep to the right side of the line most of the time, but family is most important. Someone crosses us, and we handle it in ways which citizens don't approve. Our justice is swift."

There's a tremor in her voice as she asks, "Have I crossed your club by not coming clean from the start?"

"Nah." I hug her tighter and kiss the top of her head, breathing in the flowery scent of the shampoo she must have used again. "But you've given us a problem. We need to stay on the right side of the Wretched Soulz. They're too big for us to anger. The issue is, the Warped Jokers are also set up with permission of the dominant."

"They support them?" she asks, incredulously.

"Support would be taking it too far, I suspect. I wasn't party to the discussions, but even the Wretched Soulz don't go around shooting up banks. The Warped Jokers were out of line."

"Out of line?" she squeaks. "People were killed."

"I know, darlin', I know." I hope my tone is soothing. "Leaving aside their crime, they've brought the attention of the feds down on all MCs. Motorcycle clubs like ours are classified as gangs by the feds, and when something like this happens, an easy target to take down. If the Warped Jokers get convicted, their club will be destroyed. Problem is, the feds won't stop there. In their eyes it proves what MCs will do and that they're right to go after us. We're all tarred with the same brush, whether we like it or not."

"I'm going to testify."

I smile at her firm words. "Not asking you not to, babe. But the Wretched Soulz have a different take on things. They find you? They might try to persuade you not to take that stand."

"They'll kill me."

I can't deny the possibility, so I ignore it.

"The Wretched Soulz tried to run me down? Set fire to my house?"

"I wouldn't think so, Stevie. They might want the problem with the Warped Jokers to go away, but I don't think they'd get their hands dirty. I'd place my bet we've got some Jokers in town."

Her shiver isn't due to the chill that's descended in the room.

"They're the ones who found me? I don't understand how."

"Neither do we. But they did. Somehow, somewhere, the Jokers have got information they shouldn't have. But they're not going to find you." I put emphasis on the final sentence, then take a moment to explain our plan. That for all intents and purposes I'm living here alone, and that when anyone comes she'll remain out of sight. That the story will be she's gone to the marshals and left town.

"The marshals will know that's not true. What if the leak comes from them?"

Sighing deeply, I realise I can give no guarantees. "All we can do is our best, Stevie. Yeah, we're reacting rather than dictating the situation as we don't know where the threat's coming from, but believe this, everything we're doing is designed to ensure your safety."

She's quiet for a moment, then her hand reaches for mine. I meet her halfway. "I wouldn't be here now if it wasn't for you, Beef. I'm just worried how I've pulled you into this. What if they don't believe your story? What if they come here and hurt *you*?"

I move her hand until she can feel the bulging muscles in my arm. "I can look after myself, babe. And you."

She's quiet for a few minutes, taking in what I've told her, reading between the lines of what I haven't said. That in continuing to protect her, the Satan's Devils are pitting themselves against the dominant club. I really wish I could speak to Drummer, get his take on events. In my heart I'm sure I'm going in the direction he'd be taking. In my head, I want to be certain. But I need to let Demon assume the lead. It's not my place to approach the mother chapter prez. Unless... As Stevie stays quiet, I realise I am here as Drummer's enforcer. If I don't think things are being done the right way, I can alert him to any problems. But first, Demon has to make a mistake, and so far, I can't criticise him.

"Can I ask you something?"

"Of course you can."

"Will you come to bed with me?"

Fuck! I didn't expect her to ask that. Immediately my cock goes from the zero it's been at for this serious discussion to eighty. It feels impossibly hard, obviously eager to get inside her. But is that really what she's asking?

"Darlin', what is it you want?" She shifts as though feeling awkward, but my arms keep her imprisoned. "Speak to me," I encourage.

"I don't want to be alone. I just want to be held, like this, all night."

Christ! That will fucking kill me. "I can do that."

She swallows. "If you wanted to make love..."

"Darlin', I'm not going to push you to do anything you don't want. But I have to warn you, I'm a biker. I don't make love. I fuck." I got stuck in that trap with Sally. Had I warned her about my needs from the start, she and I may have recognised our incompatibilities and the whole darn mess wouldn't have got off the ground.

Stevie grins. "You know, you're not putting me off."

I'm not? For once I'm glad she's blind and can't see me grinning like a fucking loon. Jeez, but my cock wants in her. A few deep breaths, a stern mental admonishment to that traitorous part of my body, and my head is back in control. "I'll keep you company, Stevie, but that's it. Much as I wouldn't want to turn down any offer, I can't afford any distractions. Not when my job is to keep you safe." *Mad fool,* says my cock.

She stands, picking up her makeshift cane in her hand. "I'm just paying a visit to the bathroom."

I stand as well. While the outside of the cabin is always dark to her, at night unseen dangers can lurk. She nods as she hears my footsteps following her. I stand by the door, eyes scanning for any wildlife that might be a risk, waiting patiently until she returns. Once she's safely back inside, I look down at her, my fingers of one hand curled around her shoulder, those of the other taking the liberty of stroking her hair.

"Go to bed, Stevie."

"Will…?"

"I'll be there in a moment."

I watch as she walks across the room to the stairs, then as she makes her way up, trying to keep my eyes off the way her ass flexes as she takes each step.

Can't go there. I remind myself. *I'm here to do a job, not to get my rocks off.*

Having taken a piss and washed my hands, I try to keep to that resolve. Questions are going around my mind on a loop. *Does she sleep naked? PJs? Tank and shorts? Will she expect me to lie under the covers with her, or fully clothed on top?*

Will I be able to keep my hands to myself?

I can't be quiet, not a man my size. My boots clunk up the wooden stairs warning her of my approach.

Man, she's blind. I have to remind myself. *She doesn't know what she looks like.* Or, maybe she does. As I enter she's leaning over the bed pulling back the sheets and comforter, tiny sleep shorts rising high on her ass, leaving her cheeks on display and emphasising her crack. *Oh boy.* My hands itch.

Does she like being spanked?

Oh, what I could do to that ass.

"Stop staring." She stands, straightens, and turns toward me.

How does she fucking know?

Then I realise. Two steps take me straight to her. I haul her up tight against my body, leaving her in no doubt how hard I am for her. "Minx. You did that on fuckin' purpose."

She doesn't even try to deny it. "I want, need, you, Beef. Have you any idea how long it has been since I've been with a man? Show me what I've been missing, please."

"Stevie, this is a bad idea. I'm not in the market for a woman…"

"I'm not in the market for a man," she parrots.

"Stevie…"

"Beef. Just tonight. Give me tonight. Talking about what happened has dredged up all the bad memories, help me put them to the back of my mind. Tomorrow can take care of itself. I just need you, now."

She's so fucking tempting. But still I try to walk away. "This is a bad idea, Stevie. You and me? There's no future. You'll be off fuck knows where, and I'll be back in Tucson getting on with my life. Sleeping together will only complicate things. We do this? Fuckin' sure we'll regret it in the morning."

"It's only as complicated as you make it, Beef. I'm a woman, you're a man. Tonight, I need you. I'm not asking for a ring or a commitment. I know you're not looking for a wife. Please."

Please. It's that word that does it. Unleashes something inside of me.

Pushing her back toward the bed, her hands trustingly resting on my biceps, I pause at the edge. "Sit." If my voice doesn't sound quite normal, there's a good reason for that, the constriction of my jeans around my swollen dick.

Clearly wanting to be an active participant, her hands start to move toward me, zooming in at a point below my waist.

"Uh uh." Bending over I speak into her ear. As I admonish her, moving her hands and placing them at her sides, I continue in a low, but firm voice, "I'm in charge." Her sharp intake of breath suggests she likes the idea.

Keeping my mouth by the side of her head, I instruct, "Arms up."

She obeys without hesitation. That flimsy tank top is easy to pull off, revealing ample, perky breasts. Her nipples are erect and perfect, her aureole pink and quite large.

"Wanna play with your tits. Offer them to me."

In the light of the lamp she's lit, presumably for my benefit, I see her cheeks pinken. But she does what I ask, cupping her hands around those smooth round globes and raising them to me.

Careful not to touch her anywhere else, I lower my mouth and suck a nipple right in between my lips. There's no finesse as my tongue traps it to the roof of my mouth.

"Oh!"

I'm watching every reaction. She pushes against me as if wanting more, so I close my teeth applying a little pressure until it becomes almost a bite. She writhes, moans, making me think of possibilities as I release that nipple and pay the same attention to the other.

"Beef, I…"

Yeah, baby. Incapable of forming words. That's what I like. I'll be fucked if she isn't getting enjoyment from me playing with her tits. Tits or ass? I've never known what I like best, but I'd be content to play for hours. That she seems happy enough to let me is just what I want.

"Undo my zip, darlin'. Free him for me. But don't touch."

A moan of protest, but she does exactly what I've requested. I palm my cock once it's able to breathe, feeling the drop of pre-cum at the end. I wipe it up with my finger and press my digit to her mouth. "Lick."

She does, and groans appreciatively, the sound making my dick twitch.

Her skin looks so pure, so white and tender. I begin palming her breasts with my calloused hands, my tanned skin looking dark, used. The combination of innocence and biker making my cock swell more.

Again, she leans into my touch. Lowering my head once more, I suck, lave and bite one nipple then the other.

"Beef! You're making me so wet." She squirms, her hips moving against the bed as though seeking relief.

"You need something, baby?"

"Yes. You. I need you!"

CHAPTER TWENTY-THREE

She needs me? If only she knew how much I fucking need her too. I push her back down on the bed, then using my strength, haul her up until she's lying across it, giving me space to kneel over her legs. In one movement I yank away those tiny shorts which had taunted me.

The contrast between her small naked body and me still fully clothed does something to me. I feel like a marauding beast taking something I shouldn't, but I'll be fucked if I can stop. Since I met her, although I tried to deny it, I've been dreaming about this moment.

"Get naked, Beef. I want to feel your skin against mine."

Lightly I smack the top of her leg. "I think I said I was in charge."

She giggles, as I meant her to. My soft tap has done nothing but arouse her further.

"Please?"

My mouth is beside her ear again, the vibration of my voice causing tremors to cross her skin when I reply, "Seeing as you asked so nicely."

"Describe yourself, Beef."

Standing, I take off my cut, folding it neatly and placing it on a chair. Then I rip off my tee. While I'm toeing off my boots I comply. "I've got tats darlin', as you know. Lots of them. A hand of cards on my biceps which represents my brother Rock, on my biceps, the Marine insignia, the Satan's Devils patch on my back, the names of my brothers lost in service." I continue to describe each and every tat that I may not have told her about before, while her face becomes whimsical, and I wonder if she's regretting that she can't see them for herself. Muscles she can feel, but not my ink.

"Any girls' names on you?" she asks brazenly.

"None." There's no hesitation in my truthful reply. Never met a woman yet who I wanted to mark permanently on my body.

She holds out her arms. "What's keeping you, Beef?"

I slide a condom out of my pocket, then push my jeans down and off. Then stand, watching her laid out for me like an offering. She's so small compared to me. "How long has it been for you, Stevie?"

She knows what I mean. "A couple of years."

"Fuckers are crazy down in LA." They must be. Why has she not had a boyfriend in so long? Her confidence, her encouragement shows it isn't for the lack of her wanting.

She shrugs. "Once they know I'm blind, men seem to think they'll get stuck caring for me."

Shit. Wasn't that what I'd been thinking as well? But now I know her, she doesn't want a slave to run after her. Nah, Stevie will do as much as she can for herself.

"Then," she continues, "there are those which can't get a sighted girl because of their appearance. Obviously that doesn't turn me off, but their desperation does. And others, well, a blind woman's a notch on their bucket list. Pity fucks, when they're offered, are the worst. Or sometimes they act as if what's wrong with me is catching." She giggles. "Then there are those who seem to prefer my dog, and want to pet him, not me."

"Crazy." I can't wait to get closer, get near, get inside her. But

I'm going to have to go slow. Like the rest of me, my cock is large. Not boasting, just fact.

She's up on her elbows. "Let me touch?"

"Uh uh," I say again. "No touching. You're gonna get a surprise little girl."

"Huh." She shakes her head making her long hair fly. "You're probably all bluster. How am I to know it's not a teeny wiener?"

A startled laugh bursts out of me. "You're going to have to wait to find out."

I've been interested in, but never really understood the dynamics of BDSM before, but having Stevie effectively blindfolded is turning me on. By not allowing her to touch, she's got no clue what I'm about to do. She's breathing fast, her skin is nicely flushed, and I bet her heart's beating fast in anticipation. This isn't just an act to get off, nothing like going with a sweet butt or the boring missionary position where dirty talk was discouraged. My head's running through ways of how to drive this, to make the experience good, not just for me, not only for her, but, for us both.

I move fast to take her by surprise, raising her legs, bending them then pushing her knees apart so she's completely open to me. She gasps as I've startled her, and then again when I huff warm breath against her clit. She hadn't been kidding when she said she was wet, she's dripping. Her moisture is dampening her inner thighs, glistening in the light spilling from the lamp.

Lazily I circle my fingers down from her knees, in no hurry to reach that part where she wants me to touch her. I don't think I've taken the time to examine a woman's reactions in such depth before. Stevie's eyes might be sightless, but the rest of her body is so expressive it more than compensates.

Her nipples are pert, her stomach softly rounded, her pubic hair neatly trimmed. She's a natural redhead.

She shivers, but it's not with cold. Her mouth starts to open, but before she asks what's taking me so long, I lower my face, breathing in that perfume that's uniquely hers. Her labia are like petals surrounding a prize underneath, my tongue parts them, and her taste… If I thought the aroma was perfection, when my taste buds start getting some action my cock jumps as though it's alive. I could become addicted to this. Eating pussy is one of my favourite things to do, but sometimes it's just mechanical. Stevie? I could stay here for hours devouring her.

Her hands come down, her fingers start running through my short hair, then she tries to move my head, but this is my show. I delve deep inside her, but there's no way I can get the last drop. Her body's reacting to me as mine is to hers, and she simply produces more cream for me to lap up. I love the effect I'm having on her. No lube needed tonight, that's for sure.

Her clit. Yes, can't ignore that. As soon as my lips close around it, she arches her back, pressing up into my mouth. I toy with it, licking around, then flicking across the top. She's flexing, seeming unaware that she's grunting and moaning, giving me clues as to what she likes most.

"Beef," she wails. Then, more urgently, "There, Beef. There…"

I could pull away and make her wait, but my cock's leaking pre-cum as much as her slit's leaking cream and I don't want a delay. Another suck, nibble, then my tongue works the spot and with the action she seems to like the most, she's tensing, her muscles tight, then she screams and comes.

I continue to work until her convulsions cease.

Easing my head up, I stare at her, able to drink in the view of a fully sated woman. As she has no clue I'm watching her, I can take my time, enjoying the flush to her skin, the sheen of sweat on her brow, her mouth half open as she draws air down into heaving lungs. Like a slap around the head it hits me. *I'm not going to be able to let her go.*

I must.

This is the only time I'm going to be weak and let my cock have its way. Just this once. Too many issues if we do a repeat. My hand idly strokes that appendage as I indulge in the view I promise myself I'll never see again, committing the sight of her head thrown back in ecstasy into my brain. If I use the image to fuel my alone time in the shower in the days, weeks, months to come, who could blame me.

I can't hold back any longer. As I tear open the condom packet, a little smile curves her lips. *Appreciation I'm taking care of her?* Or anticipation of what's to come.

"Ready for me?" I ask her.

"What's taking you so long?" she replies, impudently.

Well, that's it. I sit back on my haunches and pull her toward me, her feather-light weight proving no problem at all to slide her hips up over mine. In this position she's completely open to me.

Christ she looks tiny. And for her, it's been a long time. *Take this slow.*

I line myself up and push in. She's as tight as I expected. Her eyes squeeze shut, her brow furrows. "Relax. Breathe."

She attempts to obey, as I start making headway. Her scrunched-up face shows it may not be pleasurable right now, but once I'm in, I know ways to make it better. To distract her, I play with her clit.

A small thrust in, a slow pull out, then repeat. It's not my normal style of fucking, but I love it. Her tightness is strangling my dick, ramping up my own pleasure, it's taking all my control to prevent this being over too fast.

At last she's taken all of me. Leaning forward I take her mouth in a gentle kiss, our lips meeting and melting, our bodies as close as they could possibly be.

When I pull away, I ask, "Are you ready?"

She wriggles for an answer which I take as a yes. A slow slide out, then I push right in, butting against her cervix. I do it again, again and again, each thrust getting more powerful, making sure I find that special spot inside her every single time.

Studying her, every reaction is encouragement. I ramp it up, my movements become fierce and powerful, a punishing rhythm that not every woman likes, but she takes it, encourages it, allowing me to fuck how I want. Her hands grip the comforter, her fists clench, her mouth twists as though she's in mid-scream, and her internal muscles clench down on my dick. *Christ, she's going to take me over.*

As her body goes taut and starts spasming, I lose it myself, my body jerking erratically as cum rises from my balls, up through my shaft. The swelling of my dick inside her seems to be all she needs to start flying.

I grunt, she cries out. It's a perfect moment. Both of us coming together. Both of us heaving to get breaths into starved lungs. I swear I see stars for a moment. It must be because she's so tight, but I can't remember coming this hard in my life. Or pumping so much cum into a condom.

It's her that recovers first and is the one who gives voice to my own realisation. "That was amazing. I've never come like that before. Utterly, incredibly, amazing."

"It was." I'm barely able to respond. My mind fighting with two thoughts, one that I'd like to try round two just to see if it's really her that makes the difference, and the second, that I have to leave her now, before I become addicted.

My dick, now soft, starts slipping out of her. With one hand I hold the end of the condom. "Got to go deal with this."

"Yeah." She can't see but must have enough clues to know what I mean. Propping her elbows beneath her, she raises the upper half of her body, and frowns. "Are you coming back, Beef?"

I slip off the condom and tie a knot in the end. She's pre-empted the conversation we must have. I close my eyes, knowing she can't see my expression or how much I regret this. "No. Stevie, this was—"

"Don't you dare say it was a mistake."

"I wasn't going to. This was one time, Stevie. You needed a release, so did I. It stops here, it has to." Her bottom lip quivers, so I add more. "Soon you'll be able to move on. We'll never see each other again. I won't know where you are, you won't even be able to check in. Safest that way for you, darlin'. One fuck and I already know I could get hooked."

"Me too," she inserts fast.

"So it's best we put this behind us. Before neither of us want to walk away."

I wait, but she seems to have accepted it. Me? I'm already wondering whether it's too late.

CHAPTER TWENTY-FOUR

Although Stevie seems to have a sixth sense and can often somehow feel my eyes watching her, I've learned how to sneak peeks at her without her knowing I'm there. Right now, she's busying herself in the kitchen preparing lasagne for dinner tonight. As usual, I'm transfixed by her effortless actions as she feels her way through the preparations. It's only because I'm watching carefully that I see the clues that give away she's blind; the way she finds the right implement by touch.

The first time I saw her chopping an onion I thought she'd surely cut herself, then saw she'd learned or taught herself a technique by which she could safely do it.

She doesn't object to my help when I offer it, she only protests if she feels I'm contributing assistance if I don't think she can do it herself, when she's perfectly capable of performing a task. I've learned to wait until it's obvious, or only aid when asked. She knows her limitations better than I.

Already I know how far off the mark I was to ever think she'd be needy and clingy. Daily she demonstrates far more independence than Sally ever showed. Moving to Pueblo alone with only her dog beside her should have been the first clue, it had been there from the start. But so fresh from leaving Sally, I'd looked for something that wasn't there, a reason to not fall for the first woman who crossed my path.

Have I fallen? A range of emotions must cross my face. At least, with her, I don't need to guard them. I admit it, I have. I've fallen hard. Since the night before last, we've not touched, not kissed, and not spoken about the out of the world sex we'd experienced. The next morning started as each subsequent one has with us avoiding the issue completely. If at times I believe I see a wistful look on her face, it could be my imagination.

I know the words said in the dark of the night were right. As soon as it's safe, we'll be handing her back into the care of the marshals. Anything started now would have an expiration date. If I feel this way after just one night, how would I feel if we repeated it, not once, but twice, a hundred times or more? A feeling tells me, this woman is one I'd follow to the end of the earth.

It makes me admit, there was never a time I wasn't faking it with Sally. From the start I'd been trying to make her into someone she wasn't, trying to see her as the right woman for me, simply because she strayed into my path. Now I know why my Tucson brothers knew their old ladies were their one. It's the same way I know Stevie could be that for me.

It's easy to dream of taking her down to Tucson—on the back of my bike, she wouldn't complain about the long ride. I'd introduce her to Sam, Sophie, Marcia and the rest of the old ladies. Oh, and Becca. Becca would be so happy I'd found someone for myself at last.

That thought pulls me up. While I've been with Stevie, I've not thought about Becca once, or not with the regret that she was with my best friend and not me.

But taking Stevie to Tucson, well, that's never going to happen.

I've been staring down at my hands, something makes me raise my eyes.

Stevie's standing, spatula in hand, her head quizzically tilted toward me. "You alright?" she asks.

Wondering again how she can tell, I lie. "I'm fine."

"You gave a heavy sigh." She frowns. "Are you getting bored, Beef? Staying here with me?" She gives a brief chuckle. "Getting cabin fever?"

How could I be bored? It's easy being here with her. I read Harley magazines, planning upgrades to my bike while she listens to her audible books using headphones. Those are some of the best times, my attention often drawn away from what I'm reading, to watch the expressions crossing her face. Tenderness, arousal, anger. Yeah, the latter amused me. One night I was sure she was going to throw her iPad across the room. Or, if she's not reading, we watch a film. I've become used to describing scenes where there's action but no conversation. It's natural for me to say something like, yup, she's going down to that basement, to which Stevie will scream out, 'No', and, amusingly, cover her face with her hands.

Daytime I chop wood for the fire and clear up around the place outside while Stevie tidies the interior. This cabin has been neglected for years and there's much I can find to occupy myself.

"Not getting cabin fever, Stevie. In fact the opposite. Probably the most time I've had to decompress for years. Can't say I'd like staying here forever but it will be a while yet before I get bored."

Her lips curve. "You done anymore on that old bike?"

Hmm. She remembers too much. Some of my clearing up might have revealed the frame of an ancient Indian. I've been scrounging around to see whether there are any other parts for it. Someone obviously brought it up here and dumped it. Perhaps they were going to restore it, but then gave up? Or, considering the early days of the Colorado club and the loss of members to prison or bullets, maybe they never got the chance to return for it. I remember how Sam, Drummer's old lady, had restored her Vincent from nothing much more than I have found.

"Well, I might have found me a project to work on." I laugh.

Then I wonder about her. "How you doing? You finding time dragging?"

"I would, but you're good company, Beef. Like you, though, it won't be long before I want to get back to real life. It's great having a chance to relax, and these couldn't be nicer surroundings, but I do want to get back to work." Her face falls. "Not that I probably have a job now, I just disappeared."

"What do you do?"

"I'm designing a program to make doing taxes easier for blind people. Most of the time I work on my own, but I give email reports and updates. As I haven't been able to do that, well, I suspect they'll be looking for someone else now."

They may well be. "The marshals got you that job?"

"Yes."

"Then I suspect they'll help you get something else. It was on their watch you almost got killed."

She looks thoughtful and brightens as if I've given her hope.

My phone pings with a text. "Prospects are coming tomorrow," I tell her as a warning. I haven't been back to church, but Demon's given me updates. Wills and Dan were ecstatic to be patched in, something I'd have loved to have witnessed. Always a good feeling bringing new brothers to the table. As a result, Beaver and Karl were given prospect cuts.

"I'll make sure I'm ready," she acknowledges. We've found a place where she can stay out of sight. Not very imaginative, just the spare bedroom. I've piled up furniture so it looks like a storeroom. No reason for anyone to go looking, but if they did, a cursory glance wouldn't reveal her inside. Before they arrive, I'll make sure there's no feminine shit hidden around.

The next day I've got Stevie comfortable in her secret nest, well before our visitors are due. She's going to listen to her book until she hears the bikes, then will just have to wait it out. I need to get her new headphones as the cheap ones she's got leak sound. I promise to get rid of the prospects as fast as I can, but she waves me off, telling me to take as long as I need. She's right,

I've got to be careful not to raise suspicion, or for the prospects to suspect I'm not here alone.

It's almost exactly the time Demon had told me when Beaver and Karl come driving up in the truck. Immediately they get out and drag on their brand-new cuts proudly displaying that they are Satan's Devils prospects.

Beaver's next action is to light a cigarette. Belatedly he waves the pack toward me, putting it back in his cut when I shake my head. I've never smoked, and the fresh mountain air immediately seems tainted. I step around him, putting myself upwind of the stench. Karl shakes his head at his traveling companion, then walks around to the back of the truck. I notice his eyes scanning the surroundings.

Looking for someone? Nah. Stevie arrived in Pueblo long after these two started hanging around the club. No one could have predicted Satan's Devils and her paths would have crossed.

"This is the back of beyond," Beaver says, conversationally. "Ain't you going stir-crazy out here?"

"Not at all." I don't need to explain myself to a prospect. Oh, in time, if he looks like he's going to make the grade I'll look on him as a friend before he advances to being one of my brothers. Right now and just starting out? I need to see what he's made off. "My bike got dusty coming up the dirt road. Go and clean it." I point to the lean-to where it's currently protected from most of the elements.

I'm pleased to see he stubs his cigarette out on the heel of his boot, pockets the stub, and steps smartly off in the direction of my Harley. *Learning already.* Good sign. Of course, I could have asked he clean the outhouse with his toothbrush. Maybe I'll tell him to bring it with him next time. My lips curl behind his back. Always good fun fucking with new prospects.

"Beef!" Karl's deep voice draws my attention to him.

He's still leaning in the back of the truck, sorting out provisions I suspect. Well, if he expects a patched member to help his sorry butt carrying shit, he's got another think coming. If he hasn't learned the crap part of being a prospect yet, I'm happy to teach him. If I'd truly been alone, I could have asked him to cook me dinner and he would have to jump to it. Probably wouldn't be edible though, unless he's got hidden talents.

Prepared to educate him on the facts of prospect life if all he wants is help, I move around to the back of the truck, coming to an abrupt halt when I see what he's brought.

Staring at the contents, Karl shakes his head. "Fuck knows why you want this beat up piece of shit. Think Demon thought you might be lonely."

Curbing my instinct to put my fist in his face at his disrespectful mode of speaking, I crouch, then reach out my hand. A long pink tongue comes out to lick it. "Hey, you remember me, boy? You were in a fuck of a state when I last saw you."

Max has got a cone thing around his head, his back leg is bandaged, and he's got shaven bare bits on his front legs, presumably where the catheter went in. But his eyes are alert and bright, and when I reach behind his ears to give him a scratch, he leans into me.

Karl reaches into his back pocket. "Got instructions here from the vet. He told you to call him if you've got any problems."

I hold out my hand. When the piece of paper is in it, I unfold it. Max is to be kept quiet and rested. The prospects have brought a crate for that purpose. There are instructions for his meds, and for his maintenance diet so he doesn't eat too much and put on weight which would stress his healing leg.

"Okay, boy," I mutter, half to myself. "Let's get you inside." It's not the first time I've been close to him. Whether he remembers me or not, he doesn't protest or struggle as I pick him up and take him inside.

Behind me comes Karl carrying a folded-up crate, and some blankets. There are other bags full of treats, toys, food and his meds, but at least the prospect's got a head on his shoulders. We need to get Max settled and comfortable first. *Stevie's going to go ape-shit when she sees him.*

"Don't know why you want the mutt," Karl mumbles as he sets up the crate. "Doesn't the seeing-eye dog place take them back or something when they can't work?"

Damn. He knows it's Stevie's. Well of course, he would. He'd have heard the talk around the clubhouse that I was the first on the scene of the accident. I wonder what I can say, and come up with, "You're right, he can't work. His mistress has moved on. I liked the mutt and offered to take him."

"Your bike's done, Beef. Got off all the dust." Beaver points to the dog who I've placed in his crate. "I suppose the bitch left him as he was no good to her."

"That's right," I say, firmly, keeping up the pretence, but unhappy to have even a fictional slur on her character. "A guide dog's no good if it can't work."

"So, you, what? You wanted company?"

"I like dogs," I repeat. Truth is, the closest I've ever been to a pet dog is Grunt, the wolfhound on the Tucson compound. I turn away dismissively. Conversation over. There's a point when you start offering too much explanation that it becomes suspicious.

Beaver starts carrying grocery sacks into the kitchen. When he starts opening cupboards to put stuff away, I stop him.

"I'll do that later. You'll only put everything in the wrong place." Places where Stevie wouldn't think of looking. I'll put everything away under her instruction later.

"Neat fuckin' freak, ain't ya?"

I swing around, suddenly seeing what he is. Tins stacked neatly by their contents. I simply glare at him. Whether I am or not is none of his business.

Wanting them to be gone, anticipating the delight on Stevie's face when she finds out her friend has been brought back to her, I open the front door pointedly and follow them out. Then watch them go to the truck.

They've got their hands on the door handles when I shout, "You really want a beatdown? Be out of the club before you've fuckin' started?"

Two men turn around fast. Karl holds up his hands as if to ward me off. Beaver looks perplexed. Then it suddenly dawns on them. In unison they give each other sheepish looks, take off their cuts, and only then get into the truck.

"Be sure to hide the fuckin' gate once you're out," I add as they close the doors.

A wave of Karl's hand out of the driver's side window shows me he's heard.

Fucking prospects.

CHAPTER TWENTY-FIVE

I give it a few minutes before returning inside, making sure that the new prospects haven't forgotten something or other and decide to come back. Then, with a huge fucking smile on my face, and unable to hold back on the surprise any longer, I go inside.

Taking the stairs two at a time, I call out before entering the bedroom where Stevie is hiding. I'm so impatient to show her what's waiting for her, I can barely hold myself back from yanking her into my arms and carrying her downstairs.

"What's the matter, Beef? What the hell are you doing?" Stevie's face is tight. "Have they found me? Why the rush?"

Shit. I've scared her. She can't see I'm beaming from ear to ear. "Nothing's wrong. Fuck, sorry, Stevie. I'm happy is all, and you will be too."

There's a thump thump from the crate. Stevie stops dead, her brain computing the sound. The conclusion she comes to is confirmed when Max, eager to see his mistress, gives a small whine. Several emotions pass across her face, disbelief, then hope and finally, pleasure.

Taking a step toward the sound she asks, "Is he alright?"

"Yeah. He's in a crate. His leg's bandaged, he's got one of

those cone things on presumably to stop him gnawing the bandage off. He's supposed to take it easy. But he seemed to be able to walk okay."

"Can he come out? I'll try and keep him calm."

"Of course. You sit on the couch, and I'll let him out, okay?"

Max is so thrilled to see his mistress that he bounds out of the crate in a way that makes me wince. But as soon as he reaches her, she gives him a command, "Down." Within a second, he's lying at her feet.

Sliding off the couch, she sits on the floor beside him, her face buried in his fur, her body shaking. When she looks up, tears are falling down her face. She sniffs loudly. "I didn't let myself believe he'd be alright. Is he going to make a full recovery?"

"Looks that way," I reply, sinking to my haunches beside the pair. "James' note said he's coming on really well."

She can't stop touching Max. I eye her carefully, then place a box of tissues beside her, remembering to tell her they're by her left hand. She's not going to want to leave him anytime soon.

"I'll go start dinner. You stay here with Max."

I don't need to tell her twice. Thinking that food will probably be the last thing on her mind, I defrost some chilli I find in the freezer, then heat it along with some rice. After plating it I take it back into the main room.

"Mmm. Smells good." Her nose wrinkles in appreciation. "Thanks Beef."

"It's not much. You want it there?"

She eases herself back onto the couch and holds out her hand to take it. Well-trained dog that he is, he wags his tail, licks his lips, but Max stays put. When I sit down beside her, he inches over so he's lying against my feet as well as hers. Guess he's adopted me too.

"Where's Max's food?"

"Prospects brought it. Load of shit lying over there. Collar and lead. No harness, but he won't be up to working for a while yet."

"I know that. But at least he's here and with me."

She's still pleased and excited, while I view Max with a frown. I'm delighted she's happy but seeing Max on the road to recovery just reminds me that as soon as he's able to guide her again, it will be time to say goodbye. I don't say anything though. The dog's still got some way to go yet. I can enjoy this idyllic interlude for a while longer. It's just an unwelcome reminder that I'm one step closer to losing her.

When we've finished eating, she insists on taking our plates and washing them. I watch her walk away, accepting at some point she'll disappear forever.

My arms itch to hold her again, but I can't. If it's that difficult to imagine her leaving as it is, if I allow myself to get close to her again, I won't want to let her go at all.

Stevie wants to do everything she can for Max herself. She knows about his needs far more than I do. After cleaning up, she takes him outside, the dog limping along by the side of the woman finding her way with the stick I'd made, while I'm hovering close by in case she needs help. I'm intrigued by the practicalities.

"Get busy," she says.

Max immediately squats. Stevie reaches her hand down and strokes his back.

"I thought male dogs cocked their legs," I observe, having seen Grunt water the plants back in Tucson more times than I can remember.

"Guide dogs are trained to squat."

"And you touch him, why?" It seems overly invasive to me.

"So I can tell whether I need a bag. I know he's peeing now as his back is straight. If he was having a poo then it would be curved, and I'd be ready to scoop it up. Normal dogs don't like being touched when they're doing their business, but he's been trained to accept it."

Clever. I nod admiringly.

"This is why not all blind people want the hassle of having a dog. Owning a dog anyway is a responsibility, but it is harder when you can't see. Max pays me back a thousand times over. If cleaning up after him is my payment in return, it's the least I can do." She raises her head, and sniffs the air. "Storm coming. I can smell the ozone."

I glance up. Clouds are gathering, darkening the light from the moon. She could well be right.

"Best get back inside. Max should be off that leg anyway." We're not long back in the warmth of the cabin before raindrops start to hit the roof hard.

There's something comforting about sitting in front of a log-burning stove while lightning flashes, and the sound of rain hitting the cabin vies with the rumble and crack of thunder for which can be loudest. Stevie jumps when there's a loud crack right overhead, and again my arms ache to hold her.

Max, completely unperturbed, lies at her feet.

Ignoring the elements outside, we put on a DVD and watch it. Well, I view and describe. It seems the most natural thing in the world now. Then it's time for bed. Not wanting to strain Max's healing leg, Stevie goes up alone, satisfied with my promise I'll look after her four-legged friend tonight.

She doesn't know I'm observing her take every step, recognising her reluctance to leave him and to sleep alone. But it's for the best. She knows it is too.

As the days pass I notice there's a change in Stevie now she has her dog back with her. She seems lighter, happier, and her smile comes to her face quicker. It's as if he completes her, as thought he was a missing limb. Max stays glued to her side, staying so close I catch myself feeling jealous of a fucking dog.

Demon keeps in touch, I make sure to give him a list of things that we need which the prospects will bring up in a few days and reassure him all's as it should be on the cabin front.

Max is walking better as every twenty-four hours pass. I checked with James and the vet told us we could remove his bandage now, and his cone if he doesn't worry the stitches. Carefully unwrapping his leg, I describe it to Stevie. The operation scar is quite small, looks good and clean, and the stitches are dissolving just as they should. Being a good dog, when his cone is removed Max licks the wound then ignores it when told.

I continue searching for parts of the Indian I'd unearthed. I find a box of treasures and start sorting them out and cleaning them; the oil pump, the engine. Why someone stripped it down and left it I've no idea. The thought grows that they hadn't come back because they couldn't.

I decide I'll do the work, put it back together again; I'll finish the job they started as a tribute to an unknown biker. Maybe Hellfire would know who it was? I'll ask next time I see him.

If Stevie is bored with our simple life, she doesn't show it. She finds pleasure in small things, like sitting in the sun with her dog by her side, her hand ruffling his fur as she listens to me tinkering with the bike. I've grown used to hearing her giggle when I swear at something that's not going the way I want it. Her lack of complaint, her amusement at my frustration rather than fearing my outbursts are yet more things I admire about her. Despite her disability, living with her is easy, comfortable. Things I have now were exactly what was missing with Sally. Stevie's independence shows in everything she does. I don't think I've ever admired a woman more in my life.

Why is it when I've found someone who seems perfect, I can't keep her?

Briefly I toy with the idea of going wherever she goes. Taking on a new identity, giving up everything I am. Leaving the brotherhood of the Satan's Devils. Much as I admire Stevie, I'm not sure that would be fair to either of us. I'd be restless, lost. I've been a Devil most of my adult life, and don't know if I'd be the same man without the patch on my back. Despite Stevie's hopes of returning to her old life, I'd have to take that step knowing the chances are it could be permanent. I'm not ready to commit to that.

Damn it.

I'm sorting through the parts I've found when my phone rings.

"Prez."

Demon's tone is sharp, and he wastes no time. "Got Warped Jokers on the way. Looks like they're heading in your direction."

Fuck!

"Where are they?"

"Still on the highway, about twenty minutes out. Could be wrong, Beef, but you need to get out of there."

He's right. I do.

"Go straight up from the cabin. There are tracks you can follow, and then veer off out of sight into the forest. Hopefully the Jokers won't have a tracker with them. We're getting together now and coming up behind you, but you're on your own until we get there."

"Got it, Prez." I'm already outside the door when I end the call.

I march straight in. "Stevie. Get your shoes on. We've got to get out of here. Got to go on foot and find somewhere to keep low."

Her eyes widen, but the urgency in my voice means she doesn't protest or argue, asking simply, "Max?"

"He's coming too. He can make it, Stevie." He's been getting stronger, and that leg is weight bearing now. I can't risk leaving him for those sadists, and if he does do any damage to his healing leg, it's better than him, or us, being dead. "I'll grab his collar and lead."

I know he's well trained, but don't want him running off on the scent of some animal or other. As Stevie gets her trainers, I go to the pile of doggy stuff the prospects had brought and which we'd so far left untouched.

Picking up the collar I stare at it. "What the fuck is this, Stevie?" There's a square shaped object hanging from it.

"It's a…" Her hand covers her mouth, and she swallows hard

before completing her sentence. "It's a GPS tracker. In case he gets lost."

Swearing, I rip it off the collar, then place the leather around Max's neck and buckle it and attach the leash. *Someone has known exactly where Max was since he came to the cabin.* They must have been biding their time to arrange an attack assuming where her dog is, that's where she'll be. *Fuck.*

There is no time to waste. Quickly I herd both Stevie and Max out of the cabin, eyeing the slope above us. The ground is rough.

"I'll make it." Something in the tension of my body must have conveyed my concern.

"The ground's uneven."

"I'll be okay."

The first hundred yards isn't too bad. Then she stumbles and almost falls over a root which I hadn't noticed in time to warn her. Luckily my grip on her elbow prevents her tumbling to the ground. We carry on, making slower progress than I'd have liked. While Demon thought we'd be able to find somewhere to hide, there's nothing but tree trunks to shelter us here.

I stop and crouch down. "Get on my back, Stevie. We'll move faster if I'm carrying you."

"I'm too heavy…"

"Stevie. Just do it. I carried packs heavier than you in basic."

She's not heavy at all, or at least, not now. Maybe if we go too far I'll start to feel it.

"Is Max okay?"

"He's fine. Now hang on."

I've got a weight on my back and one hand on the leash, but at least we can start moving faster. I take care to watch my step, not wanting to trip and hurt either of us, and turn off the trail into the trees. Now I don't have to watch Stevie's every step, and I don't need to find an even path. I just have to remember to tell her to duck when there are low-hanging branches.

Behind, in the still air, I hear the sound of motorcycle engines. I try to count them, more than a couple, definitely. Four, five?

My gun is loaded. Extra ammunition carried in my cut. My knife is in my belt. I strain my ears for the sound of the Devils Prez promised to send, but the sudden silence of the engines means the Jokers have arrived at the cabin, and, for now, as I'd been warned, we're alone.

At last we come to a clearing. My eyes scan, settling on something. Telling Stevie I'm putting her down, I crouch so she can slide off. "Stay here."

As I thought, camouflaged and almost hidden from sight is what looks like an old deer blind, presumably used by hunters in hunting season.

I lead her over to it and settle her inside. "I want you to stay here, Stevie, you and Max."

"Don't leave me, Beef."

"Stevie, if they're out searching then I can lead them away from you."

"What if they catch you?"

"I'll make them think I'm out here on my own."

"They might shoot you, then come for me." She sounds so understandably terrified it breaks my heart.

While I yearn to stay and hold her, I know that's not the best way to keep her out of their hands. All I've got to do is hold them off until the cavalry arrives.

Shamelessly I play on her love for her dog. "Max is limping," I tell her, exaggerating his condition. Actually, Max looks like he's thoroughly enjoying his forest walk. "You stay in the blind and get him to rest awhile. All this clambering over rough ground isn't doing him much good."

She's scared at the idea of being left alone and I can't blame her. But she gives me a resolute nod and reluctantly agrees as I've convinced her it's best. For Max.

CHAPTER TWENTY-SIX

I didn't want to leave Stevie scared and alone. But I didn't think I had a choice. I've never been one to run away from a fight, and if we carried on, it's possible the Warped Jokers might be able to follow whatever track we'd left and find us. At least by leaving her in a safe place I can go back and see what they're up to, maybe take out one or two with my knife.

I wouldn't have the least repulsion in killing them up close, certain if they caught up with us, they'd take Stevie out. The stakes for them are far too high. If the RICO indictment goes ahead, every member of that club is looking at twenty years behind bars.

Even if those on the outside don't get rounded up and convicted, they'll still be giving their all for their members currently inside. I'd do whatever it takes to free Drummer, Wraith or any of my brothers. But would I kill a woman to keep her silenced? No, I couldn't do that. Find some other way to persuade her not to talk, perhaps, but not take her life. The Warped Jokers, though? With their reputation, if Stevie is kept alive, she'll spend the rest of her days working on her back wishing she was dead.

There is no way in hell I'm letting them get to her. I can't take the risk of them finding and ambushing us.

I'm a big man, but I can be quiet if necessary. It's only Stevie with her heightened sense of hearing who can catch me out. I descend the route we'd taken carefully, keeping to the shadows of the trees and the scrub, my eyes now on the ground checking for twigs which would snap and betray me.

I've been walking for a good few minutes when I hear a voice calling out.

"Looks like someone's come this way."

Fuck. I strain my ears as another voice shouts back.

"How the fuck can a blind bitch find her way in the forest?"

"Got the biker with her. Found some tracks, bike boots. I'm following them."

Not for long you're not. I take my knife out of its sheath, running my finger over the edge, reminding myself how sharp it is. Even Blade, the Tucson enforcer, would be impressed.

Jeez. I'd hoped they'd have no one with them with tracking skills, but again I'm reminded how big I am, and carrying Stevie's weight, must have left a trail in the damp earth. Soon I hear footsteps, I shrink back behind a massive tree trunk and almost stop breathing.

I analyse the sound. Only one set of footsteps. He passes me without a look in my direction, it's easy to put my arm around his neck, crushing his windpipe, and slicing my knife across his jugular. As expected, he slumps in my arms, dead.

One down. How many to go? I feel no remorse as I pull the body into the undergrowth and out of sight.

In the distance I hear more motorcycle engines. Demon is on his way. Until then, they'll have to go through me to get to Stevie.

"Buck? Where are you, man?" a hoarse whisper carries in the air. "I think I'm following you but give me a sign to show me where you are." Silence, then, "Buck? Where the fuck are you?"

Sounds of rustling and twigs snapping warn someone is getting close. "Buck?"

I haven't heard anyone else. I take a chance. As soon as he's close enough, I karate chop his arm making his gun drop to the ground, the strength of my blow having a paralysing effect. Almost in the same movement I have my arm around his neck, crushing his windpipe so he stays silent. The blade hovering close to his jugular makes him show the whites of his eyes.

"You're going to answer my questions," I tell him in a conversational tone. Then hiss, "If you want to play hero, this blade is going to make a pretty mess of your throat." I don't add I've already dispatched his brother to meet Satan. "Uh uh, I wouldn't try to nod if I were you. When I take my arm away, don't scream or call out. Don't think there's anyone close enough to save you before I slice into your neck."

His face is going red because of the pressure I'm applying to his neck. I ease my arm away a fraction, and he takes a deep breath.

"How many of you are there?"

"Four."

"Who are you working with?"

"No one," he lies.

One thing Blade had taught me was to always be prepared. Using just one arm to crush his windpipe again, I reach into my back pocket with my free hand and extract a zip tie. None too gently I then use my legs to sweep his out from under him. Whatever little air he'd managed to take into his lungs is knocked out of him as he falls to the ground. I come down hard on his back, and yanking his hands behind him, zip tie them together.

I then pull him up.

"I've got my knife and gun at your back. One wrong step and you're dead. One shout of warning and you'll wish you'd never been born. Now walk."

I hear motorcycles, lots of them. They seem to be close. Then the engines cut out. Help has arrived.

Then I hear shots, screams come then are suddenly cut off. An automatic rifle firing followed by silence. All I can do is walk my captive down in the direction of the cabin, hoping the right side has won.

I walk into the clearing behind the old building, sidle along the walls, then pause and peer around the front, my gun held at the ready. I inhale a lungful of relieved air at the sight meeting my eyes. Demon is standing, his arms folded, staring at a man writhing on the ground.

As I step into sight, he grins in my direction and calls out, "One dead, one wounded. What you got, Beef?"

"One dead, one alive." I grin. *Stevie's safe.* We've come out on top.

"Buck," my captive breathes out, his shoulders slumping. I ignore his reaction. A man wanting to kill an innocent woman deserves no sympathy.

"What we going to do with them?" Ink asks.

"Torture the truth out of them, then kill them," Pyro suggests as he walks up and relieves me of my burden.

"Got the prospects coming with a truck," Demon tells me. "Want to talk to them yourself?"

"Stevie?" I'm not leaving her alone in the cabin.

"This place is compromised, Beef. Fuck knows how they knew she was here, but they did. Best bring her back to the club." He raises an eyebrow. "She is safe, I take it?"

"Yeah, got her stashed away in an old hunting blind." My lips press together. She'll have heard the shots and will be worried sick. "If you've got it under control here, I'll go back and get her. Then I'll bring her and the dog back in the truck. I'll get my bike later."

"Christ. A fuckin' dog on the compound. Not sure how Bitch is going to take to that."

"Twenty bucks says the cat wins," Rusty calls out to Ink.

"My money's on the dog," Thunder joins in.

Demon throws them a look of disgust. His own tone is serious as he gets back to business. "Don't know how the fuck they knew you were here, Beef. Been no leak from our end. Unless," his face goes dark, "Beaver or Karl said something."

I want to know how the Devils knew the Jokers were coming. But I'll ask later, the fact is, they did, and quite possibly saved our lives with the information. Now, it's time to come clean.

"Nah, you haven't got a loose mouth in the club. Beaver and Karl didn't see shit." I take a breath. "Dog wasn't wearing his collar, didn't need it. I didn't think to check out any of his stuff until we had to move. As he's a service dog, there was a fuckin' GPS tracker on his collar. Mystery is how a bunch of fuckin' bikers knew of it, and how to track it."

He stares as if estimating my level of culpability in risking the club members' lives. Then nods. "Would have been useful to know about that earlier, Beef, but can't blame you for not looking. We know the how, but apart from this sorry foursome, we don't know who the fuck else knows you're here. You need to get her out of here as soon as possible. Get her back to the club, and we'll take it from there."

"Hold up, Prez." I raise my hand to stop him walking off. "What about the Wretched Soulz? They want her silenced as much as the Warped Jokers."

He meets my eyes for a second, then looks away. "Shit." The twisting of his mouth shows he's realised giving Stevie our protection openly would be pitting us against the dominant club. "I'll need to have words with Drummer. For now I want her where we can keep an eye on her. She's blind, Beef," he reminds me as if I wasn't aware of the fact. "A helpless woman. Who in their right fuckin' minds would turn her away?"

His words ring in the air for a moment.

"I could..."

"Nah. Whatever you're going to say, Beef, wait until we've sorted this shit here out. We need cleanup for a start."

"I'll sort that," Skull offers. "Christ, did it enough when I was prospecting.

"I'll help."

"Sure, 'Ro." Prez nods at Pyro, then Skull. "When we get back to the clubhouse we'll see what we can get out of the Warped Jokers, then have church and decide what the fuck to do."

"I need to get Stevie." I'm anxious to return and tell her the right side won.

Demon beckons to Thunder, clearly intending on him and his acting VP to accompany me. Not bothering to be quiet, we retrace the steps I'd carried Stevie earlier. Without the weight of my precious burden, we shave minutes off the time. As soon as we draw close, I call out to warn her it's me and that she's safe.

I repeat it again as I draw close to the blind. "Stevie, it's me. Nothing to worry about now. You're safe. Demon and Thunder are with me, the Jokers have been dealt with."

Instead of Stevie, a man steps to the front of the rickety construction, a Glock held in his hands, and it's pointed straight in my direction.

"Stop right there."

Who the fuck is this man? He's wearing a chequered button-down shirt tucked into jeans. He certainly doesn't look like a biker, or someone who'd ride with the Warped Jokers. But from the way he's holding his gun, steady and unwavering directed at its target which happens to be me, he's no stranger to violence. I can detect a military bearing in his stance.

Ignoring the personal threat toward me, I call out, anxiously. "Stevie, you okay?"

"I'm fine." Her voice reaches me from inside the blind.

Relief fills me. There's trepidation in her voice, but no fear. Whoever this man is, she doesn't seem to be afraid of him. *Who could he be?*

"Stay there," the stranger instructs, presumably to her.

"They're the good guys." She's obviously talking to him not to us. "They've been keeping me safe."

A disgusted snort comes from the man with the gun. His full attention doesn't waver from us even though he's having a conversation with the woman still hidden behind him. It's me he addresses. "I suggest you turn around and go. I'll be keeping Ms Nichols safe from now on."

Over my dead body. I don't move an inch. "And who might you be?"

Impatient, Stevie appears, peering around him. "He's Marshal Lennox. He's my contact."

"Stevie, come here," I instruct.

"No, don't..." But Lennox didn't expect a blind woman to move so fast and assuredly in my direction. He's clearly flummoxed that she's now direct in his sights. His momentary confusion allows Demon and Thunder to draw their weapons and step forward.

The marshal's eyes go from one to the other, then to Stevie who's now in my arms. Even Max turns traitor, sliding out from the hut and coming toward me. Stevie's hands trace the contours of my face, and then down my arms and over my chest. "I heard shooting..."

"I'm fine. We're all fine, Stevie. Don't worry, babe."

"I thought I lost you," she sobs.

"You need to start talking," Demon addresses Lennox. "If you're her contact, how the fuck did anyone know where she was? Where's the leak coming from, Lennox? That you? Mighty suspicious you and those motherfuckers being here at the same time."

The marshal begins to go red. "There's no leak from our department. It must have been Ms Nichols who gave herself away."

Stevie, quick to recover having completed her investigation and seeing for herself I've not been injured, turns around to face him, spitting out, "I'm not stupid. I did nothing."

Lennox shakes his head. "You must have done—"

"Whatever." Demon's hand slashes through the air. "You haven't done a very good job of protecting her so far."

"Neither have you," Lennox retorts. "You led the Jokers right to her."

"That was Max," Stevie enters the conversation. "It had to be the tracker on his collar."

"How did *you* find her?" I ask, suddenly realising what's wrong with this scenario.

A short laugh. "I found her because unlike the Warped Jokers, I can track someone and be quiet about it."

Demon looks at me and raises his brow. I shake my head. He takes the lead again. "I suggest we put away our guns. Seems like we need to have a conversation rather than re-enacting the shootout at the OK Corral."

"You've got your gun on them?" Stevie rounds on the lawman. "Beef saved my life. Twice. Where were you then?" She reaches her hand back and takes hold of mine.

"Come over here, Stevie," Lennox instructs.

"No." The strength in her voice is impressive. "Just because I can't see doesn't mean I'm not a good judge of character. Something's wrong, Leon. Beef's done his best to keep me safe. His club came here today to rescue me. I feel safe with them." She bites her lip. "You told me what would happen while we were waiting in the blind. That you'd give me another new identity. If I go with you, I'll have to start all over again. Max isn't fit enough to work yet. He needs a few more weeks of rest before he can go in a harness again."

She's trembling in my arms. It doesn't take a genius to understand why she's upset. She was assured that a new identity would keep her safe. She moved, left everything and everyone she'd ever known but danger had caught up with her just the same. Now she's being asked to do it a second time.

Marshal Lennox looks flustered, as if he doesn't know what to do. He knows as well as I do, if pushed too hard, Stevie could refuse to testify. She's not a criminal who's got the threat of a prison sentence hanging over her head, she's one of the few put into the witness protection program because she can help put some bad guys away.

I exchange a look with Demon. Putting the onus for her protection on the club puts the Devils right in the sights of the Wretched Soulz. Will he take the easy out offered and encourage her to put her life in the hands of the US Marshals again? The people who've already failed her once.

The prez pinches the bridge of his nose. "Look, I'm not happy staying out here. Fuck knows who's on their way to the cabin even now. It's as compromised as shit. Let's move this conversation back to the compound. Marshal, you're welcome to come back with us too. Far as I can see we've all got one thing in mind, keeping Stevie alive."

As I let out a sigh of relief that for now, at least, Demon appears to be on my side, Lennox looks completely flustered and I don't blame him. It's not often law enforcement is invited into the heart of an outlaw MC.

But as we start walking down the track, Demon pulls me to one side, nodding at Thunder to take my place by Stevie.

He's brief and to the point. "I want to know why and how the fuck Lennox was here. Want him under my eye until he comes clean."

CHAPTER TWENTY-SEVEN

The five of us make our way slowly back down the mountainside, making allowance for Stevie who's picking her way carefully along the trail with the aid of my arm, and yet another makeshift stick Thunder had spied and thoughtfully picked up. By the time we get back to the cabin there's no trace of the Warped Jokers, either dead or alive. The ones still breathing for now, will have been transported back to the clubhouse where they'll be contained in Demon's notorious soundproofed basement. The dead, I'm confident, have been buried somewhere they won't be found. I do see a suspicious shovel with damp mud on it leaning against the wall, but if Lennox notices he doesn't draw attention to it.

We hadn't expected to have Lennox with us, so I'm doubly grateful the prospects have acted fast and have loaded the crash truck with the Joker's rides. Only three bikes remain in sight, Demon's, Thunder's and mine. Those belonging to our enemy will probably, if I know anything about the man at all, have been taken to the auto-shop Pyro manages to be stripped down.

Lennox's car is apparently parked at the bottom of the track. I could make him walk, but that would be petty, so I give him a lift, the air seems easier to breathe when the lawman's out of the truck.

When it's just Max, Stevie and I, I notice she's very quiet. I rest my right hand on her left. "You doing okay?"

A quick glance shows her face scrunching. "When's this going to stop, Beef? I've been run down, fire-bombed and now nearly shot. I gave up everything to be safe, and now it's obvious I'm not. I should have stayed in LA and taken my chances." She's as down as I've ever seen her, tears are leaking from her eyes. "I know we couldn't stay at the cabin forever, but I felt safe there, you know? Now that's just one more place where they've found me."

I don't know what to say to her. Quickly I try to process everything in my mind. I end up speaking my thoughts aloud. "You should have been safe, Stevie. Your new identity should have held up. It should have been easy. You'd have stayed here until the court case, then given your testimony and be free to get on with your life." I don't tell her she'd likely never be able to go back to her old one. She's got enough to worry about for now. The top priority being staying alive until she can testify.

Demon had it right. I don't like how Lennox turned up today either, the timing a coincidence unless, like us, he was keeping track of the movements of the Warped Jokers. Demon made a good call inviting him back to the compound. If there's something suspicious about him, I'd rather have him under my eye so I can keep tabs on him. If he's innocent and as much in the dark as us, pooling our resources could keep Stevie out of the line of fire.

"Do you trust Lennox?"

"Of course." Her answer comes fast. "Leon arranged everything, got me settled here in Pueblo. He's the only one who knows everything about my new life…" Her voice trails off, and then she says simply, "Oh."

"I'm not saying anything, darlin'. But it's the knowledge he possesses, which is what I don't like."

I'll get Cad looking into him. If he can't find enough out, I know Mouse, back in Tucson, would jump to the task. He's got deep web contacts Cad might not have. I want to know whether there's even a sniff of a connection between Lennox and the Warped Jokers' members? Is one a relative? Brother or cousin perhaps. Or maybe he owes them a favour. Talking about the marshal makes me glance in my rearview mirror, yeah, there he is, right behind. Would he put his head in the lion's den if he's guilty? He might, if he was trying to get close to Stevie, to persuade her to leave with him so he could take her out.

Stevie goes quiet again. I wish I could say something to comfort her, but the future's unknown. One thing I feel in my gut, I'm not letting Lennox move her, not while we still don't how her new identity was discovered. Until we know the who and why, she could be found again in another location, and I wouldn't be there to help her out.

No. For now she's sticking close to my side.

We come up to the compound. Beaver's eyes open wide when he sees my companion. Guess he bought the story about her moving on. *Or did he think the Warped Jokers would have killed her this morning?* Nah, doesn't fit. He'll know by now there were no losses on our side, and that would include anyone who we were protecting.

For a moment as I drive around the back and park, I wish I was back in Tucson. Here I don't know who I can trust or put my faith in. Not that I've actually spent long enough on the compound to find out.

I lift Max out of the truck and clip his lead on, then help Stevie down. She sniffs the air and gives a weak grin. "Well now I know we've arrived. I can smell oil and gas."

"Yeah, we're here," I confirm, needlessly. "Ready to go inside?"

"How many men in the club, Beef?"

Hmm. Mentally I count them up. "Fourteen, nah, sixteen.

There's two just been patched in as new members. And me, for now."

"You outnumber the Warped Jokers, or those on the outside."

"Sure do, darlin'."

It's clear she's searching for something to give her confidence, so now's not the time to remind her about the dominant club who also doesn't want her to testify.

Having witnessed her depression on the drive here, I'm heartened when she draws in a deep breath and straightens her back, before demanding with lips curved up, "Lead on, then." I have to smile at the instruction that's becoming familiar.

I take her arm. As I've parked the truck at the rear of the building, it's quicker to take her through the entrance that leads to the kitchen, rather than back around to the front. The kitchen is full of women. Most I know from the times I've been here before, but there's a new woman who catches my eye. She's wearing respectable clothing so she's certainly no sweet butt.

"Hi Stevie. Remember me? I'm…"

"Jayden. And I can hear Violet, can't I?"

"Yup, I'm here."

Stevie tilts her head toward the stranger who'd been speaking as we walked in.

"I'm Melissa," the new girl replies. "I'm with Skull."

Oh, yeah. He mentioned he had a woman. "He claimed you?" I ask, wondering whether in the time I've been gone she's been officially added to the ranks of the old ladies.

"He has." It's Jeannie who answers, putting her arm around the girl she appears to have taken a liking too. Jeannie's been in the club getting on forty years now. If she's okay with the newcomer, that probably means she'll be alright.

"I'm Jeannie, I keep everyone in line." The way she says it means Stevie doesn't need to see the wink she gives to Violet, the prez's old lady, to know she's joking.

"Melissa likes cooking," Violet explains with a gleam in her eye, "especially baking. Get ready to put on some weight when you taste her muffins."

"My mouth's already watering." Jayden licks her lips, then leans over. When she straightens, she stands with a baby in her arms. "Think Theo's teeth are bothering him, Vi."

"Oh, give him to me," his mother requests and starts fussing over him.

"How old is your baby?" Stevie asks, and it seems to be from genuine interest and not her just being polite.

Violet answers, at the same time as Jeannie bends her knees to kneel on the floor, her knees creaking. "Who's this?"

"Max," I tell her. "Stevie's seeing-eye dog."

"He okay?" While I've foregone his bandage for a few days, his shaved legs and scarring show he's been through the wars.

As Stevie crouches down by Jeannie's side, affectionately stroking her dog and explaining, I sum up the scene. There are things I need to be doing, but I reckon Stevie will be fine if I leave her with the women for now.

"I gotta talk to the prez, babe. You gonna be okay?"

Violet's eyes meet mine and she raises her chin in a gesture she must have caught from Demon. "Stevie will be fine. But the dog…"

I swing around in time to see Bitch with her back arched and her fur erect walking into the kitchen. Max tilts his head to one side, then starts stretching out his nose. Then rears back with a yelp.

"Max! Beef! Is he alright?"

I kneel quickly. Bitch slapped him in the face, but he's only got a slight scratch. "Max is fine. I think Bitch just put him in his place."

"Come here, Max," Jeannie coaxes. "Oh you poor boy, beaten up by a cat. You're never going to live it down."

Bitch, seeming to have successfully conveyed that the clubhouse is hers, and Max only here on her sufferance, sits down and starts washing herself. Max inches closer to Jeannie, lapping up any sympathy he can get while keeping one careful eye on the cat.

"I'll be fine," Stevie answers belatedly. "You go and do your manly stuff. Just one thing, Beef. If it's about me and my safety, please don't keep me in the dark."

A reasonable request, and one I can agree to. Won't be able to share club business, or perhaps how we get to know what we do, but if it's information she needs, I'll happily share it with her.

Leaving the kitchen, it doesn't surprise me to see money is already changing hands. Rusty's grasping a fistful of dollars as Bitch's antics had clearly been observed.

"Cat knows who's boss," Rusty's saying sagely to a disgusted looking Ink.

"Dog's hobbled," Ink grumbles. "He's only got three working legs. Dynamics might change when he's back to form and can chase her."

"It was who'd win today we bet on," Rusty insists.

I catch the eye of the marshal who's got a mug of coffee in his hand, seeming unamused by the antics. The bikers are holding beer bottles. Guess he wants to remain sober while on duty.

"Beef! Prez wants you."

"Sure thing." I wave my hand toward Thunder, then go to see Demon.

He nods me to the seat opposite and wastes no time on pleasantries. "Lennox is chomping at the bit to get started. He wants to know what we know, and what we're going to do about it."

I shrug. I'm not surprised. I am shocked he's giving us time to get our stories straight and isn't busting the door down. But then he is here on sufferance and must know that.

"Demon, if you hadn't come today… How the fuck did you know to warn me?"

"You can thank Cad. He's been checking the camera feeds from the CCTV over town. Caught a whiff of the Jokers yesterday. Had Ink tailing them. Soon as he saw the direction they were heading, he called me. I called you." He breaks off and shrugs. I'm just fucking thankful they did.

I nod as I digest that, then ask, "What are we going to do with our Jokers?"

"Leave them in the basement for now. They're not going anywhere. I think we'll question them *after* the marshal leaves." As I grin in full agreement, Demon continues, "Told Lennox he's going to have to kick his heels for a few. Thunder's keeping a close eye on him. Need to do something first and want you sitting in." He takes out his phone, presses a couple of keys and puts it halfway across the desk.

It's answered almost immediately. "Drummer."

"Need your advice." Demon doesn't introduce himself. "Got Beef with me."

"Yo, Beef."

"How you doing, Prez?" Fuck, it feels good to give the right man that name.

"Drum. Got a problem. Need direction on how you want to play it." Demon quickly summarises what's gone down today, the Warped Jokers, the Wretched Soulz, and how our paths have crossed.

There's silence on the other end of the line, then, "What's the bitch like, Beef?"

"Good woman, Prez. Deals well with her disability. Not someone who deserves to be caught up in something like this."

"Okay, let's talk this through. The Warped Jokers have earned a reputation that the Devils try to steer away from. Last I heard they were running drugs, guns and women. Got a brothel or two set up in LA where the girls aren't all willing. We may not walk the right side of the line, but we don't go so far in that direction."

Demon shudders. "That shit only brings down trouble."

"I couldn't call them, brothers, Drum."

"I hear you Beef. Our problem is, where do the Wretched

Soulz stand? I can see their point, let the feds take an MC on a RICO ticket, might get them casting their net wider. On the other hand, throw the feds a bone, let them take a dirty club down, and maybe they'll have satisfied their quota. At least for now."

"Be bad publicity for any MC."

I can imagine Drummer's lips quirking. "Or good in some circles. Not good to be seen as weak."

"Get recognised for a fuckin' bank job where people were killed?" I say incredulously.

"Your woman, Beef. She can hold her own in the courtroom? She being coerced by the feds?"

"Nah, she's doing this because she thinks it's the right thing." I ignore his reference to her being my woman. "She willingly got into the witness program to keep herself and her family safe, and so she can stay alive to give that testimony."

"Demon. You say you're getting pressure from the local Wretched Soulz chapter?"

"They're acting on what's coming out of LA from what I can see."

"Okay. Their chapters are basically autonomous, and I don't know many folks from the LA branch. Let me get Chaz's thoughts on it."

Chaz is the president of the Arizona Wretched Soulz. It would at least be useful for Drummer to talk to him.

We thank him, then end the call.

Demon gazes at me thoughtfully. "Don't know what will happen if we have to go head-to-head with the Wretched Soulz. That's why I needed to give Drummer the head's up."

Fuck. This is serious. Satan's Devils would not survive a war with the Wretched Soulz, that's something I don't even want to think about. Lennox could take Stevie, set her up somewhere new, but can we trust him? I'm not convinced. The wheels in my head turn fast. Visions of Stevie so competent at the cabin, thoughts of her under me in bed. The realisation I'm not ready to lose her.

I reach the only solution I can. "I'm not leaving Stevie to go somewhere alone." I bow my head for a second, then look up decisively. "If it comes to it, I'll turn in my patch and go off the grid."

His hand crashes down on the desktop. "She's not even your bitch, Beef. How could you think of doing something so fuckin' drastic? How would you survive? No club, no brothers behind you?"

Another rise and dip of my shoulders. I could have lost her today. Third time she's come far too close to being killed. I couldn't live with myself if anything happened to her, not if I could have been there to prevent it. She means more to me alive, than my being a biker. "Doesn't matter, Demon. I've made up my mind. Nah, she's not mine, but how could she survive on her own?"

"She was doing okay in a strange city until they caught up with her. Cad could sort her out with a new ID, we do it ourselves. Find somewhere new to send her."

"That was before she was looking over her shoulder all the time," I reply, firmly. "She's scared out of her wits now. You wouldn't think it to look at her, but she's had her confidence shaken. Wit Sec should have been fuckin' fool proof, that's what she was told. She agreed to lose contact with family and friends, everything familiar so no pressure could be brought on her to not testify. Now it's all fucked up, she's never going to trust she's safe ever again. She'll always be waiting for someone to catch up with her. Someone she literally wouldn't see coming."

Demon's finger and thumb find the top of his nose. A minute or so passes before he next speaks. "We need to be able to reassure her it won't happen again. Trouble is, I don't know how much time we have. Word gets out she's here on the compound, we might have the Wretched Soulz knocking at our door before we're ready." He breathes in deep, then lets it out as a sigh. "What if you persuade her not to testify?"

"Don't think I'd be able to do that. Look at everything she's lost getting this far. She'd have given up everything for nothing."

"Or, she might be safe if she agrees to keep her mouth shut and be able to return to her family."

She might be able to at that, but my gut tells me Stevie would find it hard to live with herself if she didn't bring the bad guys to task. She still has nightmares of shots firing and people screaming. She'd be adding guilt on top of her uselessness at the time to do anything to help, she won't be getting justice for those who lost their lives. Knowing the woman as I've come to, I don't think she'd rest easy doing that.

My face shows I'm dubious that such a suggestion would work.

Slowly, Demon nods. "Keep that thought to yourself for now then, but it's an option. Now," his voice lightens, "shall we see what our marshal has to say?"

"Yeah. How do you want to play it?"

He inhales sharply, then the corners of his mouth turn up. "Shall we subject him to church?"

As long as Demon is confident everyone can mind what comes out of their mouths, why the fuck not?

While Demon gets a prospect to round everyone up, I go out to grab a beer from the bar. Lennox steps forward sharply as soon as he sees me, and steps in my way. Takes a brave fucking man to impede my progress to the bar. A warning growl sounds in my throat.

"What the fuck is going on?"

"What's going on is I'm going to get myself a fuckin' drink." I go to push past, then take pity on him. "Prez is calling the brothers together now. You're going to be invited into church."

He rears back a little. "I take it that's what you call your meetings?"

I grin evilly. "Or it could be where we torture the truth out of somebody."

To give him his due, he doesn't flinch. "I've got nothing to hide. You, on the other hand…"

"Run a clean club," I finish for him. "You won't be finding any skeletons in our closet."

CHAPTER TWENTY-EIGHT

While Beaver is gathering the troops, I check on Stevie. She's still in the kitchen but now sitting at the table with a can of soda open in front of her. Max is lying at her feet. As I walk in she's laughing, and I pause to listen to the sound. It's genuine laughter, signalling she feels safe and relaxed. After the trauma of the day, shit the past couple of weeks, it's good to hear her happy.

I vow there and then to work to put a smile back permanently on her face. She doesn't deserve to live with stress and fear or have a death sentence hanging over her. Briefly my fists clench at the thought of her lying cold and dead on a slab. I'll do everything I can to prevent it. If that means giving up my patch, I'll just have to make it work.

Her mirth ending, she half-turns in my direction. "Is that you, Beef?"

"Yeah, darlin'." I smile at the confusion on the other women's faces, knowing she must have recognised my steps, the way that I breathe, or just sensed my presence, just like I would her if she walked into a room. "You doing okay? Just going to have a meeting."

She waves her hand in a dismissive gesture. "I'm fine here.

Making friends." She smiles broadly. "And I've been advised not to move until those muffins come out of the oven. Apparently, they don't last long if you're not first in line."

Content she's alright, I leave her with her new acquaintances, noting Jayden's absence. Then, after having a quick word with Karl to keep a careful eye on her, I follow the brothers who are coming in and heading straight for church. Not for the first time I wish I had my Tucson brothers around me. Men, who I could predict how they would react.

I realise I'm not being fair. One hint of trouble today and these men put their lives on the line for me. Acknowledging that thought, as I walk in, I raise my chin in turn to Thunder, Pyro, Ink, Rusty and Skull. Translating my gesture, I get various reactions in return, a number of ways of saying, no problem. They'd have done the same for any brother.

Paladin's the last to enter. From the flush on his face I suspect I know where Jayden had disappeared to. I grin at him. Seems they've progressed a long way from just holding hands.

Lennox is already seated at the end of the table; I take the empty chair beside him. Wills and Dan, so recently patched in they haven't been given road names yet, can't hide the excitement on their faces as they attend their first proper church. I can still recall what it was like to progress from prospect to member. A feeling of pride, and an underlying concern they'll do something to fuck up. I don't expect them to do much talking.

Demon bangs the gavel, but it doesn't take much to get our attention. With a marshal seated at the table everyone wants to know what's going on. I wonder how Demon is going to handle this. I do notice his father, Hellfire, watching him with a mix of interest and concern.

"Right. No point starting anywhere other than introducing Marshal Lennox." The marshal gives a small nod on hearing his name but doesn't say a word. "There are several questions we want answered."

Lennox's lips narrow. "Not saying I'm going to be able to

satisfy your curiosity."

I raise my hand. Demon nods. Twisting my body slightly, I'm now facing the marshal. "I don't think you're in any position to do otherwise." As I pause, the men around me growl as I'd hoped, reminding him exactly where he is, in the lion's den. "I'll start. I'll tell you what we know, then you'll better know where to fill in the gaps. To begin with, let's get this straight. Stevie did everything she was told to do to protect her identity. She lived the role she was supposed to and did nothing to knowingly expose herself."

He raises his head and creases his eyes. "You sure about that?"

"Certain." I wait for him to take that in, then continue, "Stevie witnessed a crime." I change the direction of my focus, making sure everyone at the table understands. "A shooting so callous, she still has nightmares about it. She still hears the sounds of shots and screaming echoing in her head."

Lizard passes a hand over his face, while Bomber uses words. "Poor little girl."

I lift my chin in confirmation. "She wants to do right, have the bad guys put away so they can't do that again. Trouble is, it's an MC she's up against, so the feds decided to pursue a RICO indictment. That's something no club wants brought to their door as it takes down all the members, whether or not they were the ones actually doing the crime."

The marshal gives nothing away, no movement, no expression.

"She's blind, and she's got a service dog. A service dog with a GPS tag so he can be located if he goes missing."

"What the fuck?" Lennox pushes his chair back and stands. "What the ever-loving fuck?" He paces the room as he realises the implications. "But who would know about that?"

"Just as important," Cad pipes up, "how can whoever knew get into the right database and search for that information?"

"Let's leave that for now. Sit down, Marshal." I wait until he does so before continuing. "You want to know why this club is protecting Stevie? It's all down to me. I witnessed a hit and run, the fuckin' dog pushed her out of the path of the car, got clipped himself." I wait a second for that to sink in. "Woman was torn up about Max who not only is a companion, but her lifeline. So I helped her out. Went to talk to her about her situation. Fuckin' lucky I did. I was there when a fuckin' firebomb was thrown into the house. The backdoor was blocked. If I hadn't had been there, she might not have gotten out."

"I didn't know about the dog but knew about the fire." Lennox's voice and face are grim. "Had to wait for the fire-fighters to confirm there wasn't a body in there. That's when I lost track of her."

"Which brings us to how the fuck did you know where to find her today? I want to know why you were so conveniently there." If my tone is menacing, it's because I mean it. "Could be you're the one tracing the tag and found her."

Lennox looks stunned and quickly shakes his head. His lips press together, then he seems to come to a decision. "Look, I've been chasing my tail trying to find her. Thought the Warped Jokers had gotten her, thought she might already be dead." He grimaces, then continues, "I'd almost given up hope when I got a call from the cops they'd seen Jokers in town. I came back to Pueblo to find them. Put two and two together. If they already had her, they wouldn't be hanging around."

"Didn't you think to pick them up and question them? You knew her cover had to have been blown."

"Sure, I was going to work with the local cops, but I didn't have a chance. Almost as soon as I spotted them they were getting ready to ride out, I followed them. I'd put my own tracker on one of their bikes. A bike that's now in your auto-shop."

I let that pass, not wanting to draw attention to the sudden flare in Pyro's eyes, confident the tracker will be found and destroyed. "So, you followed them today?"

Another raise and dip of his head. "Sure did. They headed up to your cabin. I parked up, followed on foot. Didn't know at the time that that's where Stevie was hiding, they could have just been holing up there themselves. I got close enough to hear them talking. They'd expected to find Stevie there, and were making plans how to approach to catch her unawares. I was faster and skirted around them. Picked up your track immediately. You, cleverly, headed off into the forest." He gives me a brief grin. "You passed me walking down. I assumed you'd hidden Stevie, and I found her. Well, you know the rest. Now she's under my protection again."

His story sounds plausible. But there's one thing I don't like. "Lennox, she was almost killed three times on your watch. There's a leak somewhere."

He shakes his head. "Never lost a witness from Wit Sec yet. The US Marshals are tight."

"I suggest you stop regurgitating that shit as you almost lost this one." Demon's voice thunders from the top of the table, making the point better than I could. "I've not decided whether I trust you or not, but one thing we stand for is not hurting women or failing to protect them." He pauses, then his hand bangs the table twice in quick succession. "If you didn't open your mouth, who did? The dog's tracker is almost definitely how they found her. So who's got access to the GPS database where his details will be lodged. And who the fuck knew what to look for?"

Demon's final words ring around the room in the sudden silence as all eyes stare at the man who's got no real rights to be here. Lennox shifts uncomfortably, then pushes back his chair and starts to stand.

"Where the fuck do you think you're going?"

The strength and loudness of the prez's voice makes Lennox straighten his back. "I'm taking this back to my colleagues. We'll start…"

"You're not starting anything," I growl. "The leak may have come from within your organisation."

Lennox's cheeks glow red. "We're watertight. We've never…"

"Well you fuckin' nearly have now." My fist comes down so hard on the wooden table top I wouldn't have been surprised to hear it crack. "You don't know who you can fuckin' trust. You don't know if someone's got a brother, or sister, or cousin first removed with a tie to the Warped Jokers."

With his cheeks puffed out, Lennox spits out, "All my teams are background checked and have security clearance."

"So that's okay then?" My tone is sarcastic. Then my voice sharpens. "Then who else knows?"

Lennox grimaces. "Local law enforcement is informed as a courtesy when we relocate a witness into their town."

"What the fuck?" Thunder roars. "The cops know?"

"Ninety-five percent of the time, witnesses are people who have been involved with a crime, but who have agreed to testify. They get a new identity, help finding a job. But in the end, we're relocating a problem into a town. Local lawmen have the right to be given a heads up in case they go back to their old ways."

"Stevie's committed no crime," I say tensely. "There's no reason for the cops to know."

Marshal shrugs. "We just followed procedure."

"A cop could access the database with the dog's details," Cad suggests.

Lennox looks a mixture of relieved, confused and annoyed. "We haven't had problems before." He stares down at the table, then raises his eyes to meet Demon's. "Any local cop you don't trust?"

"Them all?" Pyro throws in, then sits back with a huff.

Prez answers more seriously, "Apart from you? No."

He looks down the table toward his father. Hellfire shrugs. "We try to avoid them when we can. Got a new police chief in recently, but as far as we can tell, he's straight."

"When did he take the job?" Lennox asks tersely.

When he's told, he shakes his head. "Date's don't match up. He couldn't have known at the time that we were going to place Stevie here."

The marshal slumps in his seat. Then suddenly he sits back up. "Of course, if they hadn't so conveniently disappeared, we could ask the Warped Jokers outright." His voice sharpens. "What have you done with them?"

Demon stares back at him steadily. "They got the message they weren't welcome in Pueblo. Must have headed back to whatever hole they came from."

I work hard at suppressing my grin. Yeah, for two of them, that's a nice deep hole in the ground. Our next step will indeed be to question the two still breathing, but that's something the likes of Lennox will know nothing about. Don't want anyone connected to the law poking into the way we manage that particular business.

"I'd like to ask a question." Buzzard leans forward, then twists his head. "If we're proposing to keep this woman safe, how long? When is the trial, Marshal?"

It's a good question. I hadn't thought to ask. I raise my chin toward the treasurer.

"Two months off. It's been put back once, but prosecutors are determined it should go ahead this time."

So we need to keep Stevie safe for eight weeks. Ideas start running through my head. *Take her to Tucson? Take her somewhere completely different?* I realise there's no conflicting thought in my head, every suggestion I'm making to myself has her and I inextricably linked together. Two months isn't a long time. I can put my life on hold for that. Okay, so it might be longer until I'm assured she can safely be left on her own or can go back to the bosom of her family.

There's a conversation going on around me, but I'm focused on the one going on inside my head. I'm loathe for Stevie to walk off with Lennox, not just because I don't think he can keep her safe, but because I don't want to lose her, and I can't see my views changing any time soon. She might not have been in my life long, but already I don't like the idea of living without her. Like a lightbulb belatedly going off in my head, she's not an example of the kind of woman I'm looking for in my life, she's the one. I'm not going to let her slip through my fingers.

Of course, I don't know what her answer would be, but if she's prepared to have a place in my life, I'd be willing to claim her. Put my patch on her.

In doing so, I have to accept my offer to give up my own patch and my club might not be temporary but could be permanent. I'm proposing to put my life on hold, or change it for good, all to bring down an MC which, however much I don't like that particular club, is part of the world I've bought into.

Is she worth that?

She's worth that and more.

"You with us, Beef?"

I snap back to the meeting in hand and give Demon a sharp nod.

But it seems it's drawing to a close in any event. We've achieved our objective. Lennox will be leaving with suspicions of how the Warped Jokers came to disappear, but no evidence. He'll also know we weren't the ones who traced Stevie to this town. If he's dirty he's found we know nothing that would point to him, no reason to try to take us down.

Lifting the gavel and turning it over in his hand, Demon looks first at Cad then down to the end of the table. "You go do what you have to do, Marshal. In the meantime, Stevie will stay here, and we'll keep her safe." He looks at me pointedly as he says it.

Lennox huffs, but must realise he's beaten. At the end of the day, it's Stevie's choice and he knows it. If he wants her to testify, he needs her alive. Having put doubts in his head, he can't trust his own organisation.

It must stick in his claw, I think, as he stands to leave, that the only people he can trust are an outlaw MC.

CHAPTER TWENTY-NINE

"You want to be in on questioning the Jokers?" Demon asks as we leave the meeting.

"He wanted to kill her, Demon. Went to the cabin with that intention. Yes, I fuckin' want to question them with my fists and leave nothing of him."

The prez's lips twitch. "Can't get answers if he's dead. I let you down there, you could kill him before he talks, not that I'd blame you."

I nod. He's suggesting I step back and let others lead. The way I'm feeling right now, I can see his point. "Okay. You know what I need, Prez. Any info about where and how the Jokers were getting their information."

"Mace is a good enforcer, Beef. He'll get every last thing that he knows out of him."

I purse my lips thinking. Bloody my hands to do something that anyone here is capable of, or, pursue my woman who I've neglected for long enough. "Let Mace do it."

Prez claps his hand on my shoulder as though I've come up with the right answer. "Trust us, Beef."

To my surprise, trusting this new set of brothers isn't as hard as I would have expected. I watch as Demon goes to confer with

Mace, suddenly confident they'll do the job as well, or perhaps better, than I could myself. They aren't invested in the same way or have the desire to make the man hurt for personal reasons. Pain will be inflicted, yes, but in a clinical way designed to get all the information.

I let them walk off, knowing I can rely on them to get results, and go to find Stevie.

My own thoughts are now straight in my head, and I know I want to pursue a relationship with Stevie. I suppose I need to get her views on the idea as well. I want her in my life, but I need to consider she might not want me in hers. All very well for me to decide to take her away, she might have alternative ideas.

She's where I left her, and it indeed seems like she's been getting on well with the rest of the women. When I ask her to come with me, she takes a moment to say her goodbyes, while I wonder what her relationship was like with her family, and how many friends she had to leave behind. She's not shy or awkward, in fact she seems to be outgoing. She holds up her hand to stay me for a second, while she leans in, and then laughs loudly at something Jayden says.

At last, her attention is on me. She takes my arm as I lead her across the clubroom.

"Stairs." I place her hand on the banister. "Last one coming up." I turn to watch Max who's following. Unlike the rickety steps in the cabin, he seems to be managing these well. "Right along here." I take her elbow and make sure she's walking straight, noticing it's become second nature to guide her. Doesn't hurt that I love the connection, my skin to her flesh. What had I thought in the beginning? That she'd be a burden? Far from it. Just means adjusting some of my behaviour is all and remembering to use verbal not visual cues.

That also means ensuring she knows where I've brought her. "Bedroom."

"Mine?" She sniffs the air. "Is it the same one I stayed in before?"

"There are no free rooms here, Stevie. This is mine. Last time I slept on the couch, but I can't do that every night. You'll be staying with me."

Her face tilts up. "We'll be sleeping together?" Her expression conveys neither disgust nor pleasure.

"I can keep my hands to myself." I can, but it will be hard. I remind myself she doesn't know of my decision to claim her. *Ease her in gently?* Yeah, I can do that.

She nods. Her hands stretch out in front of her. Guessing she's heading for the bed, I guide her to it, placing her hand on the comforter.

"You're tense, Beef. You want a discussion, don't you? Want to set boundaries?" She sits down. "We're staying in the same room. Sleeping in the same bed." Her brow scrunches up. "You say you can keep your hands to yourself, but what if I can't?"

I wonder if I need to say anything at all. *Where's she going with this?*

"You were right, Beef. When we made love, it was perfect."

It had been, but I wouldn't have termed it quite like that. My eyes crease as I wonder where she's going. *Ask for a repeat performance, please?* One I'd be happy to give her every day for the rest of our lives.

Her face falls. "I'd like nothing more than to make love with you again, problem is, I doubt I'd want to give you up if we did. I know you don't want a woman, and I said I didn't want a man..." The way she says it gives me hope she's changed her mind. But then she adds, firmly, "Whatever either of us want, there's no point starting anything between us. Lennox will sort out somewhere for me to go, and I'll start all over again. I may never see you again, Beef." Her voice catches.

I squat in front of her, taking both her hands in mine. "I'm not letting Lennox get in between us. Leave him out of it for now. Talk about us, Stevie. We make a good team, don't we? We're compatible in bed and out. What would you say, if I said I wanted to explore what we have between us? Take the next step?"

"You're suggesting a relationship?"

I still can't read what she thinks,. so I make sure there's no misunderstanding on my part. "That's what I want."

One of her hands leaves mine, and reaches up to touch my face, gently tracing the contours. "You're frowning."

"I'm holding my breath waiting for you to say yes."

The movement of her finger changes, now she's stroking simply to give me comfort. I lean into her touch. "I'd have been in your bed every night if it was that simple, Beef. I'd have ignored all the valid reasons you said for us keeping our distance and tried my hardest so you weren't able to resist me. But you were right then, and wrong now."

I believe it's the other way around, but I'll hear her out, then tell her why she's moving in the wrong direction. "Why, Stevie?"

"Because what I've got to do and your life don't mix. I need to present my evidence and get the bad guys the punishment they deserve. You live and breathe the club."

"Does it worry you, me being a biker?"

"No. Your club is very different to theirs. You wear leather and ride a bike. Hell, even I know there are as many different types of clubs as makes of motorcycles, probably more. I was reading about one the other day for members of law enforcement, firefighters and the like. The Warped Jokers are a long way distant from you. If I hadn't been convinced of it before, I learned a lot from listening to the old ladies."

She seems to have learned a lot in a short space of time. "You were asking questions?"

"No, not me. Melissa. I gather she and Skull are quite new, and she was trying to learn what it was going to be like to be an old lady."

"Yeah, he's only recently claimed her. Any old lady needs to be able to handle the club."

She giggles softly. "I may have learned the term, *club business.*"

"Yeah? Would you be alright with that?"

"Beef," she sighs. "We deviated from our conversation. I'm okay with club business as it will never be mine. I'm moving on as soon as Lennox can arrange it."

"Babe," I start, knowing I've got to spell out some facts of life. "It's not safe for Lennox to set you up somewhere else. You've been found once, maybe you'll be traced again. Here you've got me, and my brothers, to protect you."

"They found me because of Max's tracker," she says quickly and adamantly. "He's not wearing that now."

"Stevie," I say her name in exasperation. "What you're missing out is someone knew he had a tracker and could get into the database to trace it. It wasn't some random person, they were trying to find you. Somewhere, somehow, someone's resourceful as well as dirty. Maybe Lennox himself. Until we know who and why, there's always a risk that they'll just use another way to find you. If you're intent on testifying, you won't be any use if you're dead."

She stands, her body poised as if she's about to pace, when her brain kicks into gear reminding her she doesn't yet know the lay out of the room. I move myself, quickly lifting my duffle I'd left lying on the floor and kicking my boots under the bed. But she sits back down and bangs the cover with both hands in frustration.

"I have to testify, Beef."

"Do you?" I suddenly challenge. "Is putting the Warped Jokers away, destroying their club, worth your life?"

"You don't understand." Her voice has grown louder. "It's all I can do. *I* was the only one they left alive. Everyone else was killed because they'd seen their faces. I shouldn't be here now. If it wasn't for the fact I was blind, I'd already be dead. I have to do something. I have to. If that means taking a risk, trusting the people who should know best because we've both got the same end in mind—me turning up in court—then that's what I'll do."

Suddenly words are circling around my head. *Survivor's guilt.* "Oh, babe." I can't keep my hands off her. I pull her into me, holding her close as she begins to sob. I've spoken about it, know about it, damn, even diagnosed I suffer from it myself, but hadn't deep down appreciated why she'd given up so much. *She thinks she doesn't deserve to be here.* As her tears dampen my shirt, I try to think what I can say.

"Stevie, listen to me. You deserve to be happy. You deserve to live. You know what happened to me? I was as close to death as anyone could be. Hell, all my brothers had said their final good-byes. Fuck knows how or why, but I woke up. I've been given another chance. Three times they've tried to kill you, and three times they've failed. You stop and think for a moment. Maybe there's a reason for that. Maybe you are meant to testify, but your life doesn't end after that. You deserve to be happy."

"I'm glad you didn't die, Beef."

"Me too, babe, me too. But it has made me think about things differently. Maybe at first I made a mistake, grabbing my chance of happiness because, hey, I'd had a reminder life can be short. That's why I leapt for the first woman that crossed my path. Now I think maybe I was pushed your way, to help you and save you."

"I don't need saving…"

"Yes you do." I hug her again. "From those thoughts in your head if not from anything else. It's a fuck of a thing you're dealing with. That those bastards left you alive as a joke, because they thought your lack of sight made you useless. To my mind, your blindness saved you, just like something saved me. Mira-cles, both of us."

"Another thing in common but doesn't mean we should be together." She inhales deeply. "Am I not just another Sally? Someone you think you were saved to look after? I don't *need* you, Beef."

"I know you don't *need* me, and that's why you're nothing like Sally." I let go of her, and put my head in my hands, wondering how I can explain it. "I can investigate Lennox, and if he comes up clean, let him take you somewhere no one can find you." And threaten him with death if a hair of her head gets harmed. "That would be me doing my job and looking out for you. Max will soon be able to work again, I know you'll find your way in a new town with him by your side. You don't *need* me. But I *need* you."

"Beef." Her small arm hugs as much of me as she can.

"Listen. My sensible head tells me that's what I should do, but inside I can't let you go. How could I rest or settle, knowing you were out there, somewhere, and I could never see you? Never speak to you? Never watch you burn bacon…"

I duck her hand, then grab hold of it.

"I couldn't Stevie. I can't let you go. I didn't *need* Sally. Didn't need her to be in the room to be able to breathe."

"That's how you feel about me?" her voice sounds small.

"Yeah. Look. We can do this your way. You think the marshals are best placed to look after you. If that's the case, I'll come with you, Stevie. You'll never be alone again. If you can put up with my ugly mug in your life, I'll be by your side forever."

She's quiet. She looks stunned. "I don't know what to say, Beef. I know how this works, you don't. I'll be given a new name, a new identity…"

"I'll have one too."

"You'd have to leave your club…"

"I'll leave it."

"No." Pulling sharply away, she stands again. "I can't ask you to do that. You have no idea how hard it is to leave behind everything you've ever known."

"But I've got a fuckin' good imagination, babe. Yeah, the hardest thing in the world. You did it because you wanted justice for those people you were with at the end of their lives. Don't you think I've got just as strong a reason for changing my life too?"

"Why Beef? Why would you even consider doing something so drastic?"

I stand. My hands move to her biceps, and I grip, lightly. "Because I can't stand to see you walk out of my life. Love my brothers, course I do. But I could also so easily love you, if you let me."

"You don't know me."

"What don't I know about you? I know you're loyal. I know you're brave. I know you love fiercely. I know the type of films you enjoy and those you don't, I know which foods you prefer. I know you're hardworking—"

"Beef," she stops me. "I'm blind."

"So what? If you need me to do something, I'll do it. Whether you can see or not."

I've stumped her. But I should have known she's got more.

"I won't have children."

"Stevie..."

"No, listen Beef. My blindness is hereditary. There's a fifty percent chance of passing it on. And any child who inherited it could go deaf as well."

I can't argue with that, can't offer platitudes. Can't say it's a risk worth taking. She's clearly thought a lot about this, and the one who's lived losing her sight. I don't know how I'd feel about bringing a child into the world knowing there was a good chance they'd go blind and could lose their hearing too. Any life, as Stevie herself proves, is worth living. But she knows how hard it is, I don't.

"Stevie, babe, I want you. I want what we could have together. If there are some things we can't have, we'll deal." At that moment there's a timely thump thump on the floor as Max wags his tail. It makes me grin. "We've already got someone to care for, Max."

She chuckles as I meant her to.

"He needs to go outside."

"I'll take him."

"Beef, I don't need you…"

"I know you don't need me to do shit for you. But you haven't learned this place yet, you don't have a stick, and Max can't be in a harness right now. It's easier for me to do it."

"Easier, yes. But I don't want to have to lean on you, Beef."

I lean in, my words vibrating against her ear. "I know you don't. But if we're going to be together, we'll be a partnership, babe. You don't have to do everything yourself, and not doing it, doesn't mean you're not capable."

There's a small whine about my knee level. "Come on, Max. Let's go get your business done."

"I can't give you an answer, Beef. I don't know what the best thing to do is. I need to know it's right, for me and for you. If I take you away from everything you love, you could come to hate me one day."

I pause at the door and straighten. "Can't see that happening, and if it did? Nothing to stop me coming back. You're not trapping me babe. Think about it, okay?"

At her 'yes', I open the door, then close it. Max tugs at his leash, but I stand still for a moment. What else can I say to persuade her I'm sincere? It hadn't helped she'd seen the way I treated Sally, but the two women are poles apart. I tried, but I never had one tenth of the emotion for the other woman that I already feel for Stevie, and I'm convinced it will only keep growing.

Another tug from the leash. *Yeah, Max, I'm coming.*

Each day that damn dog seems to move easier. Wish humans healed as fast as animals seem to. Mind you, when we're told to take it easy, we're frightened to push ourselves. A dog just does what it can and doesn't hold back even if its human owners think it's too much. He's steady going down the stairs though I watch him like a hawk.

It's not the first time I've had to clean up dog poo, so I've already got used to carrying a spare bag in my cut. Lizard though barks with laughter. He's sitting outside having a smoke when I bend down, scooping up the mess and tying the bag.

"Least Bitch buries her shit," he calls out.

I walk to the trash can and place the bag inside. Max, knowing he's off duty for now, seems interested in the new smells around him. While he sniffs around, I wander over to Lizard.

"You seem in deep with the woman."

I look at him sharply, seems he sees more than others do. I could tell him he's wrong, but how can I when he's so right. Deciding to be honest, I tell him, "She's one hell of a woman, Liz. She gets me in here," I thump my fist over my heart, "man. The thought of losing her now I've found her? Can't bear to fuckin' think of that."

"Would you leave with her?"

Might as well start laying some ground work. "I might."

He shakes his head. "Most won't understand. But sometimes… I get it, you know? We've got the whores here of course, but the thought of having that one woman..." Breaking off, he huffs a laugh. "Then I 'spect I'd get bored pretty fast. Need some variety."

I'd been faithful to Sally even when she wasn't giving me what I wanted. But Stevie? Might only have had her once, already know she will be all I need to keep me satisfied for the rest of my life.

Max, either growing bored or anxious to be back with his mistress, comes over and sits by my feet. His tongue lolls out of the side of his mouth. Standing, I slap Liz on the back. "There'll be a woman for you, one day. She'll come along when you least expect it."

CHAPTER THIRTY

On my way back through the clubhouse I see Skull with his arm around Melissa. He's tall and skinny, which gave rise to his handle of Runt which had been changed when he patched in. Her head reaches just to his shoulder. He's got both arms around her and is resting his chin on the top of her head. Sparing a thought for another pair at the start of their relationship, I hope it works out. They look like a couple made for each other, the affection is shining out from them both. As long as Melissa can handle the life of an old lady in the MC, I reckon they're a pair with a good chance of success.

Me with Stevie? It's not my life I'm asking her to accept, though I wish that it were. It's me considering being the one making the changes.

"Beef? Got a moment?"

"Sure, Prez. Give me five? Just let me take Max back upstairs."

"Beef! Hold up. Stevie mentioned she needed this. Pal went and got it. Hope it's right."

I swing around and then start beaming at what Jay's holding out. A telescopic white stick, just like the kind Stevie had to abandon when we escaped her burning house.

"She'll be so grateful, Jay. Thank you."

She shrugs. Always noticed that about Jay. She'd help out with any of the kids, seeing what needed doing and doing it, but awkward when it comes to accepting thanks.

I take the stick, and Max, back upstairs. Stevie's sitting on the bed, her head in her hands. Max runs straight across to her and places his head in her lap. Idly she strokes him.

"Jay got you this." I place the stick in her hands.

She smiles broadly and extends it. "It's perfect. I feel so much better having this now."

"Demon wants a word with me. You going to be okay on your own?"

Some of her tension disappears as my absence will give a reprieve on us continuing the difficult conversation we were having. "I'll be fine. Just leave me to get acquainted with my new surroundings. With this," she holds up the stick, "I'm confident enough to go down and find the others."

I'm not letting her off the hook entirely. Going across to her I lean over and cup my hand around the back of her head. Without warning I place the fingers of my other hand under her chin and raise her face up, then my lips come down. Taken unawares she opens her mouth, not wasting the opportunity I sweep my tongue inside.

Christ, her taste. She's so perfect. How could I have ever thought I could walk away? I was a damn fool.

Her arms come up, but not to push me away. She holds me lightly to steady herself, then with a moan, she gives in, starting to kiss me back, her tongue mating with mine. It's as though our mouths are using the words we can't say out loud. Me telling her I never want to leave her side, her perhaps, even now, summoning up ways of telling me a final goodbye.

Eventually, knowing I'm keeping the prez waiting, I reluctantly pull back.

"Beef?" she begins, questioningly.

"Just giving you something to think about," I reply. "See you later, okay?"

Leaving her looking stunned, I shut the door firmly enough so she knows I've gone, and go back down to see what Demon wants me for now. On the way down the stairs I adjust myself in my jeans, her taste having had the predictable effect. That part of my body I've decided to bring into play later in a further attempt to show her how well the two of us work. Yeah, I might have a few ideas in my head which means I'm still dealing with a rock-hard dick as I enter the office of my president.

If Demon notices at least he's gentleman enough to ignore it.

"I've heard back from Drummer," he starts, getting to the point immediately. "Things have been going on behind the scenes."

"And?" I prompt. My ass hitting the seat fast, leaning forward and giving all my attention to the man in front of me.

"The issues are that no one wants the feds to drag an MC into court, nor have it disbanded under a RICO indictment."

My head starts to move back and forth, but before I can get a word out, he continues, "If the Warped Jokers had stuck to their normal trade, handled it under the radar, then they'd have had more support. But they got greedy, acted like fuckin' criminals."

I think for a moment the 'normal trade' of drug, gun running, and trafficking women could also be considered a crime, but let that slip for now. Plenty of MCs earn their money that way, Satan's Devils have got clear of it.

"Drummer spoke to Chaz as he said, who had talks with Stinger, the prez covering the LA Wretched Soulz area. Think they had a conference call with RIP in Colorado. Well, RIP was the one who's been in touch. Wretched Soulz will stand back and let this one play out. They don't want or need to be associated with any injury coming to a federal witness."

Good on Drummer. He would have explained the risk of possible blowback were it to be shown the Soulz had played an active part. Not that Demon isn't a good prez, but he, like me, is too close to the situation. Drummer, reviewing it from afar, had come up with a suggestion.

"So all we need to do is protect her from the Warped Jokers." And from whatever bastard is too close to her trail.

"Not so fast, Beef." I'd expected Demon to be pleased, but he looks anything but. "The dominant had a request in exchange for them to step back."

"Which is?"

"Except under circumstances where an MC sets up without permission or where there's a dispute over territory or direct involvement in another club's business, MCs don't turn on their own. The Wretched Soulz don't want to be anywhere close to the intimidation of a witness, but neither do they want to be seen as supporting the feds over the MCs whose charters they've agreed to."

My brow creases as I try to work through what he's just said. There's a cold feeling in my gut, and I hope I'm reading things wrong. I put one interpretation on it that's not as bad as the next. "They're stepping back and leaving us to fight it out with what remains of the Warped Jokers?" A club with its officers and half its members in jail. No leadership, just foot soldiers. No problem to take them on though I'd have preferred to avoid more bloodshed.

"Nah." Now Demon's eyes rise and look directly into mine. "They've asked that we do nothing to help her. That she's left as the US Marshals problem. Sorry, Beef. Can't risk this chapter. Can't risk this club. This is what the dominant wants. They're neither giving support to the Jokers, or to us."

"But protecting a federal witness isn't the same as offing them…"

His eyes gentle. "We're protecting someone who holds the key to the worst nightmare affecting an MC. RICO."

"I'll take her away." She's going nowhere with that motherfucker Lennox. I don't trust him. Even if he didn't directly betray her, he and his organisation failed to keep her safe.

"I thought you'd say that. Drummer did too. We both saw the way things were heading." He pinches the bridge of his nose in that familiar gesture. "Fuck this is hard, Beef. You'll need to turn in your patch. Ain't enough that you're nomad."

The words are hard for me to say, but I voice them without hesitation. "I'll do that." I mean them. There was a reason I was turned back at Satan's doorway; my time hadn't been then. I'm convinced I was brought back to take care of Stevie.

"Her dog?" Demon asks.

"We'll take him too. He's recovering fast, Prez. Better than I expected. I'll," I choke over the next words, "I'll leave my bike. Borrow a truck." Then get rid of it and swap it at the earliest opportunity. "Can Cad sort us out new identities?"

"You trust the club more than the marshals." It's a statement, not a question, but I reply anyway.

"If Cad can't, Mouse can." I'm quickly thinking through everything that's necessary. "Mouse has underground contacts—"

"Don't underestimate Cad. Nor think if he has a problem, he doesn't consult Mouse, or Hard Token in California, or Vegas's Keys."

I can respect a man who asks for assistance if something is beyond his capabilities. I raise my chin to show I'll leave my future identity in Cad's capable, if very pale, hands.

"Knew that was going to be your answer. Cad's already working on it. Should have something airtight by the morning."

At least they're not kicking us out tonight. That gives me time to talk to Stevie, to convince her and reassure her. "Once the court case is over, I'll want to come back." With Stevie in tow as my old lady.

"Agreed. The Wretched Soulz should be fine when she's no longer working with the feds. Unless there's going to be retribution…"

I just meet his eyes and raise my chin. He knows I'm accepting it may be far longer than that.

For now, I'm just focusing on the shorter period. Two months. I can manage to ride, or drive as it seems more likely, alone for that. Heart went out for six months on his own. Mind you, he went looking for trouble and eventually found it. I'll be trying to evade it.

I'm itching to get back and start talking to Stevie, but there're things I need to find out first. "You get anything out of the Warped Jokers we brought back?"

"Mace and Thunder have been questioning them. Last I heard was they hadn't said anything of importance yet, but Mace's view is that they're foot soldiers who don't know anything."

Could well be. But, "I'd like to ask them myself."

"Yeah, let's go down catch up with the latest. Might have discovered something while we've been chattering."

Offering up a silent apology to Stevie that I'd dropped the bombshell on her about my feelings then abandoned her, I follow the prez down the stairs leading to a locked and extremely well soundproofed door. He unlocks it, we enter.

There's a quiet sobbing coming from the centre of the room. A man is hanging by his wrists attached to hooks in the ceiling, the other is tied to a chair. The man strung up is bruised and bloodied, but it's the seated man who's making the noise.

Mace comes over. "They're blood brothers," he says, quietly. "That one would prefer to be hurt rather than see his sibling abused. Think he might break soon." Then he turns back around. When two pairs of distressed eyes focus on him, he jerks his head toward me, raising his voice, "Well, lookie here, rein-forcements."

Thunder's a big man, Mace not small either. But my build makes me both taller and wider and is why Drummer's used me for muscle in the past. Just one look at me and men are intimidated and start calculating their odds, which are never good. I don't just look the part, I can back it up. Not many men can best me in the ring.

I bash one fist into the palm of my other hand, a warming up gesture. It doesn't go unmissed.

The man on the chair starts thrashing at his bonds. "He's had enough. Use me. Please, not my baby brother, no more."

The man hanging can't take his eyes off me. They're wild, whites showing. His mouth opens, but to his credit, he doesn't beg as I step closer.

"Look, Seeker, this is crazy."

Hanging from arms which must be really aching, Seeker exchanges a look with his brother. "Cray—," he starts, his voice scratchy.

I interrupt. "Only one way out for you, painful or easy. Up to you whether you want to go to your grave with your teeth intact or gone."

Demon puts his hand on my shoulder. "Or we can make this even easier. Way I see it, you don't have a club to betray anymore. The question is whether the feds will take all of you down, or just those already convicted. You tell us what we want to know, I could be persuaded to let you ride out of town."

Another look exchanged between them. Then Cray's attention turns to Demon whose proposal clearly seems more attractive than mine.

"You'll really let us go?"

Demon shrugs. "Depends how much of the truth you tell us. Keep playing it dumb, I'll let Beef here take his time."

I might fight, but I don't like it. I prefer it when they can fight back. I haven't got the ability to distance myself in the same way as an enforcer does it. After Blade's finished with a man back in Tucson he throws up, that's no secret though we don't talk about it. I wouldn't mind betting Mace, who's currently looking calm and collected and ready to go a few more rounds, is similar. But if it's to help Stevie, I'll swallow my repulsion down and use that anger inside me to use an unarmed and helpless man as a punchbag. When they stay silent, I take another step forward and draw back my fist.

"Stop! For the ever-lovin' fuck of God, stop!"

"God's not here," I growl menacingly, though staying my hand. "You're dealing with Satan."

"We were just following orders," Cray cries out. His betrayal causing tears to roll down his cheeks.

"Who gave you the orders?"

"Mad Bull."

"Your president? He's in the pen."

"He got a message out."

"Your orders were to…?"

"Find the blind bitch and take her out of the picture. He gave us the info about where she was. There's an app on my phone, it traces the dog's tracker."

"Took his phone from him, Prez." Thunder steps up and passes it over.

Demon looks at it, then moves over to Cray. His hands are tied behind him, Demon manages to awkwardly get his finger on the right spot. He plays with a few keys, then nods. "Okay, I can open it myself now. I'll get Cad to look at it."

He shows me the screen. He's found the fucking tracking app easily. Every step Stevie had taken with her dog, they were able to follow.

"Why didn't you come immediately after she was reunited with the dog?" I question, harshly.

"At first we didn't think the dog would recover. It spent so much fuckin' time with that vet. Then thought she'd moved on without it. Didn't bother to check, then one day we did. Then we went after the signal. Buck came up first and was watching the cabin from a distance as we still didn't know she was with the dog. We saw you, saw your patch. Then saw the dog and the bitch. Knew we had to come prepared. Needed to get brothers up from LA."

"So you came prepared to kill her?" Demon asks, his tone more reasonable than mine. Mind you, he's not talking about the woman he's coming closer and closer to claiming.

Both men nod, or Seeker does the best he can in his painful position.

"That was my woman you were going to kill," I observe through gritted teeth. My comment makes Demon's eyes flash to mine. I reply to his unspoken question with a slight raise of my chin. No doubt about it in my head. The intense rage I feel faced with these two men tells me my gut feeling's right. *She's mine.* I'm never going to let danger come close to her again or risk losing her.

"Man, we weren't going to *kill* her."

"You threw a fuckin' bomb in her house." I round on Cray incredulously.

"We were told to silence her. After she proved difficult to take out, we came up with a different plan."

Seeker, not seeming to realise the danger he's in, adds, "She's a good-looking bitch. And being blind, she wouldn't have minded who she was opening her thighs to."

Before anyone can stop me, he has my fist in his stomach. As he tries to draw his legs up and gasps for breath, I turn on the man tied to the chair and he gets my fist to his jaw so hard I feel bone crack.

"Way to get them talking, Brother," Mace casually observes, but there's no censure in his tone. He knows, as well as I do, we've probably got all we're going to get out of them for now.

It's who gave them access to the app that's the question we need answered. We might punch them to within an inch of their lives, but they're not going to be telling what they don't know. I've been around clubs long enough to know this pair are typical foot soldiers. They follow instructions, they don't issue them.

CHAPTER THIRTY-ONE

"They've told us everything they can," Demon throws back over his shoulder as we make our way out of the Colorado chapter's basement-come-torture-chamber. Once the door is closed behind us, the sounds of partying in the clubhouse reach us, along with the aroma of cigarette smoke and stale beer. A stark contrast to the begging and pleading, and odour of fear and pain we'd left behind us.

"I agree." It's up to Cad now to investigate and find out what he can. "Be useful if we know anyone in the pen with Mad Bull."

"I'll ask around." He pauses outside his office. "You going ahead with this plan, Beef?"

"It's not that I want to, Prez. But with the Wretched Soulz breathing down your neck, can't see any other option but to take Stevie away." I'm still in the clubhouse but already I'm feeling the loss.

"You'll let us save face. But you need to be in the loop. Keep your burner phone with you so I can keep in touch."

Cad gave it to me. He'll be certain no one can trace either it or Stevie's. If they could, the Jokers would have been at the cabin long before they had. I'm glad Demon wants to stay in contact.

I'll be off the grid, but not entirely. If someone's coming for us, I'll want to get a head's up.

"You going to let them go?"

"Yeah. Don't want to pile up the dead bodies. Now the tracker's removed from the dog, they won't be able to find Stevie that way. Looks like they don't have anything else."

They might not. Doesn't mean anyone else won't.

"I'll keep them on ice until you get clear tomorrow."

Having heard what they'd planned for Stevie, I would have preferred that they shouldn't be breathing. But it's Demon's call, and this is his clubhouse. As long as Stevie and I have a chance to get far away and can't be followed, that's all that matters to me.

I'm anxious to get back to Stevie, we've got a lot to discuss. I've got to persuade her to put her life in my hands rather than that of the marshals. As Demon indicates I should follow him, I sigh, regretting yet another delay. Turns out though, it's worth my while as he leads me over to Cad.

Animatedly Cad turns his screen around to face me. There's a driver's ID on it, my picture, with the name Ben Carter on it.

"Ben?"

"Closest I could get to Beef. If Stevie fucks up, it might be close enough to pass scrutiny or give you a chance to come up with an excuse."

I shake my head, it's going to be hard getting used to a new name. At least my surname's close to my original, Carter instead of Carson.

"I was going to go with Wayne, but that would be even more alien."

To me too. I can't remember the last time I used my government name, Dwayne. Always hated it, was glad to stop using it.

"What about Stevie?"

"She's going to be Sophie. You're newlyweds. So if she slips on the surname, it will be put down to the recent change."

I'm not going to remind him Wraith's old lady is called

Sophie, and Stevie and she are about as far apart as you could get. He's gone to the trouble of getting everything organised. It will have to do.

"You're getting these printed?"

"As we speak. Got a man I use to make them authentic, he's got a stock of the right paper and ink. You'll have them first thing tomorrow. Oh, and Mouse is helping me set you up with a decent history. Once we've done that, I'll let you know the details. Keeping as close as we can to the truth."

A hand lands on my shoulder. "Had to stop Mouse putting your previous career as an exotic dancer."

I swing around fast, then slap my hand on Paladin's back, pulling him to me. "Asshole," I tell him.

He returns my man hug then pulls away. "Pole dancing was going to be your speciality."

"Yeah?" I grin back. "Like to see a pole that could take my weight."

"*That* was the reason you gave it up. You took too many steroids."

"Steroids my ass," I snarl, punching his arm. "Hard work in the gym more like." But he's made me laugh for the first time today.

"Ignore him, he's jealous. Mmm, you've got manly muscles, Beef." Jayden's sweet voice sounds as she comes up alongside her man.

"Don't hear you complaining about what I can do with what God gave me," Pal stage-whispers into her ear.

"Well, if you lovebirds are winding up to a demonstration, I got things I'd rather be doing." I thrust my hips leaving them in no doubt as to my intentions. Then, when they both start laughing, I flip them my finger as I walk off.

I'm still smiling as I go up to my room, or rather, Demon's old one. Seems I won't have spent enough time in it to lay claim to ownership. I was pleased to see Pal and Jay looking so happy and settled in their new environment. If they can move somewhere totally different, grow to call strangers friends, perhaps there's a chance for me too. Mind you, they were moving to what they could already call family. Stevie and me? Well, we'll be totally on our own.

Doesn't mean we can't do it.

And, when it's safe. We can come back.

I pause before turning the door knob. Got to get my head around it might never be safe for her to return. Tomorrow I might be walking away from the Satan's Devils forever. *Am I doing the craziest thing I've ever done in my life? Giving up everything I am for a woman I've known two weeks?* I rest my forehead against the wood, examining my feelings as honestly as I can. What I'd told her earlier is the complete truth. It might not have been long, but the time we've spent together has been intense. I may not know facts or figures, or who she was before she had to hide, but I know *her*, the woman inside. I know she's who I want to spend the rest of my life with. It's not that she's different from Sally, what I feel for her is on another level too. If I have to leave everything behind me, she's worth it. Despite my sadness, there's an undercurrent of excitement too at the thought of taking a step into an unknown future, a new reality that we can shape to our will. With her, beside me, I believe I can be happy. Yes, this is the right thing to do.

Ready, I turn the handle, mentally preparing to now persuade her.

On entering the room, all that greets me is the thump thumping of Max's tail on the floor. He may have overdone it today, as he doesn't leap up to meet me. I go to him, sinking to my haunches and stroking him. "That leg hurting, Max? You'll soon be up chasing rabbits. And where's your mistress, eh?"

My first thought is the bathroom, but the door's open and from here I can see no one is inside. Clubroom? I frown. I hadn't seen her, but she may have been in the kitchen with Jeannie, Sindy or even Mo if Hellfire's old lady made one of her rare visits to the compound. Stevie's clearly left Max here to rest. I stroke him again, seeing his large brown eyes on me. *Why is it dogs always look so sad?*

I stand, my intention to go to find his mistress. When I do so I notice a note propped up against the dresser with my name on it.

That's odd. Stevie's blind.

My senses immediately on high alert, with an unsteady hand I open it and being to read it.

Beef,

I'm dictating this note, and Lennox is writing it for me. I'll sign it so you know it's from me.

Lennox has arranged a new place where I'll be safe. He promises to take better care of me this time. Another marshal will be taking over from him (as Lennox fears he may have been compromised as my handler). He's taking me to him now. I don't know where I'm going, so I couldn't tell you if I wanted to.

I knew this would happen. Lennox has explained my testimony is too important for the government to trust me in anyone's hands but their own. It's why I know they can keep me safe. Their interest is served by keeping me alive.

That's the only reason I couldn't commit to you, Beef, though everything inside me echoes what you said. I know you too. I know you're a good man. I know you'd do everything you can to keep me safe. But at the end of the day, I have to trust the experts. The marshals have never lost a man, or woman, yet.

I'm gutted at leaving you, and also that I've had to leave Max. He's not strong enough to work yet, and I know you'll take care of him. I would be selfish to take him with me before he's healed. I've got my white stick and that will help.

I think I'm almost in love with you too. Probably more than that.

It's best you forget me. If I can make my way back to you, I will, but we need to be realistic, and this goodbye might be final.

You'll have a place in my heart forever. You deserve so much more than the trouble I bring, and which might never be over.

Yours, forever

There's a scrawled signature. A blind woman's attempt to

write her name. A name she's never seen written as it's not the one she was born with. And there, lying where I'd found the note, the phone Cad had given her.

The roar that comes out of my mouth has Max up and growling. My fist slapping into the top of the dresser makes him bark. Without taking the time to calm him, I rush to the door and back out, leaping down the steps, my mind whirling. *Did Stevie dictate that note?* Or did Lennox just write what the fuck he wanted? She'd never know. She could have been tricked into signing it. That might not even be her signature.

The only thing I'm certain of is that it was Lennox who lured her away. She wouldn't have gone with anyone else.

"Demon!" My voice thunders across the room, audible even over the blasting of the jukebox.

Sensing trouble, someone turns the music off. "What the fuck, Beef?" Demon yells almost as loudly as he walks across the room toward me.

Around me I spy men putting hands into their cuts reassuring themselves their weapons are at hand, just like my brothers would have back in Tucson. Devils are Devils. As he nears me, I thrust the piece of paper at Demon, while telling him the bare facts as I know them.

"Stevie's gone. Lennox has taken her."

"On it, Prez." Thunder circles his hand around his head. Without waiting to be asked, Liz, Ink, Pyro, Skull and even the newly patched members, Wills and Dan follow him outside. Within seconds a roar of bikes can be heard as Wills comes running back inside.

"No sign of Lennox or Stevie. Brothers have gone out to see if they can pick up the trail anywhere."

"Who's on the fuckin' gate?"

The two prospects behind the bar exchange looks and bow their heads. Not trusting myself to speak to prospects I've no authority over, I turn my back on them.

"Didn't anyone stop him leaving with her?" I'm incensed. Anyone spotting her leaving should have come running to me.

"Hey, I've been here all the time," Bomber objects fiercely. "Your girl didn't come down this way."

"The fuckin' fire escape." Paladin swears loudly. "Always said we should keep that locked after what happened to Jay."

"It's a fuckin' *fire escape*." Rusty slaps him around the head. "Can't lock it."

I don't give a damn whether we all burn to death. Right now I'd prefer it to that feeling of dread settling in my stomach. *Stevie's gone.* I might never see her again. The room's spinning around me as all the implications set in. *She's gone.* That night I had planned when my cock was going to show her how good we could be together? *Gone.* The loving I'd planned to do to her. *Never get a chance now.*

The implications cause my brain to misfire. I stare without seeing, hear sounds without listening, the rushing in my ears almost too much for me to bear. I let out a scream like a wounded animal and sink to my knees, bending my head and bowing, praying to a God I've no faith in to keep her safe.

"Beef, man. Brother. We'll find her. We'll fuckin' find her." It's Pal who's one side of me, little Jay the other. It's her arms, her touch, I lean into and take comfort from.

"Beef, I'm so sorry. She will be okay. I feel it. I know it. She'll come back to you, Beef." She repeats the words, rearranging the order, then voicing her platitudes once more.

After a couple of minutes, I feel like I can function. "You can't know it, Jay. You, we, can hope. That's all."

Tears are pricking in my eyes, I swipe them away. *I won't give up.* If it would do any good I'd be out searching, but the local brothers know more about the routes out of town that Lennox would take. That's where he'll be heading. He won't be hanging around. Now he's got her in his clutches again he'll have her far away, over the state line as fast as he can.

I've no idea of what direction he'll be heading, no clue where to start searching.

My hopes can only be pinned that he's honest, that he's genuinely doing what he hopes is right for her and that he'll do what he can to keep her safe.

What hope do I have of ever finding her?

I won't even know her name.

"Church," announces Demon, "as soon as the others return."

I don't need to ask if he thinks they'll have caught up with them. We don't know what start they've got, they could be miles away already.

Max. She left her dog. *She left me.*

CHAPTER THIRTY-TWO

Men all talking loudly enter church. As they pass by me their voices falter and looks of commiseration are passed my way. In between discovering Stevie missing and finding my seat at the table, a myriad of thoughts have run through my mind.

I had thought that, finally, I'd found my one, the person I was going to spend the rest of my life with. Fuck, I didn't care if I didn't end up with a family, just Stevie would have been enough to complete my life. Now I've got to face that what was in my head can't have been in hers. If it was, she wouldn't have left without a word. That note, written by a third party, doesn't count.

As Demon takes his place at the head of the table, the last man wanders in, but the door pushes open once more.

Hellfire laughs loudly, the seriousness of the atmosphere broken as a furry head appears, and the body follows to take its place at my feet. I reach down my hand and stroke Max. He must be feeling abandoned just like me. My eyebrow raises in challenge at the prez.

Demon stares back, then shakes his head. "Fuckin' dog doesn't want to be left out. I suppose you want him to stay?"

Not waiting for an answer, he continues, "It's not as though he's going to be giving away anything we discuss."

"Unless he's bugged," Cad says, quite seriously.

He's got a point. But even a dog as well trained as Max couldn't have been told to hang around us in church. No, he's sought out the company of the only person he now has. Nevertheless, I remove his collar, and pass it down the table.

Cad examines it for a moment, then passes it back after removing his name tag. "I'll put this outside and check it later. Can't be too careful after that fucking GPS."

Knowing he's right to be cautious, I don't object as he leaves then returns minus the tag.

"Fuckin' dog a member now, Prez?" Ink grins.

Mace reaches for a cigarette. "Nah, he can't ride a bike."

"Beef could get him a side car."

I don't bother pointing out there's no way in hell I'll be attaching a hack to my bike.

"Honorary member?" suggests Rusty.

"Whatever," Demon remarks with a sigh. "Can we now get down to Beef's problem?"

"Ain't got a problem, Prez." In some ways Max's appearance has consolidated the thoughts I'd had between finding Stevie was missing and the members having gathered for church. At the quizzical looks sent in my direction, I carry on, meeting their faces one by one. "I'm gutted she's gone. Wasn't what I wanted at all, but in the end, maybe this has worked out for the best." She wouldn't have wanted me to claim her. If she had, she wouldn't have left. *Think of the club. The brothers I've ridden beside for so many years.* "Stevie's done nothing but cause us trouble." I absorb the gasps from around me, but don't let them faze me. I've still got the floor, I use it. "She's brought us into the sights of the Wretched Soulz. My solution had been to turn in my patch and take her away, but she's saved me from making probably the worst mistake of my life. It's best, this way, for the club. She's gone, no one knows where and if the marshals do their job, no one will ever be able to find her."

"Jesus, Beef. It was all I could do to hold you down…"

"Prez, yeah. My first impulse was to go out searching for her. I admit it, I wanted to claim her. But this has opened my eyes, shown me I was going about it the wrong way. That note she left? She doesn't trust us to keep her safe. Don't blame the girl at all, blind like that, can't do much for herself. She's put her faith in the marshals—"

"She fuckin' trusts you, Beef," a deep voice snarls by my side. Turning quickly, I'm faced with a death stare from Hell not too dissimilar from Drummer's. Seems the prez glare doesn't fade once you step down from the job.

My temper flares. "Does she? Walked away without a backward glance." My voice rises in volume.

"Did she?" Thunder's question is asked in a similar tone. "Or was she fuckin' coerced?"

My fear, which I'm trying to tamp down.

"She might have thought she was keeping *you* safe. Thought her being here was placing the club in a difficult fuckin' position." Demon's snarl is much like his father's. He lets his words sink in, before adding, "You hadn't had a chance to tell her what you were planning, to go into the details of how you were going to take her away. What would you have done, Beef, if the tables were turned and you thought she was in danger? If you feel for her as much as you say you do, I think you'd have done the same thing if you were persuaded her life was in danger if you stayed."

I don't reply. I go to say I'd have found a way to keep us together, but would I? Would I really? Or would I have sacrificed my own happiness to keep her alive? Only one answer to that question.

Prez hasn't finished. "I don't like the way she left like a thief in the night. My gut feel is that Lennox didn't give her much choice."

"Could have taken her at gunpoint. Threatened you? Threatened the club? Could have played on the fact that we're an MC same as the Warped Jokers."

"Ain't nothing like them," Buzzard objects.

Mace waves his hand in dismissal. "She's a citizen. A few well-placed words about taking us down using the law could have got her on his side."

Max takes the opportunity to nudge my knee with his nose. When my hand automatically reaches down, he licks it. *What's he trying to say?*

I had a good woman once, no, I didn't, but there was one I wanted. Only she had eyes for somebody else. Am I fated never to find anyone like Rock found Becca? Have to return to Tucson and live vicariously through the lives of my married brothers? I rub my chin absentmindedly. I don't know what to think. One minute I want to race around like a headless chicken doing all I can to find her. The next, I want to forget she ever existed. Chances are, whatever I do I won't be able to find her. That's if she even wanted me to.

The table has gone silent, looking to me for direction. My gaze starts at the top, looking from Demon to Mace, then Thunder and Buzzard. Sparky has his head tilted to one side, Ink's eyes are focused on a spot on the table in front of him. Rusty looks confused, Lizard and Cad just seem waiting on me to put forward my suggestions. Skull's intrigued, and Hell just downright annoyed. Pyro and Bomber just seem poised to act on whatever decision I make. Pal, well he knows me better than anyone, his expression is sympathetic, as if he knows the turmoil in my head. Dan and Wills are keeping silent, too new to the table to challenge me.

What do I do? I've a club full of brothers who'd support any action I deem worth taking. If I say leave it, they will. I might not have my true brothers around me, but I know everyone here would have my back just the same.

"Beef?" It's Pal who gets my attention. "She it for you?"

Giving a deep sigh, I reply, "I thought so."

Paladin chuckles. "You know what the women are like, Beef. Seen enough of it in Tucson. See, we brothers think we're the protectors, that we decide what's up and what's down. That we have all the answers. Trouble is, sometimes they think that way too. Way I see it, if you want my opinion?"

I nod, to show that I do. I value his input as much, if not more, than anyone's.

"Well here it is. Stevie's handicapped, no other way of looking at it. She's limited as to what is in her power to do. I suspect it broke her to leave you, but she was persuaded it was in hers, and your best interest to go. What would happen if she just agreed not to testify? Jokers walk free, but she'd still remain a target. She has to go ahead and put them away, she's been through too much shit to step back now."

He's right. "Even if she puts them away, she could still have their sights set on her." I don't add we all know what can be achieved even from behind bars.

Pal's got more. "In her view her only option is to start anew once again. She's already left her family behind. My guess is that leaving you will be killing her, but she's got guts and will do what she has to do whatever the personal cost. She left her *family*, Beef. She's wrenched herself away before, probably was no easier leaving you."

"I was going to go with her," I tell what not all of them know. "Turn in my patch, accept whatever beatdown I was given. I wanted to be there for her."

Instead of outrage, my admission makes them go quiet. Surprisingly it's Pyro, who I'd thought was disinterested, who's first to respond. "It seems you don't have a choice, Brother. You feel that much for her, put her above your loyalty to the club? Then you can't turn your back on her now. She means too much to you."

"But we're not letting you go," Thunder steps in. "Beatdown or not, know you too well, Beef. You might not have sat around this table long, but you live and breathe the club. What we need to do is find Stevie, and a way for you to have both. Satan's Devils don't walk away when the going gets hard."

"Going gets hard?" I echo incredulously. "Impossible, more like what if the Wretched Soulz revoke our charter? I can't be responsible for that."

"No." Demon appears to think he's let everyone else speak for too long. "You can't. But you can be responsible for your ol' lady. Wretched Soulz would respect that."

"What if she puts the Warped Jokers away?" I shake my head.

Hellfire has been quiet, thoughtful. Now it's his turn to speak. "The worry has been that the Wretched Soulz don't want the feds to get greedy. They take out one club, might set their sights on more. Seems to me, if we, and that's the big 'we' including the dominant, are seen to be backing the Warped Jokers, we're only confirming we turn a blind eye to, and support those committing, criminal activities. If, on the other hand, we come down on the side of right, feds got no reason to dig deeper to see if our blood runs the same."

I have a new respect for Hellfire. He might be onto something.

Demon's eyes sharpen as he looks at his father. "I'll talk to RIP. You've made a good case, Hell. If we can get the Wretched Soulz to revoke the Warped Jokers' charter rather than ours, it could send a message they're out on their own, on the inside as well as out."

If that works, Stevie might be safe. She might be able to return to her old life. But would that be with me, or back with her folks? Could she just step back into a life she left?

It's Pal who seems able to read my mind. "If you love her, Beef, really love her. You'll want what's best for her."

His words make me feel selfish. Here I am thinking about my loss without giving a moment to think about hers. *Do I love her?* Her image floats in front of my eyes. Her voice echoes in my ears. Her courage, her ability to do so much more than I ever imagined. Her bravery, her independence, the way I feel when I'm inside her, or simply holding her, breathing in her smell, the way she makes me feel, all comes to mind.

Placing my hand over my heart, I give them the answer. "I feel her, in here." My fist taps my chest. "I've been looking for something, didn't realise I'd found it. Yeah, Pal," I raise my chin toward him, "I love her." Then my voice hardens. "And I'm fuckin' scared shitless what's happening to her. Need to know she's alright. Need to know Lennox is doing right by her." I let my heartfelt words sink in, then, aware I'm taking over but unable to stop myself, I start issuing orders. "Cad, get together with Mouse and find out who the hell found the information on Max's tracker. Prez, you meet with the Wretched Soulz. I'll get onto Drummer, see if I can locate Devil—Jason Deville—he's a consultant. Works with the feds but has been on our side before. He may be able to find shit out we can't."

Demon's mouth is quirked. "You quite finished, Brother?"

I feel my cheeks burn. "Yeah."

"Okay," he grins. "Seems like Beef here has issued instructions. Looks like a number of us have been assigned work. The rest of you, anything you can think of, any trace you can find of Lennox's car, anything that might help..."

"We'll be on it, Prez," Thunder confirms.

"Right. Let's find our brother's woman and bring her home."

CHAPTER THIRTY-THREE

Leaving church, I find Dan waiting for me outside the room. He shifts a little awkwardly and obviously has something to say. I raise my chin to encourage him.

"Didn't want to speak up in there, but just wanted to say, Beef, anything I can do to help, just holler."

Another jerk of my chin, this time in appreciation. "You're not a prospect now, Dan."

A quick grin. "I know. Still seems odd. Finding my place, you know?"

Prospecting's so far in my rearview I'd almost forgotten what it was like to first sit at the table. Now I dredge through my memory and remember. Yeah, sure, first it's elation at now having a seat at the table, but then it's a bit disconcerting as you're not quite sure where you fit.

He's offered, I'll accept. "I'm going to call Drummer. See if we can dig up some leads within the feds. You wanna sit in?"

He's eager. "Sure."

I look back into the meeting room, now deserted. "Seems as quiet a place as any."

When he follows me inside, I take the phone I'd collected from the box outside the room, stare into it until it recognises my features, then click on a contact and set it on the table.

"Whaddyawant, Beef?"

"Prez. It's Stevie." After telling him who've I've got in the room, I go onto explain what's been going on.

"You think she went willingly?"

I shrug. Though he can't see my gesture, he probably can hear the frustration in my voice. "Hard to tell. There was a note that she apparently dictated…"

"She got a phone? She could have texted you."

Yeah. A point that's been worrying me. She could have. "Her phone was left here. Presumably so we couldn't track it."

"You got Cad onto it?"

"Yeah, he should be talking to Mouse now. All we know is that she left with Lennox…"

"No. You don't know that. That's what the note said."

My eyes meet Dan's wide ones. Drummer's right. "She wouldn't have gone with anyone else."

"Not willingly, no. Have you guys got security cameras?"

Dan gestures to himself and then the door. I nod. He gets up, presumably to go and ask Cad.

Dan's back in seconds. "First thing Cad did was check the cameras on that side of the building but they didn't show anything. The footage from the gate shows the car had blacked-out windows. We don't know who was driving it."

"Fuck," Drummer and I say at the same time. "Lennox's number in her phone?"

"I asked. Cad said no," Dan inserts.

She probably hadn't committed it to memory and put it on the burner. All she had was mine and the brothers.

"I don't know what I can do from here that Demon and his brothers can't," Drummer gently admonishes me. I suppose he thinks it's a betrayal that I'm not relying on my brothers in this chapter.

"There's one thing, Prez. Devil. He in the US?"

"Devil?" He's quiet for a moment. "Man's as elusive as a pink elephant in heat. Last I heard he'd gone back to the UK. What's on your mind? His contacts with the feds?"

"Be useful if he could check Lennox out."

"Yeah. Okay. Can't rightly remember if at this point we owe him a favour or the other way around, but we've done enough for him in the past that he might feel inclined to take a look. I'll get on it."

I thank him and am about to ring off—Drummer not being someone for unnecessary small talk—when he says, "I'll do everything I can to find your girl, Beef. If you feel half for her what I feel for Sam, I'd be climbing the walls knowing she's in the wind."

It's becoming easier for me to admit it. "I do, Drum. I do."

I end the call and look at Dan. "Cad say he's got anything useful?"

He shakes his head. "What do you know about the court case, Beef? You mentioned it was in a couple of months. Where is it? What court? I know two months is a long time, but if the marshals do the job that they should, she'll turn up then for certain."

Fuck me. He's right. I look at him with new respect. We might not know where she is *now* but we do know where she'll be in a few weeks. Won't be hard finding the court details. They'll be public record. Though is he proposing that I wait six or seven weeks before I find out whether she's okay? If she's even still alive? Could I sit on my hands doing nothing in the meantime? Nah. "I can't wait, Dan."

"No," he agrees, "you can't. But there's another angle Cad and Mouse could search. See if the lawyers are still acting on the assumption she's going to appear."

If Mouse can't hack into a court computer system, he knows someone who can. Cara.

"Good point, Dan." I commend him while thinking what the fuck I'd do if her name had been removed from that witness list.

I feel like slapping myself around the face for accepting things at face value earlier today and being prepared to think I'd lost her. Even if she thought she was doing the right things, it would be all for the wrong reasons.

I stare at the new member for a moment. "How did you think of the court? You got experience?"

"Nah," he laughs, but there's no joy in it. "Or not in the way that you think. Managed to stay out of trouble with the law so far. My old man was a judge. Not that I knew him. One-night stand with my ma. But she always hoped I'd take after him. At least I didn't take after her."

"No?" There's more. I can sense it.

"Nah," he repeats. "Found earning her living on her back was easier than doing an honest day's work. Got herself killed when I was eleven. I ended up in the system. No one cared about my education then."

"Judge," I say, half to myself. Then I slap him on the back. "How's about making you one, now? Judge as your handle."

His eyes move heavenwards, and a smile comes over his face. "Christ, what a joke. I don't mind. Think Prez will go along with it?"

I have a feeling that Demon won't give a fuck. I've taken a liking for the lad, already suspecting he's got intelligence, showing he'd picked up more of his dad's traits than he did his mom's. His background isn't surprising, like so many cast adrift at such a young age, a family is all they long for. Belonging to an MC gives them what they've never had. Men like that can be trusted to have your back. They're never going to fuck up the one chance they have.

"Beef? You around?" Demon's voice bellows from the direction of the clubroom.

Dan—*Judge*—leaps up. "I'll go…"

"Not a prospect anymore. You don't need to run at everyone's beck and call. Come on, we'll both go see what he wants."

What Demon wants is to let me know he's set up a meeting

with RIP, and that it's going to happen fast. He's meeting him and his VP at a local bar tomorrow. The speed is good. If we can get the dominant off Stevie's back, then it's one less thing I have to worry about. I'll be able to make plans for Stevie and me. After I find her, of course.

"Hey, Demon." I follow him back into his office, shutting the door behind me. "Who's going to be at the meet from our side?"

"You want to be there." It's a statement so I jerk my chin. *Try and keep me away.* "I need someone to have my back."

Again, a statement. Reminding me that that's my role. Stand there and look ugly, intimidating. Not for the first time I wish I was seen as more than a muscular body and a threatening face.

But he surprises me. "Thunder won't want to go, so you'll stand at my side. RIP knows he isn't my permanent VP so there'll be no surprise there. But for a third? I was thinking…"

"Judge."

He looks perplexed as well he might.

"I've just given a road name to Dan."

"Story there?"

There is. But it isn't mine to tell. I raise my chin.

"Judge. Yeah, I like it. Kid's got a good head on his shoulders. Yeah, okay. About time we brought him on board."

I grab a chair, turn it around, and sit with my hands clasped over the back. "How we going to play this, Prez?"

"You heard Hell." He grins. "Don't mind using my old man's experience when it helps, but I don't want him there. My show now. Anyway, Hell's busy trying to keep himself out of the shit he passed on. You present it as your idea. Can you do that, Beef?"

Of course I can. Though it will be the first time I've spoken up in such a meeting. "I'll be fine," I reply, confidently. "And Stevie's mine. I'm happy to make that plain to him."

"You sure? You seemed a bit uncertain, earlier."

"Got issues, Prez. Needed a kick to get my head out of my ass. But yeah, I'm fine."

A searching look, then a nod. "Best get Dan, *Judge*, ready then. Brief him on what to do, will you?"

I can do that. After all, it's what I've been doing all my life.

After a sleepless night with a restless Max by my side, I'm more than ready to get to the meet the next day.

I've heard of RIP's reputation, who hasn't? There are various rumours about how he got his name. My personal favourite, and I think his, and why he insists his name be spelled in capitals, is that he gained it from being the last thing he says before offing someone. The more likely is that it's short for Ripper, as his legal first name is Jack. It's true that before he rose through the ranks I've heard him referred to as Ripper, so am pretty certain the second is closest to the truth. Still, who would want to argue with a Wretched Soulz prez?

I'm reminded of how much he likes theatre when, having left Beaver, the prospect minding the bikes, Demon, myself and the newly named Judge, walk into the bar, quickly seeing a trio of men sitting at a corner table. The others in the vicinity are left vacant, even though the place is busy.

RIP, president of the Colorado chapter of the Wretched Soulz stands and reaches out his hand, clasping Demon's by the elbow and then pulling him in to slap his back. Next, he turns to me, his eyebrow raised quizzically. "RIP. R.I.P." He spells out his name with a grin.

"Beef." I shake his hand.

"Judge." Demon jerks his chin toward our companion. Having schooled him, I'm pleased when Judge folds his arms over his chest and satisfies himself with a sharp nod. Muscle isn't expected to say anything.

"Charmer." The man with the VP badge is next to greet me. His name would give no clue to his appearance as he's covered in battle scars with an obviously broken nose which hasn't been set right. Maybe his character will live up to his name, though something suggests it might not.

"Bam Bam." Again, his cut gives me a better introduction. He's their sergeant-at-arms. Interesting they've brought him.

RIP catches the eye of the bartender and holds up three fingers. They've already got beers on the table for themselves. Seconds later beers appear for each of us. A civilian couple wander in and make as if to sit at an adjacent table. As Bam Bam scoots back his chair noisily and stands, they change their minds quickly.

Looking from his sergeant-at-arms to us, RIP leans forward. "So, what have you got for me, Demon?"

Demon gestures to me.

I don't miss a beat. "The woman going by Stevie Nichols. I'm claiming her."

"Jeez." RIP rolls back his head and stares at the ceiling. "You gonna think about that for a moment?"

"Don't need thinkin' time." I shrug. "Didn't mean for it to happen, but it did. I've come here with Demon to smooth the way. Don't want to find an old lady just to lose her."

"You're out of Tucson, aren't ya?" Charming motions his beer toward me. Something must give him his answer, as he shakes his head. "What is it with that fuckin' chapter that you're all about women and kids? Give me a sweet butt every time. No commitment, and she gets the job done just how you want it."

Manly chuckles from Bam Bam, though RIP stays quiet, glaring quickly at his VP. I take it he's got a woman himself. Not that he admits it, but he does take over the lead in the conversation. "Ms Nichols is a problem."

"Only for the Warped Jokers," I say quietly, mindful of keeping my voice low. "What's your take on them, RIP?"

He seems surprised I've asked him a direct question. Bam Bam stops laughing, and Charmer regards his prez seriously. RIP looks from one to the other, then at Demon, finally at me and shrugs. "They're a pain in my ass."

I didn't expect him to come out and say it so openly. I sit back, putting my thumbs through my belt loops. "Here's how I see it." I used the personal pronoun deliberately. If RIP objects to my reasoning, he'll see it as all mine and nothing to do with the Colorado Satan's Devils. "Warped Jokers are everything that citizens are scared of. This latest escapade, they got caught, but not before taking out a load of innocents." Shaking my head, I continue, "Not an MC I want to be associated with: careless, greedy and incompetent." I don't say committing a crime is wrong in itself, leaving them to fill in the gaps that what I object to is them getting caught. Heaven knows what the Soulz get up to, rumours are quite a lot I wouldn't want to know about. Not that we're angels or averse to taking a life, but only those who deserve it.

"Know your prez." RIP points his bottle at me. "Got a lot of time for the Devils. You do walk on the government side of the line but aren't afraid to cross it when it's needed. Soulz might move that line a little further over, but Jokers can't even see the road anymore, let alone the marking in the middle of it."

Now comes the hard bit. "To citizens we're all MCs. Especially one-percenter clubs. One does wrong, we all get pulled into it. Bad news for us all."

"You got that fuckin' right. Reason why we've got to stop your woman testifying. No conviction, no stain." He thinks for a moment. "She's your responsibility, if you can keep her quiet—"

"That's not what I'm sayin'." I feel Demon tense beside me, knowing this is where I'm getting to the hard bit. "The US Marshals have got her again. I don't know where she is to stop her testifying."

RIP's face gives nothing away. If that's not news to him, he's not showing it. Or is he thinking she's been easy to find once, and she will be again? Just who has these contacts with a federal agent?

"RIP, what I'm sayin' is, maybe we should throw the Jokers to the wolves. Step back from them. Denounce them. If the Wretched Soulz withdrew their charter, then they're adrift. Sends a message to the public and feds that we're not all tarred with the same brush."

"Laid a lot on me there, Brother," he responds, casually, again, no intonation to give away his thoughts.

I know when to push, and when it's time to step back. But I think I've got a chance to say one more thing before over-pressing my case. "RICO is what we're all worried about. Step away from the Jokers, disavow their activities... It strips the feds of an excuse to go after the rest of us."

Again, RIP's bottle is pointed toward me. "If she testifies, your woman is dead. Mad Bull's got friends on the inside."

"Some of those friends are Soulz." I raise and lower my shoulders again, and from then on, keep my mouth shut.

RIP looks down at his bottle as though the low level of beer is interesting, but I don't miss the sideways glance he gives his VP, nor can I read any of their silent conversation. The silence draws out until it becomes almost painful. I think all of us have to suppress the urge to fill it. Out of the corner of my eye, I see Demon draw in a breath, but I give a miniscule shake of my head which he interprets correctly.

Finally, RIP meets my eye. "Heard good things about you, Beef. I, personally, can see the benefits in what you're suggesting. Not up to me, of course. Up to LA. Our chapters run independently."

It's rumoured the Wretched Soulz have a national prez, but no one will admit to being that man. He'd only be making himself a target. As such, the chapters are thought to run autonomously with no overall control except the same binding regs. No one outside knows how much influence one has over the other. Much like the Devils though, all chapters recognise Drummer as the National Prez, in part because he's a clever motherfucker and they do well to seek his opinion. Also, as our chapters are smaller, it helps having someone who can rally the others around should we need their support. It's understandable RIP can't speak for the Los Angeles' Soulz. He may, however, be able to influence them. I can't ask. All I can do is hope he passes on my suggestion.

"Okay," he puts his beer bottle down empty. "I'll have words in ears. Can't guarantee anything. But I'll get your suggestion heard. Chaz up to speed?"

"With this? No. But I can ask Drummer…"

"Nah. I'll handle it." RIP stands. Charmer and Bam Bam are only seconds behind him. "Good to meet you, Beef. And to see you again, Demon. Judge." He raises his chin and nods at our man who's stayed silent, standing with his arms crossed. His eyes settle on him for a moment as though committing his features to memory. Just before he moves away from the table he leans in conspiratorially, saying quietly so only we can hear. "Best start saving. Hits can be expensive."

It's only when they've gone that Judge lets his eyes open wide. Demon waves him to the table.

"Hits?" Judge asks.

I take pity on him. "If the Jokers go inside, they'll still be gunning for Stevie. They'll appeal their sentence, that could go on for years. If Stevie's not around to back up her statements, they may have a chance of success. Being inside would distance them from any murder, though that wouldn't stop them pulling the strings and getting the job done." I grow cold at the thought. "Only way out is to take out those with any influence, the officers and ringleaders."

"Wretched Soulz have enough people on the inside. At the moment the Jokers can rely on the Soulz for protection. If they lose their charter, it changes the dynamics." I don't elaborate, suspecting the man can fill in the gaps for himself.

"Christ." Judge wipes his hand over his face and shakes his head. Just as I start wondering whether he's going to be a good fit for this life, he grins widely. "Now a permanent solution I like."

CHAPTER THIRTY-FOUR

"Here, boy," I call to Max who trots over, giving wide berth to Bitch who's watching him with wary eyes. She stands, arches her back and hisses as he passes just a little too close for her liking, but out of range of her claws. Guess they're never going to be best buddies.

Opening the door, I lead him outside. "Get busy," I instruct, and he does, immediately. I reward him with a 'good boy', and a pat, then stand for a moment, giving him a chance to sniff the weeds growing up through the cracks in the pavement. With half an eye on him to make sure he doesn't start tracking the trail of some small animal that's passed by, I stare around.

The outside of the clubhouse is a dismal area. The old furnace, the huge pit where they used to melt down trains, is the most interesting feature. A few picnic tables are sprinkled around, but instead of grass, they stand on old broken concrete. It's a good size area and could be made into something attractive if its current resemblance to a demolition site was tidied up. I make a mental note to mention it to Demon. It wouldn't take much more than a hired digger to get rid of the trip hazards and broken surface. Then we could use a rototiller to turn over the soil and lay some turf. Much safer for Stevie when she returns and wouldn't take much more than a weekend if we all put our backs to it.

"You'd like that, wouldn't you, boy?" Max, moving remarkably well on his injured leg, has returned to my side.

Why am I thinking about sprucing up the clubhouse? I won't be here much longer. I'll be returning to Tucson. A smile curves my lips as I think how Stevie would love the compound in Arizona. We could build a house at the top alongside the rest going up, and there's a good safe area and a swimming pool for those inevitably hot days of summer. Nestling in the valley between the mountain ranges it's a beautiful place. In my mind's eye, I'm imagining describing it all to her.

How would Max get on with Grunt? Do dogs just accept each other? I glance down at Max. Somehow I suspect he's too well trained to get into a fight. Chuckling softly, I imagine lording it over Heart when he can't get Grunt, his oversized mongrel to obey his commands, whereas Max will do anything asked of him.

"Yeah," I start quietly, not even embarrassed I'm talking to a dog. At my voice he's raised his intelligent eyes and is staring into mine. "You'd love it in Tucson. A little hot, but there's air conditioning inside. Kids who'd adore you, women who'd spoil you. Not sure Drummer would allow you into church, but then you'll be back working, looking after Stevie..." My voice trails off.

Yeah, he'll be back to a working dog if I can find that woman of mine. One of my fists smashes against the palm of my other hand. *I am going to find you, Stevie.* But will you be dead or alive? A feeling of sheer panic goes through me. Sensing my change of mood, Max whines quietly by my side. *Got to think positively.* I'd go crazy if I thought I'd never see her again. *Is she thinking of me?*

It's all the unanswerable questions which are driving me crazy. The only thing I don't challenge is that I'm going to make her mine. Whatever objections she has, I'll overcome them. I'll draw her a picture of a life she can't turn down. With me. In Tucson.

"You're deep in thought."

I jump about two feet in the air, and my hand automatically goes over my heart. "Way to scare a man half to death, Brother."

"Never thought I'd walk up on you unawares, Beef," Paladin replies with a smirk. "You seemed to be somewhere else."

I had been. "Just thinking of when I go back to Tucson."

"Yeah?" Pal looks around him. "Have to admit this place is a dump compared with what we left behind. But there is a lot going for it."

"Like what?" I'm genuinely interested to hear how he's settled down.

"Like Jay for a start. Wherever she is, that's where I want to be."

Once I might have laughed at him, but now I've met Stevie, it's something I can fully understand.

"The brothers. Just as good people as those I left behind." He pauses, and this time it's his eyes which glaze slightly as he drags up what's on his mind. "I've been able to find my place here, become a new man if you like. There's been opportunities and I've grabbed them with both hands. Got a respected place around the table."

"You had respect in Tucson."

He shrugs. "It wasn't the same. I was always the youngest member. Sure, I'm still the same age, but I'm not the kid anymore. Demon's handed me and Cad the security business since he became prez. Nice to have something of my own to build up."

"How's that going?"

"Well. I'm actually taking some classes online to learn about new methods and stuff we could do. Oh, and the legal shit as well."

I realise that everything's been a blur since I arrived, I haven't had the chance to speak with Paladin before, or not in any depth. I admire him for taking the opportunities offered by moving to a new place, settling into a new family. I'm genuinely happy for him, but can't see myself doing that, I'm longing for the men I've called brothers for years, the familiar rather than the new. I'm too old to change. Unlike Pal who still has a chance to find his place in the world, I already have mine, and it's not here in Pueblo.

Though I think he's got something right. I suspect wherever Stevie is, I'd be happy.

Max, getting restless, wanders off once again. Pal's eyes follow him. "Any news on your woman?"

I bite back my reply I'd not be idly standing here if I knew where to find her and try to summon up a polite reply. "Zilch. Cad's working with Mouse who's pulling in favours from Cara, but the marshals know how to hide their shit deep. Drummer's still trying to trace Devil who's gone underground."

"And there's been no word back from the Wretched Soulz?"

"Nah. Driving me fuckin' crazy if you want to know."

Pal's eyes crease in sympathy. "When Jay disappeared, I went out of my mind and that was only for hours. It's been a week for you now, Beef. I can't begin to imagine how you're feeling."

"Just putting one foot in front of the other and keep breathing air into my lungs. I feel so fuckin' helpless, that's what's worst."

He makes no verbal reply, but I feel the slap of his hand against the leather of my cut. The simple gesture of sympathy and support, letting me know he'll be there for me no matter what. Not for the first time I wonder how I could tolerate a situation such as this without knowing I had such men at my back. The knowledge I'm not alone is what keeps me moving forward.

Another church, the second since Stevie vanished. Ten days gone by and we're no further forward. Negative reports all around. For want of something to say that doesn't attract answers of no news, or how the fuck should I know, I bring up the ideas I've had while taking Max outside to do the necessary.

A task I need to do so often, the state of the area has been playing on my mind.

"You know you could turn the yard into something attractive?" I start when Demon asks whether there's any other business. Seeing I've got their attention, I lay out the ideas I'd thought about the other afternoon.

"Yard's been that way since we moved into the place," Rusty grumbles, jerking his chin toward Bomber and Hellfire, the original members.

"Rather like the rustic feel," Pyro observes.

"Rustic? Construction site more like." Ink sounds like he could be brought over to my side.

"Pussies from Tucson probably want a swimming pool dug out as well."

Lizard's eyes gleam at Mace's complaint. "Now you're talking!"

"Vi's always worrying about Theo when he comes to the club. He'll soon be crawling. I'm up for the idea."

I raise my chin toward Prez. Two coming around to my way of thinking.

"How much is this gonna cost, Beef?" A not unexpected question from the treasurer.

I supply the answer, "Less than you'd think. If we do the labour. Just the cost of hiring equipment for a couple of days and the turf."

"I'm game. As long as Skull's woman bakes some of those muffins and cookies to keep us fed." Mace grins.

"Get the prospects to do it," Thunder growls, seeming unimpressed by the enforcer's reference to Melissa's cooking skills.

"We'll all pitch in," Demon states firmly. "Bout time we did something about tidying up the outside. Add in fencing to go around the furnace. Don't want any dogs or kids falling inside." His pointed look toward me states volumes. *Or blind women.*

It's something I can put my back into. Sorting out what we need, getting people organised, having to draw up a rotation from the large number of volunteers who seem more like a pack of kids wanting to take their turn with the new toy, the digger when it's delivered, keeps me occupied. It doesn't take my mind totally off Stevie, but at least helps me get through the day. With everyone doing their bit—even the club girls getting involved with Titsy who shows she's got green fingers and demanding we leave part un-turfed so she can start a vegetable and flower patch—the work proceeds at a good pace. By Sunday evening the yard has been transformed. The ground has been cleared and flattened, and Kentucky Bluegrass has been laid. Just as we finish there's a rainstorm which means nature's taken care of watering it in.

Standing inside looking out of the kitchen window, Demon slaps my back. "Will you look at that? Transformed the fuckin' place. Let's have a family barbeque next weekend, put it to some use."

Like the rain drenching the newly laid grass, his words have a similar effect on my pride in the fruition of my idea. What good is a family event when you've no one to share it with?

"We'll find her," Demon states softly, but with determination. "It's only a matter of time, Beef."

The new grass barely has time to settle before it starts getting covered with loungers which, in turn, bear almost naked bodies of the club girls, and only slightly more decently attired old ladies. Jay, Melissa and Violet adorn themselves with bikinis, much to the ire of Demon, Pal and Skull while Mo, Jeannie and Sindy make do with more discreet swimsuits. Cad, strangely, as he's so pale it wouldn't be expected he'd spend much time outside, seems very taken by the new greenery, and takes it on himself to direct the prospects to move the furniture each night to avoid browning the new grass. For everyone else, the mood is cheery, and expectations of the barbeque, which is approaching fast, are high.

While Violet's overjoyed she can sit Theo on a blanket outside and is currently helping him throw a ball for Max—well, roll it along the ground really as he can't run too fast or jump yet —the preparations just serve to remind me that my woman isn't here.

Hellfire wanders over and passes me a beer. In order to stop him asking how I'm doing, which seems to be everyone's opening gambit now, I get in first.

"While I was at the cabin, Hell, I found the frame of an Indian. Engine and bits and bobs where it had been stripped. Looked like someone was going to rebuild it but didn't go back."

Glancing at him, I see a shadow pass over his face. "Forgot about that, Beef. Yeah. It was Furnace's."

"He was Blackie's VP, wasn't he? Became the prez when Blackie died?"

Hell's face blackens at the reminder of his father, and I hurriedly remember that there's some dark history in this club that I vaguely remember hearing about. *Didn't Hell kill his father?* I backtrack fast. "You were Furnace's VP."

"I was. Decent fucker, he was. Totalled his bike. Yeah, that was his Indian, he was going to rebuild it. Got as far as stripping it down before he died. No one had the heart to touch it after that, been so long, I'd forgotten about it. You want it, Beef? Doubt anyone will challenge you if you want to take it. Finders keepers and all that."

"It's the club's, Hell." It's a generous offer. If I take it back to Tucson, Sam could help me do it up.

"You're club, Beef," he says, sharply. "Only Bomber and Rusty would remember it in any event, and, I suspect, like me they'll have forgotten it was there, and even if they did remember, wouldn't want to put in the work. I, for one, would be quite happy to see it ridden again."

"I'll give it some thought." If I can't have Stevie, might need something to focus on to help me forget.

"Take it if you want it. Better than it rotting away." A quick glance, then he adds, "Furnace would have liked you." A chin lift, then he walks off.

I watch him leave, see him picking up his grandson and throwing him in the air, smiling for a moment as I realise family is as important here as it is in Tucson. I'm club, as Hellfire said, welcome wherever I am. The feeling brings me comfort, even if my heart and arms feel empty.

Mo joins Hellfire, Demon's arm's around Vi. Pal and Jayden are laughing together, Sindy's with Buzzard and Bomber with Jeannie. Fuck, even Skull is standing close to Melissa.

Whereas I don't know where my old lady is, or, even if I have one.

The sun may be shining, but I feel as cold as a dreary winter's day. This might be a celebration, but there's no pleasure in it for me.

When the time comes, I munch mechanically on a hamburger, barely tasting the food in my mouth, sneaking more of it to Max than I manage to consume. I escape to my room as soon as I feel my absence won't be noticed. Not that it's much better there, all I can see is Stevie lying on the bed.

Though she'd bundled most of her clothing and taken it with her, I'd found a pair of her panties forgotten at the back of a drawer. Clean, unworn, but still something of her. Like a pervert I twist them in my hands, imagining her wearing them, imagining her being here with me. Lying back on the sheets, I close my eyes, picturing her lying next to me, conjuring up that memory of her perfect tits, pale brown nipples, that soft rounded stomach, that pert little ass.

My cock swells. When I place my hand on it, I try to dream up her scent, the feeling of her touch, trying to make believe it's her hand that's stroking me, up and down, her fingers squeezing then loosening, her palm surrounding me as she increases the speed, pumping my dick hard.

Ribbons of cum cover my stomach quickly cooling in the draught from the air conditioning.

I feel no relief, instead I'm consumed by an emptiness. *Had it been my fault? Had I had my head so far up my ass I didn't see what was in front of me until it was much too late? What if I'd told her how I felt earlier? What if...*

What if I never find her?

What if my memories are all I have left?

They aren't enough.

Wetness on my cheeks tell me I've tears rolling down from my eyes. I lie, silently weeping, unable to bear the thought of a future without Stevie in it.

How will I survive?

CHAPTER THIRTY-FIVE

"Beef. Get your ass back to the club. We've got company."

I stare at the phone, the call abruptly disconnected. The questions I wanted to ask not even voiced, let alone answered.

"You off?"

"Yeah." I put down the wrench that I'd been using to loosen the nuts on an engine. "Sorry, Ro. Boss wants me."

Pyro waves me off. I don't need to explain more. When Demon summons, you respond. My bike is parked out front of the auto-shop, already facing away from the building. It takes but a second to get on, start the engine, and let those pipes roar as I shift through the gears and back toward the compound.

After yesterday's barbeque I'd been in a foul mood. Helping out Pyro by tinkering with an engine he couldn't find the fault with at least focused my mind and let me think of something other than the time passing with no word about Stevie. It's got so that I'm not even expecting news today. Half of me is wondering whether it's nearing the time when I'm outstaying my welcome in Pueblo, and whether I'll be given my marching orders to get back on the road.

What good am I doing here? I've not done the job I was sent here for. Demon's no closer to finding a VP than when I arrived.

My enquiries at other chapters has so far turned up nothing. I've failed both him and Drummer. Will Drummer even let me go home? It was my request to go nomad, if it suited his purposes he could send me on to another club rather than letting me return.

In truth, the nomad patch is starting to annoy me. Conversely, the thought of returning to Tucson doesn't fill me with delight. Pueblo is my connection to Stevie. Going back with her is one thing, but returning alone? Would seeing Rock and Becca be even worse, now I know I could have had what they do, but had let it slip through my fingers?

While I'm not optimistic about Demon's reasons for calling me away from the job I was tackling, I didn't expect the summons would be for anything significant. I'm therefore surprised, when I draw up to the clubhouse, to see Drummer and Wraith's bikes parked outside, alongside a few more I don't recognise.

My thoughts return to me with full force. Will I be returning to Tucson with them, knowing I've let down my prez? Or will Drummer give me orders to move on somewhere else?

Since Stevie had been taken, all thoughts of helping Demon solve his problems have gone right out of my mind. Before entering the door, I bang my fist against my head. *I've fucked up,* fucked up everything it would seem.

"In church," Beaver calls out helpfully from his position behind the bar as I step inside.

Breezy flaunts her tits at me as I walk past. I wave her off. I wouldn't be interested even if I hadn't had to get somewhere quickly. The club girls have all been willing to try fresh meat, but I won't do that to Stevie. I'm not even sure I could get hard for another woman right now, even if I had the inclination. Yeah, me, addicted to one pussy. With Sally I'd been fighting temptation to stray, which should have been my first warning sign, whereas Stevie is the only woman my dick seems to want.

I'm undecided whether to knock or just enter when I get to

the meeting room, but the decision's made for me as the door opens and Demon strides out, looking behind him, and saying, "I'll hurry him up." He bumps into me and stops. "Oh, there you are."

Was I tardy? He knows how long it takes to get here, and I came as fast as I could. But the apology I believed wise to offer falls from my lips as I view the people seated around the table.

Drummer, mother chapter president and his VP, sitting alongside RIP and Charmer. Next to them, Chaz, the president of the Arizona chapter of the Wretched Soulz and his VP, Bull. But the man who's brought me to a halt is Devil. I did not expect to see the Englishman here in person.

"Beef." Both Drummer and Wraith stand and come over to me. We share a moment of man hugs and back slapping, then they take their places again. It hits me Demon's the only one without a VP present, and for a moment I wonder why he hadn't called Thunder in.

The question is answered without me having to raise it. "Sorry I'm without a VP this morning. Thunder's dealing with a problem at the strip club."

I hear a growl from Drummer's throat, and his eyes briefly meet mine. All I can do is give an almost imperceptible shake of my head, but he understands the message I'm sending. *No progress as yet.* He won't criticise Demon, or not in front of our other visitors. No club wants to expose a weakness.

Though Demon's up at the top of the table, it's Drummer who kicks off proceedings.

"We've got business we need to bring Beef in on, but some other things to get out of the way first."

I glare at Drummer. He's here for a reason, and if it involves me, I'd prefer him to start with that.

But my prez has other ideas, continuing, "I'd like to introduce those of you who don't know him, to Jason Deville, or Devil as he is known."

Having met him before, I just raise my chin at the man with a heavily scarred face that makes him look like he's permanently scowling and wait while the others introduce themselves. It appears I hadn't missed any of the meeting.

"I run Grade A Security based in the UK along with my partners. I tend to work in the field and provide consultancy to whoever wants to pay me." Devil's taken over his own introduction. "Sometimes I work with the feds, sometimes I investigate for them. I've a team working with me who can get into virtually every computer system there is."

"Useful," RIP observes.

Devil tries to grin at him, but as only one side of his face moves, it doesn't quite work.

"You're the law?" Chaz pulls out a packet of smokes and lights one. Demon shoots an ashtray down the table.

"No," Devil answers seriously. "But I'm usually on the right side of it, though some of my methods aren't quite legal. Hence why I'm called in when there's dirty work others like to keep their hands clean of."

"I won't tell you, you can talk freely in front of Devil, but I can say he's always been straight with us," Drummer explains.

"You trust him?" RIP asks frankly.

"To some extent," the Tucson prez replies.

Devil doesn't seem upset by the response. My leg is bouncing, I'm more interested in why he's here than his credentials.

RIP and Chaz put their heads together and have a murmured conversation punctuated by grunts and growls. In the end it's Chaz who takes the lead. "You've always been a crafty motherfucker, Drummer. We've got an update, don't mind ears hearing who might pass it onto the feds. Good call, Drum." Both dominant prezes nod their heads.

RIP takes the lead. "Sorry it's taken so long to get back to you. Had to arrange a few sit-downs to thrash things out. Cutting a long story short, we've come to an arrangement with LA. Warped Jokers have lost their charter."

I breathe in sharply. *That's the news I wanted.*

"As far as the Soulz are concerned, the Warped Jokers are no longer an MC who are welcome in any of our territories. Anyone wearing their patch, well," he pauses and looks quickly toward Devil before resuming, "let's just say they won't get a friendly greeting."

The movable side of Devil's face smirks. "Wise move. I know that club calls themselves an MC, but they're acting like the criminal gang the feds lump you in with. Cutting them loose is a good step. If I have a chance, I'll drop that into conversation. Won't get the heat entirely off of you but may remove it in this particular instance."

"What does that mean for us?" *For Stevie.*

RIP sits forward. "You claimed the blind bitch, Beef. So you've got a vested interest. It means that *we* won't be on your backs. If you want to give her protection, you won't get blow-back from the Soulz."

"But," Chaz takes over, "that doesn't mean she's not still at risk. Warped Jokers may have lost their charter, but they still act as a club. They've got a lot to lose if she testifies."

"Can you confirm you're happy with that?" Drummer's voice is firm. "I want there to be no misunderstandings."

RIP shrugs. "Now they're out on their own, as Devil here said, they're just criminals. We'd like it if the feds don't use the term MC in front of the judge but can't see how we can stop it."

"Stevie's testimony will only identify the men who held up the bank. Who they are has nothing to do with her further than that."

The two Wretched Soulz prez' raise and dip their heads. "We've washed our hands of them. They're on their own."

I catch Demon's eye. Looking straight at me, he steps into the conversation. "All well and good to say there's no issue with giving Beef's woman our protection. The problem remains, we don't know where Stevie is—who has her, and whether she's still breathing. You," he nods at RIP and Chaz, "may no longer be looking for her, but that doesn't mean the Warped Jokers have stopped."

I swallow. Those are my thoughts but having them put so starkly is chilling.

"That's where I come in." Devil's voice is steady as eight pairs of eyes land on him. "Beef, I know you want me to get down to business, but there's background you need to hear first."

Drummer focuses his steely glare on me. My mouth stays shut, even though I'm starting to feel uneasy that I'm out of the loop in some way.

Devil continues, "Drummer asked me to do some investigating. I've got my best people—Sean and Nessa—working on it. One person I have been able to find is Marshal Lennox."

I breathe in sharply. "You've found him? Where is he?" I want to get my hands on him. Make him tell me everything. Hope starts to glow inside me. Maybe now I'm closer to finding her.

"Hold your horses, Beef. He's told me everything, which is nothing." Devil wipes his hand over his face while that slight burn of expectation is extinguished.

"What do you mean, he's told you nothing?"

"He doesn't know anything."

My muscles start to tense. "Just let me have five minutes with him..."

"Lennox was compromised, Beef, as much as Stevie. He's willing to help us find out how that happened, as he's close to as angry as you are."

That's impossible, my glare shows my thoughts.

My expression has no noticeable effect on Devil. "Look, this is the situation. Lennox liked Ms Nichols, admired her. He was doing his job, but as he said, this was one time his whole heart was in it. Ninety percent of the time he's providing a new cover for criminals in return for their information, a small wrong to put a huge one right. I've spoken to him at length, and I'm assured he put his everything into keeping that woman safe. He did it all by the book. New identity, new location. He stayed close until she was settled because she has particular needs. He's feeling bloody guilty. He was happy to talk to me as we went through all the steps he had taken, and I'm convinced he didn't put a foot wrong."

"He stole her away from me," I growl. "Took her away from our protection."

"He thought he was doing right. You're an MC, same as the Jokers—"

Now snarls refuting the similarity come from all around me. From the Satan's Devils denials that we're anything like them, from the Soulz it sounds more like they wouldn't have been so stupid as to get caught. But nothing fazes Devil. He simply waits for the noise to die down, then continues.

"He had everything set up. A completely new identity. A new place for her to stay. Thing is, he knew nothing about it. Because he was compromised, he handed off to a trusted colleague. The only part he played was getting her out of here. He knew she'd go with him, and probably wouldn't with anyone she didn't know."

"But he knows where she is?"

If Devil could look sympathetic, that would be his expression. "No."

"Who's the new handler?" Drummer asks.

"That doesn't matter."

"What the fuck you mean that doesn't matter?" I roar, suddenly impatient with all this pussy footing around. "I want to know who he is. I want to speak to him. I want to…"

Devils eyes meet mine. "I can tell you, it was Marshal Handson. But that won't help you in the least. He's dead."

Oh fuck. My heart stops. I can't voice the question.

My voice breaks. "Stevie?"

"Missing."

CHAPTER THIRTY-SIX

Unable to stay still, I stand. My chair topples over, I don't bother to right it. I pace up and down the side of the table, my hands raking over my head and down my face. Rage bottles up inside me.

"Give him the rest, Devil," Drum says tersely. "Whatever you know."

"Accident, murder? And when?" I'm trying to get my head around there's no one protecting Stevie.

"Yesterday. And I'm pretty sure you'd class a bullet through the forehead as murder," Devil replies drily. "Crime scene's been fully investigated. No sign of a struggle, or anyone else being there."

"So Stevie wasn't taken at the same time?" Demon asks. "And where was this?"

"Denver," Devil replies.

"They didn't take her far enough," Drummer observes.

"Could have been a staging point." The suggestion comes from Devil. "But wherever she's gone, we have to assume they've got ways of finding her. Lennox agrees with me. Someone, somewhere in the US Marshals headquarters is plying them with information. Can't be anything else."

"What the fuck do I do?" My thoughts voiced aloud.

"Beef." Wraith's there beside me. "Man, we'll find her. We're working on this."

My eyes water as I look at him. "If Lennox knows someone's dirty, presumably they're looking into it. If the marshals can't find their own leak, what the fuck is the chance we can?"

"You're looking at this wrong, Beef." Devil's voice remains calm, but not calming. "You're right. The marshals are looking to clean their house, particularly focused on who's responsible for the death of one of their own. Our problem is Stevie and finding her."

"She could be dead," I state bluntly.

"No sign of a dead body," the Englishman replies. "Sean's checked out the morgue and police reports in Denver."

"Buried out in the desert?" RIP puts in, unhelpfully.

"She's clever. She could have gone underground herself. Maybe this Handson wasn't where he was supposed to be, perhaps didn't turn up to meet her. She could have hidden."

"Unlikely," Drummer responds to Demon. "If she was fully sighted, I'd be thinking that way too. But blind?"

She might be blind, but she's resourceful. But I have to agree with Drummer. It's not impossible, but not likely. How would she know who to trust, or more to the point, who not to?

"We start looking in Denver," Wraith suggests.

"If she knew she'd been located, she'd have wanted to get away. Hop onto the first Greyhound I'd think."

"Good point. We'll check out the bus terminals." Devil makes a note on his phone.

"She could be fuckin' anywhere."

"Mouse is working with his friends on the deep web. He's trying to get a trace on her."

But it will be as hard as finding a needle in a haystack. So far we've got that she could be dead and buried somewhere no one will ever find her, or out on her own, anywhere in the US. I don't like either option.

"You're missing something," Demon states. "We're talking about the Warped Jokers. They'll still end up in court whether or not the state's prime witness is there. Could go either way, may still be enough evidence to convict them. Half of their gang is already in jail awaiting the trial. Already she's caused more trouble than they can handle. It may be they're out for revenge, and not just to silence her. Remember what Cray and Seeker told us."

For a moment I can't speak.

"Their skin trade," RIP breathes. "She could go into their pipeline, disappear forever, and spend the rest of her life wishing they'd taken her out."

Fuck. He couldn't have said anything worse. What was it Cray had said? *A blind woman wouldn't care who's between her legs.*

I remember how different it was to make love to a blind woman. The same thing I found a turn on, wanting to give her pleasure by touch, could arouse men for a totally different reason. A woman they could torture because she couldn't see what was coming. I turn, my hands smashing down on the table, tears from my eyes starting to run down my face.

"We've got to find her!" I yell in frustration, feeling so useless. This morning I woke up and Stevie wasn't there, but at least I hoped she was being looked after, that someone was watching out for her. It wasn't much, but it was some comfort at least. Now we know fuck all about where she is, only that she's been missing for twenty-four hours.

"Why now, Devil? Why didn't you tell us yesterday? Before any trail went cold?"

Devil's eyes turn icy when he lays them on Drummer. "Because it's marshal business. Lennox didn't inform me until today. Updated Drummer as soon as I got here, and he got on to Mouse. We haven't been sitting twiddling our thumbs, Beef. Until a few hours ago, I thought my update was simply that she was safely in the hands of the marshals. Got Sean looking into it.

Just before I came in I got the update that he couldn't locate a body."

Not yet. But I'm not hopeful they won't. All my dreams and plans. Yeah, I knew I'd lost her, but I was going to get her back. As Judge had suggested, if all else had failed, I'd been planning on turning up at court. One way or another I'd get her back. Or at least, give her the chance to come back to me.

RIP and Chaz have been muttering together, in such a low tone I can't distinguish their words. Nods, chin raises, shakes of their heads tell me nothing. I'm expecting the two Soulz' prez' to get up and walk out, saying it's our problem and nothing to do with them, when Chaz bangs the table and surprises me.

"Drummer. You and I go way back. Sent us some lucrative business not too long ago as well."

I remember the drug trade we didn't want to dip into but passed on the tip to the Arizona Soulz. I frown. I'd been close to death at the time. Now inside I feel all over again that I'm dying.

For a reply, Drummer raises his chin.

Chaz continues, "I fancy myself a trip to LA. Let's go capture us a Joker. Get info on their houses where they take the girls. If they've got her stashed there, we'll find her."

"Stinger might help. I'll call him, see if we can get a step ahead in this game," RIP offers. Then seeing my confusion reminds me gently, "The LA Soulz prez."

"Jokers will have gone underground, now you've taken away their charter."

"Not so sure of that, Drum. They're not the brightest tools in the box. No. I think RIP and Chaz are onto something. Anyway, us going to LA is better than kicking our heels here."

"You want in on this?" Drummer asks Devil, sounding surprised.

Devil's eyes blaze. "You know me, Drummer. I've seen enough of the trafficking business. The thought of a helpless woman being caught up in that, and for nothing but wanting to stand up and tell the truth? Yeah, I'm with you."

"We're in too." Four heads, two prezes, two VP's are all nodding at RIP's words. "Just need to get to LA. If she's with them, that's where they'll have her."

"Been a bit of time since I've been in the thick of the action," Chaz confirms.

Devil holds up his hand. "One, I can get a private plane to take us all down there. We might even be ahead of them if they're driving her down. I doubt they've got the resources for a jet and won't be able to take her commercial. Two, get Stinger spreading a net. Three, just in case she got free herself, I'll keep Nessa and Sean searching." He pauses as though to gather his thoughts. "I got a couple of men I can get on the ground there too."

"Mouse and Cad will work with Sean," Drummer confirms.

"Expected that." Devil nods, then looks around. "Am I missing anything?"

"Only that if she's got free, she might contact Beef," Wraith suggests.

I shrug. "I'll have my phone, but she doesn't know the number."

"She knows the club owns businesses. She's resourceful enough to find one of their numbers. I'll get everyone listening out for a call for help. We'll get brothers to her if she makes contact."

"You staying here, Demon?"

"Yeah. Just in case she tries to get here. I'll send Thunder with you, Beef. You need to have a brother with you."

I've already got two. My *real* brothers, Drummer and Wraith. But I appreciate the gesture and that Demon has started to see me as one of his own. Won't for long, of course, I'll be headed back to Tucson as soon as possible. I frown. Without Stevie at my side, I can't see myself anywhere.

Devil stands and leaves the room with the parting comment he's off to make the arrangements. RIP follows him out, and I know he'll be calling Stinger. Demon isn't far behind them, but he returns shortly with a tray full of beer bottles. They're only half drunk when the other two men return. Devil saying a plane will be waiting for us in two hours at Pueblo Memorial airport, and RIP reporting Stinger will try to find a Warped Joker. His grin and slight shake of his head suggests the LA Soulz prez isn't fazed by the task he's been set.

Four hours later we're setting down in LA. I'm hopeful we're not far on the heels of Stevie if this is indeed where she's been taken. The drive from Denver would take eighteen hours, and that's if they drove or rode without stopping. We're less than a day behind her.

Surely not much could have happened to her in that time?

When we disembark, it's to find three SUVs waiting for us. Stinger, himself, has arrived to escort us to his clubhouse. Chaz and RIP ride with him, I find myself in the next with Drummer, Wraith and Thunder. Charmer, Bull and Devil take the third.

Automatically I go to shrug out of my cut before getting into a cage and catch Wraith's eyes.

"Feels naked, without one, doesn't it?"

I've worn a cut for fifteen or so years, so it certainly does. But we're not in Satan's Devils territory, so couldn't bring them with us.

"You gonna be okay, Beef?" Wraith's eyes are watching me carefully.

I shrug, not knowing how to answer. If we can't find Stevie, I'll wish I hadn't risen from the dead last year. I'd believed I had something to live for, but without her, it seems I've lived only for life to have a chance to torture me. Why had it taken so long for me to pull my head out of my ass and know I wanted to claim her? If I hadn't friend-zoned her for so long, I would have been the one she'd turned to instead of Lennox.

"We'll find her." It's Thunder who sounds adamant. "You'll have her back, Beef."

He can't know whether that's possible or not, but the sentiment is something I have to hang onto.

Taking a deep breath, I force myself to be positive. "When," *yeah, when, not if,* "when we get hold of a Joker, I want to take lead, Drum."

He fastens those steel-grey eyes on me. "Know you do, Beef. And I would if I were in your shoes. But the fact is, we're in the Soulz hands now. On their territory and will be in their house."

"But—"

"Beef," Wraith interrupts. "You're likely to kill him. You're too emotionally involved and I don't fuckin' blame you for that. If it was Sophie, yeah, I'd want my fists on him too. I've no doubt the Soulz will make him hurt, but they're likely to get him to talk. You let fly? Break his jaw? Might cause him pain but won't get your woman back."

LA traffic is a bitch. We seem to be stopped more times than we're moving and I long to be on my bike. Lane splitting is legal in California and getting through this traffic would be a breeze on two wheels. On four it's hell on earth. I hate being enclosed in a cage at the best of times. At least the air-conditioning works. The way the road is shimmering as I look ahead reminds me it's high summer, and the temperature will be hot as hell. Not quite as hot as to what I was used to in Tucson. The climate in Pueblo is slightly cooler, that's one thing going for it. Though, I wouldn't be looking forward to snow in the winter. Uh uh, not this Arizona boy. Not that I'll be there to experience it.

Stupid thoughts, but I welcome anything to get my mind off Stevie and what she might be going through. I long for a call from Pueblo to say she's reached out for help, or for Devil's guys to find she's on a Greyhound bus and that they can track her. Devil managed to get a plane fast, he can probably manage to get her picked up from whatever bus station she arrives at. Yeah, Stevie's got away and is safe, and we're here on nothing more than a wild goose chase. That's the thought I've got to hang onto. The alternative is something I don't have it in me to even consider.

I swear the journey from the airport to the clubhouse takes

longer than the plane ride. As the SUV pulls up, I'm subjected to the full heat of the sun for just a few seconds before being waved on through the door without having had a chance to examine the exterior of the Wretched Soulz clubhouse. Inside it's much the same as any club I've been to. A bar in prime place, pool tables, games machines and an odour of cigarette smoke, stale beer and sweat. A man's environment. A girl is down on her knees sucking cock, a sight I wouldn't usually object to, but the thought that Stevie could be forced to do what the club whore is doing voluntarily makes me go cold to my gut. I turn quickly away.

CHAPTER THIRTY-SEVEN

Despite the heavy traffic, we arrive at the LA clubhouse only minutes behind the first SUV, and the third no more than a few seconds behind us. We're in time to see the various Wretched Soulz prezes meet. Arms clasped, backs slapped and then hugs. I try to suppress my impatience while the greeting ceremony takes place, and the obligatory small talk which follows. Then, finally, when to my mind an inordinate amount of delay has passed, Stinger comes over to us.

Gritting my teeth, knowing we could have been out searching, trying to find a man with knowledge of where Stevie is, I do my best to be polite when he gets to me.

"You're Beef."

I raise my chin and hold out my hand.

Stinger's face splits into a grin. "Got some news you might like."

I tilt my head to one side.

"Found us a Joker."

"Where is he?" I rasp.

He jerks his head as though indicating somewhere behind him. "Secure. Got my enforcer softening him up. Letting him know what to expect. Left the actual questions until you got here."

"How'd you find him so quick?"

"Assholes were still using their favourite bar." He spits on the floor. "Stupid motherfuckers."

"You going to clean them out?" Chaz calls.

"Yeah, will have to if they haven't got the message by now."

"We're wasting time," I interrupt.

"Respect, Beef," Drummer says, warningly.

Stinger lifts his head and nods in appreciation at my prez, then his eyes narrow. "Him. He's the one in with the feds?"

Him is Devil. Devil grins and, stepping forward, speaks up for himself. "Your house, your rules. But I work with, not for, the feds. Right now, I'm employed by Drummer to find Stevie Nichols."

My eyes shoot to Drummer's, he gives a confirmatory chin lift in return. I didn't know Drummer was paying him. Fuck it's good to have someone at my back.

"He straight?" Stinger asks Drummer, clearly still suspicious.

Drummer gives a twisted grin. "He's watched Blade's handi-work before, and we're still here."

"I can sit the questioning out," Devil offers. "But could be he'll let something slip I can get my guys following up on. Save time if I hear it from the horse's mouth."

"You a fuckin' Aussie?"

Devil snorts. "British."

Stinger regards him for a moment, wasting yet more time, before giving a sharp up and down of his head. He points his finger at him and snarls, "You rat us out, you're dead."

Devil shrugs as though a death threat is water off a duck's back and then, finally, we're led out back, across a yard, and into a storage shed. The walls and roof are made of corrugated iron, and to say it's hot inside is an understatement. I can immediately see why Stinger's enforcer is stripped down to a naked chest.

They've got a man tied to something I've only seen on the rare occasion I've gone to a BDSM club. I've never been into that shit seriously, but I know enough to recognise a St Andrew's cross that he's been strung up to. Arms in a V above his head, leg's in an inverted V tied apart at the ankles. It leaves him wide open and vulnerable.

"How's he doing, Brake?" Stinger enquires as we walk in.

"Sweating." Brake, who presumably is the enforcer, grins widely.

Anyone would sweat in this environment. I can already feel my tee dampening under my arms.

"Well, make him a bit more comfortable." Stinger leans back on a workbench.

I stand, my hands clenching into fists. I try to relax, but despite my efforts, each time I force them open, seconds later my fingers have curled inward again.

Clearly knowing what his prez is asking, Brake steps forward carrying a blade that even from here looks sharp and lethal.

"Stay still," he warns in a gravelly voice.

The man strung up protests, "What you doing? I've done nothing…"

Then he goes silent as the knife cuts through his tee as easily as through butter. Brake then sinks to his haunches and begins carving his way up through the denim of his captive's jeans. "Stay very still," he warns again. "Or I might cut off your balls accidentally."

Like any man would, he stills. But protests still come out of his mouth. "Don't cut my jeans, no man, you can't."

But Brake can.

It's hot, sweat is already running down the Joker's face, and his face is flushed from the heat. But I'll be fucked if he doesn't go even redder as his pants and underwear hit the floor. Yeah, I can see there are benefits to a St Andrew's Cross. Vulnerability. His legs stretched apart leaving his sensitive parts wide open.

Not that the Joker's are currently very impressive. Mind you, in the circumstances I would think any man's would wither.

Stinger leans in conspiratorially. "Blake's got some fuckin' good techniques. He put a cock cage, one of those real tight ones on a man once. He then fed the fucker Viagra and let's just say he didn't take heed of the recommended dose. You should have seen him. His eyes looked like they were popping out of his head." He's not speaking particularly quiet. The Warped Joker looks in complete distress, his eyes flicking around as if to spy what Brake has waiting for him.

"He die?"

"Nah. We let him go in the end. Took that cage off eventually, and, well, I swear this room still stinks of cum."

Can't tell whether he's joking or not, but my story's the truth. "Worse thing I saw happened to a brother." I frown, remembering Rock. "Fuckin' bastards flayed his tat off his back. He said it was the worst pain he'd ever felt."

Brake, overhearing, picks up another knife. It's long, and thin. "Haven't tried that. Sounds interesting."

"Yeah," I say, getting into it. "They took their time. He had no skin left from neck to ass."

"What do you want to know? I'll tell you," screams the tied-up man.

Stinger turns away from the man and winks at me, then steps up. "Name," he snaps.

"Fucker."

I can only see the side of his face, but all Stinger has to do is raise his eyebrow. Brake growls and steps forward menacingly.

"It is. That's my name. They call me Fucker." The Joker screams.

"I can work with that. *Fucker.*" Stinger grins. His puffed-out chest shows the president patch he's wearing. Dirty and worn, showing he's worn it a long time. "You know you don't exist, right? Yet there you were in the bar the Warped Jokers used to frequent. You got the message you've lost your charter?"

A tied-up man finds it difficult to shrug. Fucker tries his best.

"Arch said it made no difference. Just that we shouldn't wear our cuts."

"You were wearing a cut," Stinger observes, taking out a packet of cigarettes. Lighting one, he blows smoke in Fucker's face. *If you don't smoke that shit is nasty. Fucker though, he breathes in and half closes his eyes. Good way of getting him to betray, he'll be desperate for a dose of nicotine himself soon.*

"I like wearing it."

"I'm sure you do." Stinger indicates to Brake, who begins cutting Fucker's leather vest in half. "But you won't need it anymore."

Get to it, man. I'm itching to step up and take over. Stinger catches my eye. I feel a hand on my shoulder.

"Easy, Brother," Drummer's voice sounds in my ear. "He's just putting the fear of God into him. Start easy and work up to the hard. Go in too fast, and he'll clam up."

"Jokers are a fuckin' joke in this town now, got it, *Fucker*. And seeing we've got chapters in most of the states, and beyond, doubt you'll find a new home. You're done for."

"Mad Bull said he'd sort it when he gets out."

"He ain't getting out. We've disavowed him, and your brothers in the joint. You know what that means?"

As Fucker's eyes widen, it seems that he does. Without protection, his prez's lifespan doesn't look like it will last much longer.

"As for you, you're on your own. You got one chance to get away from this alive."

Now he's going to ask about Stevie. Only, he doesn't.

"I want to know your safe houses. Where you stash your girls before moving them. Every fucking one of them, you get me?"

"You're taking over our businesses?"

"You won't be working the trade anymore." Stinger neither confirms nor denies it. *I don't want to know the answer, right now I'm only interested in one woman.*

"They'll kill me if I tell you."

Another rise of Stinger's brow. He doesn't need to tell him he's got a more immediate threat from him.

Brake steps forward ominously. He's got a rubber mallet in his hand which he's bouncing against his fist. "I love the way they squeal when this hits the sac," he offers in a conversational tone. "I must be warped, but I get a thrill from seeing those balls swell up and turn purple."

"Go the size of water melons," Chaz puts in. "Seen that myself."

"Oh fuck, no. No. Not that. No."

My balls seem to shrivel in sympathy. Worse pain a man can go through. If Fucker's cock could shrink anymore, I think it probably would. It's trying to make itself even less of a target.

"Start talking," Stinger snaps.

"I, I… can't."

I suppose you have to admire his loyalty. Brake steps forward and starts an upward swing aimed straight through the V formed by his legs, then brings the mallet back down. "Just getting the right angle," he explains. "Need to get it just right. Course, I may pop one of the fuckers if I'm not careful. Hey, one of Fucker's fuckers. It's almost worth it to be able to say that."

Fucker's eyes are wild. He's looking around each of us, wanting to see sympathy. Well, that he might find, the kindred of men who know just what terrible pain to expect, but he doesn't find any for him.

Brake looks like he means business this time. He grabs the mallet with both hands taking a firm hold.

"I'll tell you. I'll tell you."

Stinger stays Brake's movement. "Everything?"

With tears rolling down his face, Fucker nods.

If he doesn't spill everything fast enough, I'll be taking that mallet off Brake.

Suddenly Stinger does what I wanted to do. He lurches forward and tugs the mallet out of Brake's hands and starts a swing which is certain to end in agony.

"I'll tell you everything!" Fucker screams before it hits him.

Stinger eases the arc but still makes contact. I wince as Fucker unsuccessfully tries to curl up. Screams of pain fly out of his mouth and tears start rolling down his face. I see his stomach muscles clench, and his balls seem larger than they were a moment before.

Without giving him time to recover, Stinger threatens him with the mallet again. "Next time I'll do it properly. Now what about the blind bitch, where's she being held?"

His eyes meet all of ours, then his chin drops against a chest which is still heaving. "A house on fourth," Fucker rasps out, each word punctuated by an intake of breath. It might only have been a tap compared to what Stinger could have done, but he's finding it hard getting air. "That's where they were planning to take her."

I note he didn't even try to deny he knew who we were talking about, and that they had her.

Stinger considers for a moment, like me, probably weighing up whether he's told us the truth, and coming down on the side that in all likelihood he has. "Get him down and dressed. Fucker can take us there."

Losing interest in the tortured man, the Wretched Soulz prez comes back to me and the rest of the interested group watching his technique.

"Quickest way to get the info." He nods at me. "Show him what's he in for, then fire the question you want answered. Now, do you want to go find your woman, Beef?"

He doesn't wait for my answer. It's obvious. I might not have been able to lay hands on Fucker, but I will on any man who's dared touch a hair on my woman's head.

I've no sympathy for the man who's struggling to get dressed, gingerly tucking his family jewels into a baggy pair of sweats that's been found to replace his jeans and struggling into a plain borrowed tee. Brake shows no compassion as he hurries him up, then, after zip-tying his hands behind him, none too gently pushes him out of the shed and into the sun.

The rest of us follow. The sun is hot, but less stifling than the shed we've just been in, and I eagerly breathe in the fresh air. My whole focus is on getting to Stevie, and luckily no one seems to want to waste time.

Could I have gotten the information quicker and saved precious moments? Unlikely. In the state I'm in I'd have had more of a bull in a china shop approach. Wraith was right. A man can't talk around a broken jaw and can be hard to understand when he's missing his teeth. I've learned a thing today about mental torture being a useful tool. Maybe I'll suggest it to Mace when I get back to base.

Why Mace? Why wasn't my first thought Blade? I've known him far longer.

"You okay, Brother?"

I give Thunder a look that pointedly asks, *what do you think?* I'll only be alright once Stevie's back in my arms and I know she's unharmed.

As we walk, he places his hand on my back which feels naked without my cut. A silent gesture of support. No need for more words.

Drummer and Wraith are walking ahead with the Wretched Soulz prezes and VPs. All following a man who looks like he knows death isn't far away, being dragged along by the enforcer. Fucker will co-operate to try to prevent it, but I'm doubtful his life will be measured by anything more than hours.

CHAPTER THIRTY-EIGHT

The house Fucker takes us to looks run down and uncared for, but basically sound. The neighbourhood around matches. As we drive by slowly, I take in a man bent over a beat-up car, attracted by the engine noise. He stands and yawns widely, the state of his teeth showing me he's clearly a meth addict.

The SUV Stinger and Brake are in along with Fucker draws to a halt around the corner. We park behind.

"Fucker says there's a rear entrance. That's how they get the girls in and out. I've sent Shift around the back to see what the set ups like." He nods to one of his members who's disappearing amongst bushes, already crouched down. At my look of concern, he reassures me. "Shift knows what he's doing. They won't spot him."

"We need to attack from both sides," Chaz suggests. The two Wretched Soulz prezes didn't need to come along, but both, together with their VPs, had decided they weren't missing out on any of the action today.

"How do you want us to split up?" Drummer defers to the LA Soulz prez.

"You, Wraith, Beef, Thunder, Chaz and Bull take the back.

The rest of us will come in from the front. Use what force you have to. You take your woman, Beef. I'll deal with any other girls."

"Deal?" Devil's frowning.

Stinger gives him a measured look. "I can find work for them if that's what they want. Don't like unwilling women, so we'll leave them alone."

"I'll arrange to get them home," Devil challenges.

A moment of consideration, then, "Yeah. Okay."

I'm not sure that's what he'd have normally done if a consultant with connections to the feds wasn't here, but it eases my conscience that I'm only intent on saving one woman.

"You're with me," Drummer tells Devil.

For an answer, Devil slides out a gun and checks it. He meets my appraisal with a lop-sided grin. "When in America…"

My weapon's already primed and ready, and I'm pleased to see everyone is in a serious mood making their own preparations. Chaz, who'll be leading our team, bends his head close to Stinger's as they make the final arrangements. I'm bouncing on my feet in a hurry to get moving, but if this isn't done right, people inside might die, including Stevie.

Stinger calls Drummer, RIP and myself to join him.

"Problem we've got is that Fucker can't tell us how many Jokers are inside. They come and go, particularly to sample new merchandise."

"Fuckin'—"

"Can it, Beef," Drummer stops me. "Deal with what you find, not what's in your fuckin' imagination. Got it?"

I've got it. But it's hard to stop myself thinking the worst.

Stinger's looking impatient. I nod, showing I've got myself under control. Outwardly, at least.

"Warped Jokers are likely to kill the woman, so she can't testify. Fucker's coming to the door with us, he'll get them to open up. Once he's inside, we'll be right behind him. I'll give you the signal, Chaz, and you can bust in the back door. I'm hoping we can do this quietly." He pauses. When Brake holds up his knife, he nods. "Our priority is to get to the women before bullets start flying."

"Where are the women being held?" Wraith asks, his eyes going to the man who's agreed to betray his brothers.

"In the back, according to Fucker."

At that moment, Shift returns. "Windows are blacked out, can't see anything. But the frames look fairly weak, and I've just picked the lock on the back door. Couldn't hear anything going on inside."

Stinger nods. "Okay. While we get their attention out front, your team, Chaz, enters at the rear. Find the women and protect them. Beef, you can help here. If your woman's there, she'll know you, and can help keep the others calm. Otherwise..." Otherwise they'll just think there're new men come to rape them. "Keep them covered and their heads down."

Sounds simple as a plan, though I know there's a thousand things that can go wrong. One thing in our favour is that we've got the manpower. Doesn't mean much if bullets start flying. But once I find Stevie I'll use my body as a human shield. Don't mind taking a bullet for her, there must be something I was brought back from the dead for, and maybe this is it.

A few last final words, then it's time. Shift accompanies us as he's already found out the best way to get to the rear without being seen.

The bushes that serve to hide the residence from prying eyes also afford us cover. Keeping low and quiet, we make our way around the one-story building. Shift points to the door he's already opened. Chaz holds up his hand. When his phone vibrates, he points to the door.

Chaz takes the lead, I slip in right behind him. The kitchen is empty. I'm just breathing out a sigh of relief when a toilet flushes in a half-bath off to one side. Chaz takes the left, I take the right. The door opens, a blade flashes, and as if we had choreographed it, I have the dead body in my arms and lowered to the floor without any sound.

Drummer and Devil have come in behind us. Chaz points to two doors, one either side of a small hallway. Drummer opens one, Chaz the other. One is empty, soiled bedding strewn all over. *Have they been warned and moved the girls?* Fuck, no. Impossible. *How could they have known?*

The other Chaz pushes against but it doesn't budge. Looking there's a bolt, top and bottom. As we slide them back carefully, there's a shot from the front, followed by another.

"We've got your back," Thunder says quickly. "Get in there, Beef."

Chaz holds the door open for me. Still with my gun in my hand, I step inside.

It's dark, dingy, the windows have been painted black. There's a light switch I flick but it doesn't work. Thunder passes me a flashlight and I switch it on to reveal a world of horror. About a dozen women are cowering together, half dressed, clearly beaten and cowed.

"Stevie!" I call out, but there's no answer.

Fuck no. Wrong place.

I turn in horror as Devil steps inside, pushing past me and rasping out, "Go find her, Beef. I'll take care of these."

More bullets are flying. Screams of pain as they meet their targets.

"Stevie!" I shout louder now.

"Beef!" Comes an answer. It's her voice. She sounds terrified. But fuck, where is she?

Chaz kicks a door open behind which is chaos and action. Men are hiding behind overturned furniture firing toward the door. Our entrance has startled them, and I get off shots before they realise they're fighting on two fronts now.

Stevie. Stevie. Where the fuck are you?

"Stop firing or she dies."

I turn, slowly. My eyes widening in horror as I see one of the

Jokers has Stevie held in front of him, a gun pressed hard against her forehead.

Quickly I analyse the scene. There are four other Jokers. Two dead or incapacitated, two alive. One of whom I recognise. My eyes narrow. It's Cray. *Fucking knew we shouldn't have let him go free.*

"Stay where you are," Stinger snaps as they try to move closer to the man holding Stevie.

Guns are pointed at Stevie and us. Guns are pointed at them. We outnumber them, but as far as I'm concerned, the only important person is the woman I love.

I might be standing in the room with four presidents, but that's my girl there. Without consultation I take a step forward, my action causing the gun to be pressed harder into her forehead.

"You're not going to get out of this," I tell the man who's obviously the leader of this group of men. "Give yourself a chance. All we want is the woman."

"Allow her to testify? We'll all end up in the pen. Nah. My prez gave me orders. See that she never gets to court."

"You haven't got a prez any longer. You haven't got an MC. It's over for the Warped Jokers and for you if you shoot her. Yeah, you might take a couple of us down with you, but you're outnumbered and outgunned. You kill her? We kill you."

"Shorty…" His comrade I don't know is looking around nervously. Cray's eyes are wild, and I'm worried about the way he's holding his gun. He's recognised me and Thunder.

"Shut it. You know what Mad Bull wants," Shorty replies.

"You let her go, we let you walk out of here." I'm making a promise I'm certain Stinger won't keep, but I'll try any ploy to get Stevie back into my arms, alive and unhurt.

Stinger's leaning lazily against the wall. He doesn't seem bothered about what's going on. Casually he takes out a cigarette and lights it. After he's drawn smoke into his lungs and let it out to pollute the air, he says, lazily, "Shorty, is it? Well, you know who I am?"

A nod confirms he's been recognised.

"We're stepping into your trade. All we want is the girls, and that includes her."

"Satan's Devils want to protect her. Want to get her to court."

For once, I'm grateful I'm not wearing my cut when Stinger responds, "You see any Devils here? All the cuts I see are Soulz."

Shorty looks left and right, and finally at me. I stare back stoically.

Cray opens his mouth. Then, for some reason he doesn't say anything. *Has he calculated he's got better odds to get out of here if he stays quiet? Thinks he's doing us a favour?*

"So who are you then?" he finally asks.

"Who they are doesn't matter. Who the Soulz consort with is no concern of yours. What matters is we've both got something we want. I want the women, *all* of them. You want your lives. Seems like a good bargain to me."

"Take it, Shorty," the man who'd spoken before insists, shifting nervously from foot to foot. "I don't want to die."

Shorty looks shifty. "How about I kill this one, you can have the others?"

"A blind bitch? I can think of a special market for her. Nah. I want her."

Stinger sounds so convincing, he's almost got me believing he'd betray us. *He wouldn't take Stevie, would he?* Nah, course he wouldn't, he's bluffing.

But Stevie doesn't know that. The whimper from her lips makes me wish she could see me, when she gasps out, "Beef..."

"Yeah, what's with that? She knows him. I don't believe you." Shorty looks like he's solved a puzzle and is patting himself on the head. "You won't be using her..."

"Beef..." she implores again, her blind eyes searching the room as if to find me.

"Sweetheart," I drawl. "Stinger wants you? He can have you.

I don't do relationships, you know that. This is just business. You hear me? Had you once, that was enough."

I'm hoping she of all people will understand the undercurrent beneath my words.

Half-turning I'm in time to see Stinger wink. Then he stalks toward me. I'm not in time to dodge the fist that comes toward my jaw.

"I told you not to touch the fuckin' merchandise," he snarls as all hell lets loose.

The Jokers' attention had been on our altercation. They've completely missed Thunder creeping up behind Shorty. Three gunshots ring out. Three bodies fall.

Stevie, wrenching from the grasp of the man dying staggers forward and into my arms. I hold her tightly. "You're safe. I didn't mean any of it. You're mine, Stevie. No one else will touch you. You're fuckin' mine and I'm never letting you go again. You hear me? No fuckin' marshals, no one else protects you. Only me. You hear me? I didn't mean what I said. I was just—"

"I know Beef, I know." She sobs against my chest. "I know. Please, the smell. I need to get out of here. Take me out Beef, please, take me outside."

I sweep her up into my arms and carry her. Soulz and Devils part ways to let me through. I know the smells of cordite and blood will be horrendous to her over-developed senses. Outside the house I put her down but keep hold of her. She's crying, weeping and uncontrollably shaking. Then, not surprisingly, she gags, and when I turn her away from me, she throws up.

Taking off my bandana, I pass it to her so she can wipe her mouth. When she turns to me, her face is white.

My teeth clench. *What the fuck have they done to her?* I want to know it all, everything, but I've seen enough sufferers of PTSD in my time to know if she went through even a fraction of the things running through my head, she needs time and space to talk it through in her own time, not be subjected to a barrage of questions fired at her right now. I have to tamp down my impatience.

"Stinger suggests we get her out of here." Thunder is by my side, pointing to where we left the SUVs. Then, more quietly into my ear, he adds, "Soulz are dealing with the clean-up. Devils are all returning to partake of their hospitality until we can get transport arranged."

"Beef. There're more women…"

"Sweetheart, we know. They'll be taken care of." Whatever she's been through, Stevie's thinking of others rather than herself. Showing that backbone again I so much admire.

"Stinger's got a doctor on call if she needs one."

Stevie hears that too and shakes her head. "I'm fine."

She might think she is, but her complexion, her trembling, suggests to me she's not. No woman would be. Right now, I don't know whether she needs to receive treatment or not, or, if she does, what for.

CHAPTER THIRTY-NINE

Stevie doesn't say a word on the drive back through LA. I take comfort that she's holding onto me as though I'm a lifeline. I could have found her abused, not wanting to accept the touch from any man, but whatever happened to her since she was stolen from the marshal, doesn't seem to have affected how she'll accept support from me.

When we arrive at the clubhouse Thunder steps up, telling me to wait outside while he sees if there's somewhere I can take her. It's a good idea. From the noises coming out it's crammed inside. There'll be drinking, smoking, fucking, and God knows what else which might set her back.

Within moments he's back. "There's a room you can use. Stinger called ahead and prospects have just cleared it."

I thank him. He leads the way and soon Stevie and I are alone. The room is a typical one. A bed, dresser, and not much else. I've carried her in, now I put her down next to the bed, taking her hand and placing it on the covers so she knows what it is and can sit if she wants. The thought runs through my head that being alone with a man and a bed might not be what she needs just now.

I don't know what the hell to do or say for the best. I wish we were back in Colorado where Jay or Vi could help. Even if there are old ladies here, I wouldn't know who the best would be.

Knowing she can't see the anguish or indecision on my face, I use the words she needs. "Stevie, babe. I'll do whatever you need. If you want me to stay, I will. If you need to be alone, I'll go. Just tell me, are you hurt? Do you need medical attention? Of any sort?"

She rubs at her arms. "They were rough, Beef. They left bruises, but no, I'm not injured. There's nothing that won't heal on its own."

Did they fuck you? That's what I want to ask. But can't. Not just yet. For both her sake and mine. If there's any way I can be, I want to be prepared for the answer.

My eyes tell me I may have got there in time, her clothes are awry from the struggle, but she's still wearing shorts and a tee. I don't want to make assumptions and be wrong.

Her hands reach for me. "I want you to stay Beef. Please don't leave me alone."

That's an easy one. "I've no problem with that, sweetheart. I'll never leave you alone. Not again."

"Where am I?"

"You're in LA, you know that?" When her head moves side to side, I narrow it down further. "You're in the clubhouse of the Wretched Soulz. Just til we can work out how we're going to get home."

Her eyes widen a little when I name the Wretched Soulz. "Am I in danger from this club?"

"Nah. Wretched Soulz have cut the Jokers loose. That was their prez there, in the house doing the talking. In fact, most of the men there were Soulz. They helped rescue you."

Her mouth opens and shuts. I realise there's so much she doesn't know, and when it's time, I'll fill her in on the info she's missing. For now, I want her thinking about just one thing. "Focus on getting home, Stevie."

She repeats the word I've used. "Home." Her teeth bite her

lip, and a tear rolls down her face. "I've no idea where that is now."

That's not hard for me to respond to, either. "Home is Pueblo. With me and Max," I respond without hesitation, but then feel driven to add, "If that's what you want?"

She had left me. There remains a niggling doubt in my head as to why. A doubt she immediately puts to rest with her next words. "I want nothing more. Beef, I didn't want to leave you. But Lennox, he said there was a war brewing between MCs, and all because of me. He said you would be in danger unless I went. He told me your dominant club gives you permission to have an MC, and that they were coming for you if you gave me protection. Now we're here, in their clubhouse. I don't know what to think."

"Come here." I pull her into my arms. *She'd left because she thought I was in danger?* Her short statement has thrown all my doubts to the wind. "In a way, he was right. But we've sorted it out. Wretched Soulz have come out on our side. It's the Warped Jokers who have lost their charter..."

"The men who took me, they said something about that. They were so angry. I didn't understand it. Back, back..."

Back there. Where she almost suffered a fate worse than death or had been killed. My eyes close and I need a moment to control myself when I think of what could have been the outcome today. Her head moves, bumping into my jaw, and I wince.

"Are *you* hurt?"

I laugh softly, realising she hadn't been able to see what went down. "Stinger, babe. He wanted a distraction and hit me to provide one. He packs quite a punch."

Her hand rises and now it's her comforting me. Smoothing away my bruises with her touch.

Putting my hands on her biceps, I turn her so she's facing away from the bed. "Sit a moment, Stevie."

Feeling behind her, she does. Then tilts her face up. "You're going to ask what happened to me, aren't you?"

"No. If you want to tell me, you can. If you'd prefer, you can talk to someone else. There's no pressure, babe. Whenever you're ready."

But it seems she's ready now. She shudders. "It was close. So close. They wanted to get me to LA from Denver fast. One of them, well, he tried, but the others wouldn't let him. Said it would hold them up too much. But once we arrived here." She shudders. "I was thrown in with the other women. Those women, Beef. I couldn't see them, but I knew enough by the tone of their voices let alone what they were saying. They were used, by all the Jokers and by other men and that was what was going to happen to me. They said no one was kept there long. They told me men chose them, then they were taken away and didn't return."

"Stevie…"

"Let me finish. They came for me. I heard them talk, they didn't attempt to be quiet. They knew I couldn't see, so they taunted me. They were all going to try me out. They were… explicit in what they were going to do. One, two, three… All of them at once. They felt my breasts, groped my ass… But you came and stopped them."

The blood rushes from my head and I feel faint when I realise just how close it had come. "Stevie…" I croak.

"You were in time." Her voice sounds stronger. "I held onto the thought that I'd be saved, and you came."

"Stevie." I drop to my knees, my arms going around her, no longer wanting to give her space. "From this moment on I swear to you, I'll always come. I'd walk through hell to be with you." Yeah. I knocked on the door once and they didn't let me in, and now I know why. I'm her guardian devil. That's my role, my place and that's what I'll be until the day I die.

We stay like that, rocking gently in each other's arms. Just taking comfort from each other, both of us lost in the thought we might never have seen each other again.

"No more marshals, Stevie," I tell her at last repeating the words from before.

"I'm still going to testify." Her jaw looks set.

I know her too well to ask her to do anything but. "I know that. And you will. We'll figure out a way."

There's a knock at the door, it makes her jump. I glance across, then back to her. "You okay? I can tell whoever it is to get lost."

Her shoulders straighten a fraction. "I'm alright."

I open it surprised to see the Wretched Soulz LA prez standing there.

"How is she?" he mouths.

"She's fine," a voice calls out from behind me.

At his confused look, I tap my ear. "Excellent hearing."

"Could be awkward." He grins. Then, seeming surer of his welcome, steps inside.

"Hi, Stevie, I'm…"

"Stinger. I recognise your voice. Apparently, you hit my man." I'm amused at how cross she sounds on my behalf.

His grin widens. "Good memory too. Yeah, that's me, and I'd say I was sorry about that, but it saved you from a bullet. I'm the prez here." His smile slips away. "You doing okay, darlin'? Those fuckers hurt you?"

"They would have," I tell him grimly, "if we'd been minutes later."

He inhales sharply, then lets it out on a sigh. The implications hitting home. He raises his chin. "I'm sure Beef here's told you, but you've nothing to worry about from the Wretched Soulz. Just wanted to tell you that in person."

"Thank you."

Stinger looks at me uneasily. He can't read if she's really okay or not, and to be honest, neither can I. She looks so unusually uncertain. His glance goes from me, to her, then back.

Finally he suggests, "You want to come down and get something to eat?"

I look back at Stevie, at her hands twisting in her lap. Then turn back to Stinger. "We'll be down later."

A look of commiseration crosses his face, a recognition that in the last day or so Stevie's gone through hell. We might have been in time to stop the worst happening, but in her nightmares? I'd place good money she'll dream we didn't get there in time.

After the door closes behind him, Stevie calls me over to her side.

"What do you want, sweetheart?"

"For you to hold me, Beef. Just, hold me."

Lying down on the bed, I manoeuvre her up against my side, pulling her into me. Tears of relief prick at the back of my eyes. Having her back with me has brought me to my knees. She's my *one*. The woman I've been searching for all my life. Knowing how close I came to losing her…

"It's alright, Beef. I'm here." Her hand smooths over my head and then caresses my cheek. "I'm alright. I'm not going anywhere." Rolling over, her arm drapes across my chest. "Is Max okay?"

"He's doing fine. His leg's about healed now. He'll be over the moon to see you again."

"I hated leaving him, but I didn't know where I was going, and I couldn't look after him. I knew you'd take care of him for me."

I assure her I have. I tell her some of his antics, how he's twisted Pyro around his paw and manages to scrounge scraps from him at the table. How he and Bitch are keeping a good distance from each other, and how tolerant he is of Theo pulling his ears—not that we encourage that of course. As I bring her up to date with news from the compound, slowly her eyes start to droop and close. Her arm, still draped over me, becomes heavy and drops away. It makes me realise she can't have got much, if any, sleep in the past twenty-four hours.

As there'd been times I never thought I'd have her close to me again, I'm content simply to hold her.

A gentle rap on the door which she doesn't hear. I slide out from under her and go to answer it, stepping into the hall and pulling it closed behind me.

"She gonna be alright?" Thunder asks, quietly.

"Sleeping. She needs it."

"Drummer wants a word."

I look back at the closed door undecided. *If I leave her and she should wake, or have a nightmare…*

"I can sit with her," Thunder offers. "She knows me."

"Call me the moment she wakes."

He agrees.

Drummer and Wraith are sitting at a table in the bar, bottles of beer in front of them. At my approach, Drummer waves to a prospect who brings over another for me.

To pre-empt the question, I formulate the answer before it's asked. Wiggling my hand in a 'who knows' gesture. "On the outside she's fine. Inside? Hell, I haven't even asked about the marshal being killed, or if that was in front of her. She's got a lot to work through."

"We found her, Beef. Just concentrate on that and that you'll be there for her."

"You claiming her officially, Brother?"

"Yeah, VP, I am."

"So she's under the Devils' protection until she testifies. Stinger," Drummer tilts his bottle in the direction of the table where the LA prez is sitting, "reckons the Warped Jokers are getting depleted—probably with the Soulz help—and those on the inside won't last long without protection. After the trial, it should be safe for her to resume her old identity."

I nod. That's something we need to talk about. I don't even know her real name. Something I need to find out is whether she'd want to resume her old life. *Does she think my commitment to her is only until the court case is over?* But I've got a few weeks before all this is over, and hopefully during that time I'll make her see her life is with me.

"You want to get that nomad patch off your back, Beef?"

I tilt my head and raise my eyebrow.

"Come on home to Tucson? Girls would love to meet Stevie."

Why isn't my heart jumping for joy? Why even the slightest hesitation? "I don't know, Prez. You gave me a job, and I haven't done it."

"Think we can give you a pass on why. You got dragged into your woman's problems before you even arrived." Wraith makes excuses on my behalf.

"Thing is," I twist the bottle in my hands until I can pick at the label, "you're right about Demon needing a VP. Thunder could step up, but he doesn't want to, so, as you've seen for yourself, he's a great guy to have at your back, but isn't doing the role properly."

"I'll ask the other chapters. Maybe someone is ready to move on," Drummer says, firmly.

"Already got that in hand, Prez." Or I would have, had I not been so focused on Stevie.

"Thought you'd jump at the chance to come home. Oh, if you didn't know, Sally's taken the kids and gone back to her family. Tash is keeping in contact with her, and she seems to be alright. She's even started dating. A regular guy, not one chosen by her folks." Wraith laughs. "Think some of you rubbed off on her. She sent them packing when they tried to set her up."

"Good to hear. I was hoping she'd find she was stronger than she thought when she didn't have me to lean on. But that wouldn't be keeping me away, Sally knows where I stand now. It's just, you asked me to do something, Drummer, and I don't like feeling I'm leaving Colorado high and dry."

Drummer's expression is unreadable. I can't tell if he's pleased or annoyed I'm not leaping at the chance to return to the fold. Then he barks a laugh. "Loyal to a fuckin' fault, ain't ya, Beef?"

CHAPTER FORTY

The thought of what Stevie had gone through and the horrors I'm sure are running through her head keeps my cock flaccid, even though I hold her close in my arms all night. I'm so fucking scared of saying the wrong thing and upsetting her. All I want to do is have my face close to hers so when I inhale all I can smell is her.

Exhausted, she sleeps, while I stay awake, hundreds of thoughts going through my mind. *Does she need counselling? Would it be safe for her to see someone?* That would mean letting someone else in on her secrets, and I'm not sure that's for the best. Reading between the lines, the Wretched Soulz are making a game of picking the Jokers off both on the inside and out, but there may still be some around. Until Mad Bull's no longer breathing and pulling the strings, they'll still be trying to stop her from taking the witness box. She'll still have to stay in hiding.

Maybe Demon would know someone trustworthy. My lips curve as I think of the surprise she'll find when she gets back to Colorado, a yard where she can walk freely, perfumed flowers that will grow and be there for her to enjoy. *But she won't be there long enough to see them bloom.* Neither will I. While we're waiting for the court case I'll get in touch with Red and Snatcher, see if I can get that new VP for Demon. Then, I can go home.

I never thought a new set of brothers would come close to those I'd left behind, but somehow they've crept inside. I'd call all of them friends. My lips curve as I think of their reaction to seeing Stevie. Yeah, no regrets that I turned down Drummer's offer to go back to Tucson. There's no rush, and with everything she's been through, at least she won't be overwhelmed by strangers.

I must have dropped off sometime during the night as I wake to a loud bang on the door and a shout from Thunder telling me to get my ass in gear as we've got to get to the airport in time to catch our plane.

"I suppose that means I've got to move." Stevie rubs her eyes.

"You slept well."

"Because you were here, Beef. I haven't been able to relax since I left your side."

That's a nice thought to hear, as she'll never be leaving my side ever again. I'll chain her to me if I have to.

"Time to get up and fly, babe." Still unsure of her reaction, I content myself with a peck on her cheek rather than the devouring of her mouth I'd prefer. *Take it easy, steady, man. Let her lead.*

Stinger's got one of his club girls to lend Stevie some clothes to change into, they're remarkably respectable considering who owned them. We shower, dress—me in yesterday's jeans and tee—then head to the airport.

Due to Stevie needing to keep her head down low, Devil's hired another private plane to fly me, Stevie and Thunder back to Pueblo, accompanied by RIP and Charmer. Who's going to end up paying for this, I've no idea, but Devil mumbled something about laying the cost on the feds as they'll be the ones to benefit if they get their RICO conviction. From what I know of him, if anyone can get them to cough up, he will.

It's at the airport that we part company with Drummer, Wraith, Chaz and Bull, as they're taking a commercial flight back to Tucson. Devil is staying in LA for a while to help sort out getting the girls who want to return home back to their folks. I clasp hands with Drummer before leaving him.

"You sure?" Drummer's hand smooths down his beard in that familiar gesture, and his eyes focus on me. "I can have that nomad patch off in a moment."

I glance at Thunder waiting for me, and then at Stevie. "I'm sure, Prez."

"Ain't your prez for the moment, Brother. That title belongs to another man."

I nod. Yeah, for now Demon's my prez. Strange how that's starting to settle with me.

"You need somewhere to relocate Stevie, we'll always have room," Wraith assures me. "And keep us up to date with the court date. Reckon you might want support there."

Yes. I can hide Stevie until she's called to give evidence, but at that point, there'll be no getting away from everyone knowing exactly where she is and when she's going to turn up. That hurdle I'll face when I have to.

"Appreciate that, Wraith."

A flight number is called, a last call to get to the gate.

Drummer looks upward and then back at me with a slight smirk. "Guess that's us, got to get moving."

"Drum, Wraith. Look, give my love to Rock and Becca, okay? To all the old ladies and kids. And a hug to my cute little niece, Rose.

"Damn it." Wraith slaps his forehead. "Forgot to tell you. Heart and Marcia are pregnant again."

My brows rise almost to my hairline. "Another miracle baby?"

"Seems that way."

"Well, I'll be fucked." Good on Heart. I examine my thoughts about yet another baby on the Tucson compound, or it might be another set of twins the way my brother's luck goes. While I've nothing against children, it is nice to be in a clubhouse where you're not constantly stepping over toys. Do I regret that Stevie and I won't have children? Nah. I'll just be a favourite uncle to the kids of those who have. I'll be quite content to give them back when they poop or cry.

Another final call sounds over the loudspeaker, Drummer snarls impatiently as if telling the plane it can wait for him to be ready. We slap backs, hug and shake hands one last time, then I stand for a few seconds watching my long-time brothers stride off to their gate before returning to where Thunder is sitting with Stevie.

As if knowing the turmoil going through my mind, Stevie's hand rests on mine and squeezes gently. Then she leans in. "I can't wait to be back on the compound. Since leaving home, that's the safest place I've been. I was stupid to leave it."

"Hey. You did what you thought was best," Thunder reassures her, a pointed glance my way to make sure I agree.

I grin and raise my chin. Water under the bridge now. She went, and I have to admit I didn't like it, but now, she's back by my side where she belongs.

I'm tense during the journey. I hate riding in a cage, and a plane is a hundred times worse. On a bike you're in control, you can see what's coming and take action to avoid it. In a plane your life is in someone else's hands. At least it's a private plane and I don't have to bump shoulders with all and sundry.

With RIP and Charmer beside us, conversation is a little stilted. They don't want to talk about their business, we don't want to talk about ours. Stevie takes the journey in stride like just about everything else she does, but I notice she's quiet, lost in her head, and I don't know the words to bring her out of it.

On landing I'm happy to see my bike where I left it. We say goodbyes in our biker way to the Wretched Soulz, then, having situated Stevie behind me, Thunder and I head our bikes back in the direction of the clubhouse.

Demon is waiting to meet us, and he's not alone. Vi is standing with him holding Theo in her arms, and Jay is hovering behind her.

I don't have a chance to greet them before a bundle of fur comes rushing across the floor, skidding to a halt just before he knocks down Stevie, and at a slower pace he finishes his approach and brushes against her. Stevie sinks to her knees and starts to cry as she wraps her arms around her faithful companion, the dog who saved her life.

I watch her with an indulgent smile on my face. An expression which changes the moment I recognise who else is awaiting our arrival.

Placing myself between the two having a reunion on the floor and the man approaching, I greet him coldly, "Lennox."

He's not stupid. He takes in my demeanour and correctly interprets I'm certainly not pleased to see him. Behind me I hear movement and am not surprised when I feel a hand feeling its way up my back, then Stevie's arm loops through mine.

"Before you say anything, I'm staying right here," Stevie says firmly.

She can't see him nod, but I do. "Words," I remind him.

"Stevie. I, I'm so sorry. You should have been safe."

"You found your mole yet?"

"With a little help, yes." The way he grimaces suggests it was probably Mouse working with Cad and Cara who'd ferreted out the traitor, and not one of his own. "Not saying anything your guys don't already know, but she was a cousin of one of the Warped Jokers. Wanted to make sure family stayed out of jail. A long-term employee, her original record was clean, but her cousin patched in only a year ago."

I huff but keep quiet. Fucker patched into the wrong club.

Stevie's agitated by my side. "What, what happened to Marshal Handson? Is he alive? There was a shot..."

Lennox eyes meet mine.

He doesn't know how to break it to her, so I say it for him, "Babe, I'm sorry. He's dead."

She turns her face into my shoulder.

"Stevie's safe now, then? The leak's been stopped?" Giving her a moment, I continue to question him.

"Yeah. Though I don't know how wise it is for her to stay here."

"As the lady said, she's not going anywhere. I've got a whole club to keep her safe. Unfortunately, your marshal couldn't."

Again his face twists, and I wonder if he was friends with the marshal who died. "I can only suggest, not demand. It's up to Stevie if she gives evidence. Our offer to give her protection until she does, and beyond that if she needs it. If she refuses to accept our assistance, there's no pressure I can bring to bear to make her."

"I'm still going to give testimony," Stevie speaks up, a little tersely as though annoyed he's been talking about her as if she wasn't there. "But I'm putting my protection in the hands of the Devils," her fingers squeeze my arm, "the Devils' security business."

A quick grin comes to my face.

He nods, then remembers. "Yes. But I'll stay in touch. Please use our expertise to get you to court. That's something we've got experience in, and with the hole plugged, I assure you, no one will get to know any of the arrangements."

"I'd accept that, Beef. We'll still be there, but as Lennox has said, the marshals have the knowhow," Demon, still hovering, butts in.

"I accept," Stevie states. "It's my decision after all."

Lennox nods. "I'll be in touch then. Goodbye for now, Ms Nichols."

When he leaves, Pyro comes into view. He's carrying something which he takes out of the bag once he reaches Stevie.

"Thought you'd like this. James told us what to get."

Stevie feels the object he's given her, and I mirror the smile that splits her face. It's a new Service Dog harness for Max. She heaves a sigh full of relief. "He okay to wear this now?"

"Yup. He may get stiff at times, and shouldn't go for long runs, James said, but he's ready to do his duty again."

Kneeling, Stevie calls Max to her. The dog seems to still as his working harness is slipped onto him, going instantly into work mode. I realise it's the first time I've properly seen dog and handler together, that split second as the car was hurtling toward them doesn't count.

It's an ideal opportunity to take her outside and show her the new yard. I watch with interest as Max leads her around obstacles and stops at the steps we had to leave in place. Although the turf has yet to settle in, she notices the new soft grass under her feet immediately.

"You've made some changes here," she observes.

"A yard. Grass, flowerbeds too. Flattened it all out."

"For me?"

Yeah. "It needed doing," is all that I tell her. "Theo's going to be able to crawl around in the sun without getting hurt. And the furnace pit has been fenced in so there's no danger to you or to him."

"I've put you to a lot of trouble."

"Want the truth? I needed something to occupy me, a hope to hang onto that you'd come back."

Her hand fumbles for mine, I help her find it. "I was hanging onto the hope that I'd be back too, Beef. I couldn't have stayed away. I kept telling myself, just until I testify, then I'd make contact again. I didn't realise how hard it was going to be to leave you behind. Even worse than it had been leaving my family."

We're both silent, each deep in our thoughts. I hate knowing we'd both been as lonely as the other, but know it's a good sign for our future.

A raindrop falls, hitting the ground with a splatter.

"Think that's our cue to go inside."

At her nod, I let Max lead her back into the clubhouse, watching as he accurately meanders his way around tables and chairs. Then I apply my hand to the small of her back.

"Come up to the room." I want to say *our* room, but wonder if that's presumptuous, wondering whether she needs more time.

"I'll look after Max," Ink offers with such an exaggerated wink, for once I'm pleased she can't see.

Leaving the dog downstairs, we go to the bedroom. I'm touching her all the way, partly to guide her and partly as I don't want to lose contact.

"Has anything changed?" she asks on the threshold.

Hastily I push past her and slide my rucksack under the bed. "Nope."

She confidently steps around me and goes to the bed, sliding herself onto it and up until she's resting against the pillows. Patting the sheet beside her, she requests, "Come here, Beef."

She doesn't need to ask twice. Kicking off my riding boots, I walk around the other side, and stretch myself out. "Christ, I've missed you babe."

"Missed you more."

Impossible. I slip my arm under her head and pull her toward me. We lie in comfortable silence for a few minutes.

"Beef," she starts hesitantly. "What's the matter? Don't you want me anymore?"

"Fuck babe. What are you saying?"

Her voice is uncertain. "I thought, I hoped, you wanted, more. They didn't get to do more than touch me, Beef. But has that turned you off?"

"Darlin', how can you think that?"

She huffs a laugh. "You're lying in bed next to me. You've not made a move on me."

"I was giving you time. Fuck, babe. I don't know what's going on in that head of yours. You've been pawed by men who wanted to use you, and I don't want you to think I'm the same."

Her mouth forms an O. "You didn't think I wanted you to touch me? You didn't think I wanted to feel your cock inside me, to know it was the man I love making love to me, rather than strangers who'd threatened to use me for their own selfish pleasure? Didn't you consider I need you to take all the bad memories away?"

"Babe…"

"Beef, I need you."

"You're mine, Stevie," I growl as I sit up, ripping my tee over my head as I do so. My cock has gone from zero to sixty in one second flat. Her permission sending blood south so fast it almost makes me dizzy. "You want me? You got me."

CHAPTER FORTY-ONE

S tanding, I take a fraction of a moment to strip out of my jeans, then I'm crawling up the bed, leaning over her, my lips crashing down on hers as I take her hand and lead it to my now rock-hard cock. With my palm I encourage her fingers to encircle as much of my girth as she can, then prompt her to start a pumping motion.

All the time my tongue is thrusting in and out of her mouth, mimicking the action my dick will soon be undertaking.

Raising my head slightly, I gasp, "That feel like I don't want you, babe?" *Christ, the feeling of her hand on my cock is making me feel like a naïve schoolboy, unable to last.* Urgently I pull her hand away before I disgrace myself.

She pouts as if I've taken her favourite toy. "I want to taste you, Beef?"

"Yeah? You want me in your mouth?"

She nods.

"Then let's get you out of these clothes." I lean back on my haunches and lift her into a sitting position.

She shrugs me away as she disposes of her clothes in a time to rival mine. She's naked and glorious, and I take too long to admire her.

"Well?"

"Fucking perfect, babe. Lie back." I ease her into the position I want after ripping the top pillow away. Then I turn. That amazing perfume from her sex that I'll never tire of hits my nostrils and I can't wait, my mouth zeroing in on her cunt.

Her hands find my cock and lead it to her mouth. I go still. The only mouth that's ever been around my cock has been that of a club whore. The feeling of it being in hers is fucking incredible. It's not a job, it's something she wants. The difference is stunning. As her tongue swirls and explores, I almost stop breathing.

Until she pulls away and whines, "Beef…"

It's a prompt that this is reciprocal. I fasten my lips around her clit while the fingers of the hand not holding my weight off of her dip inside her cunt, the dual sensations make her gyrate her hips as she tries to get the right pressure in just the right spot.

And all the time her fingers are pumping the length of my shaft she can't get into her mouth.

Fuckin' hell that's good.

The sounds we're both making are brutal. Slurping, sucking, lips smacking. Groans, moans, pleas leaving our mouths. Despite the intense pleasure I'm feeling and that she's brought me quickly to the edge, I'm determined to keep control and not go over. I have to start envisioning all the nuts and bolts on my bike, what parts they screw into. *This goes here, that goes there…*

Then, as her muscles clench and tighten, her thighs start to quiver and shake, her efforts on my dick are more frantic. She comes.

"Babe, let me go…" I try to warn her.

But she takes me in further and swallows.

Fuck. I'm a man who prides himself on iron control. Unfortunately, I've lost it with her. Weeks of pent up frustration flood her mouth as I involuntarily let go. She keeps sucking, licking, and swallowing.

I lose all ability to think, becoming nothing more than an organism who feels.

"Babe." I draw away when I've finished, and embarrassed lift my head, raise my body, and pull myself out of her mouth. "I'm sorry."

Turning, so I can look down at her, I see her wiping up the cum that's dribbled out of the side of her mouth and sucking the drop off her finger. *What a fuckin' sight. Best thing I've seen in my life.*

"First time I've done that. Did I do it right?"

There are a few ways I could answer that. I settle for, "Think you could do with a bit more practice."

"Hmm," she answers lazily. "Think your skills are a bit rusty too."

Her impudent response stuns me. I slap the side of her butt cheek. "The devil they are. Not had any complaints before."

She's giggling so hard it's making her perfect tits wobble. I let my eyes feast for a second, realising, even though I came hard just moments before, I'm ready to go again now.

"Want your biker, do you, babe?"

"So soon?"

For a reply, I lift her up, turn her, and place her on her knees, then push her forward. Taking her hands, I place them on the headboard, warning her, "Hold on tight for the ride."

Taking hold of her hips, I position my cock against her glistening, slippery cunt and push inside, struggling to get my big dick into her tight hole. Then I'm all the way home. My finger rims her asshole. "Ever had a cock in there, babe?"

"No." The word is part nervous, part uncertain, but there's a tinge of curiosity too.

"One day, I'm going to take you there."

Her skin flushes red, which I hope is anticipation and excitement. Certainly wouldn't be my first time even if it's hers.

"Hmm," I pump in, "a nice big dildo in your cunt, and me in your ass. Think you could take that, babe?"

She pushes back against me. Yeah, I reckon this woman of mine will give it a try.

"Oh, fuck, Beef. *Condom.*"

Shit! "Stay there." I was so damn close to forgetting. "You need to go on the pill or something, Stevie. Or I'll get the snip. Want to feel you skin on skin as soon as possible," I tell her, reaching over her and opening a drawer. As I cover myself, I continue, "Never ever forgot before, but you make me forget my fuckin' name, babe. Now, where was I?"

I'm back inside her with just one thrust. I'm fucking her, fondling her tits which are dangling down. She's every bit as into it as I am, giving as good as I take, proving yet again she's the right woman for me.

Having already come once, I can take my time. I give myself over to the feeling of being inside her, learning the sensations we both like the best, trying out different speeds and rhythms. It's her third orgasm that takes me over with her. As I roar out my release, she's still hanging onto that headboard as if her life depended on it.

Pumping the last few drops into the condom, I relax my hold on her hips. "You can let go now."

She giggles. "I can't move. I think you've killed me, Beef. Can you give me a while to recover before the next round?"

Removing the condom and tying it, I leave it on the floor to deal with later and flop down beside her. "Think I'm going to need more than a minute myself, love."

"Old man," she teases.

"Watch out. Else I'll show you just exactly what this old man can do."

That threat seems to work as she snuggles in under my arm.

"I'm going to put my patch on you. Marry you too. Tie you to me in every way possible. Never letting you go again, babe."

She's quiet. After a moment, I get worried. "That alright with you?" Didn't she realise I meant this was forever?

"Alright? It's perfect." Her brow creases. "I know leaving

you was the wrong thing to do, Beef, but it made me realise that if I ever got the chance, I want to spend the rest of my life with you."

They say bad things happen for a reason. Any lingering discomfort at the thought she hadn't trusted me enough to keep her safe flee at her declaration. She'd thought she was doing the right thing to keep me safe, but distance had given her the clarity that she'd needed.

Leaning over, I kiss her until we're both breathless, then lay back and haul her into my arms once again.

"Will you want me to get a tattoo? Vi said it's in the club's rules or something."

The thought of fucking her with my name on her? That might just have made my over-worked cock twitch again. "That's Colorado rules, not Tucson's."

"Oh."

Is that disappointment I hear? I test her. "I've got no objections—none at all. If you're okay with getting a tat, I'd love to see my name on you."

Another moment of silence, then, "I'd like that, Beef."

I feel like pumping my fist in the air. "There's one other thing. For now, until this business is over." I pause, thinking I'm starting at the wrong end. "When Vi was abducted, Demon had a tracker on her." Not that it helped in the end, but the idea is a good one. "It was in a necklace she wore. I'm going to ask Cad to do something similar for you. I'm going to be looking out for you every step of the way, Stevie. If I can't be with you, I'll have another brother or a prospect with you. But this is just an extra bit of security."

She laughs out loud. Not the reaction I expected. "Like Max's tag? You're tagging me like a dog."

"It's..." *not the same thing* I start to tell her, then stop. Now I'm laughing too. She's got a point.

Her mirth dies away. "Anything, Beef. Tell me what to do and I'll do it. Get Max a tag too. I know the risk I'm taking, the danger that I'm in. I'll do anything to stay with you. But Beef, are you sure about this? You really want to marry me?"

"That's secondary babe. Just to make it legal in the citizen world. I'm claimin' you. And that, to a biker, has more meaning than a marriage license. So yes, I'm fuckin' serious. I've never been more certain about anything in my life."

"Stevie can't marry you."

What the fuck? Can't marry you is all I heard. I rear up. "Why the fuck not? You already hitched? You've got a man in the wings waiting? You engaged or something?" Fuck, I never dreamed… I thought she might have a life to return to, I never thought about her having a man. Not that he'd be worthy of the name if he let her go off alone. "You…"

"No." She replies emphatically, sitting up, drawing up her knees and wrapping her arms around them. "No Beef. I just don't want you to call me that anymore. That's not me, no need for pretence between us. I'm Stephanie, okay? Steph. Stevie doesn't exist. Stevie is somebody different."

"Stephanie?"

"Or Steph. That's what my family calls me. Stephanie North."

"Stephanie Carson," I try it out. "It has a nice ring to it."

"The marshals suggested I use a name close to my own so I wouldn't ignore anyone calling me it. But I long to hear my old one again."

"Steph," I try it out. Then do it properly. "Stephanie North. Will you be my old lady and marry me?"

"Yes."

Round three, it seems, isn't delayed as long as either of us had expected it to be.

CHAPTER FORTY-TWO

"You sure you're okay with this, Steph?"

"No." Her bottom lip quivers. "But the time has come when I need to do what I have to. Lennox has explained how this is going to play out. But you've got to stay back, Beef. Let them do their job."

The marshals, it seems, are experts at getting witnesses to court and have come up with a number of ways to get them there unseen. Stevie is going to be hidden in a catering truck, the one that normally goes to the courthouse, so it won't stand out. Another car, a decoy, and escort will be going by a different route.

I pace the room, while trying to bring myself under control. We've had no trouble in the last few weeks, which leads me to think it's today when an attempt will be made on her life. I've been trying hard to stay positive for Stevie and not let her in on my concerns; she's sufficiently aware of the risk herself that she's worried enough. If I let on how anxious I am too, it won't help her at all.

Lennox has assured me his plan is airtight, it's worked before, no reason why it should fail now. Even getting her to the catering truck will involve switching vehicles a couple of times, a wig for disguise. Steph's been well versed in what she has to do. She's practiced swapping cars, so she can do so without help and give no suspicion she is blind.

Ink, Mace, and Lizard have already gone down to LA and are staking out the courthouse. They volunteered due to the skills they picked up in the Army and Marines, namely the ability to merge into the background and remain undetected.

Steph is being flown down, and Demon and I are going with her on the plane. As the nearest chapter of the Satan's Devils is San Diego, my old friend Dart, now the San D VP, will be coming along with some of his brothers; Salem, their enforcer and Grumbler, their sergeant-at-arms, along with Pennywise and Kink. As Lennox has forbidden us to carry weapons on the plane—it had been hard enough to convince him to let Demon and I tag along —Dart is bringing weapons for us in case we need to use them.

We do know, courtesy of RIP, that Mad Bull and the officers in the pen have been removed from the general population due to threats, hopefully isolated so they can't contact the outside, but I wouldn't stake Steph's life on that. As they are on remand and not convicted, they're being protected for now. We also know there are still Jokers in LA that Stinger and his crew haven't been able to pick up. Too many of the motherfuckers still breathing. Hopefully Steph's testimony will get them put away for a very long time, and the feds will round up everyone else.

The only outcome from the trial that I'm worried about, is a lack of a conviction. If the Warped Jokers walk free, they'll want revenge for having been locked up in the first place. And, of course, losing their charter from the Wretched Soulz could be laid at Steph's door.

"It's time, Beef."

As Steph used her speaking watch, I'm only too well aware. At least I'll be with her until the last moment.

Descending the stairs to the clubroom, Max scampering ahead, the only sound that can be heard is the ticking of his claws on the floorboards. The solemnity of the situation has got to everyone.

"We wanted to wish you good luck. When you get back, we're going to have a party."

"Might not be anything to celebrate, Vi," Steph warns her.

"Whatever happens it will be over, and you'll be able to get on with your life." Melissa, Skull's woman, who now seems to have found her place here, makes a good point. Whatever the outcome, we'll know what we're dealing with and won't be hanging in limbo.

"Good luck, Stevie. Steph." Jayden gives her a hug, a quick self-deprecating smile, but we're all getting used to calling her by her real name.

Pyro comes over. "I'll take good care of Max. We'll all be waiting for you." His eyes come to mine, a slightly pained look in them. They're all being positive for my woman, but there's still a risk. We all know the Warped Jokers are crazy, and loyal to their officers inside. Everything hangs on Steph making it to the court safely. If she doesn't give her testimony, it's likely Mad Bull and his cohorts will walk free. No one wants that, well, except for the Jokers of course.

"Ready?" Marshal Lennox walks into the clubhouse escorted by Beaver.

"As I'll ever be," Steph replies.

"Come on, babe." I take her hand and squeeze it, trying to convey a confidence I don't feel.

I've made Lennox go over the plans with me, threatening I won't let Steph anywhere near LA today if I wasn't involved. He threatened a subpoena, but she's disappeared once and can do it again and he knows that. I'll do anything to keep my woman safe. In the end he relented. Demon and I have poured over his plans, trying to see any weakness, but it seems as watertight as it can be.

Doesn't ease my mind any.

Vi's helping Steph put on her blonde wig, hiding her

auburn hair, making sure it's straight, and being the mirror Steph can't see herself. Blonde, red head, she looks perfect to me.

"What do you think, Beef?" She turns to me, a small smile on her face.

"Hmm." I consider. "Not sure I like you as a blonde. But I'm willing to give it a try," I answer in the light-hearted way she needs.

Even leaving the clubhouse I glance up at the roof where Bomber and Paladin are waiting, the wave of the latter's hand showing they've seen nothing suspicious. I still keep my body in front of her while Lennox puts her in the car with blackout windows that will take her to the airport. Demon and I get on our bikes to follow behind. In the front, Buzzard, Cad and Sparky are ready to get going too.

I'm tense all the way to the airport where Skull, Rusty and Thunder are waiting for us, relieved to see they give the all clear as we arrive.

Leaving my bike I approach Lennox, pulling him away from Steph so she can't hear.

"Could anyone have tampered with the plane?" I ask him, tersely.

"No. It's only just arrived, and no one would have known where it was flying from until the flight plans were filed. The pilot will only have just filed them here for the flight to LA. All's good, Beef."

"And your marshals? They're meeting us in LA?"

"They are. And we're not flying into La Guardia like they'd expect, we're using a private airport, and my team is already there." He sighs as he patiently repeats the arrangements I already know by heart. I just want to know everything is going smoothly, and that nothing has been changed without me being prepared for it.

If I could have avoided this for Steph, I would have done it. All too soon the plane is in the air, and we're heading for Los

Angeles, and there's no turning back. Lifting the middle armrest, I put my arm around her and tug her to me.

"When this is over, how about you start planning the wedding?"

"You sure, Beef?"

My lips nuzzle her hair. "Never been surer about anything."

"I'd like to go see my mom and dad, and my sisters. Will I be able to do that?" Her lips press together as she waits for my answer.

Whatever the outcome, somehow, I'll make that happen. "Yeah, babe. I suppose I ought to meet the in-laws before we get hitched."

"They'll love you."

Will they? She's been able to learn the man inside the exterior. Will her parents dislike me on sight as it's impossible to hide what I am, a scary looking tattooed biker?

She's not shared much about them before, probably because she misses them. Now is a chance to look forward instead of back. To give her a hope to cling onto. "Tell me about them, darlin'."

"Mom and Dad are both teachers. Mom teaches little kids, Dad 11th grade. He's into history and will bore your head off if you give him a chance. Selina, she's my older sister, she's married. Susanna has a boyfriend, but when I last talked to her, it wasn't serious."

"All 's' names?" I smile.

"Yes." She grins back.

"Any nieces or nephews?"

Again her lips thin. "Retinitis Pigmentosa is hereditary. My sisters grew up with me losing my sight and didn't want to risk their own children going through it. I'm the youngest, Mom and Dad didn't know there was a risk until they had me. We've been lucky in the family for a couple of generations, and before that, no one knew it could be passed on. There's a big risk. One we all agreed we didn't want to take."

No grandchildren for her parents. That seems a pity. Stevie is such a wonderful person, I don't know what my own feelings are about taking such a big risk. I'm just grateful that her parents hadn't known, and she's able to be here with me today.

"I didn't influence them, Beef." She justifies herself without being asked. "Sometimes I think it was harder for those around me to accept than me. You have to just get on with it, you know? But it is something I've lost. I've managed to cope, but what if a child of mine found it harder?"

She's obviously thought about this a lot.

"Fasten seat belts for landing."

As the pilot's words come over the speaker, I give her one last reassurance. "You giving testimony is the end of this Steph, I promise. Whatever happens, and however we do it, you will see your family again."

"And we'll be getting married."

I have to ask, to make sure. "You sure you want to be with me and not return to your old life?" I hold my breath while I wait for the answer.

"You are my life, Beef."

As she is mine. It's the right answer.

We touch down with a slight bump, guess private runways aren't quite so well maintained. Before we disembark, I pull Steph into my arms, smash my lips down on hers and ravish her mouth. She responds with the same desperation. A loud pointed cough is ignored until it comes for a second time, then, slowly, with final pecks, we part. She looks flushed and slightly dazed.

"Steph…"

Her hand reaches up and caresses my cheek. "I'll see you soon," she promises, stopping anything I was going to say.

She's right. There's no need for pointless comments like, *be safe.* Instead, with a direct look toward Lennox, I tell her, "Do everything the marshals say, okay?"

She nods and fingers the necklace I've given her—the one with the tracker in it, which only Demon, Cad and I know about.

Then, without further delay, she's hustled off the plane and into a waiting SUV.

"She'll be alright." Demon's hand lands on my shoulder. "Lennox and the feds want her to testify, so they'll do what they have to do."

"Thanks, Prez. Thanks for being here and having the club support me today." He didn't have to do that. I'm not part of his club after all.

"What else would we do? You might be wearing a nomad patch, but you've sat around our table for a while now, Beef. Steph, we've adopted her too. She's good people, a good fit for you and for the club. We've been through this Beef. I know Drummer said he'd send guys from Tucson, but we've been involved in all the planning. Made sense for us to be here with you."

Another SUV comes into sight. It stops just in front of us.

The driver's door opens and Dart steps out, already moaning about his mode of transport. "Fuckin' hate drivin' a cage."

Stepping forward, I take his outstretched hand. "Hey, you old fucker. Christ, I can't remember when I last saw you."

"Been a while for sure."

"You're doing me a solid here, you know."

"What else could I do? You were there for me, Beef, when I had problems with my own ol' lady. Now you've got one of your own." He breaks off and looks around. "Thought I might meet her."

"Nah, the marshals have already taken her off."

"Good to see you, Dart."

"Demon."

After the greetings are complete, Demon and I get into the SUV Dart's driven. To pass time, I explain how Steph's getting to court.

"They are taking a circuitous route to make sure they're not followed, changing cars a couple of times, before going to the catering company that deals with the court. Then she'll go in the back of the catering truck."

"I always wondered how the marshals got their witnesses to court."

"Yeah, seems like they're pretty practiced in being sneaky."

My leg starts to bounce. Demon notices. "We'll be there soon, Beef."

While my brothers will be keeping watch outside, Demon and I will be in court, watching the proceedings. Just in case someone starts something inside.

CHAPTER FORTY-THREE

I was proud as fuck watching my old lady give her testimony in court. Nothing fazed her. Of course, it probably helped that she didn't see the threatening glances being sent her way by the defendants. She was unwavering as she answered questions from both the defence and the prosecuting attorneys, scornfully facing down any accusation that her testimony wasn't as credible as that of a sighted person. Her voice remained calm, and probably only I could hear the slight tremor in it. She did need water handed to her as she recalled the shots and the screams she'd heard. I was gutted she had to go through it over and over again, recognising the strain on her face as she relived it.

I'd cast sideways glances at the jury, pleased they appeared to be exchanging admiring glances as she explained clearly and concisely exactly what happened, and how she could recognise those responsible. When she'd been helped to the stand, I'd seen dubious looks as if they doubted she could give reliable testimony. But those misgivings seemed to disappear as her strong, clear voice rang through the courtroom.

When it was over, it seemed anti-climactic. There'd be no verdict that day, the jury would hear more and then take their time to deliberate their findings. But she'd done it. She'd given her testimony. There was no reason for anyone to immediately come after her, retaliation at this point wouldn't do anything other than point fingers toward the guilty parties.

For now, Steph as I'm now free to call her, is safe.

As we walk out of the clubhouse into a warm but cloudy day, there's an excited squeal behind us.

Steph spins around, her head tilted in the direction the sound came from. Almost under her breath is the word, "Susie?" Then it comes again louder. "*Susie?*"

"Sis!" A woman comes up at a run, her arms going around Steph whose arm I'm holding, tugging her away from me. "Steph, it's so good to see you!"

"You came?"

"I had to, how could I stay away? Mom and Dad wanted to be here as well, but they're working, Selina too. I was able to take a few hours off. I've been following the trial. Knew you were due to testify." She pulls back a bit and holds her at arm's length. "You look good, baby sister."

"I *am* good. Now that's over, at least."

I clear my throat.

"Susie, this is Beef. Er, Dwayne Carson. He's my fiancé."

Fuck me, but it's good to hear her introduce me like that.

"Dwayne." Susie's eyes narrow suspiciously. I'm not surprised. On looks I'm not much of a catch for any woman.

"I prefer Beef but take your pick." I try to soften my expression but it's not easy. Inside I'm preparing for a fight over whether I'm good enough or not for her family. The anticipation is making me tense.

"And what do you do, Beef?"

How the fuck do I answer? Whatever my club wants me to? Tell her at the moment I'm acting as an enforcer?

Steph answers before I do, "He's a biker, Susie, like out of Sons of Anarchy."

Shit. Way to make it easier.

"Not like that lot inside the court?" Her sister jerks her head back over her shoulder and looks concerned.

"Nothing like. He and his club have been working with the marshals to keep me safe."

Susie gives me an appraising look. "Well, you're built like a bodyguard." Then to Steph she asks, "You sure about him?"

"I love him."

"And I love Steph." Taking the step needed to regain my position beside my old lady, I put my arm possessively around her. My eyes flash a warning to her sister. *She's mine.*

She looks from Steph to me, then back again. Then surprises the fuck out of me when she asks, "Do you ride a Harley, or one of those plastic imports?"

Now I grin. It seems she speaks my language. "You ride?"

"Yeah. I've got my own Sportster. Didn't Steph tell you? Dad rides too. He's restoring an old Norton."

"I didn't tell him anything about the family, Susie." Steph's eyes glisten with emotion. "I had to become Stevie Nichols, and never refer to my old life. I could only keep in character if I never forgot who I was supposed to be."

"Are you safe now?" She addresses the question to Steph, but her eyes find mine.

Quickly I decide platitudes wouldn't work. "I'll keep her safe, but we don't know what we're dealing with until the verdict comes in." It's the truth. I'll be holding out no false hope that everything will be rosy. Thinking it might help win her family over, I add, "Whatever we need to do, I'll be at Steph's side. I won't leave her to face anything alone."

"Good."

"Hate to interrupt this family reunion, but our plane's ready and waiting. You coming?"

I raise my chin toward Demon. "Susie, this is my prez, Demon. Steph's staying at the Colorado chapter with me for now. Demon's offered his protection while she needs it. We've got to get back."

"Susie, I'll try and make it home soon…"

"I'll make sure she does."

Her sister nods, then winks at me. "And I'll prepare the family."

With perfect timing, Dart draws up beside us in the SUV. Susie and Steph hug, both have tears running down their cheeks, but Demon's right. We need to get out of LA before the verdict comes. Probably won't be today, but if the jury has heard enough to make their minds up fast, it could be. If the Warped Jokers go down, wouldn't be good for Steph to be out in the open, at least while we know some are still on the loose.

I give the sisters a moment alone, then go and take my woman's arm. She's crying freely, and I let her weep on my shoulder. She'd have given into tears whether or not she'd seen her sister. Today's been the culmination of a difficult few months, and now it's over. I just let her cry it all out.

Demon has a last few words with the brothers who'd ridden to LA to provide their support. It will only take us a couple of hours to fly to Pueblo, but brothers riding have a nineteen-hour journey in front of them, and will no doubt spread their long ride over a couple of days. It's Wednesday today, which means church has had to be cancelled. I overhear him telling them to take their time, but to be sure to be back by Saturday, when he plans to reschedule our meeting.

As I watch them go to their bikes, part of me is envious. A long ride in the company of brothers? Fresh air in my face? Much better than being stuck on a flying prison. One day, I promise myself, Steph and I will just take off and travel. Her and me on my bike? Can't think of anything better.

I smile to myself. No wonder she's not afraid of bikers or riding. From what her sister had said, it's in her blood.

Steph was bone tired when we returned from LA, all the stress and strain of the last few months leeched out of her. At first she slept, curled up on our bed with Max by her side. When I went up to find them there, I didn't have the heart to move them, so I spent an uncomfortable night, well over to one side, almost falling out. I might love Max, but he's not making a habit of this—darn dog takes up more space than both of us put together. *And* he was lying in the middle which meant I couldn't cuddle my woman. But I've got days, weeks, months and years ahead when I'll be able to do that.

When she wakes the next morning, she's got a full-blown migraine. Rusty told me not to worry, they sometimes come on when the stress is over. My plans to demonstrate my love for her are put on hold as she wants to do nothing more than lie in a dark room and sleep. Friday, she's a bit better, but tired with a lingering headache. It's that day her phone rings.

Unashamedly, I listen to her side of the conversation.

"Lennox. Yeah? Thank goodness. Thank you." She ends the call and inhales a deep breath.

"Well?" My voice conveys my impatience.

"Guilty on all counts. Remanded for sentencing. Warrants have been issued for the rest of the gang."

Any other MC and I'd have corrected her. But the Warped Jokers are a gang, not my definition of a riding club even though their transport may be Harleys.

"Do you want to talk about it?"

She shakes her head. "Not now, no."

Watching her carefully, I see her face is tight. Though some people might expect to see relief, I can understand her reaction. It's a lot to sink in after the months of anticipation, and the toll it's taken on her. We'll have to face a lot of things head on, but I can give her this breathing space to process.

Worries are still in my head. Is she really out the other side? Is there still any risk of blowback on her? For now I think what remains of the Jokers will be keeping down low, evading arrest. Any thoughts I have on dealing with that can be discussed with Demon or Drummer. She doesn't need to be bothered with anything other than fact.

She remains quiet, thoughtful all day, and does little other than walking Max around the new yard and chatting with the other old ladies. I don't interfere, knowing she needs to get things straight in her head, and it's best to let her do that at her own pace. If she needs me, I'm there.

It's Saturday when she wakes up refreshed seeming like her batteries have been recharged. She looks so energetic that an idea comes into my head.

"Want to take off for a while? Go for a ride?"

"Where?"

I haven't thought that far. *Do we need to have a destination?* "Just take off. See where the road leads us? Stop somewhere for lunch?"

She's jumping up and down like an excited child, her smile is like the sun coming out on a rainy day. "I'd love that, Beef. It's been so long. Will Pyro look after Max?"

"Someone will. Put clothes on suitable for a long ride."

Now I know a little about her family I understand better why she loves being on the back of a bike. "You ever go riding with your Dad?" I ask, "Or, your sister?"

"Yes, but Dad's more often got the bike apart than it being suitable for riding. And Susie's not had her bike long. I just love riding. I feel freer than at any other time."

Same way that I do. Could this woman be more perfect?

We grab a bite of breakfast, tell everyone we're heading out, getting a warning from Demon to be back in time for church, then as we're walking out of the door, Melissa comes running up.

"Here," she puffs, "Just out of the oven. Put them in your saddle bags in case you get hungry."

"Mmm, muffins." Steph breathes in deeply and sighs. "Chocolate?"

"Chocolate chip."

"Perfect. Thanks Mel." She holds out her arms and Skull's woman steps in for a hug.

"Best thing that boy did bringin' you to the clubhouse, Mel. Though you may get us fat."

Mel swipes at Pyro's arm as he walks past. "And where do you think you're going?" she shouts after him.

"Someone said muffins," he yells back over his shoulder.

She throws up her hands in mock exasperation. "I better get back to the kitchen. He'll eat the lot otherwise." With that, she hurries off.

Steph and I both laugh. Yeah, Skull did well with that one. She's a good fit for the club, and they seem to go well enough together.

I put the muffins in the saddle bags carefully so they won't get squashed. Then we're ready to head off.

I love the feeling of Stevie's arms as she puts them around me. Having started the engine, I wait, doing nothing more for a few seconds than enjoying the feeling of her holding onto me as if she was meant to be there. Then, with a shit-eating grin on my face, I turn the bike and head out west.

I've decided to go toward the mountains. Stevie won't be able to see or appreciate the scenery in the same way that I do, but I'll give her the experiences and sensations that she can enjoy. The warmth of the sun on her face, the air rushing past, the smell of pine, the thrills of leaning with the bike as I take the curves. I know she'll be mapping the road in her head as we go over the different terrain, my hand twisting the throttle and then backing off as I expertly navigate each twist and turn.

My bike is up to the job, responsive enough so it feels like an extension of myself, not a machine I'm riding on. My mind flits back to that suggestion I get one of the touring bikes. Nah, not for me, and Stevie doesn't seem to mind she's got just a small sissy bar at her back.

There's a piece of straight road, Steph must have realised when I opened the throttle as her hands leave my waist, rise in the air, and she shouts out into the wind rushing past. She's in her element, and I, in mine. I realise it will always be like this, her and I, riding together. Another good reason not to have kids, we can focus on us, with no one to say we're being selfish.

We stop and eat muffins, me kissing away the chocolate from around her mouth, then we're back on the bike again. We have lunch in a small café. It's a day to remember, and one I see us repeating time and time again. Us, the open road, and nothing to worry about.

As we ride back to the compound, I feel her relax against my back. It's been a long ride, and unused to it, she must be tired. I concentrate on the road, but part of my mind is thinking about our future, and where we'll be living it.

Drummer said I can go back to Tucson, and I admit, I miss the place. What I miss most is having somewhere I can call home. Here I'm only a temporary visitor, though I couldn't have wished for a better reception or a better group of brothers to have my back with all the trouble I had with Steph. They even go out of their way to look after the fucking dog, for God's sake. A good group of men here. I find I'm now as reluctant to leave them as I originally was to leave my real brothers in Tucson. But it would feel great to get this nomad patch off my back. At least Drummer wasn't sending me on to another club.

As I told Drummer, though, I don't like leaving things unresolved. Until Demon gets a VP, I need to be here. Now that Steph's safe, I can concentrate on that. I've approached the other prezes who've put out feelers, but so far, no one's come back with a definite answer. Red had said in his latest contact that he might have someone, but he doesn't want to lose him. Maybe this week I'll follow that up and see if I can twist the Vegas prez's arm.

I still haven't given up on pressuring someone from here to step up. Bomber, Ink or even Pyro are capable of working with Demon, if they had the ambition. Hmm. I'll bring it up in church, force the issue. These past weeks have emphasised there's a gap that needs filling, and no one can argue with that.

CHAPTER FORTY-FOUR

"Did you have a good ride?" Vi asks as Steph collapses down on the sofa with a groan, then sits slightly forward and rubs her ass.

Max immediately trots over and puts his head in her lap, his soulful eyes seeming to ask why she left him. He makes a noise that sounds suspiciously like a purr when she rubs behind his ears.

"We had a great time," she responds to the president's old lady. "It felt amazing to just let go and enjoy everything."

I look around. Beaver's behind the bar, and I saw Karl outside cleaning bikes. There are no members around. Which is strange, as it's only an hour or so before our meeting.

"Where is everyone?"

"Church." Vi seems unconcerned at her announcement that makes my face tighten.

Church? I take out my phone and look at it. Nope. I'm not late.

"They've been in and out of meetings all day," Vi continues.

What? Shit. Has something happened while I've been out having fun? If so, it's not something the prez's old lady knows about as she's happily playing with her son and doesn't look worried at all. She builds up a stack of blocks, and a giggling Theo knocks them over, the game seems to be on repeat.

Leaning over I kiss Steph quickly. "I better get in there." With half of me wondering whether I've been directly excluded as I'm not part of the club—a thought which I find more painful than I would have expected—I make my way to the meeting room. Ever since arriving in Pueblo I've been treated as nothing other than an equal member.

My fist hovers in the air. *Should I knock?* Nah, I'll just walk in. They can tell me to get lost if they don't want me there.

"Ah, Beef. Come in."

"Sorry if I'm late."

Demon shakes his head. "Nah. We just met early to discuss a couple of things. Wasn't necessary to call you back from your ride."

As I thought. Discussing things which didn't include me. Well, I'm not part of this club, they can do what they like.

"What else did RIP say?" Hell leans forward, continuing a discussion I must have interrupted.

RIP? My eyes sharpen. What have the Wretched Soulz been contacting Demon about?

"As soon as the Warped Jokers are in the general population, Mad Bull and his VP will be taken out. The Soulz have got a guy in there who's got nothing to lose. He's up for a bit of fun. The others will be given a warning. Drop any action against Stephanie North or they'll go the same way."

Now that's information I needed.

"I was waiting for you to impart that, Beef. Good news for your girl."

It is. I nod.

"So, let's get this meeting started now that Beef's here. Buzz?"

Buzzard runs through the normal stuff. Bottom line, we would like more dollars coming in, but are balancing the books.

I zone out a little as I had when I first arrived. This isn't my club, as this afternoon has reminded me. What do I care about their new tattoo parlour if I'm not going to see it in operation? Apart from Steph's tat, of course, still got to get that done. Yeah. My mind's off thinking about my handle inked on her skin, when Demon says my name. When I come back to myself and see his face, I realise it might not have been for the first time.

"You got anything you want to share, Brother?"

Yes. I have. I sit forward. "Yeah, I wanted to bring this up. I'm nomad, as you know, Drummer's traveling enforcer. Drummer is worried that you still haven't got a VP. Prez, Red might have a possible which I'm happy to follow up. Just a warning that if anyone here wants to throw their hat belatedly into the ring, now could be your last chance to do it. Otherwise an outsider will be coming to Colorado."

There. Possibly should have told him I was bringing it up, but it's time I played my part, as Drummer would expect.

"So I need a VP, do I?" It's said in the prez's deadly tone.

Maybe I should have been more circumspect, and not as direct as I was. *Damn it. He's taken it as a criticism in front of his men.*

Well, it's done now. Standing my ground, I shrug.

"And what you're proposing is finding someone with the right skills and personality from outside the club?" He sounds icy.

I send an apologetic look toward Thunder. "You've a man acting as VP who doesn't want to do it. You've others who could step up but won't. So yes, I don't see what other option you've got. What happened with Steph showed there's a gap in your ranks. You need a permanent someone sitting on your left."

Opposite me Bomber is smirking. Pyro chuckles softly and raises his eyebrows toward Ink. Judge is smiling and exchanging looks I can't read with Wills. Mace has his hand over his mouth though I can see he's amused as his shoulders are shaking.

Thunder simply sits back and folds his arms while Cad looks smug.

They're laughing at me? What the fuck have I said that's funny? I run back over my statement in my head. Nah. Can't see anything amusing there.

"What the fuck is going on?" I ask. Quickest way to tempt my fists to start flying is to make me the butt of a joke I don't understand.

At last Demon's set face relaxes and he leans his elbows on the table. "That's what we've been meeting about today, Beef. Don't need you to tell us there's a weakness in our ranks. We know that. And we also know what we want to do about it."

Well, that's great. I can leave them to sort it out themselves and point my bike toward Tucson. Yeah, that's… great.

Thunder takes over. "We've found just the man we want. All we need to do is find out if he wants to transfer to Colorado."

"You have?"

Murmurs of assent go around the table.

"Unanimous vote," Demon confirms.

That's a weight off my mind. It means I can go… home. Yeah, home. To Tucson. About fuckin' time. Steph will love it there. "So, right. Have you got the ball rolling? Have you asked him yet?"

Demon shakes his head. "Not yet, no. Had to get permission from his prez."

Of course he does. "Want me to make contact?"

Again, I don't understand the sniggers, but I ignore them and focus on Demon.

Demon gives a quick shake of his head and grins. "Nah. Did that myself. Just need one thing from you, Beef."

I nod sharply. Whatever he wants, he's got it. My parting gift to Pueblo.

He doesn't immediately continue. Instead, he looks around the table. The mirth has gone like a switch being thrown. Now brothers are sitting forward, regarding Demon, and, for some reason, me, intently.

As chin lifts go his way, as though in encouragement, Demon takes a deep breath. Then, at last, he speaks. "Need an answer from you, Beef. You want to transfer to Colorado and sit to my left? As my VP?"

I draw in air sharply, then hold it. I glance around waiting for them to all laugh, wondering who will be the first to crack. This has to be the joke. *Yeah, it's a good one.* They're pulling my leg. I'm not officer material, and certainly not a vice president. To step up in Demon's place if necessary? I'm muscle, that's my role. Nothing more than that.

My head moves side to side. "Oh, come on. Joke's over. Who are you really looking at?"

"Think they're looking at you, Brother," Hell says from my side.

"Nah, I'm not—"

"Whatever you think you are, Brother," Demon interrupts, "isn't the fuckin' point. We need a vote, but from what I've heard, every man at this table respects you and knows you'll have their backs. You're fair, but firm. You don't take shit. You stand up to the likes of RIP, and you've got a fuckin' good head on your shoulders. You're a friend, a true brother, to all of us in this club. Men will follow you as you're a natural leader. That's how we see you. How Drummer sees you as well. Why the fuck do you think he sent you here in the first place? He never let on until today, but that was his plan all along." He breaks off to shake his head. "Cunning motherfucker, the mother chapter prez. Knew we had a gap to fill, thought you could fill it. Wanted us to get to know you, and you to get to know us. We might not have a swimming pool, but I'm sure we can offer enough to compensate. So, what do you say?"

Drummer, you crafty motherfucker.

I hold out my hands, palms up. "What can I say?" my voice sounds choked. "Yes."

"Vote."

Ayes come from all around with no dissent. Buzz pulls a book toward him and writes it down. Demon reaches behind him and pulls out something which he shoots down the table to me. Two patches. One a large Colorado rocker, and the other, a VP patch. I turn them over in my hands disbelieving but grinning broadly.

"Crazy fuckers," I say at last, still clutching the VP insignia tightly, as if someone might change their mind and snatch it away from me. "Not sure I'm the right man, but I promise I'll try to live up to the trust you've placed in me, and I'll never let you down."

"Party!" Sparky yells loudly.

It seems there's going to be a celebration held in my honour. Last time it was when I was patched in, many moons back and in a very different club. As men walk out of church in a celebratory mood, I sit for a moment, pondering how my circumstances have changed. Sure, I'll miss Wraith, Drummer, Rock and everyone else in Tucson, but now I've got a new purpose in life; a role to be proud of, a woman at my side. All totally different from when I first rode into town.

I don't spend too much time in contemplation. There's someone I need to break the news to.

Steph's still talking with Vi, I go over and pull her to her feet. "Need a word."

Men are already getting loud around us, so I take her upstairs where I can speak to her in private.

"Beef, what's up? Is there trouble?"

"Nah, babe. The opposite." I'm having difficulty getting the words out, still overwhelmed by what's happened to me. "I know I said we'd live in Tucson, but would you have a problem if we stay in Pueblo instead?"

"Of course not, Beef. I really like Vi, Melissa and Jay. Jeannie, Mo and Sindy too, though I don't see them as much. Your brothers are great, it's like one big family which I already feel a part of. I'm used to this place and would have no problem stay-ing. Though I'd go anywhere with you. It doesn't matter to me where we live, as long as we're together."

"What if I told you the whole club is totally mad?"

"Mad? Angry?"

I laugh, then take hold of her hands. "Mad as in crazy, that they've lost their fuckin' minds. They've only gone and voted me in as their fuckin' VP."

"Beef!" She squeals and jumps forward, trusting me to catch her. "You're going to be great! That's wonderful news."

Suddenly I realise I can do this with a woman like Steph by my side. She's got that strength I need, and a belief in me for the times I lose faith in myself.

How the fuck did I get so lucky as to find her?

Nine months ago, I died. I came back from the dead not knowing why a miracle had occurred. Now I realise it wasn't my time to go then, I had more to live for. A woman to save, a woman to make mine, and a new club I'm going to give my all.

There's a party going on downstairs. But the only person I want to celebrate with is here.

My hands, which have been gripping her arms, start moving, fingers curving under her breasts. Her breathing begins to quicken, her skin flushes, and there's my green light.

Dispensing with our clothes, the urgency to get naked shared equally, I lift her gently, place her on the bed, then, skin to skin, start to make love to my old lady.

"Ouch!"

"Shit, am I hurting you?"

"Just a bit tender there from riding."

I'm glad she can't see the grin on my face. Of course, I'm sorry she's hurting, but it reminds me of the ride we took earlier. Such a pleasure to be with her out on the road.

I see to her needs first, then, when I'm balls deep inside her, I rest my forehead against hers.

"Love you, Steph. It scares me how much I love you."

"Beef, I love you too. So much."

At first with gentle strokes that infuriate her, and has her begging for more, then a faster pace that has her coming again, I love on my old lady, giving all that I am to her. Then, empty myself inside her.

As I roll over and gather her into my arms, I sigh in satisfaction. I'm going to spend the rest of my life making her happy, my mind whirls with the endless possibilities. Go to visit Tucson, introduce her to another set of brothers and their old ladies, and all my nieces and nephews. Go to California and meet with her parents. Then, return to a club which has made me a man my old lady can be proud of.

That day when I rode into Pueblo? Seems everything happened to a different person. A man still making sense of why his life had been handed back to him. A vow sent up, I'm not going to waste a fucking moment of my reprieve.

"Beef? The clubhouse is very noisy tonight."

Her observation has me remembering. Just as I'm about to reply, there's a banging on my door.

"You in there, Beef? Need the guest of honour down here."

"Yeah, we'll be there in a few."

"Pull your dick out of your ol' lady and come on down," Thunder roars from outside.

"My dick, my business," I yell back, earning me a punch on the arm from a grinning Steph.

As his chuckles and footsteps fade, I slap Steph gently on the ass, mindful she's feeling tender. "Come on, babe. Better get down to the party. You have to make the entrance as the VP's ol' lady."

"Guess I am at that." Her eyes widen. "Not what I expected when I was relocated to Pueblo."

"Not what I expected to find here, either," I tell her truthfully, a moment of seriousness descending. "But you know what? Getting a kick up the backside to come to this club, when all I wanted was to stay in my rut. Finding you, filling a spot where

Pueblo needs me; those are the reasons it wasn't my time when Satan closed the door in my face."

She's equally solemn. "I would be dead if you'd died."

Too much. I choke up, so need to change the tone. Trying to sound lighter than I'm feeling, I tell her, "Time to party."

Turns out Pueblo boys know how to throw a patch over party every bit as good as the Tucson brothers can. We drink, laugh, talk and even dance to some old shit playing on the ancient jukebox Ink had found after their old one had been destroyed. Steph stays by my side as she should, until it gets too much. She might not be able to see Breezy getting fucked by Ink and Pyro, but as they're not being quiet about it, she can hear well enough.

While she takes Max upstairs and out of the den of iniquity, Demon comes up.

"We're going to make a great team, Beef. Difference between you and Thunder? You're not going to be afraid to tell me when I'm being an asshole."

"That," I point my beer bottle toward him, "you can depend on." As he laughs, my lips press together. "I'll do the best I can, Prez," his title now falls from my lips easily, "but I still don't know if I'm the right man."

His chin dips then rises. "Same doubts as I had when Hell stepped down. Fuck, still not sure I'm right to sit at the head of the table. But I reckon doubts are good in a man. Means we'll keep trying to be better. And, Beef, have faith in yourself. You've given your all, fuck, damn near your life, for this club. You're due some payback, Beef. You're fuckin' due."

I'm still shaking my head as he drains his beer and tells me he's going home to his wife. *Is he right?* I've never been one to think life owed me anything at all.

Maybe it's those of us who don't expect much, happy to be the grunts doing the heavy lifting without complaint, that finally get recognised and given their deserve.

Makes it special, that's what. As brothers come and go, greeting me with the VP title that sounds strange falling off their lips and heading in my direction, I know it's going to take more than a minute to get used to it.

Me. A fuckin' VP. *And* soon to be a married man.

What more could I want?

Nothing at all.

EPILOGUE

"Yeah, show him what you're made of, VP!"

A collective groan as Rock gets in a lucky punch, followed by a cheer as I get in one of my own. Just as I'm expecting the third round to end with us showing we're evenly matched, Rock makes an error, and my fist to his jaw sends him down just as the final bell rings to loud shouts and hollers.

I help him up, then Demon jumps into the ring and holds my arm in the air. "Winner is our VP."

"As it should be," shouts Pyro. "Show Tucson what they lost."

I step down, followed by Rock who's rubbing his jaw, but there's no real damage done. He's got a rueful grin on his face. "Lucky shot there, Brother."

I snort. "Lucky, my ass. You're going soft."

Rock puffs up his chest. "Feel that," he instructs.

"Nah, not feeling you up, Rock. But I can barely see your muscles at all." I wink at him.

"I need a fuckin' drink." He slings his arm over my shoulder, and we walk across to the clubhouse.

Once we've got beers in our hands, Rock nods toward the women who keep well away from our regular bouts in the ring.

"I like her for you, Beef." His eyes shutter. "Miss the fuck out of you, Brother. Kind of got used to seeing your ugly mug, feels a loss when it's not there."

I miss him too. I know him so well, I know I don't need to say the words. "Here's good for me, Rock."

"I can see that. Got your VP patch, and a good woman too."

I raise my chin. "How's Becca?"

"Pregnant again."

Beer flies out of my mouth. "So fuckin' fast? How old's Rose?"

"Six months." He shrugs apologetically. "What can I say? I don't like wrapping it up, she wants loads of kids. Got Viper onto building a house for us now."

"Looks like it will need plenty of space."

"Yeah." Unrepentant, he grins. He swallows a mouthful of beer, then sets the bottle down. "I was worried you were staying away because of me."

"You?" My eyes crease.

"Well, me and Becca. Look, man. I never said anything, but I know how you feel about her."

"Nah," I contradict, "you don't. I used to wish I'd seen her before you, but you two were always a pair, even when you weren't." I check, but luckily I'm making sense to him. "I wanted what you had, but now I know, it wouldn't have worked." I point to my old lady sitting with Theo on her lap. "Always believed there was one woman for me, just didn't know who. Now I've found her. What I thought I'd felt for Becca, hell, for Sally too, wasn't the real thing at all."

Rock's hand lands on my back. "Pleased for you, Beef."

I'm pleased for me too.

"Ever miss Tucson?"

"Of course." I'm wistful for a moment as I look into the rearview. "But we've all got to move on. You've got your family, and I've got my VP flash and a job to do."

"Fuckin' proud of you, Brother."

I've heard that a lot over the past few weeks, but falling from Rock's lips? Means one hell of a lot.

"Proud of you, too, Brother. Seems we've both got new lives which suit us both."

Picking up his beer, he clinks his bottle against mine. "Had to grow up and settle down one day, man."

I lean in closer. "Give you a tip? Try blindfolding Becca sometime."

He chuckles and winks. "What makes you think I don't?"

Snorting with laughter, I look around the room and see Steph's face turned toward mine. As if she knows I'm watching, a smile slides over her face.

I turn to my friend. "You, Tucson, all the brothers there, will always have a special place in my heart. But that woman there? She's my home."

As his face softens, I translate he's agreeing. He's feeling the same way about Becca.

"Well, what's the gossip from back home, Rock? How is everyone?"

My question opens the flood gates as he runs through what's been going on. Luckily no particular problems for them to deal with, his update is more who's pregnant and who's not. Money's been placed that Heart and Marcia are expecting another pair of twins. I hand him a twenty saying my guess is they're not. Drummer and Wraith seem content they've completed their family. Hyde, at last, is going to claim Sarah officially.

"How's Truck doing?"

Rock's eyes shutter. "Can't tell you that. He won't have contact with anyone. Shut himself off from the club and his fire-fighting crew. He's alive and will stay that way, but that's about as much as we know. We've tried to see him, Slate, his captain has too. But… nothing."

I sigh heavily. Man needs his family around him when the chips are down. But what can be done if he doesn't let help in?

"Yeah, well. We'll keep trying." Rock raises his chin.

"Yo, Rock. Beef tells us you'd like to try your hand at cards."

Oh fuck. I glance at my best friend and see his mood has risen, laughter twinkling in his eyes as he calls back, "Yeah, Ro. Deal me in."

I start shaking my head. "I live here," I hiss.

"Aw, come on Beef. I won't rob them. Too much."

"Better fuckin' not," I rasp out under my breath. Then, throwing up my hands, walk over to join them, feeling I need to keep an eye on what's going on.

Different clubhouse. In many ways, just the same.

Then I lean back against the bar watching my old world meet my new. And doesn't that seem right?

Rock catches my eye, grins, then mouths, "Shiny side up, Brother."

I raise my beer toward him and my lips form the words, "Dirty side down."

Truck

Badly burned and injured, I've lost everything. I can't fight fires anymore, or even ride my bike.

I brood, alone, even contemplated ending my life. What do I have left to live for?

When I hit that lowest point, I decided to fight back. I needed someone beside me. I didn't expect to find a friend in Allie.

Was she like the rest of the sweet butts just wanting to become an old lady? Was she trying to sink her claws into me because she thought I was easy? Was she ignoring my scars just so I'd patch her?

Could I believe she had my best interests at heart and move past the fact all my brothers had known her intimately?

Allie

I enjoy sex. Not going to apologise for that. But Truck? He was different. It wasn't just getting off, with him, it had been something else. Something I wanted to explore.

Before I'd gotten my chance, he'd left and never returned.

The club wants him back, so I volunteered to try to reach him.

My heart shattered when I found him scarred, broken and angry, but I wouldn't let him push me away. He needed a friend, and I could be that.

I can't hope for anything more. Bikers never fall for sweet butts do they?

OTHER WORKS BY MANDA MELLETT

All books can be read as a standalone.

Blood Brothers – A series about sexy dominant sheikhs and their bodyguards

Stolen Lives (#1) Nijad and Cara

Close Protection (#2) Jon and Mia

Second Chances (#3) Kadar and Zoe

Identity Crisis (#4) Sean and Vanessa

Dark Horses (#5) Jasim and Janna

Hard Choices (#6) Aiza

Satan's Devils MC - Arizona Chapter

Turning Wheels (Blood Brothers #3.5, Satan's Devils #1) Wraith and Sophie

Drummer's Beat (#2) Drummer and Sam

Slick Running (#3) Slick and Ella

Targeting Dart (#4) Dart and Alex

Heart Broken (#5) Heart and Marc

Peg's Stand (#6) Peg and Darcy

Rock Bottom (#7) Rock and Becca

Joker's Fool (#8) Joker and Lady

Mouse Trapped (#9) Mouse and Mariana

Blade's Edge (#10) Blade and Tash

Satan's Devils MC (Colorado Chapter)

Paladin's Hell (#1) Paladin and Jayden

Demon's Angel (#2) Demon and Violet

GLOSSARY

Motorcycle Club – An official motorcycle club in the U.S. is one which is sanctioned by the American Motorcyclist Association (AMA). The AMA has a set of rules its members must abide by. It is said that ninety-nine percent of motorcyclists in America belong to the AMA

Outlaw Motorcycle Club (MC) – The remaining one percent of motorcycling clubs are historically considered outlaws as they do not wish to be constrained by the rules of the AMA and have their own bylaws. There is no one formula followed by such clubs, but some not only reject the rulings of the AMA, but also that of society, forming tightly knit groups who fiercely protect their chosen ways of life. Outlaw MCs have a reputation for having a criminal element and supporting themselves by less than legal activities, dealing in drugs, gun running or prostitution. The one-percenter clubs are usually run under a strict hierarchy.

Brother – Typically members of the MC refer to themselves as brothers and regard the closely knit MC as their family.

Cage – The name bikers give to cars as they prefer riding their bikes.

Chapter – Some MCs have only one club based in one location. Other MCs have a number of clubs who follow the same bylaws and wear the same patch. Each club is known as a chapter and will normally carry the name of the area where they are based on their patch.

Church – Traditionally the name of the meeting where club business is discussed, either with all members present or with just those holding officer status.

Colours – When a member is wearing (or flying) his colours he will be wearing his cut proudly displaying his patch showing which club he is affiliated with.

Cut – The name given to the jacket or vest which has patches denoting the club that member belongs to.

Enforcer – The member who enforces the rules of the club.

Hang-around – This can apply to men wishing to join the club and who hang-around hoping to be become prospects. It is also used to women who are attracted by bikers and who are happy to make themselves available for sex at biker parties.

Mother Chapter – The founding chapter when a club has more than one chapter.

Nomad – In an outlaw MC a **nomad** is typically a member who's been given permission/instruction by the national president to enforce the laws of the club at other chapters.

Patch – The patch or patches on a cut will show the club that member belongs to and other information such as the particular chapter and any role that may be held in the club. There can be a number of other patches with various meanings, including a one-percenter patch. Prospects will not be allowed to wear the club patch until they have been patched-in, instead they will have patches which denote their probationary status.

Patched-in/Patching-in – The term used when a prospect completes his probationary status and becomes a full club member.

President (Prez) – The officer in charge of that particular club or chapter.

Prospect – Anyone wishing to join a club must serve time as a probationer. During this period they have to prove their loyalty to the club. A probationary period can last a year or more. At the end of this period, if they've proved themselves a prospect will be patched-in.

Old Lady – The term given to a woman who enters into a permanent relationship with a biker.

RICO – The Racketeer Influenced and Corrupt Organisations Act primarily deals with organised crime. Under this Act the officers of a club could be held responsible for activities they order members to do and a conviction carries a potential jail service of twenty years as well as a large fine and the seizure of assets.

Road Captain – The road captain is responsible for the safety of the club on a run. He will organise routes and normally ride at the end of the column.

Ronin – A biker who travels alone, sometimes wearing a patch denoting he's Ronin. Not affiliated to any club, but often bearing a token which will help ensure safe passage through territories of different clubs.

Secretary – MCs are run like businesses and this officer will perform the secretarial duties such as recording decisions at meetings.

Sergeant-at-Arms – The sergeant-at-arms is responsible for the safety of the club as a whole and for keeping order.

Sweet Butt – A woman who makes her sexual services available to any member at any time. She may well live on the club premises and be fully supported by the club.

Treasurer – The officer responsible for keeping an eye on the club's money.

Vice President (VP) – The vice president will support the president, stepping into his role in his absence. He may be responsible for making sure the club runs smoothly, overseeing prospects etc.

ACKNOWLEDGMENTS

I have to admit I loved writing Devil's Due, loved finally getting to know Beef and how his near death experience had affected him. I hope you were pleased to read his story at last, and for him to end up with a woman of his own.

Sometimes stories are kicked off by just a comment. I can't remember who is was, but someone, after reading Blade's Edge, commented, 'Please don't let Beef end up with Sally, she's not right for him'. Hmm. Cue author's brain. I had originally thought that instead of writing Beef's book, I could just mention him playing happy families as I intimated in the previous book. But could he be happy with Sally?

The idea he had to extricate himself from that relationship, while carrying the guilt he hadn't been able to make it work, was intriguing. But who could he end up with? Then I thought of Steph, and her guide dog, Max.

I hope you liked Steph as much as I enjoyed writing her. I love her sense of humour and teasing of Beef. She was exactly who he should be with. It was also great to write about a well behaved dog, I don't have much experience of those. There, I definitely needed to use my imagination. (I have two Irish Setters. Enough said.)

I've got some great ideas in my head for the next book in the Colorado chapter series, but first I'll be returning to Tucson to end the main series with Truck Stopped. It might be the final instalment for the mother chapter of the Satan's Devils MC, but you won't be losing sight of the characters as they will be turning up in other books.

If you're wondering, at some point I'll be returning to San Diego to see how Lost and Dart are managing, finding out more about Red's crew in Las Vegas, as well as discovering what goes on in the mysterious chapter in Utah. I've so many ideas in my head and am trying hard to write them.

Getting the book from the very rough first draft to the finished product is a team effort.

I love working with my editor Maggie Kern. I love reading her comments, especially when they read, 'That made me laugh out loud'—luckily in parts I meant to be comedic. Her encouragement and support, as well as her great editing skills, helps me keep writing. Thank you, Maggie, once again.

At the same time as the draft goes off for editing, I also send it to my poor beta readers who have to read something unpolished. Someone always spots something everyone else has missed, so having a team is really helpful. So, in no particular order, these are the people I need to thank. Tami (my location advisor), Danena, Sheri, Terra, Zoe, Nicole, Alex and last but not least, my husband Steve.

I hope you'll agree Lia Rees has come up with another outstanding cover. Thanks Lia, always love your work.

Grateful thanks to Melanie Darrow for proofreading.

Again, I'd like to thank Tracy Wood my PA who makes my life run smoother, taking some of the burden off me so I can get on with writing.

Readers. What can I say? Without you buying my books I wouldn't be writing them. I do love hearing from you about what you thought.

The best way of telling me is to leave a review on Amazon,

Apple, Nook—wherever you read, or on sites like Bookbub. I appreciate every review good or bad. Reviews help authors make sales, sales allow authors to pay editors, models and photographers, cover designers etc, and put food on the table.

Well, it's goodbye for now, but there'll be another Devil along very soon.

Manda's life's always seemed a bit weird, starting with a child-hood that even today she's still trying to make sense of, then losing her parents in the late teens. Going from the tragic to the bizarre, who else could be unlucky enough to have had two car accidents, neither her fault, one involving a nun, and another involving a police woman?

There isn't enough space to list everything that's happened to Manda, or what she's learned from it. But by using the rich fabric of her personal life, psychology degree, varied work experiences, and amazing characters she's met, Manda is able to populate her books with believable in-depth characters and enjoys pitting them against situations which challenge them. Her books are full of suspense, twists and turns and the unexpected.

Manda lives in the beautiful countryside of Essex in the UK, the area's claim to fame being the Wilkin's Jam Factory at nearby Tiptree. She can usually find jars of jam which remind her of home wherever she goes. As well as writing books and reading, Manda loves walking her dogs and keeping fit. She lives with her husband of over 30 years, who, along with her son, is her greatest fan and supporter.

Manda is thankful that one of the more unusual, and at the time unpleasant, turns her life took, now enables her to spend her time writing. Confirming, in her view, every cloud has a silver lining.

Photo by Carmel Jane Photography

www.ingramcontent.com/pod-product-compliance
Lightning Source LLC
Chambersburg PA
CBHW070346170726
48291CB00001B/202